Stuck
in
Between

ALSO BY BLAKELY BENNETT

My Body Trilogy

My Body-His

My Body-His (Marcello)

My Body-Mine

Co-Authored

The Demarcation of Jack

Stuck
in
Between

Blakely Bennett

TandemWriters

Stuck in Between

TandemWriters

Cover design by Clarissa Yeo
Logo design by Olivia E. Bennett
Edited by Read Owl Publishing

ISBN: 978-0-61598-037-9 (Trade Paperback)
ISBN: 978-1-63173-316-1 (eBook)

My favorite part of being an author is the friends I make along the way. There is a small crew who make my day so often, lifting me up and urging me on. This book is dedicated to Serena K., Tami C., Sara S., and Ann P.—you gals rock!

AUTHOR'S NOTE

This is the first of many stand alone books in the Bound by Your Love series, which centers on the romantic lives of one group of friends.

As you will see, each chapter is headed with a song title. The melody, title, and/or lyrics inspired me to choose each song for each of its corresponding chapters. If you're into music, like I am, I hope you enjoy the accompaniment.

ACKNOWLEDGMENTS

Although writing can be a solitary process, publishing a novel is not. My first note of appreciation goes to my husband who is the best soundboard a writer can have. I'm so happy to be sharing this journey with you.

My beta/test readers never fail me. Big thanks to Serena K., Brenda L., Stephanie H., and Sara S., your feedback is invaluable.

A special shout-out to my "street team" babes for reminding me, often, why I write. Thanks for all your help and support.

I'm so happy to have found my editor, April Duffy, and cover artist, Clarissa Yeo. I'm thrilled with your work.

Warmest hugs to my daughter who puts up with me having my nose buried in my computer too often. Thanks for cheering me on.

CHAPTER ONE

Help Me

by Joni Mitchell

*D*amn, *not again*, I thought as I opened my eyes and scanned my surroundings. In one fell swoop, I had abandoned all my firmly held resolutions. I should have known better than to mix alcohol and my ex-boyfriend Bond.

My eyes swung to the left, and skimmed the rack to see if he had added any new devices for disciplining his wayward lovers. There, on the wall, hung a variety of whips, cuffs, and paddles. I had long ago vowed never to allow him to take such liberties with my body. At least I had upheld *that* promise to myself.

As I sat up, I felt my head swim from the wine, the pot, and Bond. He was like a ticking time bomb, blowing my life to pieces each time I gave in to his gravitational pull. In my defense, he had that effect on all women, not just me. Unfortunately, I was the silly woman lying naked in his bed under the black-framed *Octopussy* movie poster he had hung above the headboard.

Bond leaned through the doorway wearing fitted white shorts and a short-sleeved shirt with a white collar and blue stripes. His long, brown hair appeared wet from the shower. Seeing him dressed like that reminded me he came from money. To me, he looked funny dressed like a man going to play tennis at the country club instead of the tattooed biker he liked to portray. Neither was really him in my opinion.

"Chop, chop," he said.

1

"'Chop, chop'? Have you turned into my mother all of a sudden?" I said, slowly pivoting my body to the side of the bed to stand.

"I have *company* arriving soon."

The way he said company, it was clear it would be of the female persuasion.

"It's not even 10 a.m.," I almost whined but modulated my voice in time.

"They own a sailboat so we're setting out early. Seriously, I need you to vacate."

"Well, good morning and fuck you too." I wanted to stick my tongue out, but instead behaved like an adult.

He moved toward me with *that look* on his face.

I held my palm out, to halt his progress. "Don't," I said.

"Look Jacqs, let's talk later, okay? I don't have to be at work until nine tonight. We can deal with this at Red's before I head in."

"Deal with what exactly?" I turned my back to him and threw on my dress from the previous night. My torn panties were nowhere to be found.

"Well, you know, last night."

Last night, I sighed.

It was actually 3:30 a.m. when I had heard the first text chime, and I didn't have to look to see who it might be. I ignored the sound, rolled over and started drifting back to sleep. Bond, however, proved relentless and texted me seven more times. After the first five texts, I started to worry. I had considered turning off the sound on my cell phone overnight since knowing Bond, but I feared my sister wouldn't be able to reach me in an emergency. She frequently called at off hours, but found texting too much of a bother so, at least, I knew I wouldn't be dealing with her latest drama.

I finally gave in, snatched my phone away from its

charging cord, and headed into the bathroom. I scrolled through my newly received texts:

> **Bond:** Jacqs, are you up?
> **Bond:** Come on, sleepyhead, I need you!
> **Bond:** My father threatened to cut off my money again.
> **Bond:** He and I really had it out this time. I don't think he plans to speak to me again.
> **Bond:** I just need you to come by and bring me a bottle of wine. That will calm me down so I can sleep. Please!
> **Bond:** Now I know you're just being stubborn. Are you lying in bed trying to get back to sleep?
> **Bond:** It's not going to work. I need you, and you know you are my only real friend. Pretty please?
> **Bond:** Baby, I promise to behave, okay? I'm asking you over as my friend only.

"Yeah, right," I said to the bathroom door. I gave in and typed:

> **Me:** What kind?
> **Bond:** Merlot and thank you, thank you, thank you, you're a godsend.
> **Me:** You owe me.

Bond and I had been friends for over eight years, and he had always been there for me. I knew a lot about his family dynamic and what it cost him on an ongoing basis. I would always respond to him, even though I fought it.

I stood in front of my closet, looking for something half-decent to wear. After putting on a light sundress, I grabbed my purple hoodie. Winter weather in Hollywood, Florida, could be unpredictable. After freshening up in the bathroom, I stared in the mirror. *You'd better behave yourself tonight*, I said to my body and then rolled my eyes at myself.

As I pulled my messy, long, wavy brown hair back into a ponytail, I thought of putting on some makeup but nixed the idea. My eyes, green around my pupil and blue filling the rest of the iris, were red-rimmed from lack of sleep, and makeup couldn't fix that.

On my way to Bond's apartment, the only movement on the street was a stray cat and a section of a newspaper blowing in the wind. It was warm enough outside to let me crack the driver's side window. I drew in a deep breath of ocean air coming from a few blocks away. The surrounding silence made the volume on the stereo seem louder, so I turned it down. After pulling into Bond's parking spot, I bumbled up to his place toting the bottle of merlot.

"Here you go," I said, after unlocking the door with my own key and handing him the wine that I kept for such occasions. "Do you ever plan to get your own car?"

"No," he said, taking the bottle into the kitchen.

"Are you ready yet to tell me why?" I asked as I followed him.

"No," he repeated, uncorking the bottle.

Even with his body angled away from me, I felt the ungodly pull on my being. It had been months since I'd sex and far longer since I had received a really amazing orgasm at the hands of another. Simply, I was crazy horny, and hanging out with a past lover, specifically the one with the most magnificent cock I ever had the pleasure of experiencing, did not help matters.

My nipples tightened as Bond glanced over at me. He seemed very tall at five feet ten, but then again, at merely five feet two, almost everyone dwarfed me. He was a decent-looking man, with masculine arms and legs, who, against convention, wore his glossy, brown hair long. His face would qualify as above average, I suppose, but he wouldn't be considered exceptionally attractive. His light brown eyes, however, seemed to mesmerize us simple mortals. I had never given much thought to pheromones before I met him, but he had them in abundance. His unique scent melted the defenses of women in his presence, which, trust me, can be quite intimidating when you are the one dating him.

His low-slung, black jeans, black T-shirt and black boots made him look as dangerous as he truly was.

"Do you want a glass?" he asked.

"Sure, why not," I replied. I leaned against the counter, took the goblet from his hand, and asked, "What happened this time?"

"Honestly, the usual argument. They want me at their next event so I can play the black sheep and make them feel superior. I told my father I can't get time off, which is partly true."

"Is there some big event at the CroBar club? Do you have to be at work that night?"

"Yeah, but there are plenty of newbies who could fill in for me."

"How much longer does your father have control over your inheritance?"

"At forty, I'll get the money my grandparents left for me. Five very long years. It wouldn't be such a big deal, but you know me, I love to party and those monthly trust payments help."

I knew his emceeing job kept him busy, but it certainly didn't keep him out of trouble. He was like a spider sitting in the middle of his web, ready to capture his latest prey.

"Help pay for dates, right?" I hadn't forgotten how he liked to wine and dine. "You can't mean you spend it on living here," I said, glancing around the apartment.

His place was above the club where he worked, and it could get loud in the little abode, so I didn't imagine he paid much rent. He did have expensive tastes though. The kitchen was completely outfitted, although I'd never known him to cook. The black leather couch with plush matching recliners sat atop an oriental rug. I knew he spent some of his funds on those ridiculous toys hanging on the wall in his bedroom. His king-sized bed filled most of the space, and he used the wall of closets for his clothes and a collection of leather jackets and boots.

"Is your family thing another one of those company functions?" I asked.

"My family *is* a company function."

"The one you dragged me to was dreadful. For Democrats, they surely looked, acted, and talked like their Republican brethren. I'm pretty sure I was the only woman or man there not wearing a business suit."

"Yeah, sorry about that," he said and shrugged his shoulders.

"What does Lily say about it?"

Bond took a big gulp of wine. "Lily wants me to come because she hasn't seen me in ages, and she says she doesn't have any fun without me. They're making my brother Donny a partner, so it's going to be black tie."

"So what are you planning to do?"

"Talk you into going with me, of course," he said with a cheeky smile.

"Oh, hell no. You have years of experience dealing with hundreds of people looking down on you and asking awkward questions. I, for one, don't have the stomach for it. Plus, do you really want to encourage Lily's idea that we're the perfect match?"

"Aren't we?"

I decided not to dignify his question with a response. His need for multiple women, domination, and his general fucked up nature didn't suit me well at all. And yet, he was my best friend. My body would staunchly argue he was entirely and exactly what she needed, including the length of his cock and his aggressive sex. Fortunately for me, at least most of the time, my mind ruled my collective being.

"You didn't answer," Bond said as he led me into the front room.

"You noticed that all by yourself?" I sat down on the soft leather sofa, leaving some distance between us and took a sip of wine.

"Am I going to have to spank you, Jacqs?" He held out his big hand, and my heart beat a little faster. "Because you know, not much else would give me as much pleasure as putting you into your rightful place, over my knee."

"So what do you plan to do?" I said out loud, while my body flamed in silence over his suggestion. I could already feel my pussy throbbing, and he had yet to touch me. I swallowed a larger gulp of wine, trying to distract myself.

"I already told you," he said as he refilled his glass and topped mine off. "But since you are so inclined to change the subject, how's *your* sister doing?"

"Samantha is a train wreck, although—and it seems wrong as hell—she is as gorgeous as ever."

"And the baby?"

"My mother is taking care of Sarah, who is a love. I just don't understand why Samantha wouldn't give her up for adoption when she seems to have no interest in raising her."

"Where is she staying these days? Is she still seeing the same therapist?" He shifted closer to me, nonchalantly laying his hand on my thigh.

I stared at his fingers, feeling the energy radiating

from his palm. His touch caused wetness to gather in my panties. "Uh ummm," I said, abruptly pushing his hand off me. "She's living in an apartment with her latest criminal boyfriend. As horrible as it sounds, I'm just grateful she's not at my place. And no, she stopped seeing the therapist when he insisted she needed to grieve our father's death. She ranted on about it to me. She said, 'I'm twenty-fucking-five years old, and they want me to grieve something that happened when I was nine.' She told him to get a life and to fuck off. She never went back."

"Sorry, babe. She's a good kid, deep down," he said, shaking his head.

"Let's hope it surfaces soon ... for her sake and Sarah's."

"What about your boss? Is work any better?"

"He's still a huge asshole. I long for the days when he was still on his best behavior. Now he's just a bull in a china shop, running over everyone. But really, I'd rather not talk about work on my day off."

He threw his arm around my shoulders and said, "I've got some great dope. Want a hit?"

"I'm exhausted because some crazy man got me out of bed at three thirty in the morning."

"This stuff will perk you up."

I finished off the glass of wine and said, "Oh? Well, can I crash on your couch tonight?"

"Bed and of course." He winked.

"Couch! And stop winking at me."

"I guess we shall see?" His relentless stare penetrated my blue-green eyes.

"What about your promise to behave?"

"I'm incapable of behaving when I'm alone with you."

With sheer will I pulled away from his gaze. I wanted to swipe that confident smile off his face. It had been six months and three days since I had succumbed to his charms, and like an addict attending AA, I had no intention of starting back on day one.

Lainie, my closest friend other than Bond, remind me often, most especially when I complained about Bond to her, how ill-conceived it was to be friends with an old lover. According to her, I'd never gotten over him.

Bond handed me the pipe, and I took a hit. I held in the smoke for a bit, and when I breathed out, I, at once, felt more relaxed and energized. It didn't lessen the tug on my libido though.

"It's been awhile since you and I spent any time alone together," Bond said, pulling me back against him.

I sighed, feeling like I'd come home again. "Mmmhmm," I muttered.

He took advantage of my relaxation and drew me in for a kiss.

"Wait!" I said, trying to hold him off.

"Don't play games with me, Jacqs. I can already smell your cunt, and it's driving me insane." When his mouth descended on mine, my mind lost the fight, and my body started making all the decisions.

As I shifted my legs across his lap, I threw my arms around his neck, and took in his naturally appealing fragrance. I wanted more; I needed to be closer. My rational mind made one last attempt, trying to persuade me how much I would regret my decision to have sex with him. I mentally kicked her away, deciding to suffer the consequences later.

Bond groaned into my mouth as he schooled me with his tongue. No one had ever tasted so good; I just wanted to eat him alive. He shifted my body around so I straddled his lap, and I felt his profound interest. The forcefulness of his continued kiss compelled my submission. In those moments when my body ruled, the desire to give myself over to him resurfaced.

He grabbed a fistful of my hair and yanked my head back. "You have the most gorgeous eyes I've ever seen," he said, as he had before.

I figured he said similar things to his other women, but I didn't care in the least. All I wanted was for him to take me roughly, so the rest of my world would fall away.

He lifted the hem of my dress off my thighs revealing my white bikini panties. He rubbed my pussy through the thin cloth.

"Jesus, Jacqs, already so wet for me? You're good for my ego." He continued circling the way he knew I liked.

"Your ego … oh … doesn't need … any help!"

"Shh," he said.

I almost lost control when he slipped the material to the side and plunged his middle finger into my wetness. "Ohhh," I moaned.

Scooping up my juices, he lathered my bulging clit. "Look how hard and swollen you are already. You haven't been using this enough," he whispered into my ear as he lightly pinched my bud between his fingers. Then he laid his hand flat and made big circles, alternating between soft and slow and a hard frantic rhythm. He propelled me higher and higher.

"Stand," he ordered as I hovered at the edge of a powerful orgasm.

I quickly obeyed.

He tore off my panties and let them fall to the floor. Repositioning me on his lap, he resumed his play and placed a finger from his free hand into my mouth. "Make it good and wet."

Holding me right at the edge of release, he softened the pressure on my clit and inserted his saliva-wetted finger into my ass. As soon as he penetrated my anal opening, which had to have been his wicked intention, I screamed out my climax, "Oh, oh, oh, yes, oh Bond, you make me … ohhh!" I breathed erratically as my heart tried to beat its way out of my ribcage.

He held me tight against his chest as I recovered, slowly floating back down to earth. "I've missed you," he muttered into my hair.

That lone comment began to thaw my heart and melt my resistance. *I won't make this into more than it is*, I promised myself.

"A lot," he continued, "and seeing your face as you come, there's nothing else like it."

"I've missed you, too," I said, but could feel my mind shaking her finger at me.

"Please undress me," he said in a domineering yet quiet voice.

I tilted upright and pulled up his shirt, revealing his smooth chest, taut stomach, and small silver nipple rings. He lifted up slightly so I could yank the top out from around him. On his right shoulder was an intricate Celtic knot surrounded by the flames of the sun, which covered an earlier tattoo I had once seen before he had it reworked. The underlying faded blue tat had one Celtic knot intertwined with a heart, and flames crowning the top. It was much smaller and poorly done, but I still wondered what it meant. Bond never liked talking about it.

My eyes shifted away from the tattoo and moved down his chest, following the trail of hair leading into his pants. Shifting my butt back towards his knees, I unzipped his jeans. I stepped down from his lap to sit at his feet in order to remove each black boot. I had to tug to get them free. I then slipped the denim down his legs easily.

He wore no underwear, leaving his magnificent cock standing at attention.

"Kneel," he said, although he needn't bother. The

pearl of precum had already garnered my attention.

Obliging him, I settled between his knees and lifted his hard erection to my lips. He let me play for a few minutes, but it would be short lived. Before he took control of my mouth and his blowjob, I had time to take in his masculine scent of warm skin and sandalwood, and the musky taste of his cock, which had long been embedded in my psyche. I could have knelt there forever worshipping his phallus, but Bond didn't have the patience for that. I knew where he planned to send his first ejaculation.

Once I had worked his cock halfway into my mouth, he tilted my head up and forced the rest of his engorged dick into my throat. My eyes watered as I struggled to maintain eye contact, wanting to see him as he took from me what he needed. He shifted himself to the edge of the couch and slowly pulled himself out of my mouth, allowing me to swallow and take a breath.

"I love that mouth of yours, Jacqs. My cock belongs there. It's been way too long, don't you think?"

Before I had a chance to respond, he soused past my lips, forcing himself in until I felt his balls on my chin. Back and forth he moved, never breaking eye contact and our connection. His cock swelled even more as his orgasm hovered close.

The last time he pulled out he said, "Take a deep breath for me honey."

I nodded and did as he asked.

He immersed his shaft back into my throat and held it there as he bellowed his release. "Fuck Jacqs! Just as I remembered, oh fuuuck."

My eyes continued to tear as I watched his climax through a blur. I felt both powerful—that I could give Bond such an intense orgasm when he could have anyone—and in awe of his sexuality and the spell he cast over me.

"Jesus," he said, as he finally withdrew his cock.

I licked my lips and made a popping sound.

He chuckled as he reclined against the couch and closed his eyes.

Resting against his left leg, I snuggled close. I lifted his semi-hard cock and licked off the come oozing out of the tip.

"Do you know what will happen if you continue doing that?" he asked.

"Mmmhmm," I muttered.

After he had recovered, he reached down and pulled me back into his lap. I couldn't help but swivel my butt, making Bond laugh.

"You sure are a horny girl, Jacqs. I think you should visit me more often."

"You have plenty of women to provide *services* for you."

"First off, none are like you. And secondly, I was talking about you."

"Let's not talk," I said. I would berate myself the next day for my current indiscretions, but I had no plans on stopping at one orgasm.

"As you wish. Let's move this to the bedroom."

He stood up with me in his arms, and I wrapped my legs around his fit waist. In quick, confident strides, he entered the bedroom and placed me down at the edge of the high mattress.

"I'm always amazed at how quickly I recover for you," he said, staring down at me.

With my legs hanging off the end of the bed I leaned back on my hands and said, "Shall I believe it takes longer with the rest of your harem?"

"Believe what you want." He folded his arms across his chest.

"Don't get snarky, Bond."

"You're right, let's not talk."

Our brief conversation hadn't dissuaded his cock. Clutching my thighs, he pulled my ass just over the edge of the bed and lowered himself, propping his upper body over mine. I held my knees back, opening myself to him. His hard-on penetrated my enflamed pussy, and after two strokes, he was fully immersed.

He groaned in ecstasy and I moaned in unison, making us both smile. Bond filled me in a way no other man had, and I enjoyed every second of it.

Our pace became frantic as we slammed our bodies together, and I could feel our perspiration building.

Bond slowed his thrusts and said, "Play with your clit, Jacqs. I want to feel you come with me."

I hesitated, still feeling the discomfort that came along with touching myself around other people. Even with my history with Bond, I still felt self-conscious.

"Do you need some motivation?" he said, glancing at the rack that held his instruments of torture.

"No," I said, letting go of my right knee and circling my clit. I placed my other hand down on the bed to propel myself against Bond's delicious assault.

"Jacqs!" he grunted, and I knew what he meant. I had let my eyes drift shut, and he demanded eye contact during sex at all times.

"Yes sir!" I practically spat out.

"Good girl."

I circled my nub in time with his lunges and grunted each time he crashed against me. It didn't take long to get right to the very edge, sparking small orgasms leading up to the big one.

"Bond, I'm close."

"So am I love. Take me over the brink with you."

"Okay … okay … oh lord, oh yes, here we go! Ohhh."

My pussy clutched and convulsed around Bond's cock, causing his orgasm to fire along with mine. A roll of thunder that seemed to start in his chest escaped his mouth in a roar that deafened us both. His explosion filled me with his energy and come.

He collapsed on top of me, shifting slightly to the side. I just lay there, dead to the world, floating in the afterglow.

"Jesus, Jacqs. Do you have special powers in that pussy of yours?"

"Very funny," I said, rolling my eyes.

"I think I have sex amnesia with you."

"Sex amnesia? That's a new one. Do tell." I wondered where he came up with his bullshit.

"Well, if I remembered how great sex was with you, I'd be following you around all the time."

I laughed at him. "Uh huh," I said, scooting over to get around him.

"Where are you going?" He grabbed my waist to keep me in place.

"To clean up," I said, gesturing to my saturated labia, "and to brush my teeth."

"Okay, hurry back."

Once I had finished up in the bathroom, I climbed into bed, and we got into our usual sleeping configuration. My right cheek lay on his left shoulder, and my left leg crossed over his stomach. His left arm cuddled me in close, and we both started drifting off. I would berate myself in the morning, most especially when Bond morphed back to his usual self, but in that moment, before sleep overtook me, I felt blissful.

❀ ❀ ❀ ❀ ❀

"Last night was a mistake and shouldn't have happened. Next time call Red."

"Come on, Jacqs, don't pull away from me."

"You're kidding, right?" I said, throwing my hands out in front of me.

"I'm not."

"Bond, I love you, but you're delusional. *You* are kicking *me* out of your apartment so you can yacht with some rich chicks Red has drummed up, and yet, you're acting like I'm shunning you after you have awakened me with kisses and a warm breakfast. Really, dude?"

"Oh, no," Red said as he strolled into the apartment, "she's calling you dude. That can't be good."

"Fuck off Red. I'm not in the mood," I said, spinning around with my hands on my hips.

"Are you ever? I mean other than last night, obviously. And I had actually started growing some respect for you but now…" He swept his hand around as if the gesture said everything.

"You and the Neanderthal deserve each other," I spewed at Bond.

I punched the big brute in the stomach, and he just laughed.

At six feet two, Red towered over me by a foot. Everything about him was big. He had a large head and huge hands, and even as much as I hated him, I wondered just how big his cock might be. He had small gauges in both earlobes and full lips. He kept his beard and hair shortly cropped, which highlighted the sharp planes of his face. Bond had dubbed him "Red" when they first met at their private high school. His hair fit the name; even the hair under his arms and on his chest was red.

He, like Bond, had one tattoo. His was much larger due to the sheer scale of his size and its location; the tattoo spread out across the top of his back between his shoulder blades. It was a green Celtic tree created by a complex series of knots that illustrated the trunk, roots, and branches.

I never understood the friendship between them, but they seemed to have a history that kept them close. Where Bond had flitted between different jobs and apartments over the years, Red seemed far more stable, owning a house and a successful investment firm.

"You're still coming over to Red's later, right?" Bond asked. "We can talk then."

"There's nothing to talk about. And when are you going to start hanging out somewhere else? Don't you realize that your guard dog doesn't like me?"

"How wrong you are about that, Jacqs," Bond said.

I stared at both of them, absolutely sure they were just fucking with me, but I could have sworn Red's ears went crimson.

"It's time for you to leave, Little One," Red said.

I hated when he called me that, but Neanderthal and Little One had become our snarky nicknames for each other.

"I'm going," I said, grabbing my keys and purple hoodie off the entrance table on my way out.

CHAPTER TWO

Sweet Nothing

by Calvin Harris (ft. Florence Welch)

I climbed into my pale-green VW Beetle and drove back to my first floor, one bedroom condo off Sheridan Street. Other than the no-see-um bugs that came out at dusk and dawn, I loved my place.

To the right of the front door was the kitchen that overlooked the living room. I had painted each wall in the main space a different complementary color, which I chose because they nicely offset the dark wood furniture and brown couch. I hadn't bothered with a kitchen table and instead had two stools on the far side of the island that housed the stove.

The usual huge pile of laundry sat to the left of the entrance, and the place overall needed to be cleaned, but I just wanted to climb into bed. I thought about pounding my pillow, imagining Bond and Red alternately, until my arms were too weak for another punch. Then I'd crash until I woke up again at which point I'd decide whether or not to go over to Red's house to talk with Bond.

As I tromped to the bedroom staring at my unmade bed, my stomach growled, so I circled back to the kitchen.

A knock sounded on my door.

"Come in," I yelled from behind the refrigerator door.

"Where were you girl?" Lainie said as she closed the front door behind her.

She stood almost as tall as Red and had long, light-brown hair that became blonder in the summer months. Her legs went on forever in her black bike shorts as she settled herself upon the stool. Bending over, she unlaced her running shoes. We didn't always see eye to eye on things, my relationship with Bond for example, but she was always there for me.

"You're just in time for some breakfast. Eggs?" I placed the eggs, cheese, black olives, and tomato on the counter.

"I'm good with whatever. So?" she said, boring into me with her hazel eyes.

"How do you know I wasn't here?" I asked as I diced the tomato and olives.

"Your car was gone when I passed on my way to the beach. I stopped to see if you wanted to go for a walk on the boardwalk."

"Oh, sorry I missed you. Bond had another family crisis last night and I stayed over there." I tried to pull off nonchalance, but Lainie knew me better than that.

"Jacqueline, please don't tell me—"

I gave her a sheepish smile, and I could see her fuming.

"Have you learned nothing? Come on girl, you know better than that. He's never going to change."

"I know that, Lane. Truly I'm fine, other than wanting to punch Red again. That man works my last nerve." I poured olive oil into the hot pan and threw in the tomatoes and olives.

"But you slept with Bond, right? Don't you remember the last time?" she said, throwing her hands up in the air. "How long has it been? Five … six months? You were a wreck."

"This time was different. I made a choice. What can I say, I was horny and I just decided to go for it. I wasn't expecting anything more than a few orgasms for me." I gave her a cheeky smile and almost laughed. I looked away and tossed a sprinkle of shredded Italian cheeses and some fresh basil into the pan.

"How are you ever going to find someone else when you can't let Bond go?" Lainie walked over to the coffee maker and fired it up.

"Come on, Lainie, that's not fair, I have let him go. So what if we fuck now and again. As long as I know, and I really do know, that it will never be more than that."

I popped two slices of bread in the toaster and poured the scrambled eggs into the pan.

"Why does Bond always say you were the one who ended things and yet—"

"It's his clever way with history, but technically he is correct."

"*You* ended it? Wait a minute, I thought you said—"

"I'm the one who said, 'we're done', but his unwillingness even to try a closed relationship is what did us in. How many times should I have to watch him go off with another woman? Of course, according to him, I could have joined in. Ugh! Truthfully I have only myself to blame. He has always been upfront with me, and I guess I just hoped he would change." I sighed and said, "None of that matters now. I got laid, and things will continue as always."

"Are you going over to Red's tonight? Kev and Cat plan to be there."

"You're coming too, right?"

"Not tonight, unless my online date sucks, or he doesn't show. My offer still stands; I'll help you set up a profile."

"Thanks, but no thanks. I'd rather not suck at dating online too, and I don't have the patience for it. Besides, I can live vicariously through you, that is, if you start sharing any of the details."

I plated up the food as Lainie poured each of us a cup of coffee then we settled on the couch.

"So what did Red do to piss you off this time?"

"Just his mere presence pisses me off."

"And yet you hang out at his place often."

I laughed and said, "That's true but there are usually enough people and plenty of rooms there that we can safely avoid each other. Plus on Wednesday nights, it's usually just the gang and not a line of their latest hopefuls. How many modelesque women are there in South Florida anyway? They'll run out soon enough."

"Very funny," Lainie said.

"Something odd happened this morning though."

"With Bond?"

"No, with Red. I said something to the effect that Bond needs to start hanging out somewhere different because Red hates me. And Bond said something like I got that all wrong. I swear Red's ears went all red." Jacqs laughed.

"That is interesting. What do you make of it?"

"Eh, it's probably nothing. He could have been angry that I called him a Neanderthal."

Lainie burst out with laughter. "That might have done it."

"How are things going at Bella Boutique? Anything new I should check out?"

"Our new shipment is coming in this week. Sales have been steady so that's good."

"I might need something new."

"A hot date, I hope?"

"Bond wants me to go to another family function, but I haven't decided if I'll say yes."

"I can help you with that one. No, no, no, and no."

"I thought you might say that."

After Lainie had left, I straightened up and started a load of laundry. I then lay down on the couch and drifted off.

A loud melody swirled around me, and I blinked my eyes rapidly, pulling myself out of sleep. I reached for my cell phone.

"Hi Jacqueline," my mother said. I could already identify the tone in her voice. My sister was up to something.

"Hi Mom, what's up?" I said, sitting up.

"Samantha stopped by, and I'm pretty sure she's looking for some money."

"Did she ask you?"

"Well, no, but she doesn't have her car."

"Do you know where your purse is?"

"Yes, I locked it in the trunk of my car the first chance I got."

"Is she spending time with Sarah?" I asked, walking into the kitchen for some water.

"Yes."

"Does she seem straight?"

"Yes, thankfully."

I sighed in relief and said, "Okay, so maybe it's not as bad as we think. How long has she been there?"

"About an hour now. I fed her some dinner."

"Did she mention Darren?"

"Darren?"

"That's her current boyfriend as far as I know."

"Oh, no, she didn't mention him."

My mother's call meant she wanted to be rescued, and being a dutiful daughter I obliged. "Give her the phone, Mom."

"Okay. Thank you," she said. I could hear the appreciation in her voice.

"Hey Jackie, what's up?"

I placed the glass down on the counter and said, "Just getting some cleaning done. What are you up to?"

"Hanging with Sarah for a bit, but I was wondering if you could pick me up?"

"What happened to your car?" I asked, shaking my head.

"You don't want to know."

"And Darren?"

"Can you come get me or not?"

I paused for a minute and then said, "Do you have plans tonight?"

"Jackie, it's still early."

I took a deep breath and said, "I'm heading over to Red's in a bit, but I was planning to get some more laundry done and I still need to take a shower."

"Come get me first, and I can hang out at your place."

"I'll forgo the laundry and just take a quick shower. I'll be there as soon as I can."

"Jackie, you know Mom and I can't spend that much time alone together," Sam whispered into the phone.

"Take Sarah for a walk in the park or hang out at the coffee shop not far away. I'll try to get there as fast as I can."

"Please Jackie."

"I love you, Sam. I'll see you at around seven thirty, and if you leave Mom's, call to let me know where you are."

"Fine!"

The way she said "fine" sounded more like "fuck you", so I knew she was pissed. I hoped she wouldn't use it as an excuse to drink or worse. Our mother had a hard time setting limits with her, and I imagined Sam might get some money out of Mom if she pushed hard enough. I hoped not.

After my shower, I twisted my hair up into a knot and debated over what to wear to Red's. I refused to don any of the heels, which remained in their boxes at the back of my closet. I used to try to make myself taller in an effort to compete with all the statuesque women who seemed to frequent Red's parties, but I no longer put in that much effort. Most of those who regularly attended had become my close friends—except for Red. He held me at a distance early on and I responded in kind. I figured he didn't think Bond and me were a good match or maybe he didn't want to lose his partner on the revolving dating track. At any rate, he was a big oaf I avoided as much as humanly possible.

I ended up choosing a fitted pair of light-blue jeans and a scoop neck, bright purple blouse with five buttons at the top. In front of the mirror, I checked my appearance and decided to leave the top two buttons undone. Although petite, I loved my proportions. I had curves in all the right places and at twenty-eight my breasts were still round, full, and firm. I could get away without wearing a bra and did so often.

The dark blue eyeliner I applied made the green stand out in my blue-green eyes. I added mascara and a little tinted lip gloss. Unknotting my long, brown hair, I flipped my head over and dried the underneath as best as I could in the short time I had left. It had the desired effect of making my wavy hair fuller.

As I walked to my car, I hoped my sister was in her "good cat" mood because I didn't think I could handle her "bad cat" ways *and* deal with Bond.

I hopped onto I-95 and headed toward Fort Lauderdale. As I pulled into my mother's driveway, I felt an intense wave of angst. "Shit," I said, even before I got out of the car.

My mother flipped on the light and came out to my car.

I rolled down my window and said, "How long ago?"

"Right after she got off the phone with you."

"Did she say where she was going?"

"No."

"Did someone pick her up?"

"Not that I saw."

I shook my head, taking in the reality of the situation.

"You look nice," my mother said.

"Thanks. I guess she'll call when she's ready."

"Come in for a minute?"

"Is Sarah still up?"

"No, she's been down for a while."

"I have to be somewhere or I would." I got out of the car to give my mother a hug and she embraced me tightly.

"I'm sorry to have bothered you."

"It's not easy for either of us, is it?" I asked.

"No, I guess not."

Neither my mother nor Samantha had recovered from my father's untimely heart attack and death. I probably hadn't either, still chasing the unattainable. I had a closer relationship with my mother at the time, but it was almost like losing them both. My mother was never the same and as soon as Samantha hit puberty, she became unmanageable and the focus of our lives. I love my sister, but I often wanted to strangle her.

As I drove away, my mother waved and my heart hurt for her. I wondered if she would ever again open herself to love.

Although Red had a long circular drive, I parked on the road so I could escape at any time. I secretly loved his home, but would never tell him. From the tall palms out front to the multiple arching windows, I even found the red, barrel tile roof and cream-colored paint appealing.

No one sat in the front sitting room as I entered. The hardwood floors sparkled as I strolled through the wide doors and under the high ceilings. I wished I had the discipline to keep my small condo as clean and organized.

I followed the voices I heard into the kitchen and found Bond, Red, Kev and Cat leaning against the counters, chatting and drinking beer.

"Hey guys," I said.

"Hey Jacqs, love the purple shirt," Cat said, coming

forward for a hug. The nickname Cat, short for Catherine, fit her perfectly. She had a lithe body and blue-black hair cut in a long angled bob. Her dark black eyeliner came to a point, and her smoky eye shadow and pink lipstick finished off the look.

"Oh, thanks," I said and reached for a hug from Kevin too. He immediately placed his arm back around Cat's waist, her perfect counterpart. They both looked fashion forward, including Kev's blonde, spiked hair.

I opened the refrigerator and grabbed a Mike's Hard Cranberry Lemonade. I tried to twist off the top, but it hurt my hand.

"Here, give me that," Red said with impatience, and before I could respond he snatched it out of my hand. He used the church key hanging on the fridge.

"Thanks," I said when he handed back the opened bottle.

"Yeah," he said. He motioned to Kev and Cat to follow and they left Bond and me alone in the kitchen.

"You look like you got some sun today," I said. I wrapped my arm around myself in self-protection.

"Don't I get a hug too?" Bond asked. He wore his work clothes of black slacks, a white, button-down dress shirt and black boots. His tan accentuated his light brown eyes, which he used to bore through me. The sides of his long, brown hair were pulled back in a knot.

He looked devastatingly hot and I had to force my desire aside. I mentally urged my body to behave.

I stood up taller and said, "Well, I didn't want you to think that I thought it meant anything."

"The hug or last night?"

"Both."

"It always means something when we make love," Bond said as he moved in to embrace me.

I stepped back before he had the chance. "Make

love?" I said. "Seemed more like fucking to me. Really good fucking, I'll admit, but I'm not in the mood to be trifled with. Were you not just on a sailing vessel with other women?"

"That's separate from us and it was just sailing."

"To you, but not to me, and I don't see the point of retracing this ground. I had fun last night, didn't you? Can't we just leave it at that?"

"Come home with me tonight and I'll leave it alone," he said, holding out his hand. "Let me make it up to you."

I considered it for a second and said, "Were you with anyone today?"

"Jacqs, don't." He dropped his hand and crossed his arms.

"My answer is no. Most definitely no." My body and mind played tug-of-war in my head. My body remembered the times when we were ravenous for each other and the sense of home I found in his arms. My head pointed out all the times my heart ached for more from Bond.

He reached out again to grasp my shoulder, but I yanked it away.

"Don't give me that sad puppy dog look of yours, Bond. We can occasionally be sex buddies, but not much else at this point. Don't think I'm going to stay at home waiting for you to come back from fucking the rest of the world. Don't try to pull me back in because you'll only end up breaking my heart again. Give it a few days and a few more women, and you'll forget how much you love our sex."

"I hate when you talk like that. And you insult us both when you make it just about sex."

"You mean when I speak the truth? What do you want from me?" I put my hands on my hips and continued, "You could have stayed in bed with me this morning, making love all day, but instead you went out on a date with another woman. I don't begrudge you that, but don't act like *I'm* the one keeping this from being more. I'm just doing what I need to keep my sanity."

"I've been ready to try again for a while." When he reached out again to touch my arm, I let him. "I get why you're upset with me—Red kept reminding me all day. He's decided to take your side. Baby, please, I want to be different for you. You keep saying no."

"You've been telling me for years that you can't change," I said, pointing at his chest, "and I thought you would happy that I finally believe you. I'm fine. Go to work and find another bevy of broads to bring back for you and Red to pick over."

"Stop it, Jacqs. You're the only woman in my life, other than my sister, that I truly love."

"It doesn't feel that way to me. It feels like I could never, ever be enough for you."

"Baby, that's not true. It's not you; it's me."

I laughed but it wasn't a pretty sound. "Please don't insult me, okay. I told you this morning we didn't need to talk, and we don't. Just don't think we're falling back into our old ways. I can't and won't."

"I'm sorry. When you were in my arms last night I wasn't thinking about this morning, I'm sorry for being such an idiot. I love you, Jacqs and wish I could stop being such a fuck up. It's just when we're alone, together—"

He gazed down at me and I could see the pain in his eyes. He wanted to be better for me, but I didn't think I had it in me to give him another chance.

He checked his watch and said, "My ride should be here in a few."

"A woman?" I could tell by the look on his face I was right. I don't know why, but that hurt me more than anything else he had said. "Trying to get me in bed tonight, after you fucked me last night, and some other woman on a boat today. Now you have another taking you to work and what will she get in trade? Is it ever enough?"

Leaving my untouched drink on the counter, I ran out of the kitchen.

He yelled after me, "It's not like that, Jacqs."

I continued through the house and out the back French doors, jogging around the pool to the dock. I climbed into Red's large cruising vessel called the Adjustable Bend and went into the belly of the boat. Why couldn't Bond leave well enough alone and why couldn't I stop caring about him?

I needed to get myself together and leave. Struggling to keep my tears inside, I no longer felt like socializing, and I definitely didn't have it in me to put up with more crap from anyone else.

As if the cursed gods heard me, they sent big foot after me. I felt the boat rock with his weight.

"What?" I said defensively, wrapping my arms around myself.

"You ran through the house, so I came to see if you're okay," Red said, standing by the stairway in his aubergine, long-sleeved T-shirt, beige jeans, and leather flip-flops.

"Does it matter?"

"It matters to me."

"You're right to think I'm a stupid woman who keeps making the same mistake, over and over again. Except last night, I was fine with it being just this one time, but he wants to make it more, at least in words. His behavior says something else entirely."

"Never assume to know what I think," Red said, his jaw tight with displeasure.

"Why are you always so mad at me?"

He sighed heavily and said, "Unfortunately Bond's past will always rule his life and his choices."

"You really care about him, don't you?"

"Yes, I do."

"Do you know why he doesn't drive and why he's so messed up in relationships?"

"Only he can tell you that."

"So you know the truth but you won't tell me. Great." I stood and said, "Do you mind letting me by?"

"Where are you going?" Red asked, blocking my way.

"Keeping tabs on me for Bond?" I said, looking up at him, trying not to be intimidated.

"Why are you the most frustrating person I know?"

"Again you don't answer *my* questions and *I'm* the frustrating one? I'm going back into the house to get my purse and drive home. Between you, Bond, and my sister, I feel like crawling under my covers and hiding for a good long time."

As I passed by, he reached out and touched my arm. The contact sent a frisson running across my skin, causing my nipples to tighten. I stared down at his large hand dwarfing my arm and then back up at him. I couldn't fully decipher his expression, but he looked shaken. *Could it be possible, that through all the years, this was the very first time he had ever touched me?*

I stood with my mouth hanging open. When I realized it, and he said nothing, I clamped my mouth shut and climbed up the steps out of the boat.

I stormed through the house, noticing all the new people who had arrived. I had to get out.

CHAPTER THREE

Save Room

by John Legend

In front of Red's house, I paced back and forth until I decided to head home. I sat in my car, trying to make sense of Red and what happened when he touched me. My phone rang, yanking me out of my musings. I shook myself out of my thoughts and hit the speaker button hoping it was my sister Samantha calling.

"I'm at a pub a couple of miles from Mom's. Can you come to get me?"

"Tell me where you are, and please don't get yourself into any trouble."

"No trouble, Jackie. Let's just have a drink and then we can head over to Red's."

"I'll come get you and take you back to Darren's. Don't drink Sam! I'm on my way."

"Fine, but come into the place when you get here."

She gave me the address to Dirty Joe's and I had a feeling I knew the place. I had passed it several times on my way to the Swap Shop. It sat near Sunrise Boulevard adjacent to a bad neighborhood. She was like a homing pigeon for dives.

I found Samantha at the pool table with an audience. She had just knocked back a shot and was lining up the cue stick for her next drop. She looked so out of place.

Where I managed to get the curves, she got all the height. Her slight frame and long flowing blonde hair made her look more like teenager than a twenty-five-year-old. Our only commonality was our eye color. As down and out as she often seemed to be, she always managed to look put-together. Why she gravitated to dives never made any sense to me; men anywhere would buy her a drink.

Her tight jeans hugged her hips, and when she bent over with the cue stick in hand, the top of her blouse billowed open, giving the men surrounding the table an eyeful.

"Jackie!" she squealed when she saw me walking up, throwing her arms open for a hug.

"Sam, let's go," I said, returning the embrace.

She pulled me over to her booth and said, "Go get a drink and let me finish this game."

I really needed a drink, and didn't have the strength to fight with her. "Only if you promise not to drink anymore."

"Promise," she said, crossing her heart.

"Watch my bag," I said as I grabbed my wallet out of it. At the bar, I ordered the house blush and sighed out all of my stress.

The old bartender wearing a ratty, long-sleeved, plaid shirt and jeans that looked like they might stand on their own, asked, "That bad?"

"Worse," I said, resting my elbow on the wooden bar.

"It's good you came for your friend."

"Sister."

"Sister, then. This isn't the greatest area of town."

"I noticed."

"I'm sure you have," he said, wiping the counter down in front of me.

"I meant no offense," I said, shaking my head as real exhaustion set in.

"None taken. A piece of advice?"

"Sure."

"The later it gets, the worse it'll be."

"Gotcha and thanks."

"No problem."

I paid, left a tip on the bar, and walked back over to Sam and her entourage. "Let's get out of here," I whispered into her ear.

"The game is almost over," she said. She eyed the man next to her, and a look passed between them.

"I'm going to the bathroom, and when I get back we're leaving."

"Okay."

Fortunately the women's bathroom wasn't nearly as bad as I expected it to be, but when I came out of the restroom, the game had broken up, and Samantha was nowhere to be found. I snatched my purse out of the booth and found my cell phone.

Me: Where the hell are you?

I received no call back, so I rummaged through my bag for my keys.

"Mother fucker!" I yelled, knowing she stole my car.

"She left with Frank," the bartender said.

I just shook my head, at a loss of what to say. I had to know if my car was really gone so I tromped outside to make sure. "I am going to kill her," I said to no one.

"I can give you a lift, little lady," a heavyset man said, taking me by surprise.

"Uh, no thanks," I said as I scurried back into the bar and sat up front.

I texted her again:

Me: You better bring my car back this instant!

I dialed Lainie, but it went straight into voicemail.

"Hey girl, I hope you're having a fun time on your date. My bitch of a sister stole my car and I'm stranded at Dirty Joe's west of US1. Please call me if you get this."

Next I texted Cat and received nothing back. I imagined the party at Red's was in full swing, which would mean she probably couldn't hear her phone. I had Red's phone number on my refrigerator at home, but not in my cell. I realized I didn't even know his real name. Bond had a habit of doling out nicknames to the ones closest to him. I decided to text Bond to get Red's number. Red could relay my message to Cat.

> **Me:** What's Red's phone number? I can't seem to reach Cat.
> **Bond:** I thought you were at Red's.
> **Me:** I'm stuck at Dirty Joe's and need a ride.
> **Bond:** What the fuck are you doing there? Do you know how dangerous that place is?
> **Me:** Can we do this later? I'd like to get the hell out of here!

A few minutes past and another text came through:

> **Bond:** Red's on his way. Stay at the bar near the bartender.
> **Me:** Did you have to send him?

I wasn't thrilled to be seeing Red again, but at least someone was coming to get me. I moved over to the bar and lowered my shoulders in relief.

Even though I was still steaming mad at Bond, I wished he could have been the one to come.

Sam's previous boyfriend liked to rough her up when they partied to excess. The last time I received a crisis call from her, Bond left work in the middle of his shift to help me out.

We found her high on drugs and alcohol with a black eye in the middle of a club, barely coherent. He held her in the backseat as I drove us to my place. We took turns holding back her hair as her stomach purged her overdose. I felt immense gratitude for Bond's support and not having to handle the situation alone. I don't know what Bond said to her boyfriend that night, but he never bothered her again.

My thoughts were interrupted by a tall man looming over me and poking my arm.

"Where's Samantha?"

"I have no idea, Darren. When she was kind enough to steal my car, she didn't happen to tell me where she planned to go."

"This is all your fault!" he yelled, grabbing my shoulders and shaking me. "Why did you make her go see Sarah? Why couldn't you just leave us alone?"

"Let go of me," I yelled, trying to dislodge his grip by scratching the back of his hands. "I did no such thing. She's clearly lying to you as well. Let … me … go!"

"Samantha said you were forcing her to see her daughter. She said that—"

Darren seemed to get angrier and tightened his grip. I thought he might throw me to the ground.

"How did you know she was here?" I squeaked out.

"She told me to come pick her up. Do you know how many days she's been sober until now? What kind of sister are you? You bring her to a bar?"

"Darren, stop! I didn't bring her here! She—"

He shook me again, not listening to me. "Why can't you just butt out of her—"

In quick succession, Red entered the establishment,

grabbed Darren's wrist, and flipped him around, sandwiching his face against the bar. "Another boyfriend of yours?" Red said.

"Fuck off," I said, pursing my lips.

"Do you kiss your mother with that mouth?" he said to me and to Darren he warned, "I'm going to let you go but if you take a step towards either of us, I'm going to cold-cock you and I promise, it's going to hurt."

"Yeah," Darren mumbled.

"Jacqs, head for the door, I'm right behind you."

I lifted my purse off the bar and stomped off. *What an asshole*, I thought, and I didn't mean Darren.

Red caught up to me as I pushed my way out of Dirty Joe's. "I can take care of myself."

"You're doing such a fine job that I had to rescue you from this sleazy bar."

I turned to face him and said, "There were extenuating circumstances."

"I'm sure," he said, sarcasm coating his words.

He had parked his ostentatious silver Mercedes SUV up front. Because of his extra-large tires I had to climb to get into the passenger's side. As soon as I settled into the seat, I started to shake. The accumulation from the day exacted its toll and my tears mutinied down my cheeks. Red caught me up in his arms and I punched his chest for him to let me go, but he held me tight as I continued to sob.

"It's going to be okay," he said as he let me cry. After several minutes past, he said, "We should get out of here before any more of your boyfriends show up."

"Really? You too?"

"You're right, I'm sorry. You just don't get it."

"Get what?" I said, staring into his bright, green eyes surrounded by golden-red eyebrows and light lashes.

"Never mind. Where do you want to go?"

"Goddamn it, there she is," I said, scooting away from him. "I'm fine now and have my own way home."

"I'm waiting until I know you're safe and I can tell Bond that I took care of things."

I paused with my hand on the door. "So, the only reason you're here is because Bond sent you?"

"Would you like there to be another reason?" His serious expression gave me pause.

"Um, well, you should know I asked Bond to have you send Cat to get me."

"To this dive?" He waved his hand toward the bar and we watched a man stumble out.

"Well, I … maybe it wasn't the best of ideas, but I had no intention of bothering you."

"You bother me all the time," he said, rubbing his short-cropped beard. "Even when you're not around."

"Well, you can't blame me for that!"

"Who should I blame, Little One? Please come by the house for a little while."

"Why?"

A knock sounded on the window, startling me back to the present. I opened the door and hopped down, almost twisting my ankle. Samantha stood in front of me dangling my keys.

"Come," I heard Red say just before I closed the car door.

"You're on my shit list," I said to my sister.

"I simply gave him a ride and came right back."

"No, Sam, what you did was steal my keys and car and if you ever do something like that again, I will call the police immediately and press charges. Your boyfriend is here and practically assaulted me because of your lies. You need help and frankly, I don't want to hear from you until you get some."

I stalked to my car and threw my purse into the

passenger seat. Flopping into the driver's side, I flipped down the visor and saw blue streaks of makeup running down my face. "Great," I said out loud.

When I glanced at the entrance I saw Red waiting for me to leave. As I drove out, I realized I had never thanked him for coming to get me. I'm not sure if I rationalized a reason to see him again or not, but I wanted to know what he meant in his car. Turning off the main drag, I took the back streets to his house.

He stood outside of his SUV waiting for me and that, in and of itself, almost made me turn around to leave. He arrogantly believed I would follow.

I had to park farther down the road to find a free space. I pulled a tissue out of the glove compartment and did the best I could to clean up my eye makeup. After pushing my purse under the passenger seat, I texted Lainie to let her know I had made it back to Red's with my car.

I shook out my hair, put my shoulders back and stood as straight as possible. I wouldn't let Red intimidate me. When I strutted over to him, his expression left me confused. He'd always been as cold as a granite statue, and I couldn't read the new side to him.

"Why did you want me to come and what did you mean? Wait … no … shit, what I really wanted to say was that I appreciate you coming to get me."

"Let's go have a drink."

"A drink?"

"Yes, you could use one."

"Would you stop doing that?" I said, squinting up at him through the outside house light that cascaded around him.

"Doing what? I just offered you a drink," he said, resting his back against his vehicle and folding his arms in front of him.

"No, you said I needed one. You're so bossy."

He laughed and said, "You bring it out in me. I'll do my best to temper the urge."

"You have urges?"

"You don't want to know," he said, glaring down at me.

"Oh … I," I stuttered, my nipples flaring at his intent. I crossed my arms over my chest as well.

Grabbing my hand, he pulled me along with him into the house and through the main sitting area. *Dreamworld* played through the sound system. Cat gave me a questioning look as Red led me into the kitchen. I shrugged my shoulders back to her. He opened the refrigerator, fingered a Mike's Hard Lemonade and a bottle of Dos Equis, popped the caps and swooped up my hand again in his large palm, leading me out to the back.

I loved all the palms and the large stone deck around the Jacuzzi and pool. His two-story home sat on the Intracoastal Waterway, allowing him to keep his boat right behind the house.

Two guys I didn't recognize sat at the wrought iron table by the pool, smoking cigarettes.

"Hey Ray, Charlie, glad you could make it," Red said, pausing but not releasing my hand.

"Thanks for the invite. She's a tiny one," one of the guys said, tilting his head in my direction.

"She makes up for it with a big mouth," Red said with a smug expression.

I tried to pull my hand out of his grip, but he held on so tight I had to use my free hand to punch him in the shoulder. I would have preferred to punch his jaw, but I figured it would hurt me more than him to hit the sharp edge of his face.

His friends chuckled, leaving me even more incensed.

"And he makes up for his Neanderthal size with his small personality or at least that's what he calls it," I said, purposefully looking at his pants.

That made his friends laugh hysterically and I felt proud of myself.

"Come on, you," he said, dragging me back inside and up the stairs to his bedroom.

I had never been in there before. So neat and organized, it could have been a room in an upscale hotel except for the antique furniture on either side of the fireplace and the art on the walls. A chair sat near the entrance to the room, a pair of slacks over the back of it.

"What the hell is going on with you Red?" I said as I finally managed to pull my hand away from his. "You've never given me much notice over the years. How long has it been?"

"Five years."

"I've been putting up with your crap for five years? Jesus." I took the lemonade from his hand and took several swallows.

"Take it easy, Jacqs," he said, closing the door behind him and leaning back against it.

"Stop telling me what to do, would you?"

"I can't help myself," he said with a slight smile.

"Try." I sat on the edge of the bed, putting plenty of distance between us.

"I didn't much care for your joke."

"Your friends liked it and you started it. Don't fuck with me and I won't fuck with you back."

"Do you have to talk like that? It's very unattractive."

"What the fuck … shit …um heck do you want from me?" I drank more to boost my courage.

"I'm warning you, Jacqs."

"Warning me? From what? What will you do?"

"Don't push me."

"I push your buttons without even trying."

"I'm well aware of that."

"Are you going to answer me?" I asked. "Because, if not, I'll just head home." I stood, finished off my drink and took a step toward the door that he blocked with his massive frame.

He crossed the distance between us, swiped the drink out of my hand, and placed both bottles on the corner of his dresser. Before I had a chance to fight or protest he lifted me under my arms, off my feet, and placed my back against the wall. He groaned as if it pained him and then he lowered his mouth to mine.

I tried to push him off, but he remained determined and I finally gave over to the incredible sensations he stirred within me. I took his large face in my little hands, which caused him to groan in pleasure, deepening the kiss. As I wrapped my legs around his bulky frame, he held me closer and carried me over to the antique chair by the door. He sat down with me on his lap, and we just stared at each other for a moment.

Afraid of breaking the spell that I knew would end once reality set in, I sat, waiting. He ran his hands up my neck, followed by his mouth, kissing and nibbling. Chills fluttered down my spine and I moaned, "Oh, Red." Wetness pooled in my panties and I wanted him to take me. I wanted to know what his cock looked like, tasted like. I didn't care if we ever spoke again, or if my motivations stemmed from getting back at Bond. Red had sparked an intense need and I wanted him to take me.

Running my hands through his red hair, I pulled his mouth back to mine and he took control. Clutching my wrists with one hand, he held them behind my back freeing him to bite his way down my chest. He unbuttoned the rest of my blouse, pushing the silk down off my shoulders, exposing my breast and hard nipples to the air.

"No bra? You're naughtier than I imagined."

"You've thought about me?"

"Incessantly. Keep your arms behind you," he said as ran his hands under my breasts and lowered his mouth. "I had no idea."

"What?"

"For such a tiny woman, you have large nipples."

I scrunched my face, not sure if he liked what he saw.

"No need for the funny face, I love them." He sucked on my right nipple and I closed my eyes in pleasure. His big hands kneaded my flesh and pulled on my left nipple.

"Ohhh," I called out, arching into his caresses.

"Shh," he said, "I think I heard something."

"Don't stop," I pleaded.

"Stay the night."

"That'll go over well with Bond, for sure."

"Did you have to mention him?"

The bubble had burst and in my embarrassment, I scurried off his lap and buttoned up my blouse. I glanced in the mirror on the dresser and smoothed out my hair.

He pushed into me from behind, grasping my breast over my shirt. He nipped my earlobe and said, "I'm not done with you, but I need to check on the party below." He clutched the nape of my neck, turning my head toward him and kissing me one last time. "I'll see you downstairs."

As soon as he left the room, I ran and jumped on his bed, lying back and staring at the ceiling. "What the hell was that?" I said to the crown molding. *Is that why he has been an ass to me all these years? Why give in now? Why did I kiss him back?* My head hurt with all the thoughts, so I decided I needed another drink.

I hopped off the bed and noticed an antique Victorian wooden trunk against the wall on the far side of the room. The leather straps and rivets reminded me of a saddle. I slipped into his bathroom to freshen up before rejoining the party. Once downstairs, through the open French doors, I could see Red talking to a tall, attractive woman. They both laughed and it pissed me off. I turned right into the kitchen for another lemonade. Scanning the people scattered around the house, I strolled until I found Cat in the front sitting room. The plump couch and love seat matched the rug beneath perfectly. I plopped down on the cushion next to her.

"What was that all about?" she asked.

"Long story short, Red had to rescue me from Dirty Joe's. Well, he did and he didn't. Sam showed back up with my car at the last minute."

"She took your car? What's up with that girl?"

Taking a long swallow of my drink, I said, "Trust me, I wish I knew because if I did, I would knock some sense into her."

"I don't think Bond would've liked to see Red holding your hand and pulling you through the house. That was a first."

"I'm done worrying about what he thinks. He certainly doesn't care what I think."

"Truly? That would be wonderful, but I find that hard to believe. How many years have you been going back and forth?"

I knew I should chase the lemonade with some water, but the loosening effects of the alcohol felt great. Though with my tiny frame, it didn't take much. I took another draw from the bottle and said, "Eight, but I've long since given up hope. We are great as best friends and nothing more. I thought maybe we could have sex on occasion, but I don't think he can handle it."

"Him?" Cat said, laughing.

"Yes, him!" I said indignantly.

"Whatever you tell yourself to get through the day." She patted my shoulder like I was delusional.

"Why is every single person working my last nerve today? For your information—you know what? Never mind. I don't want to talk about Bond, or Red, or Samantha. I'm going to get another drink."

For a second, I wished I hadn't consumed any alcohol so I could've driven home and crawled into my own bed. Since that wasn't an option, I drank a full glass of water, hoping to avoid a hangover, and then opened another lemonade. I wondered if I could sneak past the people outside and hide in Red's boat. Exiting the kitchen on the far side led me into the dining room, a room I had never entered, but I only found windows and no doors to the back. Instead I went around to the front of the house and tried to walk carefully around the side, through the landscaping to the back. Some soil migrated into my sandals so I held onto the corner wall and shook them out.

"What do you think you're doing?" Red's deep booming voice startled me.

"Avoiding you. I was trying to make my way, unnoticed, to your boat."

"It's technically a yacht and why are you hiding from me?"

"That woman, is she the one you fucked today while sailing?"

"I didn't have sex with…" He clutched my upper arm, peered around the corner, and pulled me along with him.

"Let go of me! Stop dragging me around everywhere."

"Whatever you say," he said, scooping me up in his arms and carrying me the rest of the way to the edge of the dock.

"Put me down you brute!" I said, kicking my legs.

"Shh," he said, I could hear the laughter in his voice.

44

"Just because I'm smaller than you—"

"Much smaller—"

"Doesn't mean you can keep manhandling me!"

"Oh, I have definite plans to manhandle you," he said, desire filling every word.

He placed me down on the edge of the dock, in front of his yacht. With a sweeping motion of his arm, he indicated I should go ahead of him. Heading straight into the belly of Adjustable Bend, I sat on the couch to the right and placed my drink on the table in front of me. His cruising vessel belied the elegance of the house. Although very high-end, it read bachelor pad. On a raised platform at the bow of the boat was a circular bed piled with an assortment of pillows in beiges and browns.

"Cat's already wondering what's up with us, Red. Who was that woman?"

"A friend of a friend," he said, still standing by the stairs.

"And have you slept with her?"

"I didn't have sex with anyone today and I don't have sex with people I've just met."

"What, wait a minute! You and Bond pick up women all the time. You're telling me you don't sleep with them?"

"Not on the first date and frequently there's no second."

"Who the hell are you? And what has happened..." I flipped my hand, palm up, toward him and back to me. "...between us?"

"That's two separate questions, the first takes time and the second is far more complicated."

"Give it a shot."

"I think our major problem is that both of our loyalties lie with Bond and not each other."

"That doesn't tell me anything other than stating the obvious. Up until a few hours ago I thought you hated my guts. Bond seems to think otherwise."

"That's because we fought about you this morning."

"After I left?"

"On the phone before I got there." He took two long steps and sat down on the couch next to me. "I was furious with both of you, with myself too. I waited too long. I knew nothing had happened between you two for months, and I actually thought you might have gotten over him, but I'm not sure that'll ever happen."

"I'm not either, but I'm not waiting any longer for him to change. What do you want from me?"

"A chance."

"And Bond?"

"I'd like to see if there is anything here for us before we talk to him."

"I don't think he'll care," I said, shaking my head.

"You are very wrong about that."

"Then why do it? Why risk your friendship?"

He maneuvered closer to me, lifting me onto his lap and said, "I couldn't sit back and watch the way he treats you for another second. Had our fight happened in person, I probably would have decked him. When he told me you'd spent the night—"

"I didn't know—"

"I had to keep you mad at me."

"Why?"

"It was my only form of self-protection." He moved my hair away from my face and held it in one fist. "I love your petite, lovely neck," he said, nuzzling in close.

I laughed out loud.

"What?" he asked.

"I've been fascinated by your thick neck. It's almost as wide as your head. You and I … we're an illustration in contrast."

He smiled and said, "Yes and it drives me crazy."

"I thought you liked tall women."

"I like you."

"Oh." Without thinking, the liquor fueling me on, I blurted out, "Are you going to make love to me?"

"No."

"No?"

"I'd like you to get tested first. I know you're not very sexually active, but Bond is."

"Oh … okay." I wasn't sure what to think.

"Are you on birth control?"

"Yes, of course," I said and then had another thought. "Will you get tested too?"

"I have current tests."

"From when?"

"Around six months ago."

"You haven't had—"

"No."

"Oh." *Wow*, I thought.

Tilting his head down, he swept me up in his kiss. He conquered my mouth, pulling me into his world and showing me what it could be like. I wanted more.

As if hearing my thoughts, he easily moved us over to the bed, laying me down beside him. His legs hung off the end.

"This bed doesn't fit you," I said.

"No, but you do." He rolled me on top of him and enveloped me in his embrace. His hard contours felt wonderful pressed against me.

"Have you ever dated someone my size?" I asked.

"No."

"The Neanderthal and the pixie."

He laughed, rocking us both.

"I still hate you, you know," I said, smiling.

"I'm well aware of that, but at the very least you can

use me to get back at Bond."

"That's what I was thinking."

Red pushed my hair away from my face, looping it behind my ears. "Seriously Jacqs, please think about it."

"Which part?"

"You and me."

"You might have to give me awhile to wrap my head around this new you."

"We'll take this slow, but I'll leave you some incentive." Holding my head gently in his big hands, he used his full lips to coax me into considering. He flipped me onto my back, looming over me. Running his tongue along the edge of mine, he encouraged me to joust with him. I complied, dancing my tongue around his. As the intensity grew, the kiss deepened.

His hand flowed down to my hip and he used the leverage to grind his pelvis against mine.

"Ohhh," I moaned against his mouth, feeling his erection between us.

"See what you do to me," he said, taking my hand and placing it on the front of his pants.

I felt dizzy with desire as I ran my fingers along the outline of his cock. Through the pants, his felt much thicker than Bond's. "Oh lord," I groaned, "this doesn't feel slow."

"I've waited a long time, too long." Nuzzling my neck, he sighed and said, "You smell better than I imagined."

"Why did you wait so long?"

Gazing into my eyes, he said, "For obvious reasons."

"So why now?"

"Life's too short to wait forever for what you really want."

"You really want me?" I said, tracing the bulge in his pants.

"Like nothing else I've ever wanted."

"Little ole' me?"

He answered with his body. Rolling me back on top of his chest, he held his head up to kiss me and grasped my buttocks in his hands, gyrating his hips beneath me.

I felt so turned on, wet, and sure if he kept rubbing the ridge of his cock against my mound, one of us was bound to explode.

"Whoa," he said as he lay me down beside him again. Both of our chests rapidly rose and fell. "We need to stop now and should get back to the party."

"Do you know what time Bond will be here?"

"Soon."

Sitting up, I said, "He'll notice something has changed."

"I'll tell him we came to a truce."

"That's not too far from the truth."

CHAPTER FOUR

Lesson Learned

by Alicia Keys (ft. John Mayer)

After adjusting my clothing and fluffing out my hair, I asked, "Should we go back to the party one at a time?"

"No, that will look more suspicious," Red said. He swept me up in one last kiss, handed me my drink and we both climbed out of the vessel.

"Where were you guys?" Kev asked when we walked into the back of the house.

"I … we…" I said, stumbling around for a plausible response.

"Jacqs just needed a break from the party," Red said. "Her sister's boyfriend really shook her up at the pub. Literally. I thought I was going to have to punch him out."

"You didn't tell me that part, Jacqs. I'm so sorry," Cat said, giving me a warm hug.

I peered up over her shoulder and Red winked at me. "I'm okay. The three drinks have helped, but I think I'd better eat something."

Cat looped her arm over my shoulder and she and I strode into the kitchen with Kev following behind. Truthfully, I didn't know if I could eat. I knew I should, but butterflies fluttered around my stomach making me jittery.

"What do you want?" Cat asked.

At home, I would have opted for a bowl of cereal. There were chips and nuts readily available around the house, however, I hadn't eaten anything since the late breakfast Lainie and I had shared.

"Let me make you a turkey sandwich," Red said. "I want one myself."

"Count me in," Bond said, making me jump.

I wished I had stayed well hidden in the boat and had sent Red on his way alone. All the tension made me feel sick to my stomach. I didn't acknowledge Bond, still plenty pissed off at him. Instead, I poured myself a glass of water and hopped up on the counter near the sink, watching the scene play out before me.

"Neither of you texted to let me know you were okay," Bond said to Red and me.

"Oh shit," I said, pulling my cell phone from my pocket. I had six texts waiting for me. Scrolling through, I read Lainie's first.

> **Lainie:** Date went well, heading home (alone). Sounds like you had another crazy evening. Are we still on for tomorrow? Can we make it a bit later?
> **Lainie:** Home now and going to crash. Let's do lunch instead of breakfast. I want to sleep in. See you at 12?

I texted her back:

> **Me:** 12 works for me too. I'm going to crash here and then head home. Your place or mine?

Bond's texts read:

> **Bond:** I told Red to tell Cat, but he said he'd head over.
> **Bond:** Is he there yet? Stay near the bartender and avoid making eye contact with anyone.

Bond: Please let me know when you get back to the house. We need to talk later.

Bond: I'm off work and on my way to Red's.

"As you can see, I'm perfectly fine," I said. "Nothing a few drinks couldn't handle. Speaking of which, I could use another."

"Food first," Red said.

I glared in his direction. "Will you ever stop being so bossy?"

"Doubtful," he said, but I could see the smile playing at his lips.

A tall, voluptuous blonde entered the kitchen and slipped her hand into Bond's. Everyone in the kitchen, besides Blondie, turned to take in my reaction.

"What?" I said, throwing my hands up in exasperation.

"Just checking," Cat said, holding her palms out in an effort to calm me down.

"I'm not going to crumble to the ground every time Bond has a new fling. No offense, new person. Besides, I'm interested in someone new."

The expression on Red's and Bond's faces were beyond priceless. I wished I'd had a camera to capture the moment.

"You are?" Bond and Cat asked simultaneously.

Red, who stood behind the group, shook his head, shooting me a look of warning.

"Yes, and I'm not prepared to share any details until I know where it's heading."

"Since last night?" Bond practically shouted.

"None of your fucking business," I shouted back.

Frank and Charlie walked into the entrance of the kitchen but immediately turned around.

"There's beer out back in the cooler to the right of the

doors," Red called out to them.

"We need to talk," Bond said, dropping the hand of his latest conquest and stepping toward me.

"We don't, and frankly, I have no interest in doing so. What I plan to do is eat my sandwich, have another drink if I can sneak another past Red, and maybe go skinny-dipping in the pool. This is a big house Bond, take your girl and fuck off, or fuck her. Either way, leave me alone."

"What has come over you? Too much alcohol, clearly." Bond folded his arms across his chest and took a step closer.

"Because I don't want what you're selling anymore?" I said, pointing my finger toward him. "Maybe the alcohol is just making me more honest." I hopped off the counter and said to Bond's date, "I'm sure you're a lovely woman and sorry for the drama." I strutted over to Red, grateful for not tripping over my own feet, and picked up half of the sandwich that sat on the cutting board. "Yum," I said, staring up at Red.

His neck reddened and his expression told me I'd better tread carefully.

I moved to the other side of him, opened the refrigerator and grabbed another Mike's Hard Lemonade. After I had popped the cap, I stood there and downed a third of the bottle.

"Let's go," Bond said to his date.

I breathed out a deep exhalation and lowered my shoulders. "That was fun," I said.

"What the hell has gotten into you?" Cat asked.

I couldn't tell if her tone was that of awe or condemnation. Maybe both? "I've had a hell of a day."

"Apparently," Kev said. "Try not to alienate the rest of the party, will ya?"

I laughed out loud and said, "I'll keep that in mind." I

finished my sandwich and my drink.

Kev and Cat wandered off leaving Red and me alone in the kitchen.

"You are in rare form," he said to me.

"Am I?"

"You seemed to be having fun pushing Bond's buttons." He took a bite of his sandwich and added, "This is a new side to you. You've always just gone along."

"And then went home to cry. I don't feel like crying now, and I have you to thank for that."

"How is that?" Red said and chewed the last bite.

"You're going to make a mighty fine distraction, I think." I touched his arm and smiled up at him.

"Let's see what you think in the morning when you're straight instead of liquored up. Have I ever seen you this tipsy?"

"No, I don't usually have more than one drink."

"Should I cut you off?"

"You should kiss me instead."

I saw the desire flare on his face and he said, "You need to behave, Jacqs—"

"She needs to behave?" Bond asked, strolling over to us. "Is my sandwich ready?"

"Yes, I've cut her off."

"That's a good idea. I've never seen you like this." Bond narrowed his eyes at me.

I stood up as tall as I could and held onto the counter to steady myself. "It's the new me, so I suggest you get used to it."

"Plan to stay the night, Jacqs. I won't let you drive home in this condition," Bond said. "You know how I feel about drinking and driving."

"I have no plans to. Red said I could sleep in his bed … on his boat that is." I giggled at myself and neither Bond nor Red looked pleased. "Where's Blondie?"

"She took off," Bond said.

"Oops, sorry," I said. "I really didn't mean to run her off."

"I think you did, but I'm the one who asked her to leave."

"Well, you shouldn't have and definitely not on my account." I shook my head.

"We need to talk," Bond said.

"I'll leave you two alone," Red said.

"I'd rather you stay, Red. I think Bond and I've talked more than enough and I, for one, want to go for a swim. It's beautiful out."

I collected the empty bottles on the counter and put them in the recycle bin. Then I took out my phone and left it on the counter that led into the living room. I scooted past a group of people playing Cards Against Humanity and out the French doors. Finding the trunk that held the towels, I grabbed one, stripped down to my panties and jumped into the pool.

Bond and Red followed me out.

"Come in, the water's great!" I said, splashing in their direction.

They both stepped back to avoid getting wet.

"I'll join her," Charlie said, putting out his cigarette.

"No!" Both Red and Bond yelled. They looked at each other, and back to me.

"Okay, no problem, guys. I was just trying to be friendly." He strolled back into the house.

"Get out of the pool, Jacqs," Bond ordered.

I floated on my back, looking at the stars. Maybe I was a bit more than tipsy because I completely enjoyed pissing off Bond, and, being completely honest, Red too. I had spent so many days and nights lamenting my relationship with Bond that my new found strength, alcohol induced or not, felt amazing.

"There are many beautiful women in your house

looking for a good time. Why don't you boys go and have fun? I promise not to drown."

They both stood with their arms crossed like they were my father instead of my lover and a potential one.

"We aren't leaving until you get out," Bond said.

"Well then, pull up a lounge and have a seat." Diving under the water, I did a handstand and circled around to the surface. After dipping my head back to smooth out my hair, I reached underneath the water. I pulled off my panties, squeezed out the water and threw them to Red. He caught them out of the air. Both Bond and Red seemed at a loss of what to do with me and I felt powerful.

I swam to the deep end of the pool, pulled myself up over the rocks and slid into the Jacuzzi. Dutifully, they followed me around and sat on the edge.

"Now you don't have to worry about me drowning," I said, smiling up at them.

"Please get out and I'll drive you home," Red said.

I liked that idea. It would give us a chance to make out again. "What about my car?"

"You can get it tomorrow," Bond said.

"I'm supposed to be at Lainie's by twelve," I said, although I didn't know for sure the final plans.

"I'll come get you in the morning," Red said. He seemed to plead with me with his green eyes.

"That seems like a lot of driving when I can just crash in your bed or you can sleep on my couch."

"Someone will have to hold your hair back," Bond said.

I splashed him in response. "I have no intention of getting sick."

"Red can drive us both to your house and pick us up in the morning," Bond said.

"Maybe I haven't been crystal clear, but I have no intention of spending the night with you, Bond. You were silly to send Blondie on her way."

"I can drive you and Bond to your place," Red said.

My anger spiked and I thought I might cry. "Fuck you, Red and your ride. I'll sleep for a couple of hours and drive myself home. Damn, I'm just a stupid woman, aren't I?" I stepped out of the swirling water and stomped around Bond and Red to my clothes. I wrapped myself in the big, fluffy, white towel and took my clothing with me.

Tears trailed down my face as I ran up the stairs to the bathroom attached to Red's bedroom and locked the door behind me. I knew the guys followed because I could hear them arguing outside the door. I rinsed off in the shower and washed the last of the makeup off my face. After re-dressing, I inhaled deeply and opened the door.

"Where's Bond?" I said, looking around Red.

"I told him to give you space, and he listened for a change."

"I've had my fill of you both."

"What I said was ill-conceived and stupid. I'm sorry."

"I don't know what to think," I said, shaking my head. "You hurt me, Red. Don't do it again. Don't think because I've been willing to put up with Bond's crap that I'm willing to let another man make me feel less than I am. I can't, I won't."

"I promise you, that's the last thing I want to do." He hugged me, and I mellowed. Staring down at me he said, "You're always beautiful, but I like you best without makeup."

"I don't know if I should be pissed off or flattered. Why all those other women? Tall, heavily made up, adorned with the latest fashions and jewelry? I don't understand you."

"That takes time, Jacqs. Let me take you home and tuck you in." Stepping around me into the bathroom, he reached for a towel. "Your hair is still wet." He wiped away a drop on my forehead and pressed my hair between the folds of the towel.

"Thanks. And what happens tomorrow?"

"I'll have a reason to see you again."

"Hmm, how long can you stay?"

A huge smile spread across his face and he stooped down to kiss me. He pushed me back against the wall and helped me to escape from my life and problems with his lovely soft full lips.

"Hmmmm," I moaned.

He made it impossible for me to think. In his arms, I became emotion and sensation, and I wanted to see how far he could take me. His firm kiss left me mesmerized and titillated, and when he bent his knees and pushed his hardness against me, a louder groan unwittingly escaped.

"Shh," he said. "We better get moving or Bond will come looking for us."

"Okay, can you tell the gang we're leaving? I'll meet you out front."

"Sure."

I skipped down the stairs and headed straight for the front door. "Shit," I said. My cell phone lay on the counter in the kitchen. Not really wanting to deal with anyone, most especially Bond, I begrudgingly headed back into the heart of the house.

I practically ran into Red, who held my phone in his hand. "Thank you," I said as he handed it to me.

"Let's go," he said, clutching my free hand and pulling me along.

We rode in silence on the way to my apartment and I praised the universe that I had the sense to clean earlier. It seemed like the longest day of my life.

Once we arrived and I showed him where to park, he helped me down out of his SUV. I was grateful for the assistance.

"Welcome to my humble abode," I said as I unlocked and opened the door. I flipped on the hall light, and Red followed me inside.

"It suits you. Cute and bohemian. And, by the way, that ass of yours—so round and sexy—I wanted to bite it, leaving my mark."

"I wondered if you'd noticed," I said, pivoting to face him.

"I've actually noticed for a long time."

"You didn't come in and swim."

"I didn't think Bond would appreciate it, but we will definitely do it together soon."

I smiled and pirouetted.

"Ballet class?"

"Years of it." I backed up against the kitchen counter.

"That must account for your high, round buttocks."

"Maybe," I said.

"I also noticed you sitting on my counter, your feet dangling. I wanted to do this," he said, lifting me up onto the island behind me. He spread my legs bringing his clothed cock right up against the V in my jeans. "Perfect fit just like I imagined."

"You've had a lot of naughty thoughts, haven't you?"

"Too many," he said. "You have been torturing me for years, I'm done waiting."

Curling my finger to beckon him closer, I said, "You're not exactly done waiting. If you were, you would tear off my jeans, which you know have no underwear beneath them."

"You're still determined to torture me, aren't you?" he said, hovering close.

"That's the plan!"

"It only makes it slightly easier with your jeans on."

I hopped off the counter, shed my pants and hopped back up. I giggled but could also feel my mind wagging her finger at me. That time, I banished her to the corner. Alcohol is a great liberator and I was having way too much fun to stop.

The energy around us vibrated as he yanked my top over my head, leaving me naked. My nipples tightened when he pulled my pussy right up to the edge and lowered himself down on his knees. Nipping his way from my knee, up my thigh, he spread my legs wide and breathed across my wet and throbbing pussy. He ran his thumbs around my labia as he gave my other leg the same treatment.

Gazing down on him, in the throes of growing passion, I cupped his head in my hands and brought him to the promise land. "Oh lord, yesss," I hissed as he licked my clit for the first time. Even his tongue felt huge. I forced his face closer so he would do it again. "Please," I begged.

"You don't have to ask twice."

I couldn't keep from wriggling while he ran his tongue from my wetness to my throbbing peak.

"Your taste ... your smell ... so much better than I even imagined."

His hands kneaded my thighs and his fingers played at my opening while he kept his flicks and strokes slow and sensuous. I still held his head, but he needed no direction. The width of his tongue caused him to hit all the right spots. Gently and slowly he manipulated my clit as if savoring my essence. It had been so long since I had experienced that kind of attention, and I wished for it to last forever. The delicate dance of his tongue caused my climb to continue to greater heights.

He penetrated my pussy with his thick finger and swirled it around as he continued his oral saltation. Removing it he said, "So exquisite, you must taste for yourself." He held his finger up to my mouth and I licked it clean. The desire flared in his green eyes, and he said, "Oh, Jacqs, I'm so hard it hurts."

As he resumed his lovely oral torment, I didn't feel rushed to climax. He allowed the sensations to rise and overtake every inch of my body. Trembling swept over me as he edged me ever closer to my orgasm.

"Oh, oh, oh," tumbled uncontrollably out of me. "Oh Red, please don't stop. Oh, it's so, so good." I finally yelled, "Pleassseee," as my release escaped and exploded with such fierce intensity that my eyes watered. I could hear myself shout, but it sounded like it came from someone else. Transported away from myself, I floated in the ethers, never wanting to come back down to earth.

As I crumbled forward, he stood, catching me up in his arms. He allowed me the time to recover before he lowered his mouth to mine, sharing the juices that still lingered on his lips.

"Hmmmm," I moaned into the kiss.

"We must stop or I'll take you right here, right now. Have I mentioned how much I like your little moans when we kiss?" Lifting me into his arms he carried me to the bedroom.

"I can walk, you know," I whispered.

"I'm well aware. Let me take care of you. I've wanted to for so long. So much so, that I'm betraying the man who has been my best friend since childhood." Folding the covers down, he placed me on the bed and tucked the sheet around me.

"You haven't completely betrayed him," I said, curling on my side.

"You don't know what you're saying."

"Probably not," I said, yawning.

He sat down beside me, pushing my hair away from my face. "In the morning, you might regret what we've done … when the alcohol has worn off, but at the very least, be interested in getting to know me, as a man, aside from my friendship with Bond. I know I'm asking a lot, given our past, but we need each other."

"Mmmhmm," I said, drowsy from the day, the alcohol I'd consumed, and the exquisite orgasm. I melted into the bed and started to drift off. "I get to see you tomorrow," I mumbled, smiling and then yawning again.

"That you do." He kissed my forehead and let himself out.

As soon as the door shut, I realized I needed to pee. I shuffled to the door, locked it and plodded back through the bedroom to the bathroom. After peeing and brushing my teeth, I collapsed into my bed and slept soundly.

"Oh hell!" I said as I sat up and looked at the clock, 9:34 a.m. My head pounded, and I needed water desperately.

I barely had time to shower, dress, and eat before Red would be back. Red? Shit what had I been thinking? A rush of pleasure shot through me when I remembered his kisses and the way he had made me come. So, so hard.

Before Bond, I didn't think I could orgasm with a man. I never had, and it even took months for Bond to accomplish it. I figured I must have a finicky clit that only I knew how to work. Bond never cared for cunnilingus, and I usually felt self-conscious letting someone new go down on me. I had to assume that my lowered inhibitions from the alcohol worked in Red's favor. At any rate, it was one of the best orgasms of my life, and it would be hard to forget.

My gut twisted in guilt over the thought of Bond finding out. Part of me wanted to hurt him in the ways he had hurt me over the years. At the same time, I loved him more than a brother or best friend and knew there was something in his past that kept his heart locked away. Could I stop thinking that I held the key?

I slogged to the bathroom, downed two cups of water and three ibuprofen and waited for the shower to warm up.

Afterwards, I dressed and sat on the couch with a bowl of cereal. The ibuprofen had kicked in, lessening my headache, but I would still need my shades thanks to all the hard lemonade I had consumed.

I had no idea what to do about Red. It seemed unwise to date within our group, let alone Bond's best friend. I should have had him drop me off at Lainie's the night before. My common sense screamed, "Stay away from the big oaf." My confused emotions told another story. The kissing, the orgasm, and the tenderness he showed me swirled in my brain, leaving me totally confused.

I heard a familiar pounding on my door and thought, *Fuck!* Bond had come too.

Dragging myself to the door, I opened to find both Bond and Red. Red stood behind Bond, looking apologetic.

"You ready to go?" Bond asked, strolling into my apartment and looking around.

I wondered if he expected to find someone there with me.

"Let me grab my sunglasses and bag," I said.

Bond decided to use the car ride to talk me into going to his family's shindig.

"I already told Lily that you might come next Saturday and she really wants to see you."

"That's not fighting fair, Bond," I said from the back seat of Red's vehicle.

"All is fair in love and war."

"I think we disagree on which we're in."

"Very funny, Jacqs. Come on, you'll be doing me a huge favor, and we can escape early and go to Red's afterwards."

I could see Red through the rearview mirror, and

couldn't decipher his expression.

"Fine," I said, mostly out of guilt. Part of me wanted to rub Red in Bond's face, but the other half of me felt ashamed by my behavior.

We rode the rest of the way in silence. I planned to leave Red's place immediately, putting off having to deal with either of them. Lainie might not be thrilled with me showing up early, but I had no idea what to do or even what I wanted to do. Hanging around them, with my head pounding, seemed like unwarranted torture.

Once we arrived at Red's, I said, "Thanks so much for driving me home and back. I really appreciate it."

"Will you be here on Wednesday?" Red asked.

"Yeah, she'll be here. She's driving me," Bond said.

"I haven't decided yet, Bond."

"Wait a minute—" Bond said.

Ignoring him, I carefully climbed out of the SUV and walked down the street to my car.

Lainie lived on the second floor of a walk-up condo on the Intracoastal about ten minutes away from Red's house. Settled in her life, or it seemed that way to me, the only thing missing for her was the illusive good man. But unlike me, she seemed undaunted in the quest. She managed to keep a positive regard for the possibilities. I imagined she would one day make a brilliant wife and an even better mother. She loved kids and had the abundance of energy necessary to raise them. I had real doubts if I had it in me to be a good mom. My experiences with my sister left me unenthusiastic.

"Wake up!" I said, banging on Lainie's door. I waited and pounded again.

"Who is it?" Lainie said, and I could hear from the

tone in her voice that she was not happy.

"It's me, Jacqs."

"What the hell, girl!" she said as she unlocked the door and held it open for me.

"I'm so, so sorry to wake you," I said, skirting passed her. "Go back to sleep and I'll just hang out in the living room until lunch time."

She kept her place immaculate, not a pillow out of place, but it still managed to have a relaxed and lived-in feel. Over the years, it had become my second home.

"What time is it?" she asked.

I checked my phone and said, "Ten forty-five."

"Are you okay? You don't look okay."

"It'll keep for another hour. I just didn't want to hang out at Red's until we were supposed to meet." I put my bag down on the counter.

"I thought you were sleeping there."

"Yeah, well that's part of a long story."

"Well, I'm up now," she said, entering the kitchen and starting a pot of coffee.

"I need you to promise to stay calm and not ream me out."

She turned to face me with her hands on her hips. "That doesn't sound good. Not good at all. Please don't tell me you fucked Bond again."

"No, but he wanted to, well sort of, I don't know, it's a big mess and I need help sorting through it all."

"But I'm not going to like it?"

"Not in the least," I said, shaking my head.

"Let me get some coffee into me first."

"Damn that smells good. Yeah, I could use a cup myself."

We settled ourselves on the overstuffed, beige couch, and I huddled in the corner facing her.

Lainie took a sip of her coffee and said, "Okay, spit it out already."

"I'm not sure where to start."

"The beginning is always good."

I told her about Samantha and how Red came to get me. "Wait, I have to back track a bit."

"That sister of yours needs a good ass kicking. So her boyfriend blamed you for her going off the wagon?"

"Yeah and he was under the impression that I forced her to see Sarah and picked her up from his house. I'm not sure what's really going on."

"I'm sure you'll find out soon enough."

"Sooner than I would like, I bet." I placed the coffee cup on the end table and wrapped my arms around my legs.

"So what happened before the Samantha fiasco?"

"Red wanted to talk about Friday night—"

"Red?" Lainie said, scrunching her eyebrows.

"No, sorry, I meant Bond. I'm a bit hungover from last night."

"This must get good because I can't remember you ever drinking enough for a hangover since college."

"Yeah, well, I was having a rough day." I rolled my neck to get rid of some of the tension.

"Not surprising. Sleeping with Bond is never, and I mean *never,* a good thing for you."

"That was only a part of it. When I got to Red's, they left Bond and me alone in the kitchen to talk, and we got into an argument."

"Over what?"

"Now don't yell," I said, holding out my palm to her. "He wanted me to spend the night again. I think he fucked another woman earlier on his *sailing date* although that was unclear."

"I'm doing my best not to give you a ration of shit."

"I know and thank you." I patted Lainie's knee in appreciation.

"But I do plan to give him a piece of my mind. He

66

needs to learn to keep his cock to himself in your regard."

"Please don't, Lane. Let me handle it, okay? He is not the worst of it."

"Go on then," she said, shaking her head at me like she was my mother.

"I ran out of the kitchen and into Red's boat. Guess who followed me out there?" I raised my eyebrow.

"Bond? Cat?"

"Red."

"Red?"

"Yeah, he said he was checking on me. He touched my arm and—"

"Oh god no!" She threw her hands up and almost knocked her coffee over.

I laughed but really felt worn out. "His touch drove me crazy and I wasn't expecting it and he seemed to feel it too. I ran out and then all the crap happened with my sister."

"I can't take the suspense! Did you fuck him too?"

"No, not that, but we did kiss. Later, when we were at my place, I let him go down on me."

"Holy shit girl, do you have no sense?" Lainie got up and filled her coffee mug.

"Well, I had a good amount to drink and all that fighting chemistry switched on me and made me crazy hot. Oh, Lainie, his kisses—"

She slapped the counter and said, "You can't be considering this. I feel like I need to shake you to wake you the hell up. This cannot end well. What does he want?"

I faced the kitchen and said, "Me, he wants me."

"And Bond? What about him?

"He says he wants to try again. Be a better man for me."

She walked back over to me and sat down. "What do you want?"

"To be happy, to have a normal relationship where I

don't feel like my heart is being ripped out of my chest over and over again."

"Red seems like a good guy, from what I can tell, but Bond will never, ever be okay with you two dating." Lainie shook her head and said, "I'm not sure why you need so much drama in your life, Jacqueline. My advice is to forget them both and move on."

"You know I can't do that," I said, waving my hands emphatically. "We have all of our friends in common and I love Bond even though I feel torn up and twisted over him. Next to you, he is the best friend I have ever had."

"And he breaks your heart."

"Yes, there is that. And Red, I don't know what I feel about him. I always thought he hated me, but now I find out he has wanted me for a long time." I paused for a moment. "It's nice to be wanted."

"This can't possibly end well and I know you are smart enough to know it."

Lainie and I passed on going out to lunch. I headed home, and she went back to bed.

CHAPTER FIVE

The Rain Don't Last

by Hope

On Monday and Tuesday the gods of fortune smiled down on me, leaving me in the office without Henry, my boss. I tended to get so much more done without his overly controlling presence. Although my title read Executive Assistant, I did much more for the small finance firm including admin work for three other managers. I also helped with marketing and sales support when necessary. I liked those projects the best.

My desk sat in the main space surrounded by six offices, a kitchen, and a conference room. In the main area, where prospective clients were greeted, the industrial and drab décor—gray carpet, beige walls, and metal desks with faux wooden tops—was spiced up with several plants that I watered each week. The two other desks near mine housed two part-timers who helped with some of the administrative tasks.

On Wednesday, Henry showed up at the office in rare form. A major client had fallen through, and he decided to do his best to take it out on me. I could hear him yelling into the phone all day, and I even contemplated leaving early, feigning sickness or women's issues. Instead I stuck it out. I thought I had made it through unscathed, until the end of the day.

"Jacqueline, get into my office," he yelled from across the hall.

I grabbed my notepad and a pen and sat down in the

chair in front of his desk, waiting for what would befall me.

"I want you to put a hold on all of your other projects and come up with a spreadsheet for last year's data. Be sure to line item all expenses including travel."

"We have already reconciled last year's numbers and Tom has me working on the most recent marketing blitz."

"All other projects are on hold and don't make me repeat myself again," he said, banging his fist against his desk.

I jumped at the sound but did not back down. "We have a deadline for the marketing campaign and I need to spend time on that."

"Have the spreadsheet on my desk on Friday."

"That's not possible even if I did no other work," I said calmly but fantasized about diving over the desk and strangling him.

"I'm getting sick and tired of your negative attitude. Have it on my desk or you're fired."

"How do you want the spreadsheet done?"

"You figure it out."

"I'm unwilling to start another project for you, without you telling how you want it. We've been over this before. I'm not a mind reader and how you want something presented changes all the time. Just tell me how you want it."

"Friday, now get out of my office."

Although my blood boiled and I wanted to punch him or better yet have Red clock him, I modulated my steps leaving his office. I snatched my purse and sweater and stormed down the hall to the elevator.

As I steamed, sitting behind the wheel of my car, I debated about going over to Red's. We hadn't spoken since Saturday night, not really getting a chance to talk on the way back to his place on Sunday morning. I still didn't know how I felt about him, but I did want to see him again. My stress escalated thinking about finding another job, and I needed a distraction.

I ran home, showered, and changed into one of my favorite dresses I had bought from Lainie's boutique. It had a spaghetti strapped halter top that flowed out from just under the bodice. It started with red at the top and had the colors of the rainbow in wide rows, blending one after the other, ending right above my brown thong sandals. I consciously didn't put any makeup on and blew my hair out so it flowed in waves. I picked dangling earrings and slipped on two long silver rings on my right hand that went just past my first knuckles.

Hearing my phone chime, I checked to see who texted me.

> **Red:** I'm in your neck of the woods. Can I stop by for a few?
> **Me:** I don't think that's a good idea. I was planning to head over to your place.
> **Red:** We won't have a chance to talk once everyone shows up.
> **Me:** Do you know Big City Tavern on Las Olas Blvd?
> **Red:** Great place. Meet you at the bar in 10?
> **Me:** More like 20.
> **Red:** Excellent.

My pulse raced at the thought of seeing Red again. I could hear Lainie ranting in my head and I chose to ignore her. When I thought of Bond, I felt a twinge of guilt but pushed it to the side. It had been eight years and for the first time since meeting him, and letting him sweep me up in his life, I felt real hard core attraction for another. Besides, I told myself, I couldn't decide what I wanted without getting to know Red better.

I parked in front of the tavern with the bright red and black awning. Taking a couple of deep breaths, I tried to relax. Nervousness filled me as I got out of my VW and I squared my shoulders. *Don't let them see you sweat*, I reminded myself.

The dark hardwood floors, gray brick walls, and shiny oak bar gave the place a rustic elegance. I saw Red before he saw me, and I stood by the entrance watching him converse with the bartender. How had I been so repulsed by him before? He looked so striking in his blue collared shirt and chinos. He must have come straight from work. A cold, dark beer sat on the bar in front of him.

As if feeling my stare, he turned to me. A huge smile broke across his face, and he strode towards me.

"You came," he said, encompassing my small hand in his. His intense desire swept over me, causing mine to rise.

"Were you worried?" I said, softly.

"I thought you might change your mind."

I let go of his hand and said, "Didn't realize it was an option. Good to know." I turned like I intended to walk away.

"Sit, you feisty woman."

"Yes, sir!" I said, saluting him as I hopped up into the high back chair in front of the bar. "A Guinness? Do you fit all the Irish stereotypes?"

He laughed and said, "It's so good to see you and you look adorable in that dress. I've thought about you every day since we've been apart."

"Have you now?" I said, batting my eyelashes.

"Stop goading me, or I'll push you up against the bar and take you right here."

"I'll try to behave," I said, grinning from ear to ear.

"Damn, girl, what am I going to do with you?"

"I guess that's still to be seen."

He just stared at me for a few moments and asked, "What would you like to drink?"

"I think I'll stick to water for now."

He signaled the bartender and asked, "How was your day?"

"I'm sure you don't want to hear about that."

"Oh, but I do. I want to know everything about you."

I shared with Red what happened at work.

"Why do you put up with that?" he asked. He appeared charged up and angry.

"I've been working there since college and I love all the other people. Henry took over my old boss's job about a year ago. At first it seemed like it would be okay but after two months, I no longer loved my job and it seems to get worse as the weeks go by."

"I remember you mentioning that, but at some point you have to decide if it's worth it. Why don't you quit?"

"I'm pretty sure I'll be fired on Friday anyway. I have no intention of working on the redundant project he wants me to do." I fingered the sweat on the water glass the bartender had set in front of me. "I guess I need to start looking for another job. It's not so easy in this economy."

"That's true," he said and paused. "Now that I think of it, I might know of an opening in my company. I can check for you."

"Thank you for the offer, but I don't think that would be wise."

He chuckled and said, "You wouldn't be working for me, Jacqs. One of the executive assistants is leaving to have her baby. She plans to be a stay-at-home mom. I'm just not sure if they've found a replacement yet. Ted is a great boss and would never treat you poorly. No one in the office would allow that to happen."

"I think you're missing the obvious."

"And what might that be?" He lifted his beer mug and downed half of it.

"We don't know what will become of us. We might go back to hating each other."

"I never hated you, Jacqs."

"You sure acted like someone who did. If I've learned any great lessons from my relationship with Bond, it's that behavior counts the most, especially when it contradicts the words people say."

"Fair enough, but I'm asking you to let me show you differently."

I sipped some water through the straw and placed my glass back down as the music from the jukebox began to blare. "What about Bond?" I said over the '80s rock song playing. "I don't want to be the one that comes between you. Have you thought that part out at least? Lainie says that he'll most definitely care, and that if I had any commonsense at all, I'd know that this could only end badly."

"I don't have it sorted out."

"We have all the same friends. How do you think they'll feel about it? What about Blue?"

"Why bring Judy into this?" He finished the remainder of his beer and signaled for another.

Sweet Judy Blue Eyes, a woman in our group who briefly dated Red, was dubbed by Bond as Blue. Their tête-à-tête had taken place three years before.

"She might not like you dating another from our group."

"She hardly has a say about it," he said, resting his arm on the back of my chair.

"Agreed. My point is that our dating might impact our other friends too."

"You can't live your life for other people." He lightly tugged on my hair, causing chills to rush up my back.

I pivoted in my seat and said, "And you can't live

alone without them either. At least I can't."

"I'd like to see what we could be without bringing them into it." He thanked the bartender who brought him another beer. "Have I told you how much I love your lips?"

"No, and you're changing the subject."

"Yes I am. They always looked puckered, ready for a kiss."

I blushed over his compliment. "Stop distracting me."

"You've been distracting me for years, so it's only fair." He scooted his chair closer to me and towered over, sucking my bottom lip into his mouth.

"Hmmm," I moaned just as the sound got caught up in our steamy kiss. "Your kisses make me dizzy and it's hard for me to think straight."

"Don't think, just feel," he said, yanking my chair even closer to his. He buried his hands in the back of my hair and lit me on fire with another mystifying kiss.

"What are we going to do?" I mumbled against his mouth.

"Spend time together," he said with an ardent gaze that set my heart pounding. "Let me find out about that job and if it's still available—"

"You don't even know if I'm a good employee!"

"Of course I do. If it's still available you can quit or call in sick tomorrow and spend the day with me."

"Wait. What?" I pushed against his chest. "Don't you have to work?"

"I'm the boss, remember."

"But not of me, never of me."

"Only in the bedroom," he said, casting me a look of pure lust.

I felt the wetness growing in my panties and with it came great relief—and a load of guilt. I thought I would never feel desire again for another man after meeting Bond, and yet it turned out to be his best friend that now stoked my libido.

"What time is it?" I asked, trying to break the spell.

"It's almost seven. I need to get going over to the house. Stay is probably already there."

I stepped down off the stool. "Oh, Stay is coming? I haven't seen him in ages."

"His girlfriend broke up with him, so he's back in the fold."

Stayman hadn't been over to the house in months because his girlfriend didn't care to hang out with us. Although I missed him terribly, I also understand how daunting it must be for a new person to come into a group of tight-knit friends. I planned to give him a great big hug.

"Okay, you leave first. I'll follow in a bit," I said, swinging my bag over my shoulder.

"Please think about tomorrow. I'll call Ted on the way to the house and find out about the job." He stood and drew me to him, folding me in his arms. After lifting me off the ground, he gave me a fervent kiss goodbye.

Before I entered Red's house, I texted Lainie.

Me: Do you plan to drop by tonight?
Lainie: Getting ready for a second date.
Me: Can I know his name yet?
Lainie: Don't want to jinx it. Maybe after tonight.
Me: You are so silly sometimes. Make sure to tell Second Date I said hello.
Lainie: Stay away from Red and Bond.
Me: :P

Avoiding Bond and Red, I went straight through the house to the game room to find Stayman. The warm wood-paneled room held two pool tables, a dart board, a couch, a bench, and two high top tables.

"Get over here woman," Stay said as soon as he saw me. He scooped me up into a tight squeeze.

"Are you done hiding from us?" I said after he lowered me to the ground. "I'm sorry things didn't work out with Karen, but I'm glad you're back. My pool game has been suffering."

Stay stood almost as tall as Red but was far lankier. He was sexy in his own way, in a plaid button down shirt with the sleeves rolled up. Although thirty-five like Bond and Red, he had a cherub face, bright, blue eyes that twinkled with mischief and a half-cocked smile, which made him appear much younger. He shaved his head bald. I liked it best just as it started to grow in. It felt soft to the touch and smelled of coconut.

"Hiding, me?" he chuckled. "I've missed you, too. So what's up with you and Red?"

I blushed and said, "What do you mean?"

"Cat told me about Saturday night. She had the feeling something was up."

"We've called a sort of truce."

"I've always thought he had a thing for you," he said, sitting down on a stool against the wall near the billiard table.

"What?"

"No one can be *that* mad at someone for that long."

"Don't be silly. I just figured he was jealous and wanted Bond for himself."

"Oh my god, oh my god." He laughed so hard he fell out of the chair. "That has to be the funniest thing I've heard in a long, long time."

I giggled along with him. "Shall we play a game?"

"Later, let's go see who else is here." He grabbed my hand and we strolled into the main part of the house together.

Most of the gang had showed, but I didn't see Bond and wondered if he had to work.

"Hey Jacqs," Cat said when she stood to give me a hug. Sleek as ever in her tight black jeans, and fitted leather vest.

"How's it going?" I asked. I saw Kevin over her shoulder, and he had an odd expression on his face. "Is all okay with Kev?"

"We had another fight and I told him to give me some space."

"Anything I can help with?"

"No, I'm sure it will blow over. Right at the moment, however, I'm still angry." She glared in his direction. "PMS isn't helping."

"It never does." I smiled and said, "Well, if you want to talk, I'm available for listening."

"Yeah, maybe later."

I headed over to Kevin, but Blue intercepted me with a warm embrace. Sweet Judy Blue Eyes had the brightest and lightest blue eyes I had ever seen. Also petite, but a few inches taller than I, her large breasts made her appear voluptuous.

"It's been awhile," Blue said.

"Sure has. Are you doing okay?" I could see that Red stood in the kitchen, pacing back and forth, beer in hand. I took my own sweet time greeting my friends.

"Yeah, I've just been writing a lot and spending my free time working on a book."

"A book? Fiction?"

"Yeah, centered on a group kind of like ours."

"That should be interesting," I said, chuckling. "I'd love to read it."

"I'm not ready to share it. I hear you and Red have made up."

"If you can call it that," I said, glancing in his direction.

"I'm sure Bond will be happy that you guys are getting along better."

I shrugged. "I guess that remains to be seen."

"Red's not such a bad guy."

Looking back, I said, "Yeah, I know."

Kevin came over and we hugged each other tightly. Stay and I had a playful friendship but Kev had become the brother I never had. He never judged me and I loved him dearly for it. Kev wore red, skinny jeans and a black sleeveless shirt with a picture of the Kinks on it. Blonde hair, as always, spiked to perfection.

"You know what time of the month it is, right?" I said to him.

"Oh shit, I completely forgot. I guess I shouldn't have teased her."

"Probably not the best of ideas. I'm sure she will be fine in a bit. Just let her come find you when she's ready."

"Thanks, Jacqs. Do you know the group is speculating about you and Red," he said, tilting his head in Red's direction.

"I got that impression from Stay."

"Damn good to have him back."

"Yes it is. He thinks Red has a thing for me." I glanced up and saw Red staring. He looked stern and confident in his relaxed jeans and maroon crew neck shirt. I smiled slightly and saw his face transform. We would not be able to keep the truth about us hidden for long.

"That wouldn't be the worst thing in the world," Kev said.

"I'm not sure Bond would agree with you."

"I love the man, but you deserve to be happy. I was so proud of you this weekend even if it was alcohol induced."

"Yeah, well, my head wasn't happy with me in the morning," I said, touching his sleeve.

"Red's in the kitchen and I get the distinct impression

he is impatient to talk to you."

"Have you seen Bond?"

"He hasn't arrived yet. Wonder who's driving him this time."

"Good question."

Kevin and I hugged again and I headed to the kitchen. Red leaned against the counter with his arms folded across his chest. "I've been patiently—"

"You mean impatiently," I said, feeling his vibe.

He chuckled and said, "Do you think there will ever be a time that you'll cut me some slack?"

"I wouldn't count on it ... or wait for it either," I said. I imagined my beaming smile gave me away.

Speaking softly he said, "When you look at me like that, I want to kiss you so deeply that you do your sweet little moans for me."

"Shh," I said, already getting turned on by him.

"When do *we* get to hug?"

"Can't answer that. Our friends are already speculating about us. I wonder if they have shared their ideas with Bond."

"I spoke to him earlier and I would guess the answer to that is no, not yet. Would you like something to drink?" he asked, standing up straight and opening the refrigerator.

"I think I'd better stick to water. I need my wits about me around you."

"That's probably wise," he said, hunching his shoulders to be closer to me. "I spoke to Ted and they haven't yet filled the position. He'd like you to come by tomorrow at eleven. Please come meet me here after. We can take the Sessa out on the water for a few hours."

"I'm still not sure a job at your firm is a great idea."

"What've you got to lose? Do you have a resume put together?"

"I updated it a couple of months ago when I started

thinking about looking for a new job."

"Good. Give me your phone," he said, holding out his hand.

"Why?" I said, standing up taller with my shoulders back.

"So I can give you my numbers, silly, and the address to my office building."

"Oh," I said, laughing.

"Great to see you guys getting along," Bond said, slapping Red on the back twice. "Need something to drink, Jacqs?"

"I'm good," I said. Guilt twisted in my gut. I glanced at Red and he could read the expression on my face.

"What're you guys conspiring about?" Bond asked after he opened his beer.

"Jacqs needs a new job and I lined up an interview for her."

"I've been telling her for months to get the hell out of there. I'd have already punched out Henry if she'd let me. Good luck, J and let me know how it goes."

"I will. How come you didn't call me for a ride?" I asked.

"I was already in the area and had a friend drop me by."

I wondered if it might be Blondie. We women tended to come back to Bond for more torture.

"Listen, I need you to get a black dress for the party on Saturday," Bond said.

"Black? Have you seen my closet?"

"Yes, although I love all the crazy colors you usually wear, I'm asking you, begging you, to get a black dress for the event. They're having it at the house."

"I'll see what Lainie has."

Before I had a chance to object, Bond lifted me up in a big hug and kissed my lips. "Thank you so much for going with me. I owe you again."

"I've stopped keeping track," I said as I squirmed to

get down.

Softly placing me back on my feet, he said, "I haven't."

Bond and Red both stared at me, and I felt my body respond. *What the hell am I getting myself into?*

"Umm … well … Stay wanted to play a game of pool so I'm going to find him," I said, pivoting on the spot and scanning the room for Stay. I saw him out back and waved frantically for him to come inside the house.

"Pool?" I said, as calmly as possible. "Please," I whispered.

"Let's do it," he said, looping his arm through mine.

I breathed out a huge sigh of relief as we trotted to the game room. I spent the rest of the evening successfully avoiding Bond and Red.

On the drive home, I pondered whether or not I would go by Red's the next day after my interview. Wanting to see him again, I didn't think I could keep myself away.

CHAPTER SIX

Trouble Sleeping

by Corinne Bailey Rae

I dressed in my most conservative outfit and pinned back my hair. I had no idea what kind of atmosphere I would encounter at Red's office. I prayed that he chose to stay home, as he said he would, waiting for me. I didn't think I could go through with the interview if I saw him first, reminding me that he owned the business.

After calling into my office to let them know I would be out, I finished the rest of my coffee, rinsed out the cup and placed it in the dishwasher. I placed a second call to my nurse practitioner's office and the staff said I could pick up the script for blood work. They told me I should wait at least a week or more since my last sexual encounter before taking the STD tests, so I decided to wait until the following week to take them.

After briefly stopping at the doctor's office to get the lab script, I drove to Red's office building, nervousness bubbling in my stomach. I should have eaten something first.

Shock overtook me as I walked into the office building. In contrast to Red's antique filled home, the ultra-modern décor surprised me. The lobby had marble tiled floors and orange vinyl chairs and couches with a circular glass coffee table between them. Large mirrors filled the left wall, and a long desk ran the length of the back of the room with a receptionist busy at work on the phones.

"May I help you?" the receptionist asked. Noticing her

casual attire, my gray fitted suit seemed out of place.

"I have a meeting with Mr. Thompson at eleven, but I'm a few minutes early," I said, tightly clutching my purse and the folder that held my resume.

"He's expecting you. Go up to the third floor, and it's down the hall to the left." She signaled to the right of her, showing me to the elevators.

As an afterthought I asked, "Do you like working here?"

"Love it. I'm getting my degree, and I'll be able to move up in the corporation. They're paying for my schooling."

I wanted to ask her about Red, but I still didn't know his real name. "Thank you," I said as the elevator doors began to shut.

She smiled, waved, and said, "Good luck."

The receptionist must have let Ted know I had arrived because he greeted me as I approached. He ushered me past him.

The corner office held a dark wood L-shaped table to the left and a six person conference table on the right. Windows lined two sides overlooking downtown Fort Lauderdale.

"Nice view," I said, holding out my hand toward him.

"I'm fond of it myself." He shook my hand and motioned for me to sit in one of the chairs in front of his large desk. "Aidan highly recommended you so this meeting is a mere formality."

Ted had a kind face, a full head of salt and pepper hair and warm gray eyes. I liked him instantly.

"That's really nice of him but he doesn't know my work history." *Aidan*, I thought, *that name certainly fits the big Neanderthal.*

"He knows people, plus he told me you've been working at the same job for the last six years, since you graduated from college. Is that accurate?"

"Yes it is," I said, sitting up straight, making sure not to slump my shoulders, which I tended to do when I got nervous.

"He also said you have experience in calendar management, all other things administrative, marketing, and some sales support."

"Huh, yes, that's right. I also have experience with event planning and general office management."

"Well then, you're more than qualified for this position. Cynthia will be leaving in another month and a half or so. Here are the salary offerings and benefits. My card is inside. Take a look over the papers, and if you decide to take the job you could start two weeks from Monday, which would give Cynthia a month to train you. That way if she has to miss a day or two, you both will have plenty of time to make the transition."

"That's it?"

"That's it. It was a pleasure to meet you," he said, standing and walking me to the door.

"Thank you so much for your time."

"You've made filling a vacancy incredibly easy and I get the feeling we'll work well together."

"I appreciate the chance."

Once I got into my car I skimmed through the offer and figured Red/Aidan had to be behind it. I drove straight to his place without thinking twice about it. I unpinned my hair, shaking it out so it hung against my back.

I walked right in as I always had and strolled through the empty house. Red, in swimming trunks, stood out back with an attractive woman. Lowering onto the couch that faced the French doors, I watched an argument take place.

The tall woman with silky, straight, red hair gestured wildly. Heat ran up my neck, and I considered leaving. As I rose to do so, Red noticed me in the house. He held his palms out to the woman, waving for her to stop. He glided toward me in long strides and lifted me up, kissing me firmly on the lips. I no longer worried about who the other woman might be.

"A bit overdressed?" he said.

"You didn't warn me that your office dresses rather casual."

"Come meet my sister." He took my hand and led me to the back.

"She seems angry. Are you sure this is a good—"

"I have to hide you from everyone else, but not her."

"Okay," I said as I followed him willingly.

"Jacqs, this is Aideen; Aideen, this is my girlfriend Jacqueline."

"Nice to meet you," she said. "It's been awhile since Aidan called anyone 'girlfriend.'"

"Nice to meet you as well. I had no idea Red had a sister, let alone a twin."

She glanced in Red's direction and back to me. It was hard not to be intimidated by her looks and immaculate attire.

"And in all honesty, we're still sorting out what we are," I said.

"I know my brother well and when he decides, watch out."

"Yes," I said, laughing. "I've figured that out for myself as well." I looked at Red who smiled warmly in my direction. "You seemed to be in an intense conversation when I arrived. I should let you get back to it."

"Not necessary. He'd already informed me he had plans today. I was trying to convince him to call our parents. It's an ongoing fight with us."

"How is it I never knew about you?" I asked.

"I've just recently moved back to the states and he likes to keep me hidden." Her red hair shimmered in the light as she tilted her head.

"Dare I ask why?" I peeked at Red and he raised an eyebrow.

"Oh, I had a crush on Bond when we were in high school and Aidan's worried that I still intend to carry it out."

I blushed uncontrollably and felt like crawling back into Red's boat to hide.

"She's not the same one you told me about a few years ago, is she?" she shot at Red.

"Yes, she is," he said, coolly.

"You talked to your sister about me years ago?" I said with an incredulous expression.

"Oh, Jacqueline, he has it bad for you. For a long time now."

"Aideen," Red said in stern warning.

"As I told you then, given Bond's history, I'd tread carefully."

"You know Bond's history?" I asked.

"Aidan and I talk about pretty much everything and yet he failed to mention that his current interest was the same as Bond's on and off again girlfriend."

"I assumed you realized that on your own," Red said. "Her name hasn't changed."

"You know me and names, in one ear and out the other. I'll let you kids go play—"

"No dire words of warning?" Red asked.

"You didn't let me finish. Don't wait too long to tell him the truth. As incestuous as your group is, he'll figure it out soon enough."

"I totally agree," I said. "I figured I'd have a good idea whether or not I wanted to kick Red to the curb after today."

"Oh, I like her bro. She'll keep you in line." Aideen gathered her purse to leave. "Call Mom. She misses you terribly, and you know how she hates email."

"I hope I get to see you again," I said. I felt inclined to hug her but hesitated.

"I'd like that as well." She embraced Red, whispering something in his ear I couldn't hear. Then she hugged me goodbye.

After she had left, I said, "That was interesting. What else don't I know about you? Do you have a wife hiding in a trunk?" I strutted over to the container that held the towels and pretended to look inside. "More siblings in the trunk in your room?"

"Get over here, woman," he said, grabbing me up in his arms. "I definitely have something hidden in the trunk upstairs." He raised his eyebrows a couple of times.

"Oh, do tell."

"In due time. Please tell me you brought a bikini, and you plan to change out of that stodgy outfit you have on."

"Right here?" I said with a wink.

"Don't tempt me," he said, grabbing for me again.

I ran, just out of reach, to the downstairs bathroom, laughing and scooping up my purse on the way. I sat on the covered toilet seat and texted Bond.

> **Me:** I got the job, but I haven't decided if I'm going to take it.
> **Bond:** Did you like the guy?
> **Me:** Yes.
> **Bond:** Are the terms good?
> **Me:** Yes.
> **Bond:** Well then it seems like a no-brainer to me.
> **Me:** You know me, I don't usually do change this fast.
> **Bond:** Jacqs, you're being silly. This isn't fast. It's incredibly slow. You've been putting up with this asshole for months or is it a year now?

Me: Close to a year.
Bond: You've made my point.
Me: You're right. Got to go. See you Saturday.
Bond: Bye love.

I slipped into a bright blue, strapless, two-piece bathing suit that had black accents at the hips. After I had pulled my hair into a ponytail, I cleaned up the mascara around my eyes and then decided to remove it altogether. I left my clothes and shoes in the bathroom.

While I waited for Red, I reread the offer. Three weeks of vacation, plus ten personal days and thirty percent more than I was currently making in salary. His firm also included a bonus structure. It seemed outrageously generous.

"Are you satisfied with the terms?" he said as he settled on the couch next to me.

"How much input did you have on the offer?"

"I told him I thought you'd be an asset, but I didn't work on the package. I'm sure most is standard for my company. Did you like Ted?"

"He seemed great … and relieved to have the position filled."

"So what's stopping you? Me? Regardless of what happens here, we can work in the same building. We won't have to cross paths except at company meetings."

"Are bonuses standard?"

"Yes, based on our income for the year."

"Okay."

"You'll take the job?" he said as if he took pride in my decision.

"I'm desperate to get out of my job and the offer is enticing. The time off especially."

"Don't forget about the perk of having lunches with

me," he said, trying to suppress a grin.

"Oh great, so we get to shake up our group *and* your employees. Speaking of shaking up things, I'm serious about us telling Bond."

"I'm fine with that, but let's wait until after this weekend and the party at his family's house."

"Okay, that makes sense. He might not want to talk to either of us after we tell him," I said, imagining the scene. "How about Sunday afternoon? I usually have breakfast on Sunday mornings with Lainie, and I could swing by here after. Of course, that all depends on today."

"No pressure."

"None at all," I said, laughing. My stomach growled loudly, making me laugh even harder. "I need some food."

"I packed a picnic on the boat."

"You did not!"

"Come and see."

The sunny and temperate South Florida day had wisps of clouds scattered across the sky. Climbing down the steps into the cabin, I saw the grapes, cheese and crackers, some type of salad spread, and a chilled bottle of wine. "Planning to get me drunk?" I shouted up to Red so he could hear me over the loud engine.

"I'll take you any way I can get you," he yelled back.

I popped a couple of grapes into my mouth and grabbed a cube of cheese on my way up the two flights of stairs to the bridge.

As he drove the Sessa slowly through the Intracoastal, he swiveled his seat to face me. I came to him at the same time he held his arms out to me. Sitting down on his lap, I faced him and tilted my head up just as he lowered his mouth to mine.

"Hmmmm," I moaned as he lavished me with warm wild kisses. His arousal pushed against my bathing suit bottoms.

"We need to stop," he said, lifting me off his lap. "I have to concentrate until we're out to sea."

Sitting on the cushioned bench across from him, I said, "We can talk then." I rubbed my hands together with a sinister smile. "I have some questions for you."

"Shoot," he said, glancing my way then redirecting his attention to the front of the vessel.

"Do you have any other siblings?"

"No, just Aideen." He eased the boat to the left down another canal.

"Did she really have a crush on Bond?"

"Not at all. I think she just said that to see your reaction."

"Why doesn't she ever come by and hang with the group?"

"Early on we went our separate ways when it came to our social lives. We are opposites in many ways, you know. She loved hanging out with the wealthier crowd and for the most part, I couldn't stand them. Somehow they felt they were superior to everyone else simply because their parents had money. I found her friends to be shallow and not worth my time. She didn't fit in with my friends any more than I did with hers."

"Do you think she realized who I was right away?"

"Probably, there's no telling what her motives were." He maneuvered the Adjustable Bend through the red and green buoys and continued, "She's a slippery one, like my dad. Hard to tell what angle they're playing. However, I love her and would do anything for her. And I trust her."

"Anything but call your mother?"

"Calling my mother, which is bad enough, usually means I end up speaking to my father, and that never goes well. I email her often and she doesn't respond. I know she gets them all. We're in a standoff at the moment."

"Huh. Is Aideen really your twin?"

"Yep. Our mother couldn't have any more children

after she carried us to full term."

"Do you want children?" I said, crossing my legs in front of me.

"I'm not sure. I wouldn't consider having them unless I found a stable relationship. You?"

"No." I shook my head. "I don't think I do."

"Really? That surprises me. I would think you'd be a natural."

"After everything we've been through with my sister, I'm not sure I'm up for that."

"Well, you're still young, you might change your mind."

"Maybe," I said, watching the nice houses pass by. "Have you ever been in love?"

"Have you?"

"Answering a question with a question? Well, I'll tell you anyway. I'm not sure I know what love is. Certainly not healthy love. I have thought I was in love with Bond, but he always manages to twist it around into something else. I really don't know is probably the best answer I can give you. Your turn."

"I haven't." He glanced at me and then set his attention back on driving the vessel. "I certainly would never want the relationship my parents have. My father is a controlling asshole who gets off on embarrassing our mother at the oddest times. Our house parties were the worst when we were kids."

"Will they be at the party on Saturday?"

"I hadn't thought of that, but probably."

"I'm really dreading the party, other than seeing Lily. I love that girl."

"She's definitely a keeper." He gunned the engine, throwing me back a bit as the nose rose into the air. After leveling out he continued, "Yeah, I have avoided those types of events for years now. Bond doesn't have it as easy. I know his grandfather would tar and feather Bond's father if he were still alive and knew how he was manipulating Bond's inheritance." We rode in silence for a while, watching other boaters in the distance. He slowed then cut the engine, and said, "Give me a few minutes and I'll lower the anchor."

I went below for more food and to open the bottle of wine. Finding two plastic wine glasses in the cabinet, I brought them and the bottle above board along with the Hawaiian Tropic sunscreen Red left on the counter.

"Let's go sit on the back of the boat," he said.

"Will you put sunscreen on my back?"

"With pleasure."

The stern of the yacht was covered with a wooden deck. We sat, hanging our legs off the end. He took the bottle and glasses from me while I started to cover the front of my body and legs with coconut infused sunscreen. The smell of the sea mixed with the fragrance of coconut epitomized Florida for me.

The yacht rocked lazily with the tide as Red poured each of us a glass of wine. After handing me the wine, he leisurely rubbed the lotion into my shoulders and back. "You have a most beautiful back, Little One," he said, nipping my neck with small bites. "Skin so smooth."

"I used to hate it when you called me Little One," I said, angling back against him.

He wrapped his long muscular arms around me and said, "I know. Can you do my back?"

"One good turn deserves another." I scooted around and filled my hand with sunscreen. Spreading the lotion over his large back, I said, "I love your tattoo, by the way." I traced the row of knots making up the branches. "Did it hurt?"

"Not too much. It took a long time though. I had to do

it in two sessions so they could get the green just right."

"It definitely suits you and it's amazing how much depth they can create on a flat surface." I smoothed the sunscreen down to his waist. "Do you know anything about Bond's original tattoo?"

"You'll have to ask him about that." He drew me back into his arms.

"I thought that's what you'd say," I said as I leaned against his chest. "It's so gorgeous out today. I love it when it's sunny with a cool breeze."

"So what's going to be the deciding factor?" he said, running his fingers down my arm.

"About us?" I said, sitting up and turning to face him.

"Yes." He took my hand in his.

"I'm confused but I don't want this to stop. You?"

"I want this, Jacqs."

I squeezed his hand and said, "I keep expecting it to be awkward between us since we spent so many years fighting and ignoring each other. Only, the crazy thing is, it feels so comfortable."

"Yeah, for me too."

We sipped our wine and stared out over the ocean.

"So what are we going to do?" I said, breaking the silence.

"Tell him the truth."

"Which truth?" I asked. "What happened in my apartment?"

"No," he said, pulling me back towards him. "I think that will just inflame the situation. We tell him we are attracted to one another and plan to date."

"Are you aware that he wants to try again with me?"

"Jacqs, honey, that's nothing new. You guys have been doing this dance for years."

I crossed my legs and touched his chest. "He thinks he

loves me."

"In his own twisted way, I'm sure he does."

Sighing, I said, "This is going to get messy. Are you sure I'm worth it?"

"Trust me, I'm sure. I've had years to contemplate it." He lightly tugged on my ponytail and twirled my hair around his finger.

"Just not how you would do it?" I asked, searching his green eyes.

"I'd hoped he would find a good match for himself, and you guys would *really* part ways. I just got tired of waiting. I'm certain on some level he already knows. I got so angry that he called you to his apartment Friday night. He knew we had a date lined up in the morning, but he convinced you to come over *and* stay the night. How selfish do you have to be to not consider how that would make you feel?"

"You said that to him?"

"Oh, that and a lot more."

"Okay, so we can assume he knows your feelings for me, however, I think he might be shocked that I'm equally interested."

"Are you?" he said, grinning. And for an instant he looked like a young boy.

"Have you not been paying attention?"

He chuckled, lifting me onto his lap. "I think it's going to take me a little while to get used to it."

"I know what you mean," I said, running my hands up his beard into his hair. "I can't believe we wasted so much time."

"I've had that thought a time or ten."

I ran my fingers along his golden-red eyebrows, losing myself in his bright, green eyes. As I caressed his face, I felt his cock stir beneath me. "When do I get to see him?" I asked, pointing down between us.

"How did I get the impression you were all shy and

passive?" he said, kissing his way up my neck.

"You were too busy keeping your distance," I said, tilting my head and groaning with pleasure.

"That's true, but I was always watching you," he said, adjusting himself underneath me. "I love all of your little moans and groans."

"He sure does," I said, glancing down between us.

He chuckled and said, "You're different with me."

"It feels different with you. Maybe it's all those years of fighting. It's easier for me to stand up for myself and just say what I feel without any filters."

"I never thought all that fighting would work to our advantage. I like it. I like it a lot." He captured my face in his hands and we shared a soulful kiss.

As strong and masculine as I have always known him to be, he had a vulnerable side that moved me even more. Kissing him back, I threw myself into the kiss with abandon. "Hmmmm," I sighed.

"Just like that," he said against my mouth.

"Will he come out to play?" I said, reaching down between us.

He held my hand against his stiff erection and said, "I don't trust myself. I want to take this slow and do it right."

"I could tie your arms behind you so you wouldn't be tempted to mount me."

"Mount you," he said, laughing hysterically. He became serious and said, "Tying is my department."

"Oh?" I said, not sure how I felt about his disclosure. "Can I at least see him? No touching?"

"Let's skinny-dip," he said, whipping off his trunks and diving into the water. He swam around to face me.

I finished off my glass of wine and slowly unhooked the top of my bathing suit, letting it fall to the deck. Circling around, I bent over so my butt faced him and shimmied the bottoms off. I'm sure he caught a glimpse of my pussy between my legs.

"Get in here," he ordered, his voice sounding gruff.

I obliged and dove in, coming up for air facing him.

"You have a beautiful pussy and I'm a fan of your smooth lips," he said, stroking his fingers between my legs as we both worked to stay afloat.

"She's a fan of your fingers and mouth." I reached down to feel Red's cock. My tiny hand didn't make it all the way around his girth. "Wow," I said, "I need two hands with you."

"Uh … one hand feels pretty good right now."

I giggled and said, "I hope he will fit."

"We'll have fun working on it."

Wrapping my legs around his torso, he treaded water, and we resumed our steamy kisses. Even though I loved the feel of his naked skin against mine, the heat of our connection rose to volatile proportions, and I pushed off Red's chest and swam back to the end of the boat. I looped my elbow over the transom and hung, waiting for Red to join me.

"Shall we grab the food and take it to the front of Adjustable Bend?" he asked, pulling himself up onto the back of the boat and reaching down to lift me out of the water.

I tried not to stare at his magnificent cock that hung heavy, slightly to the left. I pulled on my bathing suit as he yanked on his shorts. Bottle of wine and glasses in hand, I followed him below deck. "You've never told me the significance of your boat's name."

"Yacht and it's a type of knot." Before gathering up the crackers, tuna salad, and grapes, he put two towels under his arm.

"The name is a type of knot?" I asked, picking up the cheese in my free hand.

"Yes. It's the kind of knot that can easily be

lengthened or shortened."

"You know a lot about knots then?" I asked as I mounted the steps. Turning around, I saw his devilish expression. "Oh."

He pinched my bikini covered bottom and I slapped his hand away just before trotting to the bow of the ship. After we had set down the food and spread out the towels, he poured us each another glass of wine.

I reclined back on my hands and just admired the view. "I can see why you have Adjustable Bend. It's so quiet and peaceful out here." The ship rocked against the tide, leaving me incredibly relaxed. I hadn't taken a day off from work in a long while and it felt decadent.

"I love it. It's a great stress releaser, amongst other activities."

"Just remember who is holding whom off." I popped a grape into my mouth.

"I want it to mean something."

"How would a hand job not mean something, big boy? You would come in my hands and never forget it."

He chuckled and said, "You are a feisty one. Truly, I would love to, but let's wait until we talk to Bond."

"Did you have to bring him up again? Bond who? Who knows whose bed he's currently in? And you know what? I finally don't care."

"That's excellent to hear. I actually have to get back to the office for a meeting this afternoon." He finished off his glass of wine and lay on his side facing me.

"I see. Uh huh, right, good old office meeting."

"Stop being so adorable Jacqs, you make it hard for me to fight your womanly wiles."

"I have womanly wiles?"

"In abundance." Red started to sit up and said, "You can stay up here or keep me company in the cockpit."

"Let's clean up and I'll join you."

"Great."

On our way back to Red's house, I lay on the padded bench across from him and watched. He glanced at me now and again and seemed to be mulling something over in his mind. I wondered if he was rehearsing the conversation we needed to have with Bond or if he had a presentation at work.

It gave me the opportunity to stare at him shirtless. His small nipples were hard in the wind and I wondered if he'd like to have them sucked. I wanted to finger the small gauges in his earlobes and run my hand along his chest following the trail of hairs into his shorts. I found his lips fascinating as well, so full and soft yet surrounded by a full beard that he always kept neat and short cropped.

I shook my head and sat up crossing my legs. "Thanks for the introduction to Ted, and for taking the time to spend today with me."

"My pleasure."

Once we were on dry land, I said, "You seem distracted."

"Sorry, this is how I prep for my meetings. I run potential questions through my mind and my responses. Come here," he said, reaching for me.

I walked into this embrace, and melted against his warm chest.

"Thank you for giving me a chance," he whispered into my hair. He held me for a few moments and then we parted. "What are your plans tomorrow?"

"Going into the office and giving notice. I'm not really looking forward to it. When I get home I'll email Ted and tell him I'm taking the job. I also need to swing by Bella Boutique and get a boring, black dress."

"Get one with a top like this," he said, tickling down my cleavage.

"You like this suit?"

"Very much, but I liked you better without it."

I laughed. "I feel the same way," I said, tugging on the elastic waist of his shorts.

"Off with you," he said, lightly shoving me on my way. "I barely have time for a shower. I'll call you later."

A bright smile overtook me. "Good," I said.

As soon as I arrived home, I shot a quick email to Ted to let him know I planned to start in two weeks.

Needing to rinse off the salt water from my skin, I ran a bath, hoping it would relax my amped up libido from spending time with Red. I felt on edge and raw, as if my nerve endings had been awakened in a new, more intense way. Tapping my foot, impatient to feel the warm water soothing my skin, I absentmindedly caressed my breast, tugging on my nipple. My mind wandered back to Red and me floating in the water as he caressed my smooth pussy lips. Traveling farther back, I thought of the explosive orgasm he gave me as I sat on my kitchen counter.

"Jesus," I said to myself. I really needed some relief.

Stepping into the tub and immersing myself in the warm water didn't lessen the need. I imagined all the sexy activities we could have done on the boat. Would he want to tie me up there or just in his bedroom? Never having given in to Bond's proclivities, would I, could I submit to Red?

My hands roamed over my body as if they were Red's hands, sculpting, kneading, and pulling on my flesh. Not being able to stand the heat of my desire another second, I slowly let the water drain out of the tub and restarted the flow at the perfect temperature and speed for what I had in mind.

I scooted my butt to the edge of the tub and lined up my pussy under the flow of water so it hit right against my clit, my legs held up straight against the tile wall. "Ohhh,"

I groaned. Reaching down with both hands, I spread my lips to the sides, unsheathing my swollen clit.

As the water tapped against my bud, and I pulled on my nipple, my imagination ran wild:

"I can't wait another second to take you," Red exclaimed, bending me over the living room couch.

"What if someone stops by and comes in," I said, struggling against the hand that held my neck firmly in place.

With his other hand he lifted my skirt, pulling my panties to the side. "You're so wet for me already, I know you want this and you're going to take it for me."

"Yesss," I moaned.

"Good girl. Next time, I will tie you down and have my way with you, but right now, I have to sink my fat cock deep inside you."

I felt his thick head pushing against my distended lips, and I struggled to relax against the intrusion. "You're so big," I uttered.

"Shh, you can take it … you will, for me." He reached around us, capturing some of my wetness, coating the length of his shaft. I felt him pull out slightly before thrusting more of his girth within my tight pussy.

"Oh lord … oh please … I don't know if I can stand it," I mumbled.

"Relax Little One, I'm barely in." Circling my clit with his large fingers, he forced more of his length inside me.

The water level had risen too high; I no longer felt the flow on my clit. I slid down the tub, moving off the drain, letting some of the water escape. My hands continued to massage my breasts and tug on my nipples, not wanting to lose the momentum. As soon as the water level lowered enough, I scooted back in place and continue to allow the stream and my imagination to work their magic.

"There you go," he cooed. "See, you can take it. Let me all the way in."

His breath against my neck gave me goose bumps all the way down my spine as he increased the pressure on my clit and the force of his penetration. I felt his balls swing close, and I knew he had fully seated himself within me.

"Jesus you're tight," he grunted, grabbing my shoulder with his free hand and using it as leverage. He yanked me against him for each stroke.

"I'm so close," I yelled.

"Come with me," he bellowed.

I lifted my hips above the waterline and screamed my release as the flow jettisoned me out of my body as I convulsed. After the waves of my orgasm ceased, I collapsed into the tub. "Holy hell," I mumbled. I sat up, trying to collect my bearings. As soon as I could stand, I switched the water spray to shower mode and washed myself.

While drying off with one of my clean towels, my mind tried to chastise me for my behavior. "Oh, shut up," I said to myself in the mirror.

Finally relaxed, I threw on my PJs, grabbed my phone out of my bag, some chocolate from the kitchen cabinet and plopped down on the couch. I had a backlog of cooking shows to watch and would take advantage of the extra time I had. I decided to swing by Lainie's boutique the next day.

Before flipping on the tube, I noticed a voicemail

from my sister. Not wanting to deal with her, I placed the phone on the coffee table and snuggled into the couch. I must have dozed off during the episode on making bread from scratch, because the phone startled me awake.

Without thinking, I answered it.

"Hello," Samantha said. "I've been trying to reach you."

"Hi Sam. Please don't tell me I need to come rescue you from somewhere."

"No. I just called to say I'm sorry about Saturday night and I haven't had a drink since."

"What is that? All of five days?"

"I have to start somewhere."

"That's true," I said, getting up and shuffling into the kitchen for some water.

"Don't be mad at Darren. He took my car away because he knew I was in a mood and didn't want me drinking."

"Why do you keep choosing controlling men that you need to rebel against? And trust me, his violent and aggressive display didn't earn him any points with me." I drank a couple of swallows and sat on one of the stools next to the kitchen island.

"He was just worried about me."

"Worried or not, his manhandling of me was completely out of line. Let's not fail to mention that you stole my keys and my car."

"I borrowed your car—"

"What do you want?" I said, anger seeping into my words.

"I want to tag along to Red's this Saturday."

"I think that's a really bad idea. Everyone there drinks and you're just barely sober. Give it few months and several meetings. Are you going to AA?"

"No, those meetings just depress me."

"Samantha, you know I love you, but you need help. I think your last therapist was right. You need to grieve for Dad.

103

He was your best friend when he died, and you haven't recovered from his death. I think you continue to choose older men because you still want to feel like that little kid. Help yourself, please. I can't do anything else to help you."

"Well, I guess I'll hang up now."

"Please take care of yourself and really think about what I said."

"I love you," she whispered before hanging up.

The call left me feeling like crap. It's hard when you can't really help the ones you love. I scrolled through my contacts and dialed Lainie.

"Hi girl," she said when she answered her phone.

"Hi Lainie. Will you be in the shop tomorrow?"

"Sure, all day. What's up?"

"I need a black dress—"

"For who?"

"Me," I said with a slight chuckle.

"You in black? What gives?"

"For the party I'm going to with Bond. It's kind of odd because in the past he wanted me to wear the most outrageous of my colorful outfits just to piss off his people. As a favor to him, I told him I'd wear black, but you know how I've shunned the color since my father's funeral."

"Of course, I remember."

"So do you have any little black dresses? Maybe something strapless?"

"I have a few options in your size. I still think it's a bad idea that you go with him but please, keep your dress on."

"That's the plan."

"Uh huh."

"I love you, Lainie and I'll see you tomorrow after work. Speaking of work, I have some news on that front and will tell you tomorrow."

"You know I hate when you do that!"

Another call chimed through, and I said, "I have another call and have to go."

"Who is it?"

"You don't want to know," I said, shifting over.

"Hey you," Red said.

"Hey yourself," I said, moving back to the couch and lying down.

"I miss you already."

"You do not!" shot out of my mouth before I could sensor myself.

"Oh, but I do, Jacqs. I wish we had more time today."

"Well, I've thought about you since I've been home. You left me keyed up." I adjusted the pillow behind my head and sighed.

"What kind of thoughts?"

"Let's just say, I took care of things."

"So did I. Otherwise I never would've been able to concentrate in my meeting."

"In the shower?"

"How did you know?"

"Let's just call it a calculated guess." I laughed, trying to keep the sound under my breath. "How did your meeting go?"

"As well as I expected. I was hoping to take you to dinner tonight, but we have a follow up meeting tomorrow morning, and I plan to stay in the office late."

"I understand. What time is it anyway?"

"After six."

"I guess that's why my stomach's growling."

"You do have a noisy stomach when you're hungry."

"Thanks," I said, laughing.

"Have I mentioned that I love your laugh?"

"No." My cheeks warmed. "Thank you."

"Are you ready for tomorrow?"

"Ready? Yeah. Looking forward to it? Not in the least. However, I do have a plan of action."

"And what's that?"

"Tell Henry last. I want to have a chance to say goodbye to everyone I've worked with for the past six years, and I could see it going badly with Henry and him throwing me out of the building. I plan to take all of my personal belongings to the car at lunch time."

"Don't let him give you any shit—"

"I thought you hated cursing!"

He laughed and said, "It was an easy thing to give you a hard time about."

"You are too much!"

"I'd like to give you a different kind of hard time."

"I'd like that too. A lot I think."

"No doubt we'll be great together. We already are."

"Aren't you worried about how our friends are going to take it?"

"Sure, but like I said before, we have to live for us. We aren't doing it out of spite, at least I'm not."

"I'm not either." I sighed and said, "So what's your favorite curse word?"

"Fuck is pretty good. The word can be used in so many different ways. Like: oh fuck man, that sucks. Or fuck yeah, that's great. Or holy fuck I can't believe it, or one of my favorites, shut the fuck up."

"That's definitely a good one. Motherfucker is good too, especially if you slam your toe, but shit works fine for that as well. I also like oh hell and damn." A huge grin spread across my face. Just talking to Red filled me with happiness. It was a first for me. "I don't recall ever feeling like this before."

"Like what?"

"Happy and not twisted up in knots."

"I'd like to twist you up in knots." His voice sounded husky.

"As you've mentioned. I'm not sure how I feel about that."

"Trust me, I'll change your mind. I'm happy as well, Jacqs. Were you never happy with Bond?"

"I met Bond when I was twenty. He certainly captivated me and at times I felt euphoric, but it has always been this crazy rollercoaster of emotions—extreme highs and lows. Until recently I always felt insecure with him. Never being enough for someone can really tear at your self-worth."

"I've seen it myself. I love the man like a brother and hope someday he can let go of the past and really love."

"I hope that for him too." My stomach grumbled and I said, "I need to get something to eat—"

"Yeah, I need to get going myself. I can't wait to see you on Saturday. Can I text you tomorrow?"

"Sure, I'd like that."

"Okay. Have a wonderful evening."

"You too."

※ ※ ※ ※ ※

I climbed into bed and tossed and turned for a while, mulling over my feelings for two men. Just before falling asleep, I fixated on Bond's family party and telling him about Red on Sunday. Those thoughts made giving notice at work seem easy. Having another job lined up and walking away from my boss was simple in comparison.

CHAPTER SEVEN

Skinny Love

by Birdy

For casual Friday, I threw on a pair of blue jeans and a bright-pink, three-quarter sleeve V-neck. Although I usually wore a bit of makeup to work, I didn't on that day. I packed my lunch as always, finished my coffee, and headed into the office.

Clandestinely I met with my three favorite managers and each tried to talk me into staying. They said they were willing to talk to Henry on my behalf. *Where were they this past year, when Henry was being unbearable?* I thought. *They knew what he was like and could have intervened at any time. As far as I was concerned, their time had run out.*

I spent the morning finishing the marketing package I had been working on for Tom. I took down all the pictures I had hanging on the backdrop of my bulletin board, gathered the one plant that I brought in from home and searched through my drawers for any personal belongings. My phone chimed, so I sat in my chair and looked to see who had texted me.

> **Red:** How did it go?
> **Me:** I don't know yet. I'm just about to find out.
> **Red:** Text me after if you can.
> **Me:** ☺

After depositing the stuff in my car, I steeled myself

for the inevitable confrontation.

"I already know," he said once I knocked on the door and entered his office. "Steven, Mark, and Tom have all been in to see me."

"Great, then that makes it easy enough. I can give you two weeks but then my new job starts."

"You already have another job?"

I smiled with pride, "A far more lucrative one."

"I'm supposed to offer you a raise for you to stay."

"Don't bother."

"I wasn't planning on it. Where's my spreadsheet?"

"I'm available to train someone, maybe Star or Cara would like to work full-time? I will spend the rest of my time wrapping up my current projects." I turned on my heel to leave and said, "I'm taking the rest of the day off, and I expect to get my outstanding vacation pay in my last check."

I shut his door and heard him yell, "Don't count on it." However, I knew I would get it because Steven managed the money.

Once in my car, I sent a text to Red.

> **Me:** Given how it might have gone, it was short, if not sweet.
> **Red:** That's good. How do you feel?
> **Me:** Hmm, let's see. Powerful, vindicated, and relieved.
> **Red:** All good things.
> **Me:** Thanks for checking in on me.
> **Red:** My pleasure.

I drove straight over to Lainie's Bella Boutique and found her in the backroom with the recently delivered clothing.

"I'm never using this wholesaler again. Feel this," she said, holding out a shirt for me to touch. "Cheap shit that I plan to send back."

"Sorry girl."

"Yeah, so how are you here so early?"

"I've quit my job." I clapped my hands, bursting with excitement as the words settled in.

"You what?" Her jaw fell open.

"Love that expression, Lane. Priceless!"

"What are you going to do for work?" she said, shaking her head.

"I already have another job. More money, more time off."

"When did you have time to do that? I just saw you on Sunday when you rudely interrupted my sleep."

"It happened suddenly. Red—"

"Oh god, please don't tell me you're working for Red!"

I stepped closer and touched Lainie's shoulder. "I won't be working *for* Red, but I will be working for Ted, a financial partner in his company."

"Why must you make your life so complicated?"

Another text came in and I glanced at my phone. "One sec," I said to Lainie.

> **Red:** I thought you might like to know, I thought about you in the shower again today.

Heat infused my body and I could feel Lainie watching me.

> **Me:** I'm looking forward to you thinking about me in person.
> **Red:** Oh, Little One, me too. Soon.
> **Me:** I have to run. I'm at Lainie's shop and she is staring me down.
> **Red:** K. Talk to you soon.

I turned my attention back to Lainie and said, "Me,

making my life complicated? I don't mean to. Really I don't, but it's looking that way at the moment."

"Who was that?" she said, placing her hands on her hips.

"Red." I put my shoulders back, preparing for the onslaught.

"Have you told Bond about Red?"

"We're telling him on Sunday, after you and I have brunch."

"I hope you're prepared for the fallout."

I wasn't, but I didn't care to focus on it. I would have to deal with the consequences soon enough. "So black dresses?"

"Sure, follow me."

Saturday evening came upon me all too soon. I dreaded Bond's family party and just being around Bond could turn problematic. Anger and guilt brewed an unpleasant concoction in my belly.

After slipping on the black dress I bought from Lainie's boutique, I pulled a shoebox from the back of my closet. Opening it, I discovered my black pumps. I remembered the last time I wore them. It was the night of our most recent breakup.

Bond had asked me to come by his apartment before he had to work at the club. His stupid photo album of all the topless women he had fucked or dated or whatever, lay out on the end table near his black leather couch.

Just the sight of it left me on edge. "New additions?" I asked nonchalantly but inside I bristled with anger.

"See for yourself," he said as if it was completely natural to convince all your lovers to let him take a Polaroid of them naked from the waist up.

I fanned to the back of the album and found three new

photographs. Heat infused my entire body and I struggled to hold back the tears.

"I have more film if you're ready to pose for me."

"I haven't changed my mind about being part of your photo album, but I have changed my mind about you," I said, snatching up my purse and heading to the door.

"Come on, Jacqs, we've been through this before," he said, grasping my arm and pulling me toward him. "That's just something for fun and I don't feel about those women like I feel about you."

"I beg to differ," I said, shaking him off. "You want me to be another notch on your bedpost, only for you, it's a picture in your fucked up photo album." I threw my hands in the air and shook my head. "Forget it. Why do I keep doing this to myself?"

"Come on baby, you know I love you. Please let me show you." He wrapped his arms around me, but I held myself rigid.

The longer we stood there, his scent of warm skin and sandalwood filling my nostrils and his hard cock pushing against my stomach, the more my anger dissolved. I hated that he had that kind of power over me.

Tears fell on my cheeks as he began to coo at me and grind his erection against my mound. As my body responded to him, I tried to will away my jealousy. "Don't you have to get to work?"

"We have plenty of time for me to make you feel better." He led me to his bedroom, undressed, and pulled my shirt over my head. After he had slipped off each black pump, he shimmied down my tight red jeans, pulling my panties off with them. He fingered my clit and said, "Hard and wet for me as always." Lying down next to me, he took his time caressing all the places he knew drove me wild. He suckled my neck and tugged on my large nipples, running his hand down my belly.

Like an addict, I succumbed to his advances. His penetrating stare and attention swayed me and in that moment I convinced myself, yet again, that he really did love me. That I needed him, and he needed me.

I rolled onto my side and clutched his face, bringing his lips to mine. As he thoroughly possessed me with his deep kiss, he lifted my top leg over his and reached down between us to stroke my clit.

"This is what's important," he said. "How it is between us, where nobody else matters. I love you, baby." After bringing me right up to the edge of release, my nipples taut, my pussy wet, he said, "Come for me."

My body responded to his order and thrashed against his hand as I called out, "Yesss." Swimming in a sea of bliss, I rolled onto my back to recover. Dazed by the orgasm and Bond's sole ability to bring me to climax, I welcomed him into my body as he drew my legs over his waist and penetrated me from his side position.

He reached over the top of me, grasping my shoulder for leverage and with his free hand, pushed my arm down so my palm rested over my mound.

I knew what he wanted from me as he manipulated my fingers so they swirled around my clit. The deep invasion of his steel hard cock coupled with the rubbing of my hooded bud brought me ever closer to another orgasm.

Bond began to grunt as I felt his cock swell inside me. I clutched the bed cover, careening my body against him as both of our fingers played in my wetness and he forcefully buried his cock as deep as possible.

"Oh lord," I cried out and at the same instant he deafened us both with his fierce roar. We lay there panting, flying high on endorphins and our reconnection.

After we slowly recovered, he said, "Come by the

club for a drink before you head back home."

"I would just get in the way," I said as I sat up, trying to collect myself.

"Not at all. I'm going to take a quick shower and head out. Take your time."

I dozed for a bit, dressed, fixed my hair and makeup, and went down to the club. I thought it was a good sign that he wanted me to drop by to see him. Once I opened the door to The CroBar, the loud dance music spilled out onto the street. Stepping inside, I could see all the people crowded around the main bar. I moved closer to the dance floor where reflections of lights bounced off the people gyrating to the beat.

Bond sat in the DJ booth with three tall blondes surrounding him. I watched him hand one of the women his cell and she typed something, which I assumed was her number. Just as I decided to leave, he glanced up. I shook my head in his direction and walked out.

That was the last time Bond and I had been a couple. Bond later explained the woman was a friend of Red's whom I met at a gathering at his place, but at that point it didn't matter. Even if he could manage to keep his cock in his pants, I couldn't take all the women surrounding him all the time. I took a deep breath and willed the memory back into the past.

I slipped on the black pumps and looked at myself in the full-length mirror on the back of my bedroom door. Lainie had a crepe satin, black dress with a sweetheart neckline and tapering shoulder straps that fit my small curvy frame perfectly. The hem fell to about mid-thigh. I would have much preferred the bright red one she also carried, but overall it gave me a sexy yet classy appearance.

After lining my eyes in black and adding some

mascara, I pulled the sides of my hair back and secured it with a barrette to expose my silver dangling earrings. I had a small black purse for such dismal occasions, and I filled it with lip gloss, eyeliner, and some tissues. Chucking my cell phone in as well, I took a deep breath and headed out to my car. Before taking off, I sent a text to Bond to let him know I was on my way.

"You look great," Bond said as he pulled on his seat belt.

"So do you. You know, you look great in a tux. And I'm guessing the shiny boots are a rebellious statement?"

"Ah, maybe or the lack of dress shoes." He flashed one of his dangerous smiles.

"Why do I have to dress in dreary black?" I said as I drove down the street. "I feel like we're going to a funeral instead of a party. What's wrong with one of my colorful flowing dresses or skirts?"

"Can we just blend in tonight? I'm not in the mood for conflict."

"That's not like you. You've always enjoyed razzing your people." I glanced to the right and changed lanes. "What gives?"

"I want to know who you're dating."

"You're making me wear dreary black attire because you think I'm dating someone? I just said I was interested in somebody." I drove up the north ramp to I-95.

"No, I'm changing the subject."

After I had merged with the traffic, I said, "Change it again because I have no intention of discussing it."

"I think we should try again."

"Of course you do. You love the chase when I'm unavailable. The only problem is that you get bored once you catch me again. No thanks. I'll pass."

He turned in his seat and raised his voice. "That's not

true and you know it! We didn't break up last time because I got bored. I've been thinking about us a lot lately."

I glanced at him and back at the road. "When exactly? Between each new fucking conquest? Give me a break, Bond."

"You're the one who ended it. Tell me what to do. Do I need to stop dating altogether before you'll give me another chance?"

"I just don't think we work."

"When will you understand that my dating other women doesn't take away from my love for you?"

"Well ... ummm ... how about never? Do we really need to keep going over this ground? This is not a date. We aren't going to have sex when the night is over. This is simply a favor I allowed you to talk me into, against my better judgment. That's it."

"I love you, Jacqs."

I took a couple of deep breaths to calm myself and said, "I know you do and I love you too, but that's beside the point."

"How can love be beside the point?" he said, touching my knee.

Brushing him off, I said, "Because we aren't a good fit. You know that as well as I do."

"I can change."

"Uh huh." I rolled my eyes.

"I'm serious."

As we got closer to the exit to Delray Beach, I switched lanes to the right. "Okay, so why don't you drive?"

"That has nothing to do with us dating."

"It has everything to do with it. You don't trust me with your deepest darkest secrets."

"I don't trust anyone with them."

"You trust Red," I said, turning on my right blinker.

"That's different and how do you know that?"

After driving down the off ramp, I turned onto Delray Beach Boulevard. "I asked him and he said I could only get that info from you and I got the distinct impression he knew the truth."

"Since when do you and Red talk about us?"

I swallowed and said, "Well ... you know ... we've called a sort of truce and he helped me find a new job. He's not so bad once you get past his overabundant need to control everything."

"Red said the same thing."

"That I'm controlling?" I asked, in a louder voice than I intended.

"No, that you called a truce."

"Oh," I said, lowering my shoulders and focusing on driving.

"What's gotten into you lately? You seem different."

"Nothing ... I don't know ... stress from work, Sammy, you, all of it."

Bond guided me through the streets to his family's beach home. The resort-like house with two pools and a Jacuzzi had a long meandering path that led to the ocean. It was the very home where Bond grew up.

As we drove up the street, he said, "Pull over there and park."

"How long do we have to stay?" I said, standing by my VW Bug and shutting the door.

"At least until after dinner." He took my hand and we walked up the long, red-brick drive lined with several cars.

Bond's nervous energy flowed into my hand and I prayed to the finicky gods that tonight would go smoothly. I craved a strong alcoholic drink to get me through the evening, however, Bond would refuse to get in the car with me for the ride home if I drank. He, of course, was free to drink, and it seemed a little unfair. His people intimidated the crap out of me.

Just a couple of steps away from the ten foot dark wooden doors, a man I didn't recognize slapped Bond on the back and said, "Hey there, Mitchell, I haven't seen you around in a long time."

"Hi Uncle Jack. I didn't know you planned to come into town for the event. Have you met Jacqueline?"

"No, I sure haven't but she's a looker, isn't she?" he said, reaching out to shake my hand.

"Hi," I said.

He scanned my body in a way that left my mind screaming, *Old lecherous man!*

After he had stepped away, Bond said, "Watch out for that one."

"I figured that out for myself," I said, and then whispered, "Do we have to go say hi to your parents? Your mother really doesn't like me."

"Yay!" I heard from across the entrance room. Lily slipped off her heels and ran into Bond's arms. He immediately lifted her up and spun her around in a big hug. I could see her whisper into his ear and he nodded.

Lily's white-blonde hair complimented the same light brown eyes her brother had. Perched on the edge of eighteen, she had yet to fill out to womanhood. She had slight hips and small breasts, and it was easy to see the maturity that lurked behind her eyes.

"Jacqs, look at you! Looking so sophisticated!" she said, throwing her arms out wide to hug me. "Can I steal her for a few?" she asked Bond. "I want her to see how I've redecorated my room."

"Sure, but don't keep her too long. She's my shield."

"I won't!" she said, looping her arm through mine.

"It's no longer pink?" I asked as she led me up the

palatial center staircase.

"Not a lick of pink."

Once she opened the door, I couldn't believe the transformation. Gone were the bed canopy, white furniture and pink walls. On the far side, behind the red, hardwood bed was a multicolor block graphic that filled the whole wall.

"Wow," I said. "Nice job."

"Thanks. How did you manage to drag Mitch here on this day of all days?"

"He dragged me," I responded but my heart dropped at her meaning.

We both sat down on the edge of her bed.

"I'm surprised he would come on the anniversary of the accident," Lily said.

"I didn't know—" I said, folding my hands in my lap.

"He never told you? You of all people! What's wrong with my brother?"

"I guess he doesn't trust me," I said, shrugging my shoulders.

"No, it can't be that. He probably doesn't want you to see him in a bad light."

"Maybe," I said, my heart ached for Bond.

"Mitch was engaged to be married—"

"He was? Wait … I'm not sure you should tell me."

"Too late for that now, isn't it? Celeste had a hard time with all of Mitch's flirting but he was completely committed to her."

"How long ago was that? I've known Bond for eight years—that would make you, what, nine or ten at the time?"

"I was actually younger, but I've heard the story a billion times over the years. When I was fifteen, Mitch told me himself, dispelling some of the myths I had heard. Mostly from Donny. Do you still call him Bond? That's interesting. Anyway, Mitch was twenty-three at the time and he went with Celeste and Donny to a party where they all were drinking. Celeste got sick of Mitch's flirting, so she tried it out for herself, only she took it too far and kissed a guy. Mitch punched the guy out and then he and Celeste argued in front of the whole party. Can you imagine? Anyway, they left shortly after the fight. On their way home Mitch lost control of the car. He was in the ICU for weeks, but Celeste was killed."

"Oh my god! That explains so much." Tears filled my eyes and I tried to wipe them away.

"There's more."

"More?"

"Her parents believed he killed her on purpose and he was charged with manslaughter. Her family wanted him charged with murder."

"You've got to be kidding me. So what happened?"

"He got sentenced to ten years and served three."

"He was in jail?"

"Prison, yes."

The tears fell down my cheeks and I almost wished she'd never told me. I became so angry I could barely see straight. "Why would your parents schedule this party on the anniversary of his tragedy and then force him to come?"

"Here," she said, handing me a tissue. "I can't answer that for you. I'd like to think they're just ignorant or oblivious, but I don't know."

"What about Donny? He must remember!"

"Donny has always had a bone up his ass about Mitch. I think it's because he was older, but all the girls wanted Mitch, even some of his girlfriends."

Using the tissue, I blotted my eyes. "But Bond never—"

"No, but Donny thinks otherwise."

"Jesus Christ! I don't even know what to say. It explains so much—"

"We should go back down before Mitch comes looking for us. You can use my bathroom to clean up your eye makeup."

"Okay, I'll meet you downstairs in a minute."

We embraced and I did my best not to breakdown in her arms. In her innocence, she must have shared Bond's story because she thought I had a right to know. I had longed to learn the truth for years, but it left me feeling tainted. In hindsight, maybe Bond had tried to protect me from the truth.

In the bathroom, I sat on the settee and cried for Bond. I wept for myself as well. Would I have felt differently all those years had I understood the real story? Not wanting Bond to come looking for me, I took a couple of deep breaths and dried my eyes. I removed my makeup and reapplied it. He would notice something was wrong and I had no idea how I would explain it. I didn't want him to know what I'd found out.

I squared my shoulders and stood as tall I could manage before I descended the staircase. Just as I rounded the bottom, Donny intercepted me.

Before I could stop myself, anger still boiling in my gut, I blurted out, "Why did you do it? How can you be so callous and unfeeling?" I glanced around us and felt relief when I didn't see Bond in earshot.

Somehow he knew exactly what I meant. "Don't give me your sass, short stuff. I didn't want him here and never imagined he'd show."

"You're the lowest form of maggot I have ever had the displeasure of meeting," I said, placing my hands on my hips. "Why not grow the fuck up and leave Bond alone. You are thirty-seven and still jealous. You're a real piece of work."

"I'm the maggot?" Donny said, raising his voice.

"You are a very confused little girl."

"Bond has more worth and integrity in his little pinky than you'll ever—"

"Excuse me, but you're causing a scene," Bond's mother said with her husband in tow.

"You too," I said, turning my wrath on his parents. "Have you lost all sense of common decency?"

"You will not talk to Eleanor that way," Bond's father said in a quiet but vicious tone.

"Do you know what day it is? Does any one of you even have a heart?" I couldn't stand to be near them for one more second and stalked off to find Bond so we could leave.

"I never did like her," I heard Eleanor said.

"The feeling's mutual," I said to myself as I hurried through the house. "There you are," I said, pulling Bond away from a group of older men deep in conversation. "We have to go." I tugged on his arm again.

"We can't, Jacqs. Not until after dinner. Why are you so upset? You're eyes look red."

"Your brother—"

"Donald..." he said, stretching his name out in disgust, "...is not worth your time or energy. Just ignore him."

"It's not just him, your parents—"

"Ignore them too. They'll be at their own table at dinner, presiding over the meal like the king and queen. We have to suck it up and then we can leave just before dessert."

"These people, other than Lily of course, don't deserve you! I don't know how you put up with them."

"You're cute when you stand up for me," he said, touching the end of my nose. "Let's find out how much longer until dinner starts." He clasped my hand and I thought I might start to cry again. I swallowed down the emotion and shuffled to keep up.

The staff had set up a massive white tent on the lawn

between the guest house and the beach. The stunning view and the cool air made it the perfect setting for the dinner. The china, crystal, white table cloths and elaborate flower bouquets looked more like a setting for a wedding than a promotion to partner.

"Is someone getting married?" I said.

"It sure looks like it, doesn't it?" he said, turning me to face him. "Thank you so much for coming with me."

"You don't make saying no easy."

"That's part of my charm," he said with a cheesy smile.

I punched him lightly on the shoulder and said, "I'm certain I was a poor choice given that I pissed off both your brother and parents."

"If you were defending my honor, then I love you even more for it."

Before I could fight him off, he held my head in his hands and tilted my lips to his. I kissed him back, wishing I could heal all his pain and torment. Circling his arm around my lower back, he drew me to him, bringing me back into his world.

I melted against him and followed the familiar journey of our kiss. Lainie might never understand the depth of connection that I found in his embrace but it was akin to being rescued from an avalanche and swept up in an inferno. The knowledge of his history tore at my heart and opened more space for Bond to slip inside it.

"Get a room," Lily said, laughing. "See, she's still into you. I was right."

"Shut up, Lily," Bond said, but I could hear the warm affection in his voice.

"I'm just saying!" She giggled and smiled. "Dinner starts in ten minutes and you, Jacqs, are sitting right next to me."

"Oh, that's a relief. Do you know who's on my

other side?"

"Cruella Deville, I'm sorry for you."

"I'm sure she'll give me a piece of her mind after my conversation with Donny."

Bond circled behind me and wound his arms across my stomach.

"Just talk to me and don't let her get to you," Lily said. "Patricia's a bitch, but can you imagine being married to Donny? Just gives me chills thinking about it."

I glanced past her to the guests making their way across the pool deck to the tent.

"I guess we should go find our seats," Bond said in my ear, causing chills to run down my neck.

The heels of the trophy wives clicked along the wooden floor of the tent as the crowd settled into their places.

Bond's father, Joseph, stood behind the head table with a glass in hand, and said, "Welcome to all who have come to celebrate Donald's place as a partner in our law firm. His years of hard work have been a source of pride for Eleanor and me. Let's break bread in honor of Donald!"

Many people at the tables raised their glasses and shouted, "Here, here."

Several servers delivered the first course, which was a single scallop on a bed of butter lettuce. Having watched so many cooking shows, I recognized the perfection of the sear on the butter poached seafood.

Patricia arrived late, and I could feel the tension of her immediate distaste of having to sit next to me. Impeccably dressed in her Gucci floral-lace and silk dress, she shifted her long, straight, blond hair off her shoulder as if flicking me away with the motion.

"What did you think of the scallop?" Lily asked, garnering my attention.

"I love scallops but haven't had much success in cooking

them myself. This one was perfection, don't you think?"

"She's glaring at you," Lily whispered into my ear.

"I can feel her stare on the back of my neck," I whispered.

She laughed and said, "Can you believe Mitch has to sit next to Donny?"

"I hope he punches him out."

Lily giggled again and said, "I don't think that would go over well with Dad."

"Probably not, but it would be fun to watch."

I spotted a couple talking to Bond's parents, and the man looked strikingly similar to Red. "Lily, do you see that couple talking to your father?"

"That's Mr. and Mrs. Burke. Cold people if you ask me."

"Red mentioned that they might be here."

"You *know*," Patricia said, glowering down her thin pointed nose at me, "my mother-in-law thinks you are far beneath the family."

"You *know*," I said, turning to face her and mimicking her tone, "I always consider the source."

"What are you implying?"

"You think someone like me would aspire to be someone like you and you couldn't be farther from the truth. Having money does not make you a good person, deserving of respect. It just makes you a person with money. As far as I can see, none of Mitch's family deserves my respect other than Lily and Mitch."

"Don't think you will ever be a part of this family."

"Thank god for that," I said, shaking my head at the thought.

Patricia talked over me and said, "Lily, I don't know what you see in this woman."

"Only the best thing that's ever happened to Mitch."

Patricia harrumphed and turned away. Thankfully, she ignored me for the rest of dinner.

I spent most of the meal chit-chatting with Lily and watching Bond on the other side of the table. He held himself together which had to be a minor miracle. Just before the cakes and other desserts were brought out, he rescued me from the party.

"Let's get the fuck out of here," he said.

We hugged Lily goodbye and strolled in silence hand and hand to the car. Before opening my car door for me, he held me in a tight embrace. We rocked in silence until he said, "Thanks again, Jacqs."

"You are welcome." As I drove out to the main road, I asked, "Are you okay?"

"Just a lot on my mind."

He stared out the side window and my heart broke again, knowing what that day of all days meant to him. I would never forgive Donny or his parents.

The gathering at Red's was in full swing by the time we arrived. I really didn't feel like being there, but I had to talk to Red before I could sneak away.

Bond and I entered the kitchen, and instead of choosing his usual beer he opened the cabinet above the stove and poured himself a tumbler of scotch.

"I'm going to sit outside for a while," he said.

"Okay. I'm not sure how long I plan to stay. I hate this dress and I feel my socializing quota has already been extracted. Shall I come and get you when I'm ready to leave?"

"I'll probably crash here tonight."

"I can stay if you'd rather hang out here."

"Nah. I won't be much company. Thanks again for coming with me," he said, reaching toward me for another hug.

I threw my arms around his back and buried my head in his chest. I willed my healing energy of love to penetrate his broken heart.

"Baby, I can't lose you. Please think about giving us another chance. I promise to do it right this time." He pulled away and gazed down at me. "I love you." His shoulders slumped as he ambled away to the French doors.

Damn, I thought.

After checking out back for Red, I entered the game room and found him playing pool with Stay. "Can I steal him for a minute?"

"Jacqs to the rescue from your brutal loss," Stay said to Red.

"Rematch later?" Red asked.

"Sure and maybe I can grab Blue and we can play doubles," he said, hanging his cue stick back onto the wall rack.

"Are you okay? You look distraught," Red said as we crossed the room together.

"Can we go to your room?" I asked once we were out of earshot of Stay.

"Sure," he said, drawing out the word.

"Not like that," I said, jogging up the stairs to the second floor.

"I like the dress you chose, especially walking behind you," he said as he followed me.

Once we entered the room, I took in the man before me. His slate green cargo slacks and long-sleeved shirt hugged his frame, and I felt tempted to rub my hand right over his fly. The outline of his cock tempted me, causing my pussy to twitch with desire.

Focus woman! I chastised in my head. "Do you know what day today is?"

"Ummm, the twentieth? I know it's not your birthday. Yours isn't for a few months."

After closing the bedroom door behind us, I said, "Lily told me everything. How could you have forgotten that today is the anniversary?"

"Oh shit! Where's Bond?"

"He's out back with a large tumbler of scotch. He doesn't know that I know, and I want it kept that way."

"How bad was the party?"

"Honestly, I have no idea how he kept it so together, but it explains so much. Now I understand why he doesn't drive and why he is unable to open up his heart again."

"I have to check on him," Red said, striding to the door.

"Wait."

"What?"

"We can't tell him tomorrow. There's no way."

"No, of course we can't. Fuck, I can't believe I let it slip my mind. He usually gets drunk on the day of the accident and then has a major meltdown a few days later." He leaned against the door and said, "I'm glad that you now know."

"I'm not sure I am."

"I bet."

"Please don't go yet, I have something else to tell you," I said, shaking.

"What is it? You're trembling."

"He kissed me and I kissed him back."

"Oh … well … given the circumstances…"

"I'm confused. I don't want to lose what we've started, but I don't know how I feel about Bond now, knowing what I know. I still love him and I can't imagine what he must be going through."

"Jacqs, we will work this out together. Come here." He encompassed me against his large body and I felt safe for the moment.

Looking up I said, "This is where I've wanted to be since I found out." Sighing into his hug, I wanted to stay there, hiding from reality.

Running his hands over my hips and ass, he said,

"You're not wearing any underwear!"

"I can't with this dress or they'll give me lines." I chuckled slightly.

"Jesus Jacqs, what am I going to do with you?"

"I hope we get a chance to find out."

"Yeah, me too. I need to go check on Bond. I don't want to leave him alone for too long."

"I know. I just wanted to say goodbye before I take off."

Still holding me tightly, he said, "Please don't go."

"I think it'll be best for all of us. You can look after Bond and right now I'd just get in the way."

"Come by tomorrow—"

"That could be awkward. Bond said he's planning to spend the night here."

"Text me when you get home so I know you arrived safely, and I'll call you tomorrow when I know what the day's looking like."

Red lifted me up and lowered me to stand on the chair by the door. It made me slightly taller than him. I threw my arms over his shoulders and bent my head down for a kiss. My heart had thawed somewhat for Bond; however, it hadn't diminished the lust and longing I felt for Red that had caught like wildfire. Somehow, all the anger I had felt for him became desire, and I'd already started to let him into my heart. I could no easier walk away from him than Bond.

As my lips touched Red's, tears filled my eyes and tumbled down my cheeks. My anxiety of how our situation would resolve spiked just before all my thoughts were wiped clean. As our tongues met, I willingly lost myself in Red's kiss. He lingered, softly caressing his mouth to mine. When we both opened our eyes, I saw love reflected there.

He kissed away the tears on my cheek and said, "We will sort it out together, Little One. Trust in me."

"I do."

By the time I arrived home, I felt completely drained. I hadn't been to hot yoga classes for a few weeks, and the accumulation of stress without any hardcore exercise was taking its toll. I unzipped my dress as I walked through the front door and laid it down on the laundry pile. I slipped into my robe, settling on the bed with my cell phone.

> **Me:** I'm home. How's Bond?
> **Red:** Three sheets to the wind.
> **Me:** Already?
> **Red:** Doesn't take long with scotch.
> **Me:** What's he doing?
> **Red:** Hitting on anything that walks.
> **Me:** You might try getting some food in him. I don't think he ate much at dinner.
> **Red:** Short of throwing him in the pool, when he's like this, there's not much I can do but watch and make sure he doesn't hurt himself.
> **Me:** I hate this.
> **Red:** So do I.
> **Me:** What are we going to do?
> **Red:** Bond has a staff meeting tomorrow at twelve, so can you swing by after that?

My mind said, "Leave this mess alone, Jacqueline," but in truth, I felt better when I was with Red than I had in a long time. Was I just supposed to stop seeing him? Stop hanging out with the group? I honestly didn't know the right thing to do under the circumstances. It had been a long while since I had been Bond's girlfriend so why did I still feel a loyalty to him?

> **Me:** I really want to see you and at the same time, it feels wrong. Not when we're together.

> Then it feels totally right but I'm fucked up over what happened to Bond.
> **Red:** Tell me what you want.
> **Red:** Give me a sec, I'll be right back.
> **Me:** I guess I want it to be easy and it's not, and now it seems even more complicated than before.

I flicked on my iPod station and went to the bathroom to get ready for bed while I waited to hear back from Red. After I emerged from the bathroom, I still hadn't received a text, so I climbed under the covers and drifted off to sleep.

Something startled me awake and I sat up in bed. I checked my cell phone—no texts—but I noticed the time was 1:30 a.m. The doorbell rang again and I got out of bed, threw on my robe and tied the sash as I stumbled to the door.

"Who is it?"

"It's me, Red, let me in."

I opened the door and he carried a drunk Bond in over his shoulder.

"Is he okay?" I said, following them over to the couch. "Where's his shirt?"

"I don't know, somewhere in the house. He's passed out at the moment," Red said, sitting him down on the couch and turning his legs so he fell over onto his side.

I collected a pillow and blanket from the hall closet. "Should we run him to the hospital?"

"No, he just needs to sleep it off and I didn't want to leave him alone at his place."

"What about your other guests?" I lifted Bond's head and placed a pillow under it.

"Bond and Blue really got into, it so I thought it best if I extracted him from the situation."

"Bond and Blue? That's odd. What the hell happened?"

"I think I'll leave it to them to fill in the details."

"That doesn't sound good. Don't worry about him; I'll drop him off at his apartment in the morning on my way to Lainie's."

"Thank you," he said as he pulled off Bond's boots. "I wish I was seeing you under better circumstances."

"Yeah, me too."

Together we spread the blanket over Bond.

"I think I'm going to skip the next few Saturdays," Red said. "These parties are wearing me out."

"I can well imagine."

"Cute robe," he said. "Are you naked under there?"

"Wouldn't you like to know," I said, tightening the robe around myself.

"Seriously though, can I lie down with you for a few minutes? Just let me hold you until you fall back asleep?"

"I'd like that a lot." I slipped my hand into his and led him to my room. Untying my robe, I let it fall to the floor exposing my nakedness and climbed under the covers into my side of the bed.

"I'm leaving my clothes on."

"I think that's highly advisable."

After he had removed his shoes, he joined me, moving toward the middle of the bed and spooned me to him. It was as if every molecule in my body sighed in contentment.

"Should I set the alarm to wake you? Bond finding us like this would be horrible," I said, scooting in even closer.

"Stop wiggling, Jacqs," he hissed.

I laughed and said, "Sorry."

"No alarm necessary, I won't sleep."

"Okay," I said, yawning. "I will."

"Goodnight."

CHAPTER EIGHT

Lost Without You

by Robin Thicke

W hen I awoke to my alarm, I sat up, stretching my arms above me. I smiled, recalling how Red had snuggled me to sleep. Then I remembered that Bond still remained in my apartment, and my stomach twisted. *Ugh*, I thought. I pushed off the bed and headed into the bathroom for a shower.

I let the stream of water run over my head, once again waking me to the reality of the situation. My heart hurt for Bond, but at the same time my soul longed to spend more time with Red—without all the complications. I hoped Lainie could put aside her judgments long enough to help me sort through it all.

Lost in thought, I almost screamed when Bond slid open the shower door.

"Can I join you?" he asked, propping himself up against the wall.

"No," I said, covering my breasts with my arm. "I don't think you're quite sober yet. Go make a pot of coffee and I'll drop you at your place as soon as I'm ready."

"Did we—"

"Absolutely not! You were passed out when Red brought you here."

"Are you sure about the shower? I can soap your back for you," he said, scanning my body up and down.

I physically responded to his gaze, my nipples pushing

against my arm. "Got it covered. Please shut the door on your way out," I said, pointing in the direction of the bathroom door.

Heavily, he pushed himself upright and trudged out.

What the hell! I hurriedly finished up in the shower and slipped on a pair of bright purple shorts and a red top with a colorful, funky owl decal. I gathered my purple hoodie, keys, and phone and shoved them all into my black and neon Mayan backpack.

Traipsing into the kitchen, I fixed myself a cup of coffee and perched on the island. Bond sat forward on the couch with his arms on his knees.

"Headache?" I asked.

"The worst."

"Want something for it?"

He tilted his head up and for a moment I was scared what he might say. He glanced away and said, "Sure."

"Here you go," I said, tossing the bottle of ibuprofen I kept in the cabinet. "Care to tell me what happened with Blue last night?"

"I have no idea."

"Red won't tell me, but it didn't sound good."

"Terrific," he said, followed by a long sigh. "I can't believe I have to sit through a staff meeting today."

"Yeah, bad timing."

"Sorry I abandoned you last night."

"No, it's okay," I said, sitting down next to him. "I can imagine what an ordeal it was for you. I wanted to punch your brother and have no idea how you refrained."

Running his hand through his long hair, he said, "I feel like I keep letting you down."

"Let's not worry about us right now, okay?" I strung my arm over his shoulder. "We need to get you home so you can shower before your meeting. Want another cup of coffee to go?"

"Thanks for taking care of me."

"Of course, we're family. If not by blood, by friendship and that counts more in my book. Plus, I really didn't do anything but let you sleep on my couch."

"I want to be better for you."

"Yeah, well, we all want a lot of things, but let us just focus on the possible, okay?"

"I'm serious, Jacqs."

"Let's talk about this when you're sober and rested." I stood up, taking our coffee cups into the kitchen. I refilled his mug and drank the last of mine.

Later we rode in silence, and I could feel my heart breaking over all that Bond must be going through. I wanted to help him, but I didn't know how. Wiping out that kind of pain and tragedy seemed impossible.

Bond got out of my car in front of his apartment building. Stooping down to talk to me through the passenger side window, he said, "Thanks Jacqs. Let's get together this week. Okay?"

"Yeah, sure. I'll see you Wednesday at Red's, right?"

"Yeah, but maybe we can see each other before that."

"Listen, if you need me, you know where to find me."

"I love you, Jacqs," he said, standing up.

"I love you too. Take care of yourself."

He rested his hand on the door ledge and I thought he was about to say something else. He tapped it twice and shuffled away.

I struggled to keep it together as I knocked on Lainie's door.

"Hey girl," she said but took a better look at me. "What is it?" She embraced me and I broke down in her arms. She led me over to the couch and lowered me down. "Did you sleep with Bond again?"

I shook my head as the tears spilled out of my eyes.

"Red?"

Shaking my head again, I could feel Lainie relax a bit.

"Okay then, when you can speak, tell me what's happened."

I inhaled a couple of shaky breaths and said, "Oh, Lainie, I'm falling for Red and I still love Bond. And now I know why Bond is the way he is." I held up my hand before she had a chance to protest. "I know you don't care for Bond because of all the pain I have been through with him but I'm here, needing your support, and I'm asking you for two things."

"What?" she said, resting back against the couch and crossing her legs.

"If possible, can you please leave your judgment in the other room? You can go back and fetch it after but for just today, I need your help, advice, and support."

She sat up straight and said, "I'm always supportive! I just hate to see you keep making the same mistake over and over. Bond doesn't deserve you and I have my reservations about Red too."

"See what I mean?" I said, shrugging.

She chuckled and said, "Yes, okay. What's the second thing?"

"You can never, and I mean ever, repeat what I'm going to share with you about Bond. I'm not even supposed to know."

"That's a given, who would I tell?"

"I'm just saying."

"Okay, I'm listening," Lainie said, moving to face me.

"Bond was in a car accident years ago and his fiancé died in the crash. He was charged with manslaughter and served three years."

"What the fuck? How do you know?" she said, throwing her hands up in the air.

"Lily told me. And what's worse, last night was the anniversary."

"Holy shit and you guys went to that hoity-toity party. Is his family completely insane?"

"Apparently. I went off on his brother and parents. Donny picked yesterday because he was sure Bond would never come. Unfortunately, Bond's father threatened to cut him off if he didn't show."

"Wow, I'm not sure what to say. It really does explain so much about Bond's dysfunction in relationships."

"Yeah," I said and took a deep breath. "I did a stupid thing though."

"Just one?" she said, laughing and slapping her leg.

"Very funny," I said, trying hard not to smile along with her. "I'm serious though. The night after Bond and I had sex, I went to Red's party as you know. I told Bond that I was interested in someone else."

"Meaning Red?"

"Well, yeah, but I didn't really know how I felt about Red at that time and I was just so pissed off with Bond. I wanted to goad him. However, now Bond's back in pursuit mode and I'm completely confused."

"I thought you mentioned that he wanted to try again a few weeks ago."

"Well, what I meant to say is in *hardcore* pursuit mode."

"Gotcha. So, where are you with Red?"

"Falling for him."

"And Red?"

"If I'm to believe him, and I do, he has wanted me for a long time. Years."

"I'm sure that's probably true."

"What?" I practically shouted.

"Well, come on Jacqueline, he's worked so hard to keep you at a distance."

"Am I the only one who had no idea?"

"Probably."

"Damn," I said. Tears threatened to spill again as I stood up. "Should I make us some breakfast while we keep talking? I need the distraction."

"Sure. I have some fresh cut fruit that would go well with French toast."

Opening Lainie's refrigerator, I found the eggs and cream. "Do you happen to have an orange?" I said as I rummaged in her fruit drawer. "Found it."

"So what are you going to do?" Lainie said, leaning on the counter near the stove.

"I don't know what to do. I want Red. I mean, I *really* want Red," I said as I grated some orange peel into the eggs. "I haven't felt so turned on and attracted to someone since I first met Bond, before he broke my heart the first time."

"I guess you're not planning to tell Bond about Red today."

"Most definitely not." After sprinkling cinnamon in the eggs, I dunked the first piece of bread in the batter. "I don't even know how we go about that. I told Red that Bond and I kissed at his parent's party."

"You kissed Bond?" Lainie said, shaking her head.

As I pan fried the French toast, I said, "I had just found out about his past and he kissed me. I love him, Lainie. I'm not sure if you get that part but it's always there. Even when I want to punch him in the nuts for taking me for granted, there's another side to us. The friendship, the caring. He's family, just like you are. And now I know his secret and why he's so damn fucked up. It just makes it all much more confusing."

"Having the knowledge will not change his behavior," she said, taking the plate I held out to her.

"No, but now I understand it. At least I don't have to take it so personally."

"That doesn't mean you won't," she said and then took a bite. "Wow, this is delicious. I've never had French toast with orange peel."

"I saw it demonstrated on one of my cooking shows and thought I'd give it a try."

"At least one of us likes to cook. So what's next for you?"

We settled at the circular four-top table in the corner.

"I have no idea." I took a bite and continued, "Red wants me to come by after we're done here. I had hoped to tell Bond about us so I didn't have to carry around all this guilt. Why couldn't I be more attracted to Stay? That would be much simpler."

"Stay's a great guy. I'm sure he'd be interested in you."

"Really, Lane?" I said, pointing my fork. "I think he has more of a thing for you."

"Me? I don't think so. I just don't see him that way."

"Let's not add more men to my docket, okay? I already have one too many."

"Fair enough. I'm not sure I have any words of wisdom for you. It's a tangled mess really and I'm really interested to see how it all unwinds. I'm worried for you though."

"Yeah, I'm worried for me too. Thanks for listening." I took a sip of water and asked, "So what's new with you?"

"I have another date coming up."

"Not on Wednesday, I hope."

"No, I plan to go to Red's on Wednesday. You might need a referee."

"Very funny. So who's this new guy?"

She swallowed her last bite and said, "Not worth mentioning at this point."

"Please let me know when he is."

We cleaned up the kitchen, side by side and I felt calmed by Lainie's presence. I knew her judgment stemmed out of concern. She wanted my happiness as much as I did.

"I love you," I said as we hugged goodbye.

"I love you too and keep your shorts on today," she said, laughing.

"Okay, Mom."

Before I started the car, I texted Red.

> **Me:** Still okay to stop by? Any other casualties from the party?
> **Red:** No. House is all clean. Bond?
> **Me:** He still seemed under the scotch this morning, but the coffee helped. Let me stop texting so I can get to you.
> **Red:** Please.

I crossed paths with Red's house cleaners as I entered, holding the door so they could exit.

"So *that's* why your home is so clean," I said walking into the kitchen. I stood there, awkwardly, not knowing what to do.

"Sorry, I was just texting Bond back. He survived his meeting and was planning to crash for a while. That should give us plenty of time."

"Plenty of time for what?"

"For us to spend time together."

"I'm emotional and confused, and I'm not sure I'll be great company."

He sauntered toward me, lifting me up on the counter.

"Let me make you feel better," he said as he appropriated my lips.

Swept up in his kiss, I savored his taste as if it was an elixir that could protect me from the realities that threatened to rain down on us. He settled himself between my legs and I could feel his desire. The kiss deepened and the heat between us became too much so I shoved him away from me.

"Kissing doesn't solve anything. I talked to Lainie, but she didn't have any advice for me."

"Try me. Let's sit outside. It's beautiful out." His warm smile encouraged me.

"You must realize, you're part of the problem," I said, following him to the porch glider loveseat.

"I'd hoped to be part of the solution," he said, sitting down. "I'm not going to deny it's complicated and there's a good chance it will get much worse once Bond knows. What I need to know is what you want."

Slipping off my sandals first, I sat down next to Red and pulled my knees up onto the cushion. He stretched his legs out in front of him and rocked us.

Looking down at my hands, I said, "Like I said, I wish it were simple."

He placed his finger under my chin and lifted up my face. "You need to decide if we're worth it."

My throat tightened, tears filled my eyes, and I could barely speak. I felt like I could lose control at any moment. "I want us. I want you. When Lily told me about Bond, all I wanted was to hide in the safety of your arms and the calm I find there. I wanted to talk to you."

He pulled me onto his lap and held me against him. We rocked back and forth in the silence.

"I love him too," I said.

"I know you do." He paused and stopped the rocking.

"Wait, are you saying—"

"Look, I'm upset and I don't know what I'm saying." I scooted off his lap and pulled in my legs, wrapping my arms around them.

"I've loved you for a long time, Jacqs." He reached out and touched my knee, his energy penetrating in.

"It's too soon, it's too fast."

"To the contrary, it's long in coming."

"No." I stuck my chin out in defiance.

"No?"

"Maybe if you didn't know Bond and weren't the hub of our group. Try as I might, I don't see how this will work."

"And yet, here you sit with me. You aren't at Bond's; you're with me. I'm not asking you to stop loving him, what I'm asking is for you to give us a chance to see what we can be."

I paused, taking in his words and said, "Have you really taken the time to think about what it will do to him? Your friendship? Our other friends? I mean really think about it? Because when I think about it I get so damn scared that I want to crawl in a hole and hide."

"Jacqs, believe me, I've thought about it for a long time and there is no clear answer. We're going to have to ride this out together. Bond will be angry, and our friends will take sides. That's the reality."

"I don't know if I can handle it. It was so much easier before I knew about what happened to him."

"You knowing changes nothing. He won't be any different tomorrow."

"That's what Lainie said."

"I knew I liked that woman for a reason."

"Hey, wait!" I said, pushing on Red's shoulder.

"What?"

"You told me that you've never been in love."

"It wasn't an appropriate time to tell you how I felt."

"And now is?"

"You told me first, Jacqs."

"I did no such thing," I said, jumping up and causing the loveseat to rock.

Red put his foot flat on the ground to stop the movement. "Come here."

"No," I said, turning slightly away and folding my arms.

"Get over here. Don't make me chase you, you little pixie."

I sauntered up to him and stood between his legs. He ran his hands up my calves and over my thighs, playing with the hem of my shorts. Trailing his hands around my legs, he snaked his fingers under the back of my shorts.

"You're wearing underwear today?" he groaned.

"My undergarments seem to be of great concern for you," I said, squirming from his touch.

"Spread your legs." When I hesitated, he said, "Now."

I complied and he immediately tracked his fingers up the inside of my thighs, skimming my covered pussy.

He teased along my panty line and pushed underneath, feeling my wetness. "So silky," he said.

"Ohhh," I said, when he circled my clit.

"Have you submitted to Bond?" he asked, continuing to finger my labia.

"You ... want ... to talk ... about him?" My legs shook as he ran repeatedly over my arousal.

"I'm aware of his tastes." He reached under my shirt and plucked at my nipples as he continued his other manipulations.

"It's ... it's hard to ... miss them. They hang on ... the wall!"

"Jacqs?" he said, dragging out my name with obvious impatience.

"No, I haven't ... oh lord, no ... oh, that feels so,

so good."

"Why?"

I stared at Red and he stopped his touching. "Because I don't trust him."

"You could have said, 'because I didn't want to.'"

Breathing out deeply, I said, "I could have, but that wouldn't have been the truth."

He grunted and resumed his play. "You will for me." He pulled and pinched my right nipple and captured more moisture, coating my pussy. He took his time petting my clit, hitting all the right spots.

Bringing me right up to the edge, I squirmed in my stance, bucking my hips in time with his rotations. "Oh … ohhh … oh hell … I'm so, so close!" He tugged on my nipple, sending me sky high. "Ahhh," I yelled as I exploded, not caring about anything else. Life ceased to exist and just then lust ruled my world.

He held me up as I recovered and said, "I want to see all of you. Please get naked for me."

Dazed and still wholly aroused, I lifted my shirt over my head and stepped out of my shorts, drawing my panties down with them.

"You are beautiful, Jacqs."

My nipples peaked again, drawing my areolas in tight. "Please let me take him out," I said, pointing down into Red's lap.

The obvious bulge strained against his shorts. "Come here," he said.

Stepping forward, I unsnapped the waist and lowered the zipper. The head of his phallus—so thick—stuck out. So wide, I wondered if I would be able to take him into my mouth. I wound my hand inside and touched his silky hardness.

He removed his shirt and let me slide his shorts off.

"Wow," I said, taking in Red as he lounged on the loveseat. "Are your nipples sensitive?"

"Come find out." He held his arm out to me.

I sat on his lap, staring at the seductive smile on his face. I touched his cheek, running my hands to his ears. I fingered the small gauges in his ears like I had dreamed of doing. I felt down his neck and touched the red hair on his chest. "It's softer than I imagined." His tiny nipples stood erect, and I brushed over them, watching his expression change. "Oh, you like that." I smiled.

"Suck it," he said.

Shifting to the right, I lowered my mouth over his nipple.

"Yesss," he groaned.

I had a destination in mind and so I trailed my fingers over the line of hair that ran down the middle of his stomach. "Oh," I mumbled. "I'm not sure I've ever been so turned on." Lifting his manhood, I held it in my right hand.

"Your little hand makes my cock look big."

"Your cock is big!"

"Easy," he said as I moved my hands in tandem, up and down. He stopped me. "Do you come with Bond?"

"Yes, of course."

"I remember, in the beginning, he mentioned that you didn't."

"He told you that!" I was indignant. "Must we talk about Bond?"

"Yes, Jacqs, I need to know a few things."

"Like? Are you trying to kill my arousal? Because it's working."

"I was trying to kill my own."

"We need to get him from between us," I said, adamantly.

"That's just not possible, so let's be honest."

"Fine." I stood up, placed my shorts down beside Red and sat on them. "It was a few months before I came with

Bond and he was the first."

"Your first sex?" he said, his eyebrows rising.

"Well, no—not like there were many—but I meant my first orgasm with another."

"You don't seem to have trouble coming with me."

"Yes, I've noticed that as well. It's different with you."

"How so?" he asked, placing his arm behind my back and using his outstretched leg to rock us again.

I glanced down and said, "Am I supposed to have this conversation with him standing at attention?"

"We'll take care of him in a few. Answer me."

"It's really hard to put in words. Sex with Bond is great—hey, don't bristle, you asked."

"Go on," he ordered.

"But it feels different. I mean ... not that you and I've had sex yet. Bond requires eye contact all the time but it's more a thing of control than connection. Does that make any sense?"

"Sure. Continue."

"Why do I feel like I'm going to get into trouble for this?"

"You might," he said and he looked serious.

"Before you, I thought I would never feel desire for another person again. You know I've tried dating since him, but it never felt more than lukewarm."

"So how does it feel with me?"

I turned to the side to face him and said, "The heat index is definitely off the charts."

A smile transformed his face, and he said, "For me too. If it weren't for Bond, I'd ask you to move in with me now. I can't stand spending time apart from you."

"I'm not sure how to respond to that. That's pretty much over the top."

"How about the truth?"

"I'm scared, overwhelmed, and confused. Feel free to

throw a couple more verbs in there if you'd like."

"And falling …"

"Yes, there is that too."

"Before I let you make me come, which I know you want to do—"

"Badly," I pleaded.

"I want you to do something else for me."

"Why did I just get scared … yet my clit twitched at the same time?"

"I guess you can read my intention."

"Tell me."

"I want to spank you, Jacqs. And, I want you to willingly take it from me."

"Why?"

"Because you love us both and it'll make me feel better."

"You mean because I haven't let him?"

"That might be part of it, but my hand has been itching to spank your bottom for a long time. Alright … over my knees."

"Do I have to call you Daddy too?" I said, laughing.

"Only if you want to."

"Will it hurt? I've never been spanked before."

"I have a feeling you'll enjoy it." He stood up, his cock still fully engaged, and locked the loveseat so it would stay stationary. "However, feel free to stop me any time past five."

"Five spanks?" I said as I rose up.

Red sat down in the center of the couch and said, "Lie over my lap, now."

He sounded serious so I hurriedly climbed onto the love seat and draped myself over his thighs.

"Okay, Jacqs, I'm going to start."

I felt the air move when he lifted his large hand and then felt the smack across both butt cheeks. "Ohhh," I moaned. His cock swelled under my stomach and that turned me on as much as the spank did. The second one landed just slightly harder and I could feel my pussy pulse. The next three came steadily and I enjoyed the experience.

"Will you take more from me?" he asked. "I went light on you."

"You did?"

"Yes."

I lifted my head up and said, "Give me the real thing. I want to see if I can take it."

"Are you sure?" he said, but he didn't wait for me to answer.

I lowered my head, anticipation swirling within me. My nipples pushed against the cushion and I imagined Red taking me, penetrating me with his thick cock.

Instead of spanking me right away, he fingered my clit, slowly at first and then at a steady pace. "Oh my lord," I muttered until I exploded again.

Before I had a chance to recover, *thwack*, sounded and the spank caused my heart to race even more wildly. It didn't hurt exactly, but it did sting a bit. His big right hand continued the spanking and I could feel myself panting and my pussy swelling even more.

"That's ten. How are you feeling?"

I lifted my body, still unsteady and knelt next to Red trying to catch my breath. "Like I want you … to fuck me … hard … up against the wall."

"When is the lease up on your apartment?"

"Very funny," I said, chuckling. I took a couple of deep breaths, finally feeling more grounded.

"I'm serious."

"I own it, it's not a lease. How are we going to explain *that* to everyone? Plus, I'm not sure I want to live with you," I said, slightly shrugging my shoulders.

"And why is that?"

"Besides the obvious?"

"Enlighten me." A grin played at his mouth.

"Well, there's your controlling nature—"

"And…"

Pointing down, I said, "You haven't let me finish playing with him!"

He spread his arms across the top of the couch and motioned with his head.

I took the cue and clutched his heavy dick in my hands. I loved how hard and soft it felt at the same time. Moving up and down his shaft with my right hand, I fondled the bulbous head with my left. "Can I put him in my mouth?"

"Yesss," he hissed.

I hopped off the couch and knelt between his legs. Burying my face against the side of his cock, I breathed in his heady masculine scent. I palmed his firm heavy testicles as I ran my fingers around his cock. He kept the hair trimmed and I appreciated the effort. Lowering my mouth, I kissed his tip, slowly sucking his head past my lips.

He arched his hips up and uttered, "That feels incredible."

Forcing as much as I could take in my mouth, I pumped my hand up his shaft as I raised my mouth and lowered my fist as I plunged my mouth back down. Up and down my mouth and hand went in unison. He let me take my time and enjoy his cock. I knew he would never fit down my throat like Bond did, and I loved that they were so different.

"I'm close," he muttered. "Make sure … you hold … the come in your mouth. Don't … don't swallow."

I had no idea what he wanted me to do with his ejaculation, but the idea of holding it for him turned me on even more. I increased the tension around my lips and circled my tongue around his head as I pumped frantically; using my free hand to caresses his balls.

"Oh Jacqs, motherfucker, I'm coming!" He thrust his cock through my hand into my mouth, exploding his release. He jerked and convulsed until he finally lay back against the couch, breathing heavily. "Kiss me," he said.

Climbing onto his lap, I pressed my lips against his and opened my mouth. We shared his jism as he rolled his tongue against mine. "Hmmmm," I moaned into his mouth. After we broke off the kiss, I said, "Wow! That was hot."

"You have no idea," he said, shaking his head. He draped his arms across my back and pulled me in close. He reached over the side of the couch and unhooked the stopping lever which caused us to start rocking again. "I love you, Little One."

"Mmmhmm," I mumbled.

"Spend the night with me," he said as he ran his hand up and down my back.

"We both have work in the morning and what if Bond drops by?"

"It's highly unlikely."

I tilted my head up and said, "But not impossible."

"No, not impossible but I can check out his plans for the evening."

"What happened between him and Blue?"

"I told you, I'll let them tell you."

"Bond doesn't remember." I continued to rest against Red but lifted my head. "You know, I'm not sure we can work if your loyalty stays with him. It won't work for me."

"This isn't about loyalty, it's about respect and privacy and I only know what I saw. They argued and Blue was fuming. I've never seen her that mad."

"Well then, I already know what happened, at least

part of it. I wonder if Blue will confess."

"Are you upset?" he asked as he stroked my hair.

"You assumed the same thing? Why are we so worried about upsetting Bond when he is so busy fucking everyone, even my friends?"

"Because he's like a brother to me and yeah, he's fucked up and he makes a lot of mistakes but I don't want to hurt him."

Breathing out heavily, I said, "No one seems to have that concern for me."

"Not no one. You *are* angry."

"Damn straight. I can't live my life the way I want and yet everyone else does. They certainly aren't taking *me* into consideration!"

"Come on, Jacqs. Wait to see what Blue has to say. Maybe we're both wrong." He brushed my hair away from my face. "What time do you need to be home in the morning so you have time to get ready for work?"

"Breakfast and shower there?"

"No, here."

"Oh. Why don't I run home and take care of a few things and then meet you back here after dinner?"

"And you'll spend all night in my arms?"

"I'd love to."

CHAPTER NINE

Near to You

by A Fine Frenzy

After I had entered my apartment, I rested my back against the door. I slid into a sitting position on the floor. It all seemed so doable when Red had me wrapped up in his arms or dizzy from his kisses and orgasms. Away from him, the brutal facts resurfaced and my relationship with him seemed impossible. "You think too much," I said to myself. My body chimed in and said, *Way, way too much! He rocks our world.* It didn't matter what my mind or body said, I knew I would go back to his place.

I pushed myself up and headed to the bedroom, opting for a nap. Lack of sleep and all the stress worked their magic, and I slept until my phone went off.

Fuck! I opened my eyes and blinked a few times.

> **Bond:** Come by the club. Stay is here and we can all hang out.
> **Me:** I have plans.
> **Bond:** With? Bring them along.
> **Me:** You guys have fun. I'll catch you later.

I took a quick shower and gathered my work clothes for the next day. I didn't feel like taking the time to cook so I texted Red.

> **Me:** Have you eaten?

Red: Sure haven't.

Me: Should I pick something up on the way?

Red: Sounds great.

Me: I heard from Bond.

Red: So did I.

Me: Oh shit. What did you say? I said I was busy.

Red: I said I needed a break from all the partying.

Me: Oh, that's good. What should I get?

Red: You know what? Just come over and we can order something from here.

Me: Okay. See you soon.

❀ ❀ ❀ ❀ ❀

I pulled into the circle drive at Red's and found him waiting for me on the front step in plaid pajama bottoms and a T-shirt. Sitting down next to him, I said, "I like the outfit. I forgot to grab PJs."

"You can borrow a pair of mine."

I rolled in laughter. "Oh yeah, that'll work."

"I'm frustrated," he said, rubbing the side of his beard.

"About us?" I said, shifting closer.

"Impatient to be *us*. I've been thinking—"

"Uh oh," I said.

"No, really, I'm serious."

"Yeah, I know, that's what scares me. You've already waited so long, so why the impatience now?"

"Because before it was merely what I thought we could be and now I know," he said, placing his hand on my knee.

I glanced at his broad hand and back at him. "Okay, so tell me."

"What if you date both of us?"

Standing and throwing my hands up in the air, I yelled, "You've got to be out of your fucking mind!"

"Why? It makes the most sense. You love us both and—"

153

"Jesus, Red, you aren't thinking clearly. First off, Bond and I aren't dating and secondly I can't even imagine what it would be like to try to juggle the two of you. No! I'm saying no! Are you hearing me? Stop smiling at me!"

"If you'd just listen, you'd see it's the perfect solution."

"You're crazy, the both of you."

"Baby, just hear me out."

I crossed my arms over my chest and contemplated leaving Red sitting on his front step with his cheeky smile.

"Come sit," he said, patting the ground next to him.

I sat, keeping my distance.

"You and I would be the primary relationship and Bond could continue to date other people."

"Oh, you cannot be serious. What about STDs? I thought—"

"We would have to address that with him. He'd have to agree to use condoms with everyone other than you and get tested regularly."

"That's not fail proof," I said, shaking my head.

"I'm aware of that."

"What makes you think he would even go along?" I stood again and started pacing.

"Because he could have his cake and eat it too."

I stopped and pivoted to face Red. "Oh great, so now I'm cake?"

"You know what I mean."

"I don't think you've thought this through. How are you going to feel when I'm out with Bond?"

"I don't know. It might just turn me on. At the very least, I can punish you once you get back."

"I don't even know how to respond to that. How the hell is it going to work when we're all together? I'm not interested in a tug-of-war. Whose lap do I sit on? Who gets my attention at any given moment?"

"All of that would have to be worked out, Jacqs."

"I don't know what I'm worried about," I said, sitting back down. "Bond will never go for it."

"Let's not worry about him for a moment. Are *you* open to it? We could live together. Bond could keep his place and have a room here too."

"This seems way worse than just confessing that we like each other."

"Love each other, Jacqs."

"I still maintain that I haven't said it yet." I shook my head.

"You implied it. The real question is: do you want to live with me?"

"I've never lived with a man before. Have you?"

"No, I don't date men, but I've never lived with a woman either."

"It seems like a complicated mess to tackle all at once. You've had years to think about it but it's still very new to me."

"What is?"

"My feelings for you ... our chemistry and attraction ... the truth about Bond's past ... all of it."

"Let's order some food and you, can think about it," Red said as he stood and held out his hand.

"The only reason I'm coming in is because I'm starving. This in no way means I'm considering your crazy idea."

"Sure. Got it."

He led me to the kitchen and pulled open the drawer by the phone. "Chinese, Italian, Thai, bar food or—"

I placed my belongings on the counter, including my cell phone and said, "I vote for the bar menu. I could use some comfort food right now." He handed me the menu and I perused the sandwiches. "The smoked turkey panini sounds incredible. It has cheddar, bacon, and cranberry jalapeno jam on sourdough."

"Would you be up to sharing that and the parmesan fries?" Red asked.

"Perfect."

"I'll call it in."

I walked out the French door and slipped off my shoes. Sitting on the edge of the pool, I slowly kicked my legs in the water.

"It's going to be about twenty minutes and I ordered key lime pie for dessert."

"Oh, that's my favorite." I smiled up at him.

"Yes, I know."

"Have you been secretly stalking me all these years?" I asked over my shoulder.

He rolled up his PJs and sat beside me. "I've been paying attention."

"Apparently."

"Look Jacqs, I know you think I'm crazy but just think about what I've said. It's the best way for all of us to get what we want." He swung his foot through the water and hooked mine.

His touch jolted my body awake and threatened to weaken my resolve. Jerking my foot away, I said, "Lainie says I make choices that completely complicate my life but this ... this is even beyond crazy for me. Two alpha males and one woman do not work. Surely you can see that."

"I'm not saying it will be easy, but we'll get through it." He rested his palm on my knee.

"Please, don't touch me right now," I said, moving his hand to the side.

"Why? Are you angry?"

"I'm not angry; I just can't concentrate when you

touch me."

He bellowed out a laugh and said, "I love you. Let's table this discussion for later." Not waiting for me to respond, with his legs still in the water, he lay back against the ground and rolled me on top of him. He shifted me up and down and said, "See what you do to me?"

I felt his hard cock and wondered again over the chemistry between us. "Now I get it," I said. I crossed my arms over his chest and rested my chin on top of my hands.

He ran his fingers through my hair and said, "What's that?"

"How you came up with your lame brain idea."

He chuckled slightly, rocking me as his chest moved. "And how is that?"

"You lose your mind like I do when we're together and can't think straight!"

Laughing harder, he said, "I've never been clearer about anything in my life. I want you with me from now on, and I don't see another way that'll work. If I didn't care about Bond and your feelings for him, I never would have suggested it. I'd just kidnap you, make you live with me and forget everyone else."

"That would go over well, I'm sure. We'd have to become recluses and our friends would have to find a new place to hang out."

"You're making my point for—I think I heard the door," he said, shifting me to the side. He grabbed a towel, dried his lower legs and tossed the towel to me.

I entered the kitchen as Red came in carrying two bags. "Can we postpone this discussion?" I asked.

"Sure, would you like to eat at the table or sit on the couch and watch a movie?"

"I vote for a mindless comedy."

"Have you ever seen Grosse Pointe Blank? It's a shoot

'em up romantic comedy."

"Is that the one with Minnie Driver? I've wanted to see that."

"Yeah. Let me get some plates—" he said, stepping to the far cabinet.

"Let's just eat out of the containers. Do you have ketchup? I'll grab the napkins and a fork."

We settled on the brown leather couch, facing the big, flat screen TV. I found it endearing that we could simply share a meal and a movie together. It left me really considering what it might be like to live together. The rest of his crazy scheme, I couldn't even begin to digest.

After we had finished off the key lime pie, he angled himself against the side of the couch and pulled me back to rest on his chest. I sunk in next to him and loved the comfort I found in his arms.

"I've dreamed of moments like this," he said.

"You mean it wasn't always about sex?" I said, laughing.

"Well, most of the time."

"Hey!" In his arms, I spun to face him. Lying on his chest, I could see his devilish smile. His expression shifted and I felt it pull on my heart.

"I won't let you go, Jacqs."

"I don't want you to."

He kissed my forehead and my eyes. Fear, love, and excitement all churned around inside of me. When he finally touched my lips with his, I moaned in contentment. "Hmm."

As he kissed me, I wondered if Bond would even consider Red's idea. I wasn't sure I wanted him to.

Red must have felt my wayward thoughts because he deepened the kiss, clutching my ass, pushing my pelvis up against his hard cock. All thoughts ceased to exist and in that moment, I probably would have considered anything.

After we broke apart, both of us slightly panting, he

rolled us to the side, with my back pulled tightly against his chest, and we finished watching the movie.

"Are you ready for bed?" he asked, turning off the TV.

"Yeah, I told Tom I would come in a bit early to go over the last details of a marketing blitz I prepared for him." I also wanted to get my blood drawn for the STD tests on the way in, but I didn't mention that.

"What time do you need to leave?"

"I should be out of here around seven forty-five or eight."

Red locked the doors and turned off the downstairs lights. Holding hands, we strolled up the stairs together.

"Did you remember a toothbrush?" he asked after we entered his bedroom.

I rummaged through my bag and said, "Got it."

"I have a new one you can use and leave here." He opened the medicine cabinet above the sink and handed me a brand new toothbrush.

"I've only ever had a second one at Bond's."

"Now you have one at my place too," he said, through gritted teeth.

"If I can't even mention him without you getting upset, how will I be able to date him? Have you even considered that I might not want to?"

"Date him?" He squeezed a line of toothpaste onto his toothbrush and handed me the tube.

"Yes."

"I just assumed—"

"A dangerous occupation," I said and started to brush my teeth.

He held his toothbrush out from his mouth and said, "Now that you know about his past, I figured you wouldn't take his philandering ways so personally."

"In theory," I mumbled with a mouth full of toothpaste, "that might be true." I rinsed my mouth and said, "He seems sincere in trying again, but I'm not sure anything has changed. The bullshit gets to me."

He placed his toothbrush down, and said, "Bullshit?"

"Yeah, him making it seem like I'm the one keeping us apart. It drives me crazy. I love the guy but he's delusional." I left the bathroom and sat on the edge of the bed.

"But aren't you the one saying no?"

"It's his behavior that's keeping us apart. I'm starting to wonder if you're equally delusional."

"Excuse me?" he said as he entered the room.

"There you go again, folding those arms across your chest. As long as you mention Bond, all is fine, but if I bring him up, you react. Yet, you think we can all be a happy threesome. I call foul."

"I never said it wouldn't be a process, and I don't expect it to be easy. It's just the best solution for all of us concerned. I'm certain it will suit Bond well."

"And you?" I asked.

Red took a giant step to stand in front of me. He yanked his bottoms down, and his cock stood straight out, hard and erect.

"Oh," I said, running my hand down the length of him. "It pisses you off, but turns you on at the same time?"

"Yesss," he hissed.

"I didn't realize. That's kind of hot."

"Will you do something for me?" He covered my hand with his and stopped my movement along his shaft.

I looked into his eyes and felt his love and desire. "Anything."

"Take off your clothes and sit in the chair by the door. Cover it with this towel."

My heart started to race as I stripped off my clothes. Lining the seat, I sat and watched Red ceremoniously open the trunk.

He strode toward me with a gold rope in his hand. Lifting me and the chair, he moved us away from the wall. "Put your arms around the back, behind you."

My nipples hardened and my body tingled as I did what he asked of me.

"Normally I would take my time, tying a series of knots to secure you but it's late and I have to taste you again. Right now." First he wrapped the rope around my torso, just below my breast, placing another revolution across my chest. He secured my wrist behind the chair leaving me with little recourse to move my upper body. "Not my best work but it will do. How are you feeling?"

"Muddled."

"Muddled?"

"Titillated and scared, but safe too. My breathing feels erratic, and my heart seems to be bouncing in my chest."

"Perfect." Sitting in front of me, he drew my hips to the edge of the chair, and spread my pussy lips with his thumbs. "I love your taste and smell. I get stone hard just thinking about it."

"Ohhh," I said as he brushed over my clit. "Is that what you think ... about in the shower?"

"Yes, but you're usually affixed to the pool table or against the wall of the boat where passersby can see you."

"I don't know what to say."

"Just feel." Standing, he scanned me from head to toe, taking in my breasts that were pushed forward between the rope and my nipples taut in excitement. "You're panting," he said. "And your eyes are wide and dilated."

Stepping close to me, he bent down, moved my long hair off my shoulders, draping the brown waves behind the chair. Cascades of warmth and stimulation migrated across every surface of my skin. I was needy with want and lust.

He stared directly into my eyes and my pussy pulsed

with the intensity. Kissing me ardently, he marked me as his. He caressed with both hands down my neck and kneaded the flesh of my breasts. Finally breaking away from our sultry kiss, he lowered his head to my nipples.

"So hard and ready for me," he said just before he sucked my right nipple into his mouth. He simultaneously plucked at my left, and the dual sensation caused my hips to lift.

Settling between my legs again, he softly touched his way down my sides and stomach. He breathed across my swollen nether lips and lightly bit his way from between my legs, around my mound, avoiding the spot that needed the most attention. "I love your pussy lips," he said, as he tugged them.

"Oh please," I cried.

"Shhhh. I'm going to take my time." He hands trailed back over my stomach and cupped my breasts, squeezing both of my nipples as he finally tongued my sensitive clit. Spreading my legs wide, his fingers plucked at my labia again just before he penetrated me with his finger.

"Ohhh," I moaned as he found my g-spot, rubbing ever so gently as he flicked his tongue over my aching center.

He paused and said, "You're so fucking sexy and I love all your moans and groans."

"I'd push your head back down if I could."

"I think you need more incentive to behave," he said, kneeling up and sucking my bottom lip into his mouth. He stood, striding back to the trunk and immediately returned.

With my eyes opened wide, I said, "What are you going to—ahhh," I yelped, when he placed a clamp on my right nipple. "Oh lord, oh my god, oh lord that's so intense."

"Here goes the other one. Now behave."

My body shuddered from the acute pressure on my nipples, which caused my pussy to throb.

He bent forward and sucked my clit into his mouth as

he reinserted his finger.

I strained against my bindings as the heat in my nipples, combined with his tongue lashing and finger fucking created a new tightness building in my core. I felt my wetness spilling down the sides of my legs. Shaking uncontrollably, the convulsions started at my clit and ripped out through the rest of my body. "Oh please … I don't know … so much … oh fuck. Ahhh!" My hips arched with the force of my climax, every muscle in my body straining. My heart pounded in my chest, my breathing erratic as my orgasm slowly subsided.

"That was so hot. I'll give you a minute to recover and we'll do it again."

"No … no … no," I mumbled, shaking my head, my eyes still closed. "I don't think I can."

"Of course you can. Did you feel your gush?"

"I gushed?"

"A first?"

I glanced down and nodded.

"You have no idea how happy that makes me. Now close your eyes and come for me again. This time I want to watch your face." He ran his fingers over my fleshy mound, making large circles with one hand as he pulled on the right nipple clamp.

"Ah … Uh … oh please."

"I don't think it will take you much longer to—"

"Oh please, don't stop, don't stop! Here we go!" My hips gyrated in synch with his manipulations and my pelvis shuddered against his hand. The deep contractions rocked through me until I finally collapsed against the chair. "Holy hell," I groaned.

"You are loud, Little One."

"Is … that … bad?" I asked, struggling to open my eyes.

"Incredibly hot."

"Oh … good then." I closed my eyes and continued to float in the high of my release.

He unknotted the rope and massaged my arms as he brought them back around. After removing the clamps, he held my nipples tight, letting the blood return slowly. He scooped me up into his arms and used the towel to dry me off.

"I haven't taken care of you," I whispered.

"Tomorrow is another day," he said as he lowered me down on the bed.

I yawned and said, "If you're sure."

"I'm sure," he said, getting in on the other side.

"I don't have my phone up here. Can you set an alarm?"

"No need. I wake up at the same time every day." He snuggled in next to me, spooning me close.

I fell into oblivion until I felt a shake on my shoulder. "Huh?" I struggled to open my eyes. "Is it morning yet?"

"No, love. I heard your phone."

"Was it a melody or a chime?"

"A chime I think."

I rolled onto my side and sidled my butt against his leg. "I'll worry about it in the morning."

He spooned me to him, and I fell back into a deep sleep.

Nibbles along my ass and back woke me in the morning. An arm over my torso played with my nipples and a rock hard cock jutting against the back of my thigh. "Good morning," I mumbled.

"That's the best sleep I've had in a long time," Red said against my neck which caused me to shiver against him. "I've dreamt of your mouth all night long."

I turned around in his arms and immediately began sucking on his tiny nipple and reaching for his hard-on.

He groaned and pushed my head down. Knowing what he wanted, I scooted lower, taking the flared head of his phallus past my lips. I gripped him at the base of his cock and cupped his testicles in my other hand. Red rocked his hips back and forth as he held and guided my mouth over his silky erection.

"Jesus, woman, I love that mouth of yours."

"Mmmhmm," I mumbled against him.

I fondled his balls as he found a rhythm that pressed him just to the back of my throat. I followed the propulsion with my grip, up and back. I reveled in his tender control and the safety I found there.

In and out he pressed as I concentrated on sucking his cock, jerking his shaft and massaging his balls. As the speed accelerated and the movement became frantic, he groaned, "Damn, I'm close." He slowed his pace, and I could feel the head swell. "Oh fuuuck," he grunted and then filled my mouth with his warm come.

As soon as the last squirt fired, he rolled over onto his back and sighed heavily. He opened one eye and peered over at me, "How'd I taste?"

Moving up close to him, I lay my head on his chest. I chuckled slightly and said, "Like cucumber."

"Cucumber?" he said, raising his head as if offended.

"Relax," I said, laughing and patting his shoulder. "You've sampled it yourself. What would you say it tastes like?"

"Definitely not cucumber."

"Men and their egos," I said, shaking my head. "Cucumber is a compliment you silly man. Some men taste dreadful, I mean really bad. Thick and pungent." I glanced around looking for a clock. "What time is it?"

"Just after seven."

"We need to get moving. Time is a wasting!"

"You should probably check your phone. I'll run the shower."

"Oh, did my phone go off during the night? I thought

that was a dream," I said, jumping out of the bed and circling around it. I hopped down the stairs and retrieved my phone from the kitchen counter. Scrolling through, I saw text from Bond and Stay.

> **Stay:** Heads up, Bond's insisting on going by your place. You know how he gets once he gets a bug up his ass.
> **Stay:** Are you up? Text me so I know you got this.
> **Stay:** I couldn't talk him out of it. We will be there in 10 mins.
> **Stay:** Bond is losing his mind that you're not here. Text me!
> **Bond:** Where the fuck are you? Are you in there? Wake the fuck up!
> **Bond:** We're pounding on your door, Jacqs. Are you at Lainie's?
> **Bond:** I want to see you today, after work. We need to talk.

I ran back up the stairs and into the bathroom. "They came by my apartment last night."

"Who? Stay and Bond?"

He stood naked in front of me and I got distracted momentarily. His cock hung heavy, still full with blood and his muscular legs and toned physique thrilled me.

"Don't look at me like that, Jacqs, or we'll never get to work."

"I'm … yes, I know. Here, read the text. That man always wants to talk."

"I suggest that you call him on your way to work. He'll probably still be asleep. We're lucky they didn't decide to stop by here last night."

"We don't have much time left to deal with this."

"No, we don't." He hugged me, and I had to stand on tiptoe to receive it. "Let's shower and eat something. I want you in my bed tonight."

"Let's talk about that later."

"Either your bed or mine, Jacqs; and I mean it."

We showered and I found it difficult not to respond as he washed his cock and balls. "I want to do that next time," I said.

"Our next shower will be very different. You can count on it. What would you like for breakfast?"

"No meetings today at work?"

He wore a casual pair of beige chinos and a khaki, short-sleeved, button down shirt.

"I'd make us an omelet, but we don't have much time. Cereal and a banana?" I asked.

"No, no meetings. I don't have any cereal, but I can pick some up for the future or better yet, we can go shopping together. Yogurt and toast?"

"Sure. Coffee?"

"We'll have to grab that at the store as well."

We ate in silence and then straightened up the kitchen.

"Please call me after you talk to Bond," Red said as he escorted me to my car.

"Yes, of course." I rose up on my toes and kissed him goodbye.

"I love you," he said.

"I know you do. Thank you so much for last night."

"Come back tonight." He kissed my forehead before shutting my car door.

CHAPTER TEN

Another Again

by John Legend

I dialed Bond and placed my cell on speaker as I pulled out of Red's driveway. Waiting for his voicemail to answer, the breath caught in my throat when Bond actually picked up. "Oh … I thought you'd be asleep."

"Where were you?" he said, his voice husky from sleep.

"I'm on my way to work and we can talk about this later. I just wanted you to know that I'm fine."

"Did you spend the night at Lainie's?" he asked, but his voice told me he doubted it.

"No. Look Bond, I told you last night that I had plans."

"Who is he?"

"I already told you, I'm not ready to talk about him. Hang on a second." I turned onto the highway and merged in the traffic.

"I want to see you today. When do you get off work?"

"Why Bond?"

"You know why."

"Because I'm seeing someone else?"

"Have you fucked him?"

"Bond, really? My sex life is no business of yours, just like you keep telling me that yours is no business of mine."

"That's not the same thing."

I laughed but not because it was funny. "It's exactly the same thing."

"I'm serious, Jacqs. We need to talk."

"That's become your mantra these days and yet nothing gets resolved when we do."

"What time can you pick me up?"

I breathed out heavily and said, "Five thirty, and you can take me to dinner."

"We should talk at my place."

"Definitely not. Neutral territory."

"It's good to know you still don't trust yourself with me." I could hear the gloat in his words.

"Don't let it go to your heads." I hung up not giving him a chance to respond.

After swinging by the lab for the blood test, I headed into work. One of the part-timers was already in the office.

"Hey Star, did either you or Cara decide to go full-time?"

"I don't get along with Henry any better than you do and Cara is focusing on finishing her degree."

"I completely understand. Has he come in yet?"

"No, it's just me and Tom so far."

"Okay, thanks."

I retrieved my phone from my bag and texted Stay.

> **Me:** Sorry I didn't text back last night. I didn't have my phone with me.
> **Stay:** Bond was losing his mind.
> **Me:** Shit. I probably should have dropped by for a drink. I just figured he would never let me leave.
> **Stay:** He thinks he's lost you. He said that you've never stayed over at another guy's place.
> **Me:** That's true.
> **Stay:** If it's Red, you're treading on dangerous ground.
> **Me:** Why would you say that?

Stay: I'm observant.

Me: I've got to go.

Stay: I'm here if you need to talk and please be careful. I don't want to see you get hurt.

Fuck! I wasn't looking forward to the anticipated confrontation with Bond at dinner. I thought of calling Lainie, but figured that she would just say I was crazy for considering any of it. I called Red instead.

"Did you reach him?" he said.

"Hello to you too."

"Sorry. Hello, love."

"Hi. Yes, we talked, and he wants to see me after work. He's angry that I slept out at some man's house. We're going to go out to dinner."

"Come over after."

"Let's play it by ear. I'll need to shower off the—"

"Let me shower you."

Henry tromped into the office and stopped in front of me with a scowl. "Do you plan to be on the phone all day?"

"One second," I said to Red. To Henry I asked, "Have you hired my replacement to train?"

"No, that's now left up to you."

"I'll get on it as soon as I'm done with the call."

The short and stocky man pivoted on his foot and slammed his office door behind him.

"Sorry, my lovely boss was being his usual kind self," I said into the phone.

"Just two more weeks."

"Listen, I have to go. I'll call you after my dinner with Bond."

"I loved having you in my bed last night and this morning. See you later, Little One."

I hung up the phone with a smile on my face.

The day sped by at the usual hectic pace of Mondays. I reviewed the most current applications and opted to call a staffing company with the hopes of getting someone in as soon as possible. I skipped lunch altogether and finished a small project for Steve before the day was through.

While driving over to Bond's apartment, my thoughts bounced all around. I had no intention of sharing Red's identity, but I was scared what might slip out. I planned to keep my distance and not give into his crazy whims and sexual magnetism.

He met me downstairs, and I swear I couldn't help responding to the man sauntering towards me. He wore his hair down, because he knew that was a weakness of mine. His dark blue jeans hugged his hips and his tight, tan T-shirt highlighted his fit and lean physique. Over his shoulder rested a brown leather jacket, just like the one Daniel Craig wore in *Skyfall*. He seemed calm and confident strolling towards me. He managed to look sophisticated and dangerous at the same time.

"Can't imagine you'll need the jacket tonight," I said as he entered my car.

"The temperature is supposed to drop this evening. Plus it goes with the Crockett & Jones Islay boots." He lifted the leg of his jeans to show me the fancy brown leather boots.

"More 007 attire?"

"James Bond has class, what can I say? Your outfit? Did you come straight from work?"

"Yes, I skipped lunch and I'm famished. Where shall we go?"

"Anywhere you'd like." He buckled his seatbelt.

"I've wanted to try Lola's on Harrison Street."

"We won't have much privacy there."

"Perfect." I pulled out into the road and followed it over the railroad tracks. I found parking along Hollywood Boulevard and Bond paid the parking meter.

He captured my hand in his as we moseyed to the restaurant.

When his intoxicating energy pulled at my sex, I tried to yank my hand away. "I don't think—"

"I can't hold your hand anymore?" He stopped walking and faced me.

"Look … I … I just think we should talk first." I continued to move forward, and he stepped along with me.

"Who *is* this guy?"

"I need some food first. Please get us a table while I go use the bathroom?"

He held the door for me, and I had to skim by him to get into the restaurant. My body began to vibrate against my will.

I escaped to the bathroom, which was thankfully empty and bent over the sink for a second to collect myself. "No touching," I said to my reflection in the mirror. "And no drinking." I used the toilet and checked my hair in the mirror on my way out.

The small restaurant had one large room filled with tables of different sizes and a long bar on the left side. The white tabletops had lit candles, and the white walls and ceiling had accents of yellow. Bond sat at the farthest table against the back. I straightened my shoulders and made a beeline to take my seat. Bread and water had been served.

"I ordered us some wine and the portobello mushroom tacos for an appetizer, which the waiter recommended."

"No wine for me thanks, but the tacos sound great. Besides, since when will you get in the car with me if I've had anything to drink?"

"It's only a few blocks from my place. I figured we

could walk back."

"No thanks but help yourself."

"You seem different, Jacqs. I'm not sure this new guy is having a good influence on you."

I laughed out loud and said, "You mean because I won't just go along anymore?"

"Yes." He reached out to touch my hand and I placed it in my lap, avoiding his grasp.

"As my friend, you should see it as an improvement. I certainly do. And the change came from you, not him."

"What do you mean?" The smile vanished from his face.

"Calling me to your place and asking me to spend the night when you have a date the next day? Really?"

"Jacqs, it was stupid of me and I regret my decision. In the past you never seemed to mind my comings and goings."

"I've always minded, Bond. Every single time. Now I'm just saying it."

"Well, I knew it probably bothered you, but I just thought—"

"What? What did you think? Because I'm dying to know."

He took a sip of water and then responded, "That you could separate the deep love that I feel for you, from the rest of it."

"You would be wrong. I do have a question for you though; one I can't even believe I'm going to ask." I felt the push and pull of my body and mind debating, but shook them both off.

"Ask," he said as he held out the basket of bread toward me.

I took a slice and said, "I don't know how to put it exactly because I'm not sure I even want it, but I guess I'm curious about your response."

"You're talking in circles."

"Okay. How would you feel about us spending time together, on occasion, you could continue to do your thing, and I would continue to do mine?" I blurted out then added, "Could you pass the butter?"

He handed it over to me and asked, "How's that any different than that we're doing right now?"

"I would be seeing someone else." My heart pounded in my chest as I buttered my bread.

"You can't be serious."

I looked up and said, "I'm not sure what I am, but I definitely plan to continue seeing the man I'm involved with."

"How involved?"

"I'm falling for him and according to him, he loves me." I took a bite of the bread and regretted it. My saliva had dried up, so I washed it down with water.

"You just met this guy. I'm the one who's loved you for eight years."

"Me and the rest of the female population in Hollywood, Florida."

"That's just sex."

"And here we go again. I don't want to have this same argument over and over—" I stopped speaking when the server returned with the appetizer and wine.

The man in black tuxedo pants and a crisp, white shirt with a button-down collar opened the wine bottle with flair and offered a taste to Bond.

I covered my glass with my hand and watched the ritual.

After the waiter had moved away, I placed one of the tacos on my plate and took a bite.

Bond took a long sip of wine and said, "There's no way I'd go for that. Not for a second."

I swallowed and said, "Then why the hell should I?"

"Because I don't love any of them."

"Honestly, I'm relieved. I never thought you would go

for it, so that makes it all much simpler."

"Meaning?" he said, leaning forward toward me.

"Our dance is over now. Besides, you'd have to be willing to use condoms with the bevy of broads in your revolving door."

"Over? I don't think so. You still love me, Jacqs."

"And I probably always will, but now as a friend." I nodded my head and said, "We are no longer lovers, Bond."

"I don't believe you."

"I'm serious," I said, wiping my mouth with the napkin. "Don't you want me to be happy?"

"Of course I do. I want you to be happy with me."

"That's not possible. I've tried, we've tried, over and over again. No, we don't work."

"Let me get this straight, your *boyfriend* is okay with you dating someone else at the same time? He sounds fucked up."

"Jesus, dude, look at yourself," I said, pointing at him. "It's the very same thing you want."

"Is he free to date other people?"

I licked my lips and said, "No, I don't think so."

"Oh, so now it's making perfect sense. You chose some whipped pussy."

"I'll tell him you said that," I said, chuckling inwardly.

"Let me tell him myself. I want to meet him."

I finished the taco and stared at Bond. "Let's order. I'm still hungry."

"You didn't answer me."

Scanning the menu, I said, "I think I'll get the herb roasted chicken. You?"

"Flat iron steak."

"You didn't look at the menu. Have you been here before?"

"Yep, a handful of times," he said, shrugging his

shoulders.

"With other women, right?"

"Uh ... yeah."

"See what I mean?"

"I don't. Plus it's different for a man and a woman."

"Oh please, don't give me that bullshit. Let's just agree that we're going to stay friends and move on. We've tried it for eight years and it hasn't worked. I'm done trying."

"Why would this guy let you spend time with me?" He rested back against his chair and crossed his arms.

"Let's just finish our meal, okay?" I raised my hand and the waiter came over. "I'd like the chicken and he'll have the flat iron steak medium rare."

After the man had moved away, Bond said, "If you're still *allowed* to have sex with me, why won't you come back to my place?"

"Like I said, I thought it was a stupid idea and I was just wondering how you'd react to it. I never thought it could work."

"Maybe we should try," he said, trying to persuade me with a seductive smile.

"You're just saying that so I'll agree to go home with you. The answer is no."

"I'll tell you one thing: I always use condoms with other women. Every single time. You're the only one I make love to without them."

"I don't believe you," I said, glaring at him.

"Have I ever lied to you, Jacqs?"

"Well ... no."

"You're not scary enough for me to lie to."

"Huh." I looked away and glanced back. "I don't know what to say."

"Does this guy know you're out with me right now?"

"Yes, of course," I said, pulling off a piece of bread.

"So why are you hiding him from me?"

"Because I wanted to see what we might be to each other."

"You said wanted, not want. So you already know?"

"We're still sorting things out, but it looks promising."

That seemed to shut him up for a while. We finished our meal in relative silence and I felt grateful for the reprieve.

On the way back to the car, he reached for my hand again. "If I have permission to have sex with you, holding your hand shouldn't be a problem."

"Being near you is a problem, Bond," I said, letting him take my hand anyway. I shivered in the cool wind.

The temperature had dropped since we had entered the restaurant.

"At least there's still that." He draped his brown leather jacket over my shoulders.

I felt enveloped in his warmth and energy. "Thanks," I sighed, lost for a moment in the scent of Bond surrounding me. I pulled myself back, shaking off the power of his allure. "Every woman has the same problem of being sucked into your lair."

"I'm not interested in talking about anyone else. I want to meet this guy and soon. I'll decide after that. Come up and let's—"

"I have plans."

"With *him*?

"Yes."

"Fuck. You really know how to cut deep."

"It's not my intention."

I let him kiss me goodbye and part of me wanted to follow him up the stairs. I felt the tug on my heart that had kept me close to Bond, the same tug that left me crying on many nights. I handed him back his jacket and waved.

After dropping him off at his place, I stopped off at

my apartment to gather clothes for the next day. I tried to sort out my emotions on the way over to Red's. Did I actually want to date them both? I couldn't see past all the problems it would stir up and just being with Red alone was highly problematic.

Hearing Lainie in my head, I knew I should walk away from them both, but sometimes you are so far down the trail that making it safely back through the forest seems impossible. I couldn't turn back now.

Barefoot in relaxed jeans and a red T-shirt, Red asked, "How did it go?" After I put my stuff down on the counter, he scooped me up in his arms.

I couldn't help contrast the two men in my life. Red, so tall and broad, could have been a fit linebacker in another life. And Bond, long and lean in his bad boy attire. So different and yet each drew me into their sphere of masculinity.

I sighed into Red's embrace, balancing on my tiptoes. "Bond wants to meet you. I mentioned the idea of me dating you both and initially he was completely against it." I stepped back and said, "He thinks my other guy, meaning you, must be … what did he say? I think whipped and pussy are the words he used." I chuckled into my palm.

"He has a shock coming." Red ran his hand through my hair that draped over my shoulder, twirling the end around his finger.

"No kidding. So when do we tell him? How do we tell him?" I said, trying to ignore the chills running down my neck.

"I'm certain the moment will present itself. Right now, I want to concentrate on you."

"He said something else I wanted to tell you first."

"Okay."

"He said he always uses condoms with his lovers, just

not with me."

"That's interesting. I didn't realize that."

"I got tested today," I blurted out. I hadn't meant to share that information until I received the results.

His broad smile lit up his face. "When do you expect to get the answers back?"

"Maybe by Friday."

"I'm not sure I can wait that long." He looked so serious I started laughing. "What are you laughing at?"

"Sorry," I said, trying to suppress my glee. "I wanted your cock inside me that first night. Of course, I didn't expect us to speak again after that. Besides, I thought we were waiting for the test results *and* delaying until we told Bond. Which to me is a bit silly, the Bond part, I mean because this..."—I drew a line in the air between us—"...will in no way be a walk in the park. If we're waiting for him to come around, we might be waiting—"

He reached over and began unbuttoning my shirt.

"What the hell are you doing?"

"You've convinced me, we needn't wait."

"Hang on a sec," I said, pushing his hands away. "Care to catch me up?"

"Am I going to need to tie you down?" He slid my shirt off my shoulders.

"I need a shower first."

He reached behind me and unhooked my bra, letting it fall down my arms. Looming over me, he sniffed and nibbled my neck. "You taste and smell incredible."

"I'd rather not be tied down for our first time," I said, glancing up at the towering muscular man in front of me.

"Agreed. And I want to take it slow, even if it kills me."

"Very funny big boy. I think you'll survive."

"Let's go upstairs," he said, not waiting for me to respond. He lifted me in his arms and took the stairs two at a time.

"You sure are in a hurry," I said as he placed me down in his room.

"I'm impatient to get started." He pulled his shirt over his head and removed his button-fly jeans.

"Apparently!" I stepped out of my slacks and panties.

He stared at me intently until he gently cradled my face in his big hands. Tilting my head to the side, he started with sultry nips along my neck until his smoldering demand possessed my mouth. The intensity of his kiss threw me off balance, and I reached out for him, gripping his shoulders. He enveloped me in his arms, pulling me tightly against him as he delved into my mouth, caressing my tongue with his. His kiss provoked every nerve ending to spark, leaving me helpless. He disarmed me yet again with his powerful presence, making me pliable and weak in his arms.

I struggled to breathe, to think, to calm my pounding pulse. Red had the ability to render me to my most submissive form, and yet, I trusted, foolishly or not, that he wouldn't take advantage of the opportunity.

"Damn," I breathed out, once we parted. "How do you do that?"

He shook his head. "It's not just me, Jacqs. It's us together." His chest rose and fell rapidly too.

"I…" I paused.

"Tell me."

"I'm scared."

"Why?" He sat on the edge of the bed and held his arms out to me.

I huddled on his lap, glanced away and said, "Because the last time I said it, my heart was chewed up and spit out. I couldn't take it if—"

"Baby, look at me."

I scanned his face, losing myself in his bright green eyes. His expression told me what I needed to know.

"I love you and I have no doubts," he said. "This will work, with or without Bond."

I touched the whiskers on his cheeks, fingering his beard. "I love— What was that?"

"Shit, that was my phone. I need to get it." He sat me to the side of him and picked up his pants. He fumbled in his jeans pocket and grabbed his cell phone. "How was Bond when you left him?"

"How do you mean? We hugged goodbye and—"

"Was he drunk?"

"He had wine at dinner … most of a bottle I guess, but I'm not sure. He didn't seem drunk to me."

"Did he head up to his apartment or go into the club?"

I shook my head and said, "Look, I don't know, I didn't wait to see where he went. What's wrong?"

"He sent an SOS. I have to go." He thumbed a response on his phone keypad.

"Yes, of course."

He stepped into his jeans and retrieved a clean shirt from a drawer in his dresser. "Please wait for me here."

I slipped into my pants, and said, "No, I'll go home and wait there. You can call me when you know anything. You might need to bring him back here and well—"

"Okay." He stepped into a pair of boat shoes and said, "This is not how I wanted this to go."

"Maybe it's a sign," I said, crossing my arms over my naked breast.

"Don't be silly. I'll see you in a little while and we'll continue…" he said. He hunched over and sucked my bottom lip into his mouth. Letting go, he finished his thought, "...right where we left off."

We walked down the stairs together and I retrieved

my bra and shirt and put them back on. I lifted my bag off the counter and swung it over my shoulder.

"Come here, Little One."

I shuffled over to him, keeping my eyes downcast. He lifted my chin and swooped down for a steamy goodbye kiss. I fell against him, my need simmering to the surface again, but it couldn't completely dispel the concern that *I* was the cause of Bond's call.

"It'll be okay, love. I'll call as soon as I can."

As we walked to our separate cars, I whispered, "I love you," knowing he couldn't hear me. Tears filled my eyes as I got into my car. My overwhelming angst told me that this was the calm before the storm and I wasn't sure I had anything solid to hang on to.

I drove home with the radio blaring in an attempt to drown out the thoughts that threatened to tear me down. I shouldn't have mentioned the dual dating scenario so soon after the anniversary of the accident. *What the hell had I been thinking? Why did I feel so comfortable with Red, the man who for years did everything in his power to piss me off? Why did it still hurt that I was not enough for Bond? Could never be enough? Would Red get sick of me too? Would he decide that he too needed other women?*

"Fuck," I yelled as I slammed my fist against the stirring wheel.

Once I arrived home, I paced back and forth across the living room. I needed to talk to someone, and I didn't know if I could withstand Lainie's judgment. I thought about calling my sister, but I still hadn't forgiven her for stealing my car. I couldn't call any of our mutual friends; I didn't want to put them in the middle of anything. They would be there soon enough, unless Red came to his senses in my regard. I still worried Red might change his mind about me because of what loving me could cost him.

My breathing felt erratic and forced. Giving in to the pressure, I dialed Lainie.

"Hey girl," she said when she answered my call.

"Hi Lainie." I perched on a stool, flipping the stack of mail back and forth.

"What happened?" she asked.

"Is it that obvious?"

"Tell me."

"I think I just needed to hear your voice. Trust me when I say, you don't want to hear my latest drama." I got up and started to pace.

"That's probably very true, but I love you anyway. Tell me and I'll try to do my best to be helpful."

"Red came up with this stupidly brilliant idea that I should date both him and Bond and—"

"I'm certain you said fuck no, if I know you, but there is actually a kind of—"

"Who the fuck are you, and where is Lainie?"

"Very funny, Jacqueline. What I mean to say is, very few people in the world have success with just being a couple, so three people in the relationship would make it an even bigger long shot. But since, after all these years, you haven't made even the smallest progress towards getting over Bond, it sort of makes sense to me. Of course, that doesn't factor in the hell that will break loose once Bond knows the other guy is Red."

"You've twisted my brain with all of that. Are you saying you're for it, but you don't think it will ever work?"

She laughed and said, "Yes, something like that. So other than that, what has you so freaked out?"

"Red and I were about to make love and Bond sent an SOS, so Red left to make sure Bond is okay. I'm worried that Bond is freaking out because I mentioned the dual dating scenario."

"You did?" Lainie asked. I could hear her breathe

out heavily.

"Honestly, I'm not sure I'm even considering it, but I figured Bond would never go for it."

"What did he say?"

"That he would never go for it." I circled toward the couch and back to the kitchen. "But then he said he would consider it *after* he met the guy I'm seeing. I figured it was just a ploy to find out who the guy is. He wanted me to go back with him to his apartment tonight. I told him I had other plans."

"So he knew you were headed to see the other guy?"

"Yes."

"And Red is with him now?"

"Yes," I said again. I sat on the edge of the couch, my knees bouncing to expend the pent up energy.

"Well, girl, the drama is running amok with you these days."

"Tell me about it. Why did I have to fall for his best friend?"

"That's a really good question, Jacqueline, only you can answer."

"Ugh! Enough about me ... what's up with you? Any new dates lined up? Please tell me you're still going to Red's on Wednesday."

"Nobody worth mentioning and of course I'll be there. Sounds like you're going to need some moral support."

"You mean immoral support," I said, laughing.

"Yeah, that too." She laughed along with me.

"Thank you, Lainie. Truly. I thought you would tell me what a complete idiot I'm being."

"I'll leave the name-calling for the next time I talk to Bond."

"Lainie—"

"Yeah, yeah, I know, he's had a horrible past and all

of that. I'm not without compassion, but it's been years and it's time he started working on getting over it. I can't excuse him because of his past. He put you through hell and not just once, Jacqs. I'm not sure he's worth this experiment you're considering, but since you seem to think he is, I'll just make sure he treats you right. That goes for Red too. So, how's the sex with Red?"

"What we've done so far has been amazing, but we haven't had intercourse yet." I hopped up and made a circle toward the door.

"That's interesting," Lainie said.

"We were waiting, and then we weren't, but then Bond interrupted and now, I'm—"

"Are you pacing again?"

"Yes, sorry. I'm scared Red is going to tell Bond and it will all be set in motion before I've had a chance to prepare for it."

"Buck up girl and get ready. The storm is a coming. I need to get going and get ready for bed. Stay in touch and I'll see you Wednesday."

"Thanks Lainie, for your love and support."

"Sure thing," she said just before ending the call.

I tried to watch a cooking show and then read a few pages in my latest romance novel, but neither could provide distraction from the turmoil stirring within me. Why wasn't Red at least texting me? I decided to shower, so I stripped off my clothes and tossed them onto the dirty laundry pile. I turned up the volume on my phone and left it by the bathroom sink. Climbing in, I let the shower pelt me with hot water.

The longer Red took to contact me, the more my worst fears reared up, threatening to consume me—for the sake of his friendship with Bond, Red would choose to end our relationship. Not only could I lose Bond, but I could lose

Red too and all of our friends. I consoled myself by remembering that Lainie was my friend and would always stand by me. My sister, if she ever got her shit together, might be there for me too.

Without giving the task much attention, I couldn't recall if I had washed my body. Forcing myself to focus, I finished the shower and wrapped a towel around me. I checked my phone for the umpteenth time and plopped down on my bed.

After I had dried my hair, I climbed into bed and pulled the covers up to my neck. Maybe I could force sleep to come. I checked my phone one last time, plugged in the charger, and eventually dosed off.

Watching from a house across the Intracoastal from Red's, I could see his home, and the one Bond must have purchased, right beside it. They shared the double yard, kids running around and swimming in the pool. They each had a tall beautiful wife with blonde hair. One of the thin, statuesque women handed Red a beer and I could see the way he smiled at her. The same way he had once smiled at me. I saw Bond laughing when a miniature version of him did a cannonball into the deep end of the pool. They'd forgotten all about me and had moved on to create wonderful lives for themselves.

I shuffled away from the view, ambling back to my car as my heart broke into a million pieces. *You should be happy for them*, I chastised myself. *You're the one who set out to ruin everything. You deserve to be alone.*

The sob caught in my throat waking me out of my

dream. I scanned my room, getting my bearings. My breathing felt labored so I took a few deep breaths in an effort to calm myself. Scrambling out of bed, I went into the bathroom. I splashed water on my face and brushed my teeth in a feeble effort to get my shit together.

Back in my room, I sat on the bed and saw that my clock read 11:32 p.m. Red had left his house around eight o'clock, and over three hours had passed. I couldn't wait any longer and sent a text to him.

Me: Is everything okay?

Five minutes turtled by ever so slowly.

Red: I'm here.

I jumped up, wrapped my robe around myself, and snatched my phone away from the charger as I ran to the front door.

Me: Here?
Red: Just parking.

"Oh god," I said out loud. I leaned against the wall beside the door and listened for his approach. With apprehension coursing through my body, I had two thoughts—I wanted him here, more than anything, and yet I was frightened of what he might say.

Hearing his footsteps, I unlocked the door, opening it for him. He passed through the doorway and spun around to face me.

He scanned me from head to toe, taking in my dejected appearance. "It's going to be okay. It might take a while but—"

"You told him?" I stayed put, afraid to approach him.

"I had to. He kept going on and on about who this guy might be and I couldn't keep it from him. Why are you shaking, love?"

I stared up at him, wanting him to touch me, wishing he would reassure me.

"We'll get through this together," he said, taking my hand in his and leading me over to the couch.

I willed my shoulders to relax and sat down next to him. "You haven't changed your mind?"

"About us?" he asked as he scrunched his eyebrows together.

"Yes," I said, glancing up at him.

"Baby, you're stuck with me. I'm sorry I didn't contact you sooner. I couldn't text in the middle of us arguing, and I just wanted to get to you as fast as possible. Come here."

I scooted closer, and he lowered his mouth to mine, sweeping me up in his lust and love. Tears eked out of my eyes as he squeezed me in close. Pressing against him, the fear of losing him dissipated, but I felt emotionally raw and on edge.

He kissed my forehead and eyes, tasting my tears. "What is it, Jacqs?"

"I … just got worried … you might change your mind and—"

"I love you. I told Bond as much."

"I love you, too and I'm just so scared what this might do to all of us."

His beaming smile helped to ease some of my fears.

I had finally said it.

He lifted me up and kissed the tip of my nose. "You've made me so happy and it'll all be worth it in the end." He carried me to the bedroom, slipped off his shoes, and we lay down facing each other.

"Tell me what happened." I reached out and touched his arm.

He lifted my hair away from my face and looped it over my left ear. "Like I suspected, he went next door to the club and started drinking scotch. I found him there, and we went up to his place. He looked crazed, going on and on about losing you, and the creep you must have hooked up with."

"How did you tell him?"

"I said, 'That man is me and you haven't lost her'. He just looked at me as if I had spoken a foreign language. He continued his rant until I stopped him."

"What was he ranting about?"

"That you'd hooked up with some wimpy imbecile that's willing to share you."

"How did you get him to hear you?"

"I said, well actually yelled, 'Bond, shut up for a minute. How drunk are you? I'm trying to tell you something.' He said, 'What the fuck? I'm not drunk; I'm angry.' And then I said, 'Just sit the fuck down for a second.' And he finally did, and I told him, 'We've been like brothers since we were kids, and I'm asking you to hear me out.' He just looked up and didn't say anything. So I said, 'I'm in love with Jacqs, I have been for years but out of respect—' Then he yelled, 'Respect? You love Jacqs? Wait a minute.' He stood and took a swing at me."

"Oh, hell."

"He'd had enough to drink that his aim was off, so I was able to duck under his fist."

"But you were gone for hours."

"We argued for hours. He said he would never forgive me for approaching you in the first place. He asked about our sex life, which I didn't answer. I tried to explain that it's the perfect scenario for all of us, and that he could still see you and date other women. He said he would never be willing to share you."

"That doesn't sound good at all." I felt like the wind had been knocked out of me.

"Look, I've known the guy for a long time. He doesn't make decisions quickly, and he needs time to think it all through."

"Did he mention the accident?"

"No." He threaded his fingers through mine and held my hand. "In a way I think you did him a favor."

"How's that?"

"You gave him something else to focus on. I think the accident is the last thing on his mind right now."

"That's an odd favor, I must say. So you think he'll change his mind? What're we going to do on Wednesday? When do we tell our friends?"

"He said that he wouldn't be coming by on Wednesday and that he never plans to talk to me again."

"Fuck, so now what? Should I call him?" I sat up in the bed and let go of his hand.

"I'm sure you'll be hearing from him."

"You should go then," I said, pushing him out of the bed. "Bond might come by. It's a far walk, but not an impossible one."

"Let's go to my place and—"

"No, Red. As much as I'd like to resume what we started earlier, I think I need to be here for Bond. We will have plenty of time to be together."

"Promise me that tomorrow you'll spend the night."

I touched his cheek and said, "I promise."

After walking him to the door, he swept me up in a steamy kiss, branding me as his. He lifted me up by my lower back, and I wrapped my legs around him. With my back against the door, he nudged his clothed hard cock into my mound and ravished my mouth with his tongue, leaving me breathless.

"If you are trying … to get me to change … my mind. You're doing a great job of it." I lowered my legs to the ground. I wanted to follow him home but knowing Bond, he would be showing up sooner or later. I opened the door and pushed Red through. "I love you and I'll see you tomorrow after work."

"Come straight over. I want that shower!"

"Yes, sir," I said, saluting.

"Do you need another spanking?" he said, prowling back toward me.

"Maybe," I said with a grin, closing the door before he reached me. I laughed out loud.

"I can hear you," I heard him say through the door.

CHAPTER ELEVEN

Turning Tables

by Adele

Red left me with a huge smile on my face. How I got so lucky with him remained a mystery. All my fears regarding him changing his mind were for naught, and I couldn't miss the fact that my relationship with Bond had caused many of my insecurities. At the same time, I worried about Bond and what he must be going through. I started a text to him five different times and erased each one. *What could I say? What should I say?* I finally settled on:

> **Me:** Checking in. I spoke to Red and wanted to make sure you're okay.
> **Bond:** How do you think I am? I know I've put you through a lot over the years, but this is bullshit.
> **Me:** This isn't punishment.
> **Bond:** What would you call it?
> **Me:** I didn't mean for it to happen and neither did he.
> **Bond:** Maybe you didn't but he definitely did. I know that man better than anyone.
> **Me:** He waited a long time according to him.
> **Bond:** He should have waited indefinitely. I'm almost there.
> **Me:** Walking?
> **Bond:** Cab.

Fuck! I ran into my bedroom and threw on a pair of

purple, plaid PJ bottoms and a white T-shirt. After checking myself in the bathroom mirror and fluffing out my hair, I plunked down on the couch to wait and texted Red:

> **Me:** He's almost here.
> **Red:** You said you thought he would come by. Tell him the truth.
> **Me:** Now I wish I hadn't sent you home!
> **Red:** It's better this way, love. I'm here if you need me.
> **Me:** Okay. I think I need a drink.
> **Red:** You'll be fine. He won't try to punch you.
> **Me:** Here's hoping you're right.

I hopped up and tromped to the refrigerator. Scanning the shelves, I found a partially filled bottle of moscato wine. I grabbed a cup and filled it with the clear liquid. Drinking it, I refilled it with water and downed that as well.

I jumped up and down a couple of times and shook out my arms. I felt like I was gearing up for battle. I knew he would show up; I just didn't know what else to expect. In some ways, the tables had been turned, and now I was the one having to deal with the hurt lover. Bond was much more proficient in dealing with that scenario. Me, I had no idea how to navigate through it.

His intense knock startled me even though I knew it was coming. When I opened the door, he blew through it, running his hand through his long hair, still in the clothes from earlier in the night. He sat on the edge of the couch and propped his arms on his knees. I stood facing him with my arms folded across my breasts.

He peered up at me and said, "If you were trying to get my attention, it worked."

"No, Bond. I'm just trying to find some happiness

for myself."

"*He* makes you happy?" he asked, the lines intensified across his forehead and there was a slight quiver at the corners of his mouth.

"Once we stopped fighting, we realized we were attracted to one another. I'm not sure what you want me to say."

"Neither do I."

I moved over to the couch and sat next to him. "Look, we both love you, and it was actually his idea that I date you both. I thought it was ridiculous at first. Being sandwiched between two alpha males sounds like a recipe for disaster, but even Lainie sees the genius in it. She pointed out that I've never been able to let you go and—"

He turned his head to face me, "I agree with Lainie, we're meant to be together."

"That's not what she or I meant, Bond. You and me, we don't work."

"That's horseshit and you know it."

"Do we have incredible sex together? Sure. Are you a good emotional fit for me? Absolutely not."

"And Red is?" he said, his arms gesturing wildly.

"Yes, actually, he is, at least as far as I can tell. I love you, Bond, but you've spent years taking me for granted, and it left me feeling so insecure about myself. With Red, I don't feel that way. Maybe all those years of fighting helps me tell him exactly what's on my mind. With you, I'm always scared you'll reject me again, leaving me in the morning to fuck someone else."

"That's not fair."

"What's not? Which part?"

"I've always been straight with you, Jacqs and for the last time, I didn't sleep with anyone that day." He touched the side of my thigh.

Brushing his hand away, I said, "That time. So what?

I've always wanted more from you; you were never willing to try. Now you want to because I'm involved with someone else. Why be angry at Red? He's not only willing to give me the love I need, but he's also willing to let us still be involved. If anything, you should be thanking him."

"That's a stretch for any sane person, and as far as I'm concerned, Red crossed a line that can't be uncrossed."

"This isn't a normal situation."

"No, it's not. I do plan to take advantage of his supposed generosity, but I don't ever plan to speak to him again." He shifted closer to me.

"Meaning what?" Even with my guard up, his proximity revved my libido.

"This." He pushed me down on the couch and covered me with his body before I had a chance to protest. He stared down at me with his light brown eyes and plundered my mouth with his kiss. His aggression jolted through me, causing the familiar pool of wetness between my thighs.

I tilted my face away and said, "Wait, wait!" I shoved against his chest, but he didn't budge.

"I'm not going anywhere. Either we can be together or we can't."

"I don't know how it's supposed to work and—"

"It works like this…" He stood, lifting us both to our feet. Spinning me around, he tucked my back against his chest, pushing my long hair to the side. He kissed and sucked his way along the nape of my neck causing thunderous vibrations to cascade over my body. My nipples hardened as he slid his hands over my covered breast. As if losing patience, he lifted my shirt over my head and resumed his fondling. He plucked at my nipples, which caused me to groan and collapse against him. Cupping my breast in one hand, he held me securely, while the other slid under the waist of my PJs.

I gasped in anticipation as he delved into my wetness, spreading my labia. Instinctively I opened my legs, offering myself to him. Held in his tight embrace, he filled me with his fingers, and cradled my ass against his erection.

As it happened every time he drew me into his sphere, my body reigned supreme and my mind shut off. Being with Bond was the most exquisite mixture of decadence and degradation. Feeling at once redeemed by his attention as if his very energy could wipe away all the past hurts, and scared he would withdraw again, leaving me bereft.

I somehow managed to yank my mind to the surface and said, "Wait! Wait!" I scrambled away from him.

"What?"

"We haven't established the rules and I just got tested for STDs. You can spend the night, but I don't want to have intercourse."

"Listen, Jacqs—" he said, sauntering up to me with his beguiling smile.

I held up my palm and said, "Those are my conditions. Take them or leave them."

"Okay then, get back here." He grabbed my arm and tugged me toward him. He pulled off my pants and drew me back against him. Wrapping one arm across my stomach and settling his other hand between my legs, he stroked my smooth lips and said, "This is my favorite part."

"Ohhh," I moaned.

"Do you get this wet for him?" he asked, dragging me back to the couch, which caused me to land on his lap. He used his knees to spread my legs wide as he resumed finger fucking my pussy. With his other hand he massaged my clit in time with his penetration. "Jacqs?" he said, imploring me to answer.

"I don't … want … to talk … about him," I muttered.

He stopped moving, and I squealed in protest.

"If you want to come, you'll answer me."

"Fuck! Bond, what is it with you men? Yes, he makes me wet. Does that make you feel better?"

"No, it doesn't. He and I are so different. I don't see how you could—"

"Really? Is this supposed to inspire me to want to spend time with you both? Because it's not working!" I got off of his lap and went to the bathroom. I sat on the toilet, but I couldn't pee. All I could do was wipe away the excess wetness.

Bond leaned against the doorframe and said, "We have to talk about this stuff."

"Not in the middle of sex, we don't. And I'm not willing to do this with you guys until you can talk with each other so we can sort all this out. Since I was dating Red first, you're the one who'll have to wait."

"What the fuck are you talking about? We were dating first."

I shoved Bond out of the way and climbed into the bed, covering myself with the sheet. "Our occasional fucks don't count. It has been over six months since we were *trying* again. Sleep on the couch if you'd like."

"Jacqs, come on," he said, sitting down next to me on the edge of the bed.

"It's too easy for me to give in to you, Bond. I'm not doing it anymore. You have to sort this out with Red. I get that you're angry and I understand why you would be, but had you taken me into consideration, even the least bit, I would never have been open to a relationship with him in the first place. You can decide to stay mad and make all of our friends choose sides or you can let go of your pride and see that we can all get what we want. But let me be crystal clear with you; I'm not willing to be stuck in between the two of you and some feud. You have to decide if you can love me enough to let me love him too."

"No man would put up with this shit." He stood up, undressed, and got into the other side of the bed.

"Maybe not. Trust me, my first response was, 'no fucking way' and I never thought you would consider it."

"I'm not considering it."

"Well then, that makes it very simple. I'll be right back." I got up and retrieved my pajamas that were left by the couch. I slipped them on and climbed back up on the bed facing him.

"How can you possibly think this would be simple?" he asked.

"Like I said at dinner, you and I will remain friends, but no longer lovers."

"No, Jacqs, that just means I need to change your mind and win you back."

"For what purpose?" I asked, crossing my legs and hunching forward.

"Because we love each other, and we're meant to be together."

"If you mean as friends, then I totally agree. If you meant more than that, then no. We've been over this so many times." I felt exasperated. "I'm not built like you. Sex means something to me. You need to find a woman who wants to fuck around all the time, but will stay involved with you. I'm sure she's out there somewhere."

"I love you, Jacqs."

"I know you do, in your own twisted way. I believe you."

"And you love me too," he said, scooting closer to me.

"Yes, I do, but I won't let you hurt me anymore."

"I don't mean to hurt you. Why Red? Why did it have to be him?"

"I really don't know how to answer that. Proximity,

compatibility? I don't know. At first I was just angry with you and he made me feel better but now—"

"Oh, so like a revenge fuck?"

I ignored his comment and said, "But now it feels like something … more … something with potential."

"Why not have a fling with Stay or Kev? I hear he and Cat are into sharing. Even Dawg would be a better choice."

"Are you even listening to yourself? Dawg? Now that's funny. He rivals you with his womanizing." I laughed at the image of me and Doug, aka Dawg, together. I loved the man, and he was way closer to my height than either Bond or Red, but seduction dripped from every pore of the handsome, short, black man. His French-Canadian accent seemed to woo even the most innocent, but I had successfully sidestepped his charm.

"Who is out with me every night, picking up women? Red, or have you conveniently forgotten that part?"

"According to him, he never sleeps with a woman on the first night," I said, sitting up straight.

"Oh, is that the line he used on you?"

"Are you saying it's not true?"

"It's not like we're holding hands while we fuck, but I think he has grossly stretched the truth."

"He also said that he hasn't been with a woman for months."

"I don't know what game he's playing, but we have been out with many different ladies over the last several months."

"Are you saying he's lying to me?" I placed my hands down in front of me and glared at Bond.

"That would be my guess. We don't talk about our conquests, but it sounds like a load of bullshit to me."

"Is this what it's going to be like?"

"What?" he said, shrugging his shoulders.

"You poisoning the well?" I said, pointing at him.

"Why should I make it easy for him?"

"You should make it easy for *me*. If you love me as you say, then let me be happy."

"Be happy with me. I'll try to be what you need." He reached out to me.

"No more other women?" I said, shaking my head.

"Yes, I'll try."

"Try? I'm going to crash. I need to get up early and it's already ungodly late. Sleep where you want but no sex."

I took my phone into the bathroom and got ready for bed. After I had brushed my teeth, I texted Red.

> **Me:** Crashing and I'll call you in the morning. Miss you.
> **Red:** Is everything okay?
> **Me:** Not really, but like you said, it's going to take time.
> **Red:** Can you meet me for lunch?
> **Me:** Can we play it by ear? I'm not sure how tomorrow will go.
> **Red:** Sure. Love you, Little One and thanks for texting.
> **Me:** Night. ♥

Crawling under the covers, I rolled onto my side away from Bond.

"Come on, Jacqs, we can sleep together at least."

He tugged me to him, and we took our usual positions. As he hugged me to his chest, I sighed, loving his natural scent. Part of me still wished Bond could be what I needed and at the same time, even with permission to date Bond, it felt like I was being disloyal to Red. I wanted to heal all of Bond's pain and hurt and show him enough love that his past could live in its rightful place. Cuddling against his neck, I wondered if I could stay open to the possibilities and still protect my heart. With Bond's arms wrapped around me, I drifted off into a deep sleep.

When my phone alarm went off in the morning, I struggled to open my eyes and noticed Bond wasn't next to me. After using the bathroom, I plodded into the kitchen. I poured a cup of coffee and added cream, noticing that Bond sat out on the screened in porch. I rarely went out there.

"Did you sleep?" I asked, sitting in a chair across from him.

"Not much." He took a sip of coffee.

"Are you working tonight?" I brought my legs up on the seat and tested the temperature of the coffee.

"I'm not up for chitchat, Jacqs."

I placed my coffee down on the glass tabletop between us.

We sat in silence until he said, "I want you to stop seeing Red and give us a real shot."

"And how will that work? What's changed?" I brought up my knees and wrapped my arms around them.

"I'm willing to date you exclusively."

"Why now? Because of Red?" I drank some coffee and waited for his response.

"Isn't that what you've wanted from me?" he said as he furrowed his brow.

"That's part of it. A bigger part is that you really want it and I don't believe that you do. I think you're scared of losing me and will say just about anything. I'm not saying you're lying, maybe just desperate. I don't even want you to try to change any more, because I already know how that ends up."

"And how is that?"

"With me hurt and you apologizing."

He stood and walked to the edge of the screen. "This is about Red, not about me. Like I said, I'm willing to try."

"No Bond. This is about me and what I need. Maybe someday you'll be ready to do and not just try. I sure hope so, because I truly want you to be happy."

He turned to face me and said, "Do you plan to tell the group on Wednesday?"

"What do you want me to do?"

"I think you should tell them about you and Red and his horseshit plan. Did he somehow think I would be grateful because he's willing to share? It's an insult to both of us."

"I'm not sure what we'll do on Wednesday, honestly. It's clear to me that you're unwilling to date me while I date Red. I mean, I get it. I do think you're being shortsighted and yet at the same time I think this will be good for us. You can find a woman who wants what you have to offer without me making it difficult and I'll finally get to feel like I'm enough."

"Jacqs, how many times do I have to tell you that it's not you?"

"I get it Bond. It's you. Maybe you're not enough for me."

"And Red is?"

"I guess we're going to find out." I stood and said, "After my shower, I'll drop you off on my way to work. Thanks for making the coffee."

Exhausted from the all the talking and lack of sleep, Bond and I didn't speak on the way to his apartment. When he got out of my car, he said, "This conversation isn't over."

"It never is, is it?" I said through the passenger window before I pulled away.

CHAPTER TWELVE

Magic

by Colbie Caillat

M y boss was ensconced in the office by the time I arrived.

"You look like hell," he said as he strolled by my desk.

"Thanks so much," I replied.

I had showered and threw my hair up in a twist. My eyes were red-rimmed so I hadn't bothered with any makeup that might further irritate them. I thought my beige, low-slung pants and wild multi-colored chiffon blouse looked fetching given that they were my work attire. I was, however, sure I looked as exhausted as I felt.

Instead of packing lunch, I decided I would text Red when I got to the office and see if he was still interested in lunch.

> **Me:** Made it to the office but I skipped breakfast and will be very hungry by lunch time. Hint hint!
> **Red:** What time shall I pick you up?
> **Me:** 12:30? I should probably warn you, my boss said I looked like hell.
> **Red:** Duly noted. Did you get any sleep?
> **Me:** Not much. I should run. I need to check in with the employment agency.
> **Red:** I'll let you go but I'm anxious to hear how it went with Bond.
> **Me:** As you might imagine. Later. ♥

By twelve o'clock I had lined up three interviews for

Thursday. Propped up on coffee and nothing else, I felt tired and jittery at the same time. Wishing I could crawl in bed and take a nap, I decided I needed a distraction to keep me up. I dialed my mother.

"Hi," she said.

"Hi Mom, how are you and Sarah?" I swiveled in my office chair as I held the phone to my ear.

"We are both doing great. How are you?"

"I have some news. I've given notice at my job and I'm starting at Burke and Associates in a couple of weeks."

"I didn't know you were looking."

"It happened suddenly. A friend knew of a job opening and I interviewed for it. The money's better and I get more paid vacation."

"Oh, Jacqueline, that's wonderful. I know you haven't been thrilled with your new boss."

"Thanks, Mom. I'm excited about it. Anything new with you?" I shifted some papers to the side and opened my computer.

"Samantha has been coming by almost daily to spend time with Sarah. And she hasn't once asked for money."

"That's excellent news. Has she mentioned Darren?"

"No. She has never talked to me about the men in her life. She did say that she would need to find a new place to live soon and that she was looking for work."

"That all sounds promising, but I don't think we should get our hopes up."

"I've been thinking about letting her move back here."

I sat up straight and said, "That's a big step. Is she going to meetings?"

"I haven't asked. Would you consider asking Lainie to hire her? She's great with clothes and people. I'm sure she could help with the window displays."

I rolled my eyes and shook my head. I loved my

mother dearly, but she had far more faith than I did of a possible transformation from Samantha. "I don't know, Mom," I said. "What if she steals from her or worse, lets her criminal boyfriend ransack the place?"

"Well, Jacqueline, if she moves here, she'll be away from that man. You could let Lainie decide for herself."

"I'll think about it. I need to go in a few minutes," I said, loading up my work email.

"Please consider calling your sister. She told me what happened between you and she would like to make amends."

"I love you, Mom, and stay in touch."

"I will sweetheart and I'm very happy for you. Take care."

"You too," I said and ended the call.

I poked my head in Henry's office to let him know I would be gone for lunch. He just grunted at me. I popped into the bathroom to check my appearance and groaned. After removing the clip that kept my hair fastened, I smoothed it out around my face. It was a vast improvement.

I took the elevator downstairs and waited outside for Red. I felt antsy about seeing him again. Some of the things Bond said about him still bothered me.

He pulled up in his gargantuan SUV and stepped out of the vehicle. He looked very handsome in his gray slacks and a white collar button-down shirt. "Your boss doesn't know what the hell he's talking about because you look good enough to eat." He swept me up in a big hug and gently kissed me. "You taste good too."

I quickly let go of his embrace and stepped back.

"Whoa, what's going on here, Jacqs?"

"What do you mean?" I looked up at him, my arms hanging down by my sides.

"You seem different. Tell me what's happened," he said, touching my shoulder.

"I ... I don't know what to say." I looked away.

"For us to work, you need to be honest with me."

I glanced back at him and said, "Are you being honest with me? Bond said some things about you that has me thinking."

"Like?"

"Well, he said that business of you not sleeping with women on the first date was a line you were using on me."

"Some of his knowledge comes from when we were younger and we used to share a lot more about our conquests."

"You really didn't answer my question, Red. If you feel like I can't handle it or you can't be honest with—"

"Then let me be clear. I haven't had sex since before you and Bond broke it off the last time. *And* I stopped sleeping with women on the first date years ago. It's not like I discussed that change with Bond and I'm certain he's not letting on to what he really knows. I won't lie to you, I've enjoyed the flirting and meeting new women, but as I've gotten older, sex without connection has completely lost its appeal."

"Oh. I don't know what to say."

"Trust takes time, I understand that. In the future, just check it out with me and I promise to be honest. I'm invested, Jacqs. I have no intention of lying to you or jeopardizing what we've—"

I threw myself into his arms. "I'm sorry, Red. I believe you. I'm just scared that what we have isn't real and—"

He lifted me up onto the front of his car and cupped my face in his hands. "Trust in this."

As he kissed me, I lost my fears and insecurities. I resolved to trust what I felt in his arms and not let Bond or anyone else taint my experience. After we had parted, I said, "I think you must be magic." I beamed at him.

"How's that?"

I breathed out a long sigh and said, "You're willing to

talk out anything with me and really hear me. Once I'm in your arms, all my stress melts away, and it all seems possible again."

"This is happening, Jacqs. You and me. I want to hear the rest of what happened with Bond, but I have no doubts about us. My gut is telling me, he'll come around. I'm sure it'll have to be on his terms, when he's ready."

"Well at least one of us is positive about that." I shimmied forward a bit and slid down to the ground with Red's help. "Let's get some food, I'm starved."

"For such a little person, you do have a large appetite," he said, twitching his eyebrows.

I laughed. "Well, with you I'm insatiable."

He hoisted me into the passenger side and said, "That's why you need to move in with me ASAP." After closing my door, he strode around to the other side of the car and continued, "That way I can feed all your needs."

"As enticing as that sounds, I believe we need to take things slowly."

"I plan to change your mind about that and soon. So where to?"

"Red Thai and Sushi on Hollywood Boulevard? Do you know it?"

"I've never eaten there, but I've passed by it," he said as he drove out of the parking lot. He reached over and took my hand in his.

I stared at his profile, feeling the warmth of his energy mixing with mine. Tears threatened to surface, but I held them back.

When he stopped for the red light, he glanced over and smiled. "Are you okay?"

"Yes," I said quietly. "This might sound silly but I feel like part of a couple. I've only ever felt like this with Lainie. Wait, that didn't come out right."

"I get your meaning. It's a first for me too." He squeezed my hand and pulled through the intersection.

"Seriously? I mean, there have been others for you?"

"And you? Right?"

"Not like this."

"Not even with Bond?"

"No, definitely not. We were a lot of things, but I never felt … I don't know the right words."

"Safe?"

"Yes, that's part of it."

"Connected?"

"I have felt … feel connected with him but not secure." I watched the buildings pass by outside the window. "I've changed and I think you're a big part of it."

He parked in front of the restaurant, unbuckled his seat belt and faced me. "In what way?"

"I'm not afraid to say what I feel with you and it's spilling over into my relationship with Bond. I'm not hiding anymore."

"You never need to hide from me. I want the real you, Jacqs. All of you."

"And yet you're willing to share me with Bond."

"That still needs to be sorted through. For this to work, our loyalties have to be with each other, first."

"I won't share you, Aidan."

"Baby, I don't want you to," he said, touching my cheek. "We don't have much time so let's order lunch and continue talking. I want to hear all about what Bond had to say."

"Okay."

He helped me down out of his car and we walked hand and hand into the restaurant.

The Red Thai happened to be one of my favorite eateries. The yellow walls, warm dark wood flooring, elegant red decorative tapestries, gold laughing Buddha and the beaded drapes exemplified Thailand. The full-bodied aromas of varying Thai cuisine filled the air. The hostess immediately greeted us and escorted us to our table.

"I liked it when you called me Aidan. That was a first," Red said, taking both my hands in his.

"I didn't know your name until I meet Ted."

"Really? Well, that makes sense. Bond's been calling me Red for such a long time." He rubbed his thumb across the outside of my hand.

"Yeah and I didn't know your last name until I arrived at the job interview and saw the marquee. Aidan Burke … I like it."

"I know your last name. It's Worth, right?"

"Yes, how did you—"

The server brought to the table tea, water and soup. "Are you ready to order?" she asked.

"Jacqs?"

"I'll have the Pad Woo Sen, two stars, and thanks."

"Red curry, four stars with shrimp for me, and I'll have a Thai coffee too. Thank you." After the waitress stepped away, he said, "I've made it a point to know everything about you."

"Apparently. You continue to surprise me. I guess I didn't know the real you. Based on the things that Bond has said about you, does he even know the real you?"

"He knows me better than anyone. We've been through a lot together. What else did he have to say?"

"He said he would never consider sharing me and that I should stop seeing you and give him another chance. He also said that you crossed a line with him and that there was no going back. He thought I got involved with you to get his attention."

"Sounds similar to our conversation."

"He wants to keep seeing me but according to him, never

plans to speak to you again." A knot synched in my stomach when I remembered what I had done with Bond. I sipped a couple spoons full of soup in an attempt to calm down.

"Your energy has shifted again. What is it?"

"We fooled around ... well sort of ... but—" I peered up and saw his cheeks and ears redden.

We sat in silence and I could hear my pulse pounding in my head.

"Tell me," he said.

"He kissed me at first and I stopped him. We never discussed the rules of how this all would work and I said as much but then—"

"Then?" He stared at me with his green eyes and I could have sworn they became a shade darker.

"I ... we ... he fondled my breasts—"

"Did you fuck him?" His gruff voice scared me.

"No ... no ... no one orgasmed and I stopped him because he started talking about you and I didn't know what was allowed and he pissed me off and this whole situation is confusing the hell out of me."

Red drummed his fingers against the table as I waited for him to speak.

The server came back to fill our water glasses and clear our bowls. I took a sip of tea, hoping to settle my nerves.

He moved his chair from across the table to cattycorner to mine. Grabbing my hand, he forcefully placed it over the zipper of his pants so I could feel his erection. He whispered in my ear, "I owe you a spanking, Jacqs. Do you understand me?"

I looked into his dilated eyes and said, "Yesss." I felt his accelerated breathing against my neck and ear.

"Did you let him touch your pussy?" he said as he rubbed my hand over his cock.

"Red," I moaned, trying to pull my hand away.

"Answer me," he demanded.

"Yes."

"Did you get wet for him like you do for me?"

"Please!" I pleaded. I scanned the restaurant to see if anyone was watching us. "What the fuck is up with you guys and women getting wet."

"Not women, Jacqs. You. Tell me," he whispered, feeding his free hand up the back of my hair and twisting it slightly.

"Yes, and that's exactly what he asked me about you, if you make me wet like he does. What the hell is it with you alpha men? Anyway, that's when I stopped everything," I said, feeling scared and aroused at the same time.

He crushed his mouth against mine and I groaned out loud. "You're coming over after work and we're going to settle this." He moved his chair back to the other side.

I put my hands on the edge of the table, leaned forward and said, "I … um Red … are you angry?"

"We need to establish some rules here," he said in his normal voice. "Moving forward you need my permission to fuck Bond. Is that clear?"

"Yes, I think you've made that perfectly clear," I said in a curt voice.

"Are you giving attitude? Don't make me come back around the table," he said with a smile.

I laughed at his expression. "Don't expect that to change."

He laughed with me. "I have no delusions on that front."

"Seriously though, it will help if we establish how it's going to work between us all. That is if Bond ever does come around to the idea."

The waitress approached the table with our entrees and Red's coffee.

After eating a couple of bites of my meal, I said,

"Bond thinks we should tell everyone on Wednesday."

"We should wait. You know Bond, he's going to take a couple of days and then it will be like it was his idea all along."

"I'm not so sure about that."

"Trust me on this. I've known this guy a long time. He'll never give you up. In spite of everything that's gone on, he's in love with you. He just doesn't want to take the risk of commitment."

"Because of the accident?" I no longer felt like eating.

"Yes. How would you feel?"

"Yeah, I get it. Did you know her?"

"Yes, I knew her well. I expected them to settle down and start a family."

"I can't imagine Bond with children."

"He's a different man now." Red ate a few more bites before taking my hand again. "I want you to know something. I'm dead in love with you, and I want you to think about that and really take it in."

"Wow, I mean ... I love you too. This is so overwhelming."

"Even with all that's going on right now, you and me, we're a great fit."

"Undoubtedly, so why are we trying to include Bond in this?"

"Because you love Bond and I love Bond and I know how he feels about you."

"I can't eat another bite. Do you want the rest of my meal?"

"No. Let's get the check."

Red drove me back to work, my hand in his the whole way. We didn't speak much. My mind whirled around with all that he had said. He loved me and in a way I had never been loved before, a way that left me feeling whole instead of bereft. I felt surrounded by his love and hoped that we would all make it through the next few days.

He helped me out of the car and said, "Pack a few changes of clothes and whatever else you'll need. I want you to be comfortable in my home."

"Okay, sounds great. Thanks for lunch."

"My pleasure."

As he kissed me goodbye, I knew I would miss him until I was in his arms again. "I love you," I said.

I felt in a daze for the rest of the day and left work an hour early. I shopped on the way home and then took a much needed nap.

I let Red know I was heading his way and he met me out front. "I bought groceries and thought I would make us dinner," I said as I got out of the car.

"We need to settle a few things first," he said, lifting my suitcase out of the trunk.

I grabbed the two bags of food and we walked into the house together.

"Stick whatever you'd like into the fridge and the pantry." He left my suitcase by the stairs.

As I attempted to put away the food in the refrigerator, Red approached me from behind, cupping my breasts in his hands.

"I've thought about you all day," he whispered into my ear.

I squirmed. "Hey, I'm trying to put the food away," I said, a grin twitching at my mouth.

He ran his hands under my blouse and tweaked my nipples through my bra. "I like it better when you're braless."

"I'll keep that in mind for when I'm not wearing a sheer blouse," I said, almost dropping the milk.

He unhooked my bra and trailed his warm hands up my stomach to my nipples. "Are you going to take all day putting the food away?" He tugged. "I have plans for us."

"Stop distracting me!" I tried to push his hands away.

"You've distracted me all day. I've thought about making that little pert ass of yours all red." He reached over me and pulled the last item out of the bag. "You eat sprouts?"

I turned in his arms and said, "I'm addicted to clover sprouts on my sandwiches. You should try it."

"I think I'll pass. Come with me."

"I haven't put the other food away."

"Leave it, Jacqs," he said, taking my hand. He lifted my suitcase in his free hand and led me up the stairs.

My pulse had already started to race. Would we finally make love? I desperately wanted to feel him inside me, filling me with his girth and his passion.

Once we stepped through the threshold and into his bedroom, he began unbuttoning my shirt. "I love knowing your body is mine." He opened my blouse to the sides and bent down, sucking my nipple into his mouth.

"Oh, yesss," I hissed.

As he swirled his tongue around my hard bud, he unbuttoned my pants. We parted so I could step out of them. He kicked off his shoes and shed the rest of his clothes. Standing in front of me with his cock jutting out, he said, "I missed you today."

I reached out and circled my hand around his erection. I loved his flared head and veiny shaft. "He sure has."

"The correct response, Little One, is that you missed me too."

I tilted my head, gazing into his eyes and said, "Not a second has passed today that you weren't on my mind. Let me show you." I went up on tiptoe and threw my arms around his neck.

He embraced me around my lower back, pulling me in tight. As our mouths met, he tangoed his tongue against mine and I swayed into his dance. Our oral incursion caused me to moan.

He kissed me with an impassioned reverence that not only amped my arousal but allowed me to meet him equally with an open heart. Dizzy from his kisses, I clung to him, feeling at once wilted in his arms and energized. As the intensity climbed, he grasped my ass and pulled my mound against his thick cock. "I don't think I can wait much longer."

"I don't want you to, Aidan."

"We need to take care of a little matter first."

"Oh, I…" I mumbled.

He sat down on the edge of the bed and motioned for me to lie across his lap. I draped myself over his thighs, my body shaking in anticipation.

"This is to remind you that you now belong to me, Jacqs. Do you understand?"

"Yes."

"Good," he said, rubbing his large palm over my ass. I felt the air move as he raised his arm. The first spank landed across both cheeks of my butt, spreading heat over the surface.

"Oh, that hurts so good," I groaned.

His hand landed on each buttock in a repetitive rhythm that left me wet and panting. With each spank my desire climbed, spiking my need for fulfillment.

"Nice and red, Little One. Now come to me."

I crawled over and sat on his lap, wiggling my hips against his steely erection. My slick wetness had me sliding over his length without penetration.

He growled deep in his throat as he clutched my hair in his hands, bending my head back. He kissed and nibbled his way down my neck, taking his time to savor me.

"Please, now," I moaned. I lifted my bottom, and he positioned himself underneath me.

We stared into each other's eyes as I slowly impaled my pussy down on his cock.

"Oh lord, oh yes," spilled out.

Holding my hips, he helped guide me.

Hitching up and down, to fully coat him in my juices, I finally became filled with his manhood.

"Don't move," he grunted. "Give me a minute." Our eyes still locked, I felt his need and I obeyed. "Okay, now," he breathed out.

I rolled my pelvis against his, shifting up and down. His exquisite thickness filled me completely, and I lost myself in the feel of him inside me. "So good," I moaned.

"I want you to come first," he said, shifting us to the middle of the bed. He lay back as I still straddled his waist. As we resumed the friction between us, he reached over to my pussy and fingered my bulging clit.

I continued to ride his cock as he used his free hand to tug on my nipple. Angling my hips so that the ridge of his head rubbed right against my g-spot, he simultaneous thrust to meet me. The tangled sensation of his incredible invasion along with his clitoral massage and the pull on my nipple had me riding the edge of a most fantastic release. Increasing the pace, I clutched onto his chest, crushing his nipples underneath my little hands.

"I'm close, so so close, oh Aidan, please. Don't stop!"

We slammed our bodies together in unison, causing the titillating current to crest ever higher. Our orchestrated rhythm thrilled every cell of my body, and Red's exalted expression told me I was not alone. Hovering in all the sensations, my body expanded and my heart opened as my orgasm billowed through me. I held Red's gaze until my eyes rolled back into my head and I collapsed over him.

"Holy shit," I whispered. My body vibrated from the climax, my pussy twitching against his firm cock.

He chuckled beneath me, wrapped his arms around my back and held me as I slowly recovered. "Take your time," he said, as he stroked my hair.

I sighed heavily in bliss, knowing that Red wouldn't be slipping out to fuck another. Laying my head against his chest, I could hear his rapid heartbeat. Wanting more, I said, "I'm ready," and swirled my sopping pussy around his erection to let him know I meant it.

Taking me completely by surprise, he flipped me over on my back and jutted his cock into me with force. "Wrap your legs around my waist," he ordered.

Clasping his sides with my thighs and grasping his arms with my hands, I stared up at the sexy man looming over me.

"Far better than I imagined," he said. He bent over and pressed his lips against mine, sucking my bottom lip into his mouth.

I had to hold up my head to return his sweltering kiss. Dropping my head back down, I ran my hands over the red hair on his chest and plucked at his nipples.

"You keep doing that … I'll explode inside you," he groaned, still hitching his cock in and out of me.

"Fill me, you … Neanderthal. You know … you've wanted … oh lord." His cock thickened inside of me, and I knew he was close. I squeezed his nipples and watched the ecstasy in his expression.

"Damn, Jacqs, I'm going to come. Hold on," he growled as he increased the intensity of his thrusting.

"Oh … yes … fill me," I groaned, meeting his penetration with equal fervor.

"Jacqs," he yelled as he jerked rapidly and then slowly moved in and out as his orgasm continued to fire. He lowered down beside me, settling on his back, eyes closed, breathing heavily. "Holy hell, what am I going to do with you?"

"That, I hope ... over and over again." I rubbed my hand over his chest.

"No doubt about that." He stopped my hand from moving and looked over at me. "Thank you."

"What for?"

"For loving me back."

"You didn't give me much chance to refuse," I said, touching his cheek. I scooted closer and lay my chin on his chest.

"The Neanderthal comment was a nice touch." He smiled up at me.

"You liked that?" I asked, thumbing his full lower lip.

"It made me want to fuck you from behind, your long hair wrapped around my fist."

I laughed out loud and said, "Next time, big boy. Shower and then I'll make us some dinner?"

"Let's."

I gathered my soap and hair products from my suitcase, and once we entered in the shower, Red took control.

"I want to wash you," he said, soaping up a washcloth.

"I haven't been bathed since I was a little girl."

"You still are, Jacqs," he said, laughing.

I punched his shoulder and said, "Just in contrast to your gargantuan size."

"There's some truth to that." He washed under my right arm that I held up for him. "You're a perfect fit for me."

"I have to agree with that," I said, raising my eyebrows and glancing down at his cock. "Do I get to wash him?"

"If you behave, I might let you. I have a policy you should know about."

"What's that?"

"Two to one." He spun me around so he could soap my back.

"Huh?"

He lingered and reached around me to wash my breasts and stomach. He placed the wash cloth down on the tiled ledge, maneuvered me under the stream of water, and rinsed his hands in the flow.

"I owe you another," he said, reaching between my legs.

"Ohhh, that. I … don't think … I can argue … with that."

He massaged my clit, pushing me back against the tiled wall. Crouching down, he lifted my right leg over his bent knee. "There, that's better. Your clit is still so swollen. I love how hard it gets for me."

"She likes you too. Oh, yes…"

"Pull on your nipples for me, love. Yes, just like that. You're so fucking sexy, Jacqs."

My hips rocked uncontrollably against his hand as the heat in my pussy grew.

"How do you feel about anal sex?" he asked.

"I … don't know."

He stopped moving his hand and said, "You've never had anal sex?"

"Nothing more than a finger. Bond's not in to that, or at least he's never asked me to do it."

"We'll have to rectify that and soon."

"With him?" I asked, pointing down at his semi-erect cock. "I'm pretty sure he won't fit."

"Trust me, we'll have fun trying."

"Ohhh," I moaned as he continued to circle around my arousal. The idea of his cock in my ass spiked my libido.

"Let me know when you're close."

"I'm almost there." I continued to yank on my harden peaks. Warmth spread out from my mound and nipples, encompassing the rest of my body. "Oh, Aidan, oh please."

"You like that idea, don't you? Give it to me, Jacqs. Come for me."

I struggled to hold myself up while the convulsions began. Reaching up, I clutched his shoulders as I hollered out my orgasm.

He lowered my leg and held me against him as I tried to recover enough to stand. "So sexy," he said, kissing up my neck and nipping my earlobe.

"You bring it out in me," I whispered into his chest.

"Let's finish up in here so we can make dinner together."

"Kiss me first," I said.

He lifted me off my feet and ever so gently kissed my lips parting them with his tongue. He mesmerized me with his soft kisses of love and then lowered me to my feet again.

I threw on a pair of purple PJ bottoms and light blue T-shirt, and joined Red downstairs. I loved him in his plaid PJ pants and white shirt. Easing up behind him, I snaked my arms around his torso. He had already begun prepping the salmon.

"Hello love," he said over his shoulder.

"You cook?"

"It relaxes me," he said, spicing the fillets with garlic salt, red pepper, and basil.

"Yeah, me too and I also see it as a challenge. There are a few recipes I'd like to master. I watch several cooking shows, and I like it best when I can cook for other people. I tend to do the expedient thing when I'm making food for myself."

"We should plan a dinner party after all the dust has settled."

"I love that idea," I said, hugging him again from behind.

"What were your plans for the veggies?"

"We can bake them after the salmon comes out to rest."

"I've never had them that way."

"I think you'll love it. We'll just lightly coat them in olive oil and spices."

After placing the salmon in the oven, Red said, "Let's go sit outside while this cooks." He led me through the French doors to the loveseat glider. "This is my favorite time of the year."

"Mine too, especially when it's breezy. How was the rest of your day?" I sat and tucked my legs underneath me.

"Uneventful. We had a staff meeting at the end of the day. You?" He rocked us with his outstretched legs.

"The time crawled by and I ended up leaving an hour early. I needed a nap." I cuddled in close.

He looked down and said, "I love having you here— I think I heard your phone go off."

"Oh?" I glanced up. "I guess I'd better check it. It could be my mother or Sam or Lainie."

"Or Bond."

"Right," I said, a knot forming in my stomach.

I ran up the stairs and retrieved my phone from my bag. *Shit*, I found a voicemail from Bond. Pressing 1, I waited for the message to play:

"Hi Jacqs. I hope you've been thinking about giving us another shot. I have to work tonight but want us to make plans for later in the week. I ended up sleeping most of the day away. You must be beat. Have you crashed already? If you're with *Aidan*, tell him his time is running out."

I trotted down the stairs and walked outside. I held out my phone so Red could hear the message. "Doesn't sound like he's coming around to me," I said, plopping down on the rocker. "He called you Aidan."

"I caught that." He pulled me back to him.

"He also wants to spend time with me," I said, tilting my head so I could see Red's eyes.

"Yes, Jacqs, I heard that as well."

"Well?" I said, sitting up straight.

"Well what?"

"How do you feel about me spending time with him?"

"Baby, I don't expect you to stop seeing him; however, I'm not okay with you having sex until we have all of this sorted out."

"Does that include holding hands and kissing?"

He didn't answer right away, and I couldn't decipher the expression on his face.

Sitting back, I pulled my knees in and closed my eyes, swaying into the rocking and the breeze on my face. I waited silently for his response. My indifference felt odd—to be in our twisted scenario and not know exactly what I wanted from it. Not even sure if I cared if Bond came around. Did he really want to see my exclusively? I would have jumped at the chance just a few weeks ago. I hoped he would forgive Red and get past us being together, but I still hadn't sorted out if I wanted to date Bond too. At the same time, I'd never spent time with Bond alone without at least holding hands and kissing. Maybe it was time to go cold turkey and stop it all. Would it make the transition easier or more difficult?

At least I was sure of one thing: I wanted to be with Red.

"I'm okay with hand holding and kissing. Nothing more," he said, laying his arm across the back of the loveseat and crossing his legs.

"Why did it take you so long to answer?" I turned to the side to face him.

"Just making sure I could live with my response."

"We seem to be moving forward with the assumption that one, I want to continue to date Bond, and that two, he'll come around. I'm not sure of either of those things."

"Really? Are you sure you're not just mad at him right now?"

"I ... I'm not sure what I am. He said he wants me to

stop seeing you and he'll date me exclusively. *Try to* that is."

"You're kidding, right?"

"Sadly, I'm not. And I don't even know if he means it."

"The man's an idiot. I'm not about to convince you to give him a chance, but I do know how he feels for you. It's been torture for years, hearing him go on and on about you."

"What good is it if he doesn't *show* me? In all fairness, I'm not sure I'm open to letting him at this point," I said, burying my face into my hands.

"You'll have to decide that for yourself."

We rocked for a few minutes as my mind tried to decipher what I really felt. "Crap," I muttered and stood up. "Shall we prep the veggies?"

"Sure."

I vowed to myself not to think of Bond for the rest of the night.

Red and I enjoyed a relaxing dinner together, and I managed to let go of most of the stress I had been carrying around.

When we were cleaning up the kitchen, he asked, "How are you feeling?"

Placing the last plate into the dishwasher, I said, "How do you mean?"

"Are you tired?"

"Oh that. No, the nap really helped." I hung the dish towel over the oven handle and faced him.

"Good because there are two things I haven't been able to get off my mind, and I think now's the perfect time to take care of them."

"Oh," I said, batting my eyes.

"Are you taunting me?" He stepped forward and towered over me.

"Maybe," I giggled, running up the stairs to get away

from him. I tried to shut his door, but he just laughed and pushed through it.

"Get over here, Little One."

I walked backward away from him with my hands on my hips. "What're you going to do to me?"

"If you would stand still for a minute, you'd find out."

He started to take a step when I blurted out, "I'm still and you stay there," I said, pointing at him by the door. "Tell me."

"Damn, you're cute when you're nervous."

"I'm not nervous," I said, stretching up taller. "I just see that devious look in your eyes and I want to know what you're getting up to."

"About here," he said, holding his hand just above his head and striding toward me.

I hopped up on the bed and jumped out of reach.

"First—once I catch you—I'm going to bind you in rope. I've been fantasizing about tying your tiny frame in a chest harness and rope corset." He stomped around to the other side of the bed, and I shifted farther away.

"Will I have use of my arms?"

"Yes, you will need them."

"Okay then." Just as I was about to hop off the bed, I stopped myself. "And the second thing?"

"That ass of yours is mine."

"This little ole thing?" I bent over and mooned Red.

"That's it!" He scooped me up into his arms and carried me over to the trunk. "First things first, get naked."

As I peeled off my PJs, I felt my pussy pulse in anticipation.

Red flipped open the lid of the chest, which held a variety of ropes in various widths and colors, and said, "Choose two colors from the pile on the right."

I reached down and touched the cotton rope finding it

much softer than I imagined. "Purple and teal, I love that combination." I handed the two coils of rope to Red.

"Hold your hands up at chest height with your elbows out," he said as he spun me to face away from him. Using the teal rope, he ran the double folded cordage along the top of my breast and then underneath them. He did that twice before securing it behind me.

Heat rushed to the surface of my skin, and my nipples tightened.

"You can put your arms down now." Over my shoulder he draped the rope and threaded it under the bindings that crossed above and below my bust.

I watched him twist the rope a few times and run it back through the top binding before fastening it in the back.

"See how sexy your hot little body looks," he said, leading me to the mirror over the dresser. My pert breasts were more pronounced between the crisscross of rope over my chest, and the coils above and below them pushed them up and out.

He plucked at my nipples. "You look incredible, Jacqs."

"Ahhh, thanks," I muttered and closed my eyes. His warmth disappeared from my side, and when I opened my eyes again, he sat on the edge of the bed with the purple rope in his hand. "What's that rope for?"

"The corset. Come here."

Obliging, I sauntered up in front of him.

Pulling on the center of the harness, he looped the purple rope through it. He circled the rope around my back, making sure that the double layers lay flat against my torso. On each pass, he threaded it through the loop above creating the corseted effect.

"How does that feel?"

"Are you done?"

"Yes."

Turning toward the mirror, I stood on tiptoe to see the finished product. My waist and hips looked more pronounced, and my nipples protruded, waiting for play. I looked and felt sexy. "So you don't always use rope to tie people down?"

"No, sometimes I just appreciate the art of knotting and binding. You look incredible, Jacqs. Come here."

The corset kept my back completely straight, so I had to rock on my knees to straddle Red. He grabbed my buttocks in both hands and commandeered my mouth. Just tying me up had aroused him, and he wasn't alone. Through his pajama bottoms, his hard cock tapped against my wetness. Dizzy from his kisses and the fervor raging between us, I yanked on the elastic at his waist.

"Not so fast," he said, lifting me off him and placing me down to the side. "That pouty lip isn't going to work on me."

"Can't you just slide into my pussy a few times before we, you know?" I asked, lying back on the bed and spreading my legs before him.

"Not if you can't even say it, Jacqs. I'm going to play with your anus, with my finger first and then my cock. Say it."

"You plan to play with my ass and then try to get your gargantuan penis in there."

Red burst out in laughter and said, "Good enough." He rolled on top of me, bending my knees back toward my chest. "So fucking wet. Your body sure likes the idea of what's about to happen." With the tip of his cock, he rubbed against my opening and around my distended clit.

"Ohhh," I groaned.

"Only a few strokes because I don't want you to distract me from my mission." He pushed his bulbous erection into me, resting before slowly pulling out.

"Again," I ordered, clutching his ass in my hands and

drawing him forward.

"You are quite the demanding one when you're turned on."

"Please?"

He towered over me, bending so he could kiss me as he reamed my pussy hard and fast.

"Oh lord," I mumbled against his lips.

We merged together in force, his thrusts meeting mine until he abruptly pushed off the bed and stood.

"I'll be right back," Red said. He stepped away and returned from the bathroom.

"What's that?"

"Coconut oil. It's great for anal play. Here, put this towel under your hips." He scooped some out of a small jar and spread it over my anus. "Rub some on your clit."

Straightening the folded towel beneath me, I hunched forward to look in the jar. "Why?"

"Because you'll be playing with your clit while I play with your ass. Don't get shy on me now."

"It smells great." I used my finger to get some of the butter and rubbed it in over my pussy lips and clit. It easily melted as soon as it touched my hot flesh.

"Lie back and relax."

"Uh huh," I said, as if my libido and racing heart planned to let me relax.

Without hesitation, Red circled his finger around my anus and gently pushed in.

My clit hardened from his anal attention as I swirled around the protruding pearl. "Oh lord, that feels good."

In and out he stroked, loosening the area. "I need you to take two fingers before we can try him," he said, laying his thick heavy cock against my labia.

I glided my slick fingers over the flared head. "Okay, I think I'm ready."

Dipping his other finger into my pussy, he coated it in my natural wetness. Pushing past my resistance, he plunged two fingers into my anus, twisting and turning to stretch the opening.

"Oh, I feel so full."

"Should I stop?

"Ummm, maybe, oh no, don't. If you keep doing that ... I think it will make me come," I groaned. My hips bucked and shook in time with his barrage of sensual torment. Thrusting even deeper, in and out; I sped up my fingers to match his pace. "Don't stop, don't stop. Just like that! Oh ... my ... oh ... fuck!" My back arched up from the bed, and I came with abandon, squirting and gushing with each contraction. I saturated the towel beneath me as I struggled to catch my breath. "Please give me a second to recover," I said, as I felt Red slide his fingers out.

"Take your time." After washing his hands in the bathroom, he returned to my side with a fresh towel. He ran his hand down my chest, circling my areolas. "Your nipples get so hard and distended when I play with your ass."

"Do they?"

"You looked so incredibly sexy coming for me like that. Your squirt hit me straight in the chest." He plucked at my nipples as we continued to talk.

I blushed and said, "You make me feel sexy."

"There's no doubt about it. Does the binding still feel okay? Are you ready to continue?"

"Where do you want me?"

He grabbed my legs and pulled my butt to the edge of the bed.

Spreading my knees wide for him, I was thrilled to be taken in a new way. I stared up at him, my love blossoming further.

"Let me know if it's too much, I don't want to hurt

you." The head of his cock pressed against my anal opening, and I gave over to the sensation of being stretched and full. "You're so tight, it won't take me long to explode."

My nerves caught fire, and my whole body felt wide awake. "Uhhh ... uhhh ... that's sooo intense ... and oh ... oh my god ... slowly."

"Do I need to pull out?"

"Are you all the way in?"

"Almost," he said, hitching back gently and then plunging forward. "All the way now."

"Oh Aidan, that's ... that's like nothing ... oh fuck ... don't stop!"

"I want you to come with me, Jacqs." Standing at the edge of the bed, Red clutched my thighs, just under my knees, using my legs as leverage to penetrate me fully.

I reached down and found the right spot on my bloated clit, rubbing up and down. My stomach clutched as my orgasm climbed and my anus squeezed Red's cock.

"I can't hold out much longer," he said, slowing his strokes.

His cock swelled within me, and I knew he was very close. "You ... don't ... oh, Aidan, I'm so going to ... oh fuck me!" I screamed as my orgasm joined with his.

His green eyes held mine as he yelled out his release, his chest puffing out. He stood up straight and laughed.

"Stay right there," he said. "You kind of look like a rag doll there."

My legs hung over the side of the bed and I melted in bliss, drifting in the afterglow.

A warm wash cloth pressed against my pussy, and I took hold of it. "Thanks," I said. After wiping myself clean, I used the bathroom and got ready for sleep.

Back at the bed, Red waited for me. "How was that?"

"Amazing," I said, cozying up next to him.

"*You* are amazing. Shall I untie you?" he said, pulling me in close.

"I'm sure I'll sleep better without the rope on, but I must admit that I enjoyed being bound."

"Good, now turn around before I take your cute self again."

"That wasn't enough for you?"

As he untied my bindings he said, "Enough for now, tomorrow's another day."

I yawned and stretched up on my toes once I was completely naked again. "Look at all the lines," I said, tracing over my skin.

"Those will be gone by tomorrow. Let's spoon."

Wrapped up in Red's arms and just before drifting off into a content sleep, I thought about Bond and wondered if he was doing okay.

I awoke in the morning to the soft play of Red's hands roaming over my body, caressing my thighs and butt trailing up to my shoulders and around to my stomach and breasts. The nibbles along my back and neck sent shockwaves, stoking my desire. My giggles erupted as his breath tickled my neck.

"That's a wonderful sound first thing in the morning," he said, rolling me around to face him.

"Your breath smells minty," I said, pushing against his chest and jumping out of bed to head to the bathroom. I used the toilet, brushed my teeth, and easily curled back into the warmth of his arms.

"This is how I want to wake up every morning," he said.

I reached down and grabbed hold of his erection. "He sure likes it."

"*He* almost woke you in the middle of the night."

I laughed and asked, "But you stopped him? Why?"

"I thought you needed the sleep and I plan to convince you to stay again tonight."

"Oh, do convince me."

He covered my mouth with his, causing me to moan out loud.

"That's a good start," I said, practically gasping.

"Go onto your side for me," he said, moving me into place with my back facing him. He resumed his erotic massage, fondling my breasts and tugging on my nipples.

I wiggled my hips uncontrollably against him as he nipped down my neck.

His hand migrated lower to my stomach and pulled my upper leg over his thigh, spreading me wide.

He groaned deeply when he delved his fingers into my wetness. "You're so damn sexy, Jacqs, and I love how your body responds to me."

"I'm rather … fond of it … myself," I said as he swirled his finger inside me.

"I want you to come with my cock inside you. Let me know when you're close."

My back rested against his chest, and he freed the arm underneath to wrap it around my torso and tug on my nipple. He used the long thick fingers of his other hand to knead my clit, making it swell under his touch. As his heat surrounded my body from behind and I mewed in response to his manipulations, I rose higher and higher to the edge of climax.

"I'm close," I muttered.

"Roll over on your stomach and raise your hips and play with your clit for me."

Desperately wanting to please him, I did what he asked, causing my arousal to climb. I vowed not to be shy with him and how could I be after last night. I rested my forehead on my left arm as I reached underneath with my right hand and rubbed against my clit. I could feel him positioning himself behind me.

"You have the most beautiful pussy and I love that you're letting me take you this way." He penetrated me with his thick cock, filling me deeper than before.

"Oh yes, that feels sooo good," I moaned.

"Keep working that clit of yours and let me know when you're about to come."

"Yes, sir," I said, pushing my pelvis back to meet his incursion.

Red chuckled but didn't break stride. He gathered my hair in his fist and pulled my head back toward him. Clasping my shoulder with his other hand, he rode me hard.

The force of our coupling intensified, and I reveled in my submissive position—face down, ass up. "Oh lord … I'm going to come … oh please! Yesss!" I yelled as my orgasm finally stole my breath and shut me up.

Letting go of my hair, he wound his arm around my stomach, holding me tightly against him. "Take your time recovering; we are going to go again."

"I don't know if I can, that was so intense—" I breathed out.

"You can and you will," he said, brushing my hair off my back and draping it over my neck. He cupped my breast that dangled under me and pinched my nipple while biting my shoulder. He resumed the sway of his hips, still fully erect, pulsing inside me, sliding in and out of my wanton pussy. Wetness coated my inner thighs and as the pace of his strokes increased, my lust flared again.

Nonsensical groans spilled out of me and I knew it wouldn't take much longer.

"Are you close … because if not I need to slow—" he said.

"Now!" I screamed as my orgasm spasmed, causing

me to convulse and thrash in Red's arms.

"Jacqs," he growled, his release chasing mine.

Once he finished pounding out his ejaculation, I buckled. He fell out next to me, both of us breathing heavily.

"Holy hell woman," he whispered.

"No shit," I said, trying to catch my breath. I felt spent in the most exquisite way. Every muscle in my body relaxed and I melted into the bed, drifting back into sumptuous sleep.

"Jacqs," Red said, lightly shaking my shoulder.

I opened my eyes and it seemed much lighter out. "What time is it?"

"Late. Sorry, I dosed off with you. A first for me."

"Sleeping after sex?" I said, stretching my arms overhead, trying to shake off the nap.

"Sleeping as well as I do, when you're in my bed."

"I think we might need an alarm clock in here."

"Yeah, maybe. It's almost nine o'clock."

"Oh hell, I need to take a quick shower and get out of here," I said, scooting off the bed.

We showered, and I grabbed a yogurt to take with me to work.

"Plan to spend the night," Red said as we exited his house together. We shared a sweet kiss before we set off to our separate cars.

CHAPTER THIRTEEN

I'm So Heavy

by Florence + The Machine

Henry gave me crap for being late for work, but otherwise the day was pretty uneventful. I left as early as I could so I had the time to throw in a load of laundry, shower, and dress before heading over early for the gathering at Red's.

My phone rang as I pulled on my wide-band, purple hippie skirt that I wore low on my hips and the off-the-shoulder red peasant blouse. I forewent my bra and underwear to torment Red.

"Hello," I said.

"Hey girl," Lainie said, her voice sounding shaky.

"What's wrong?"

"I'm not sure about going to Red's tonight."

"What's happened Lainie? Do you want me to drop by on my way?" I walked into the bathroom to check my appearance and slipped on sliver hoop earrings.

"It's not worth talking about."

"Something's going on with you. You haven't shared anything about your dates lately, and that's not like you. I'm forever dumping my problems in your lap and lately it's been one sided —"

"It's not something I can talk about."

"I'll be there in twenty minutes. Don't go anywhere," I said and hung up. I had been so wrapped up in sorting through my own drama that I'd dismissed Lainie's general withholding of information.

I gathered a couple sets of clothing to bring to Red's and grabbed my bag.

"You didn't need to come by," Lainie said. She flipped the bolt lock and followed me into the living room.

"I was worried and you know you would've done the same thing. What's going on?" I sat down on the couch and looked up at her.

She appeared agitated, which was not at all like her. She said, "It's not something I'm free to talk about at this point."

"That doesn't sound good. Are you okay? Are you safe? Are you worried someone is going to show up here?"

She glanced over her shoulder, and I could tell that I got that right.

"I can blow off Red's, and we can go out if you'd like," I said, shrugging my shoulders. "You can stay at my place. Tell me how I can help you."

She shook her head. "I just need a drink. Give me a few minutes, and I'll get ready."

I trailed after her into the bedroom and plopped down on her bed. "I don't want to push you to talk about it, but you should know that I'd never share what you tell me with anyone."

"Jacqueline, it's not a matter of me trusting you, which I do, I just made a promise and—"

"Okay, but I'm here when you're ready—any day, anytime."

"Thanks for understanding."

I didn't understand, but whatever she was keeping from me couldn't be good. Maybe because my life currently revolved around two men, I assumed her mood and upset had to do with a lover. A lover she had been keeping a secret.

She kept on her jeans and slipped on a gray-blue,

long-sleeved top. "Is it cold out?"

"It's a warm night. Are you up for going to Red's or shall we do something else?"

"Red's is ok—" she started until her phone signaled a text. She retrieved it from the bed and read. She pursed her mouth and turned it off. "Let's go."

I drove us to Red's and we rode in veritable silence. I hoped hanging out with the gang would brighten her mood.

"Park along the road in case I want to take off early," Lainie said.

"Sure."

"Will Bond be here tonight?"

"According to him, no, but that remains to be seen."

"Yeah."

"Lainie?"

"What?"

"Thanks for coming. It means a lot to me."

"Yeah, I know. Let's get me that drink."

Lainie had never been given a nickname from Bond because she made her feelings clear regarding his behavior towards me, and I loved her for it. It was like having my own personal bulldog.

When we walked through the house into the kitchen, we could see Red, Blue, and Stay through the window to the back. Lainie took two hard cider bottles out of the refrigerator and handed me one.

"Thanks," I said, twisting off the cap. I took a sip and observed my friends out back. My gut twisted over what I might find out from Blue; however my heart filled with joy over spending the night in Red's arms again. As if he could hear my thoughts, he turned my way and smiled.

When Lainie and I headed out back, Blue mumbled a quick hello and stole inside.

I witnessed Stay's face light up when he saw that

Lainie was with me.

"Hey ladies," Stay said. He hugged me close and whispered, "We need to talk."

"Hey to you too," I said, stepping out of his embrace.

"Lainie, are you up to some pool?" Stay asked.

"Sure," she said.

They left Red and me alone outside. We stood facing each other.

"This is weird," I said.

"Let's go upstairs for a minute." Not giving me a chance to respond, he grasped my hand and pulled me along with him.

"You're so pushy," I said, once we entered his bedroom. I tried to suppress my laughter.

"This is probably our only chance to steal away for a few minutes."

"I brought a few more clothes with me." I took the items out of my backpack.

"Top drawer on the right is empty."

"That's so sweet," I said, putting my belongings away.

He cornered me against the dresser, and pressed his body to my back. "There's nothing sweet about it."

"Oh," I said, twisting in his arms to face him. "You're happy to see me?" I batted my eyelashes.

"Oh, yes," he said, lifting me onto the chest of drawers. "I've missed you."

"I've missed you too." I fingered his bottom lip and ran my hands over his bristly, red beard.

He dipped his lips to mine, and I sighed into his mouth. Our kiss rapidly escalated, scorching my libido and sending an aching heat to my pussy.

Breaking off the kiss, I declared, "Unless you plan to take me, right here, right now, we had better stop."

"Sorry, love. It's hard not to get carried away with you."

I cupped his erection over his jeans and said, "Yes, *he* is hard."

"Behave yourself, Little One, or I might have to punish you," he said, moving back a step.

"Promises, promises." I hopped off the dresser.

He grabbed my arm, flipped me around and smacked my ass.

"Oh, you Neanderthal!" I said, pushing him away. "You behave or take off your pants."

"Downstairs with you Little One or everyone will find out sooner than later."

"I'll leave, but you should know," I said, first lifting my skirt, so he could see my naked pussy, and then lowering the top of my blouse exposing my uncovered tits. I left him with his mouth hanging open as I slipped out the door.

Once I made it to the bottom of the stairs, Blue rounded the corner. "What were you doing in Red's bedroom?"

"What were you doing with Bond on Saturday night?" I said, staring her down from the bottom step.

She sputtered and finally said, "What do you know? Wait, come here." She led me to the sitting room in the front of the house.

"Just that you and Bond got into a huge fight and that he was too drunk to remember what happened."

Her face flushed red. "What the hell do you see in the man?"

"Are you going to tell me or shall I continue to assume?" I said, placing my hands on my hips.

"We both had been drinking a lot—"

"So that's the excuse?" I could feel my jaw tighten and my pulse race. "Just say it."

"Alright, we fucked. Is that what you want to hear?"

"Is that what the fight was about?" I asked. At the

same time, I didn't know if I truly wanted the answer.

"He called out your name as he came."

I almost felt sorry for her, but only almost. "You shouldn't have been fucking him in the first place."

"You don't get to take dibs on all the guys, Jacqs. Word on the street is that you and Red are riding the hobbyhorse."

"Fine, fuck him to your heart's content. But if you thought it was okay, you wouldn't have had a hard time telling me about it. You had to have realized he was three sheets to the wind. Why would you do that to yourself?"

"That's none of your fucking business. Who do you think—"

"Ladies?" Stay said, ducking his head into the room.

"I'm done," I said, slipping past Stay through the main part of the house. I stamped straight out the French doors and sat on the loveseat rocker. I curled my legs up onto the cushion and covered them with my skirt. Rocking back and forth, I tried to soothe my anger. Did I have a right to be mad at Blue? I couldn't fathom why she would choose to fuck Bond when he clearly wasn't in his right mind. Not that I should be excusing his behavior, either.

"A lot on your mind?" Stay said as he approached.

"The soap opera called 'Jacqueline's crazy life.'"

"High drama these days," he said, sitting down beside me.

"Yeah, no kidding."

"Don't be too hard on Blue. She's searching for something."

"Aren't we all? Couldn't she have picked outside of the pond?"

"Couldn't you?"

"Point taken." I unfolded my legs and rocked us. "Has Bond told you?"

"He didn't need to. So he knows?"

"Yes, Red told him."

239

"I don't imagine it went over well."

"Not in the slightest. Of course, I never thought it would. I mean, I didn't plan for any of this to happen."

"Love is never planned. Sometimes it works out well for us, but other times, not so much."

"Are you doing okay?" I wondered if he was grieving the loss of Karen.

"I have my moments. Being a way from Karen has given me great perspective. We weren't a good match."

"Yeah, I know how that is."

"You mean Bond?" Stay reached out and touched my arm. "He can't handle the thought of losing you."

"He's had over eight years to figure that out. I love him, Stay, but I'm not going to spend my life wishing he could be what I need. He can't or won't and in either case, it means the same thing. Sometimes I wish I could just rewind—" I stopped myself mid-sentence and glanced up. "Please don't tell the rest of the group."

"They already suspect, and I don't imagine the guys will care. Blue and Cat are another story. I don't know how they'll take it."

"At this moment, I don't give a shit what Blue thinks. Cat on the other hand…"

"Other than Bond, I'm sure the rest will come around. However, Bond is the binding force that's brought us all together. If he shuns Red, we might be hanging elsewhere. Or more likely taking turns like in a divorce."

"Fuck."

"Yeah."

"You remind me of Lainie sometimes."

"How's that?"

"You both are excellent listeners and supportive and cut right to the point."

"I like her a lot," Stay said and looked back into the

house. His expression became grim.

"I've gotten that impression."

"Dawg's here," he said his tone gruff.

I followed his gaze and saw Lainie laughing at a joke Doug must have told. "I'm ready for another drink. Shall we go in?"

"Sure."

We strolled back into the house, arm and arm. I walked off to the kitchen, and he headed back toward the game room.

After retrieving another hard cider, I leaned on the counter and observed Lainie and Doug for a few minutes. They made an odd couple. She towered over his short, stocky physique.

"Can you bring me a drink?" she called over to me.

I opened another bottle for her and joined them on the couch. "Long time, Dawg."

"Was dealing with some business in Canada. Should be staying in town for a while."

"Nothing too serious, I hope."

"Nah. I'm glad you dragged Lainie along this time, eh?" Dawg said, throwing his arm over her shoulder.

"I'm sure," I said to him. "Watch out for this one," I said to Lainie, raising my eyebrows and hoping she would heed my advice. "Let's play doubles with Red and Stay." I stood and pulled up on Lainie's arm.

"In a bit."

I wandered to the front of the house to see if anyone else had showed. Finding it empty, I walked back toward the game room.

Red, Stay, Cat, and Kev were playing a round of pool, so I took a seat at the table closest to them. "Where's Blue?"

"She went to get supplies for making margaritas," Cat said, sashaying toward me. She hugged me tight and whispered, "Forgive her."

I shrugged my shoulders and asked, "Are there chips and salsa to go with them? I'm getting hungry."

"I'm hungry too," Red said, staring directly at me.

I could feel heat spread across my face so I turned away. When the others were focused on the next shot, I mouthed to Red, "Behave."

He winked in response. "Text her. I have the salsa, and there's cheese, and leftover chicken too."

"I will," Cat said.

I smiled to her in thanks.

"If you all plan to indulge Blue's plan for a tequila romp, you need to spend the night," Red said while he lined up his next shot.

"Nice one," Stay said. "I don't plan to drink so I can be the designated driver for those in need of a ride."

Red stood next to me, looking down the cleavage of my shirt.

My nipples responded and when his penetrating gaze lassoed mine, I lost myself in his bright green eyes. For a moment, I forgot myself and where I was; so did he.

"Yo, Red, it's your turn," Stay said.

We both turned to see the rest of the group looking at us.

"I think I'll check on Lainie," I said and left the game room before we made our growing relationship even more obvious.

I wasn't thrilled to find Lainie and Doug cozying up on the couch. "Can I talk to you for a minute?" I said to her.

"I'll be right back," Lainie said and followed me to the front of the house. We flopped into the couch. "What gives?"

"You seemed upset before, which I can only assume is over a man, and Dawg is definitely a bad choice to take it out on."

"I'm a big girl, Jacqs. So if that's it?" She moved to

stand up.

"He's a player and I'm worried—"

"I know who he is and what he's like. I'm enjoying myself so please back off. He's assured me that he doesn't let emotions get in the way of great sex."

"If you know what you're doing," I said, holding up my hands. "Please do the sensible thing and use a condom. I can ask Red if he has—"

"I feel like you've taken over my mother hen role."

"Yes and it feels odd." I chuckled.

We both stood and hugged. I hoped she wasn't going to do something she would regret later but who was I to talk?

When Blue came back with the supplies, the party ramped up. I nursed my one margarita and ate a pile of nachos. I had three interviews to do the next morning at work and planned to avoid a hangover. Red stuck to his beer and Stay abstained altogether.

"I'm making another pitcher," Blue said after she refilled everyone else's cup.

"Let's go swimming," Dawg said. "It's a warm night out and the pool is heated."

"I don't have my suit," Cat said.

"Let's all go skinny-dipping," Lainie said.

I looked over at her with my eyes wide. Clearly she had been drinking a lot to suggest such a thing. I had never known her to get naked in front of a group of people.

"Perfect," Kev said.

We all watched him shed his clothes, walk outside and dive into the deep end of the pool.

I glanced over to Red to see his reaction. "Fine by me," he said.

"Should we turn on the outside lights?" I asked.

"No, let's leave them off, eh?" Dawg said in a hurry.

Everyone wandered outside, leaving Red and me alone.

He drew me into the pantry and immediately grasped my ass, pulling me into him. "You're a naughty girl to tease me like that."

"Me? What did I do?"

"Sauntering around naked under those clothes."

I laughed out loud and said, "I'm glad it worked."

"It'll be challenging for me to keep my hands off you in the pool."

"Good," I said, sauntering a few steps away. I flipped up the back of my skirt and mooned him.

"Now you deserve more than a spanking," he said, stalking toward me.

I giggled, ran outside and shed my clothes. I stepped down into the shallow end of the pool watching the others swim around.

Doug still had on his boxers until I saw him slip them off quickly before lowering himself down the side into the water. I got the impression that he didn't care to be seen naked.

Cat and Kev chased each other around the pool and Lainie and Blue stood next to each other chatting. I wondered what they might be talking about.

My attention was immediately drawn back to the door when Red strolled out of the house naked. His cock hung heavy and I longed to have him alone again. I wanted him hard in my hand, mouth, and pussy. I tried to shun the lust that screamed within me by diving under the water and swimming to the deep end.

"This was a good idea," Cat said. "It's an incredible night and it's sobered me up a bit."

"You and Kev seem better," I said, hanging from the ledge that separated the pool and the Jacuzzi.

"Oh yeah, we're doing great. I was just having a bad night on Saturday."

"That's good. He's definitely a keeper."

"That he is."

We watched Lainie and Doug take turns swimming on the bottom of the pool between each other's legs.

I let go of the edge and swam back toward the shallow end and Red. Once I surfaced beside him, my breath caught in my throat. Everyone's attention faced the house.

"Isn't this a pretty picture," Bond said. He held Blondie's hand, who stood rigidly by his side.

"We weren't expecting you," I said, dipping down so my breasts weren't exposed.

"Clearly," he said. "So have you told everyone? Have you all heard?"

"Bond, maybe—" Stay started.

"Then let me do the honors. Red and Jacqs are now an item." He paused and swayed just slightly. "Sprouts in the refrigerator and toothbrush in the bathroom. How sweet." Making sweeping eye contact with the rest of the group, he said, "And get this, he's allowing me visitation. Isn't he generous? Let us raise our glasses. Oh, nobody has a glass? Everyone out of the pool so we can toast Red." He waved vigorously for the clan to follow him.

Nobody moved.

"You've been drinking. Why don't we go inside and talk," Red said, climbing up the steps.

"I got nothing to say to you," Bond spat.

Red ignored his comment and walked over to the trunk. After drying off and wrapping a towel around his waist, he grabbed a stack of towels and handed them out to the rest of us as we got out of the pool. Doug stayed in the water.

"You're a piece of work," I said, stopping right in front of Bond.

"Me?" Bond said, dropping Blondie's hand. "You must be seriously confused."

I pointed directly at his chest. "What man shows up to

pursue a woman with another woman on his arm?" I pivoted to face his date or ride or whatever she might be to Bond. "You must be quite exceptional. We never see *Mitchell* with the same woman twice. Exceptional, or maybe a glutton for punishment? Bond's into that, you know."

Bond grasped my arm and spun me to face him. "There are rules and Red broke them."

A derisive laugh erupted from me. "Rules? Really. You've broken every single relationship rule in the book in my regard. I think Blondie might agree with me." I glanced her way and she looked down at her clear high-heeled shoes.

"So you *are* fucking them both?" Blue said when she strutted up next to me.

I'd forgotten for a moment that we had an audience. "Thank you for reminding me of your *special* night," I said to Blue. "Here's a refresher for your convenient lack of memory, Bond, you fucked Blue just a few days ago. Do the rules not apply to you? Any rules? I can't believe I'd even considered continuing to date you. The deal is most definitely off the table." I stepped around Blondie and said, "He's all yours."

"Wait," Bond demanded.

Turning to face him, all the anger boiling through me steamed out of my mouth. "You can't keep breaking my heart, Bond. I won't have it anymore. If you cared even a bit, you'd see that Red is good for me. He never leaves me feeling like shit like you do, over and over again."

"And you don't think I feel like shit right now?"

"I don't know what the fuck you feel. Take your date and get the fuck out!" I pointed to the door.

"This isn't your house," he said, glaring down at me.

"I've asked her to move in with me so as far as I'm concerned, she has every right," Red said.

"Live with you?" Blue said, throwing her hands up in

the air.

I could vaguely hear the rest of the group mumbling about the newest revelation.

"Look, this is a private matter," Red said to Bond and me. "Let's take this inside and let the rest of them get back to partying."

"Sounds good to me," Dawg said. "Blondie, get naked and get into the pool."

"I'll go grab a stack of cups and the pitcher of margaritas," Blue said, running past us into the house.

I could hear bodies jumping into the pool as we entered through the back.

"Let's go talk in my bedroom," Red said as he approached the stairs.

"Right," Bond said. "Like I want to talk in the place where you're fucking my girlfriend."

"I'm not your girlfriend!" I shouted. "When are you going to get that through your thick skull?"

"Let's try to settle down and sort this out," Red said, climbing the first step of the stairs.

"There's nothing to settle," Bond said, crossing his arms across his chest. "Jacqs has to choose."

"I already have," I said.

"Come on, Jacqs," Bond said in a quiet voice, dropping his arms to the side. "We have history together."

"Which you seem to be hell bent on rewriting," I said, wiping the tears off my cheeks. "I can't do this. I don't want to be stuck between you two. I'm unwilling to be the one that tears our group apart."

"That was his doing," Bond said, tossing his head in Red's direction.

Lainie popped her head in the door and said, "Is everything okay?"

"Yeah," I said. "We're heading upstairs to talk."

"Good. You two better behave yourself," she said, pointing to Red and Bond. "You know where I am if you need me."

"Come on," I said to Bond and tugged on his arm.

The three of us climbed the stairs and walked into Red's bedroom.

"How can you defend this man?" Bond said, taking up space just inside the door.

I sat down on the bed and faced Bond as Red settled on top of the trunk on the far side of the room. I took a couple of deep breaths trying to settle all the anger that still threatened to emerge. Speaking calmly and slowly, I said, "Bond, have you taken a moment to look at yourself and what you're offering me? Think back on the last few weeks and ask yourself, would I want to be with you under those circumstances? Would any woman for that matter?"

"I'm not any different than I've always been with you and I told you I'll stop fucking anyone else if you stop seeing Aidan." Bond took a step towards me. "If he'd have stayed out—"

"That's the point. We've been doing this back and forth dance for way too long. Maybe I'm partly to blame because I've been willing to put up with your lack of consideration for way too long. But this can't come as a surprise to you. There's no way."

He jabbed his finger in Red's direction and said, "We would've work this out at some point had he not—"

"I get it now. I'm not sure why I hadn't realized it before." I shook my head over the revelation.

"What?" Bond and Red asked simultaneously.

"Bond, you're incapable of really looking at yourself. Too scary maybe? Instead of really trying to understand why we don't work, you choose to focus on Red. He's given you a convenient out."

"There are things about me that you don't know," Bond said, sitting down next to me.

"Only because you've been unwilling to share them with me. Please don't pull us all apart. I know you're hurting, Bond. I…" Tears pooled in my eyes and overflowed down my cheeks. My anger melted as he wiped away a tear.

"Damn it, Jacqs, you know I can't stand it when you cry."

"You're one of my … best friends but … but you hurt me too." I sobbed. "Even if I hadn't fallen in love with Red … I couldn't go on with you the way we've been."

"You love him?" he roared, jerking upright from the bed.

Red came over to us and touched Bond's shoulder.

"Don't," Bond said, slapping Red's hand away. Bond lowered himself down in front of me and hugged me toward him.

I cried against his shoulder and then glanced up at Red. He appeared devastated and lost. "Oh god, I can't do this." I pushed myself out of Bond's arms and sat in the chair by the door. "This will never work. I love you both, but I can't … I won't be the wedge that drives you apart."

"Wait, Jacqs, give it some time," Red said, stepping towards me.

I held my palm out as my tears rapidly fell. "No," I said, shaking my head. "Why do I keep putting myself in situations that rip my heart out? What's wrong with me?"

"Jacqs, come on. You know it's not you," Bond said, standing on the other side of me.

I rose up between them and faced Red. "I'm sorrier than you can know because I thought we were on our way towards something amazing. I'll miss you every second of the day."

"Thank god," Bond said, sighing in relief.

I turned to face him and said, "I'm done with you too. Until you both can work something out, I'm out of the picture."

I circled back to Red and threw myself into his arms. He lifted me off the ground and whispered, "I love you and I understand."

My sobs resurfaced as he lowered me down. Pushing past Bond, I grabbed my backpack from the dresser. I ran down the stairs to find Lainie. She wasn't in the pool with the rest of the group.

Stay came out of the water, wrapped a towel around his waist and followed me inside.

"Where is she?" I said, drying my tears on my sleeve.

"I'll make sure she gets home. Are you okay?"

"No, not in the least. I have to go." I glanced up the stairs and headed to the front of the house.

"Please phone me tomorrow so we can talk," Stay called after me.

I waved my hand above my head and closed the front door behind me.

❀ ❀ ❀ ❀ ❀

For the first time that I could recall, I turned off my phone. I couldn't stomach hearing from anyone. Once I stepped into my condo, I found it hard to breathe. I crumbled onto the couch, clutched the pillow to me and wept. I lay in a vortex of misery until the hiccups of my purged emotions started to lessen.

The pounding on the door startled me. I had no intention of letting anyone inside.

"Who is it?" I shouted through the door.

"It's me," Lainie said. "Stay dropped me off."

"Jesus," I said, and let her inside.

"You look like shit," she said, placing her purse on the counter.

"Thank you so very much." I went over to the sink

and splashed water on my face. Drying off with a kitchen towel, I spouted, "Did you fuck Dawg?"

"Don't you think there are more important things to talk about?" She opened the refrigerator and poured herself a glass of chilled water.

"There's nothing to talk about. It's over."

"You missed quite a show after you left."

"I don't think I'm up for hearing about it," I said, lying back into the corner of the couch and pulling in my knees.

"Oh well, you might like this. First I didn't hook up with Dawg. He and Blondie seemed to have hit it off."

"Sorry Lainie. I mean, I'm relieved but I know you were—"

"It was good to feel desired, but I had decided before Bond's grand entrance that I wasn't really interested."

"I appreciate you checking in on me, but I need to crash."

"Mind if I spend the night?"

"Still not wanting to be home?"

"That ... and I don't have my car."

"Oh right," I groaned, the pain in my chest resurfacing.

"Stay found me in the game room and told me that you'd left. We were getting ready to leave when Bond and Red stormed down the stairs. I heard Red say to Bond, 'I hope you're satisfied. You got what you wanted.'

"Then Bond said, 'She didn't pick either of us.' His hands were in fists by his side and I was worried he might deck Red. Red responded by saying, 'And whose fault is that?'

"I'd never seen Red look so hurt. Did you tell him it was over?"

"Yes and you were right. I can't be with either of them unless they sort this out between them. But Lainie, I love Red, and I don't know how to get over him."

"I don't know either, girl. I know what it's like to be in love with someone who you can't be with."

"You do?"

"So back to Bond and Red. Bond then said, 'You betrayed me and I'll never forgive you.'

"Red said that he didn't betray him but fell in love. He said he had tried to ignore it for years but he couldn't continue to let him treat you like shit; that you deserve more. Bond said, 'Oh and you think you're it? That's laughable'

"At that point I thought Red might punch Bond out. Red's face and ears got all red. Somehow he managed to get himself under control and said, 'If you ever get to speak to her again, ask how she feels about me, what it's like when we're together. You may be unwilling to see the truth, but if you truly do love her, as you say you do, you'll have to open your eyes and see that I'm good for her.'

"I could see that Bond was close to exploding. Stay and I exchanged looks but then Bond stormed out the French doors searching for his ride. We stood in the doorway watching him. 'Let's go Stacy,' he grunted out like an order.

"Then Dawg wrapped his arm around her waist and said, 'She's staying.' So Bond yelled, 'Fuck you; fuck all of you!'

"He stormed past us and out the front door, and we left soon after."

"At least I don't have to worry about Bond driving anywhere," I said, rocking back and forth like a patient in an asylum trying to soothe herself. "I'm not sure that story made me feel any better."

"Maybe not but I think you did the right thing. I feel pretty confident that Red will wait for you and you know how Bond is, he can't go a week without trying to make things up to you."

I sighed out loud. "I have three interviews tomorrow

morning, and I need to drive you home before work, so we need to get up early. Lainie, I can't think anymore."

"Okay, girlfriend. Let's crash."

CHAPTER FOURTEEN

Re-offender

by Travis

The next morning, I fell right back into the throes of heartbreak. Sleep had not lessened the pain in my chest or the feeling that gravity might suck me down into the core of the earth. It certainly didn't remove the lump lodged in the middle of my throat. Tears had sprung anew as I scooted out of bed and went into the bathroom for a shower.

"You clearly don't deserve love," I said to my reflection in the mirror as I dried off. I wished I hadn't scheduled back to back interviews because a brooding depression beckoned me back to my bed, to block out my life, and the world and everyone in it.

"My turn," Lainie said as she entered the bathroom. "Do we have time to catch some breakfast on our way out?"

"I couldn't possibly eat." I wiped away my tears with the towel.

Lainie touched my shoulder and said, "I'm not saying it'll happen right away, but I think this will eventually sort out. Give it some time, okay? I started the coffee, by the way."

"Thanks," I said through the sniffles as I blew my nose.

Mindlessly going through the motions, I managed to get dressed and to make myself look somewhat presentable. I didn't bother with my hair other than twisting it up into a clip. I prayed to the gods of grief and sorrow to allow me to keep it together long enough to get through the three interviews. Once that was accomplished,

I planned to ditch out of work early, pull all of my shades shut, and slip back into bed.

After dropping Lainie off at her apartment, I drove back toward the office and recalled the acting class I had taken in college. I had a role as a secretary in one production, and I thought maybe I could channel her character to get through the day. I'd have to drop the southern accent and the gum chewing, but the rest might work. I rolled my eyes at myself over my musings.

I ended up feigning a cold during the interviews, which accounted for the occasional teary eye and runny nose. I left my notes on the candidates on Henry's desk, and made it out of the office by 11:30 a.m. Instead of succumbing to the oblivion of sleep, I forced myself to go to a hot yoga class. It had been way too long since I had a really good workout, plus I could cry all the way through without anyone the wiser, the tears mixing in with the sweat.

The gods of grief and sorrow decided to have a joke at my expense, either that or my broken heart caused my pheromones to spike.

"I haven't seen you around for a while," said a deep voiced, Scandinavian guy with muscular legs, as we walked out of the heated room, into the lobby.

I rested my rolled up yoga mat against the bench and wiped the sweat off my face and neck. "Yeah, life's been busy and I haven't made the time to come around." I pushed out the front door with my towel and mat in hand. Holding my arms away from my sides, I allowed the winter's breeze to cool me down.

"Don't you usually come in the evenings?" a very cute Italian guy asked as he joined us outside.

"Yeah, I left work early today and decided I needed a good sweat." I sat down on the top step, waiting for my pulse to settle enough so that I could change into my dry clothes and head home. I felt light headed and slightly dizzy from the heat and lack of food.

"Well, I was hoping I would run into—" Cute Italian Guy started.

"Me too. I was just about to say—" Muscular Legs cut in.

"Look gentlemen, I'm certain you're great guys, but my dance card is—" A wave of nausea assaulted my stomach and I bent forward over my knees. "Is there any chance you can get one of the women inside to grab my bag? It has my other bottle of water in it. It's the purple one all the way on the left in the middle cubby. My phone is in there too. Please. Thanks."

"Sure," Cute Italian Guy said and immediately took off through the door.

"I'll get you some water," Muscular Legs said, and followed the other man inside.

"What the fuck is with me and two men!" I said out loud to the passing cars.

Muscular Legs returned first with a small paper cup of water, which I drank in one gulp.

"Thank you," I said.

Cute Italian Guy followed soon after and said, "Your phone was off, so I turned it on for you and it chimed several times. I think someone is really trying to reach you."

"Thank you," I said again, but really, I felt annoyed. "Nice to see you both and thanks for your assistance," the polite side of me responded. Truly, I just wanted to be left alone. I took out my water bottle and placed my phone down beside me.

"You aren't going to check your messages?" Italian Guy asked. He didn't seem so cute anymore. I shot him a look and he said, "I'm just sayin', it went off several times. Seems like there might be an emergency."

I forced myself to stand up and lift my belongings. Still

feeling a bit queasy, I grabbed the handrail to steady myself.

"You going to be okay?" Muscular Legs asked.

"Yeah, I'm good. I just need some food. Thanks again guys, I gotta run." I hobbled to my car and crumbled into the driver's seat. As I took a couple more sips of water, I stared at my cell phone on the dashboard. I didn't want to deal with anything just then, but I imagined that Lainie and maybe a few others were checking in on me, and so, being me, I gave in and checked the phone.

There were a plethora of texts from Bond, which I ignored, several from Lainie and six voice mails, three of which were from Bond. I found neither a text nor a voice message from Red. *Should I take this as disinterest or respect?* Truly, it left me sad and feeling alone, much more alone than I had in a very long time. The other three calls were from Lainie, Cat, and Stay to whom I sent a group text.

> **Me:** I won't say I'm fine, but I'm hanging in there. I need my space right now, and I'll reach out when I'm ready for company. Thanks for checking in on me.

I placed the phone in my lap and continued to stare at it. I knew I should leave Bond's messages alone but at the same time, I wondered what they hell he could come up with to woo me back. Against my better judgment, which was my pattern where Bond was concerned, I clicked my phone back on and read his texts.

> **Bond:** Baby, you know I can't live without you. I don't know the right thing to say to you anymore.
> **Bond:** I took a cab back to my place. Please come by so we can talk.

Bond: I'm sorry for crashing the party Wednesday. I shouldn't have had so much to drink. The thought of losing you is killing me.
Bond: You need space? Fine, I'll give it to you.
Bond: I called your office, and they said you already left. Are you okay?
Bond: Please call me ASAP so I know you're okay.

There were several more texts from him, but I stopped reading. They just made my heart break more. I wasn't only hurting myself but him too.

I turned the ignition key, drove out of the parking lot and picked up a sub on the way home. My stomach clenched in protest after I ate a couple of bites. At my condo, I carried my belongings to my front door and found a vase filled with multi-colored roses and a note attached.

Dear Jacqueline,
I know you need time, and for Bond and I to figure things out. Please forgive me this intrusion. I won't bother you again until you're ready for me. I'll wait for you, am waiting for you. Our love is for a lifetime, not just mere minutes. You are in my thoughts always, and I love you.
Aidan

The waterworks resumed as I made the two trips necessary to bring everything into my apartment. I immediately stripped off my wet workout clothes and showered. For some reason, as the water cascaded over me, I thought of my sister. She too seemed to struggle when it came to love and relationships. Could our father's death have led us to pick the wrong men? In the case of Red, I believed that he and I made a great match, making it the most difficult part to swallow.

The pain in my heart erupted, and my breath caught in my throat as I stepped out of the shower. After drying my hair with a towel, an errant idea floated through my mind, which completely shifted my mood.

I threw on my pink silk robe and went to the living room to admire the flowers Red had left for me. I smelled them for the first time, realizing each color had its own unique scent. I loved the peach colored ones the best.

As my plan formulated in my mind, the tightness in my chest eased, and I became excited. Clearly Red loved me, and he wasn't going anywhere. I would give Bond time to come around, but not indefinitely. I had no plans to see either of them, but I would leave my own present at Red's. In my mind's eye, I could see him laughing as he approached his front door.

I opened the utility closet and sifted through all the junk I stored there. Once I found the white rope I searched for, I turned on my laptop and found a YouTube video on tying an adjustable bend knot. It was easy to see why Red chose that particular knot to name his boat. The knot could be easily lengthened or shortened but also locked in place so he could secure his bondage partners without worry of the rope getting too tight.

Following the instruction video, I did the knotting technique on either side of the double folded rope which created a loop. I delved back into the messy storage closet and found a left over red tag I used to mark holiday gifts. After widening the hole on the top of the tag and making sure it would slip onto the rope, I sat at the counter and contemplated what I should write. I finally came up with:

Dear Aidan,

In knots over our parting,
the roses cast a fragrance of hope,
Don't leave me too long smarting
or I will be left to cry and mope,
My heart full of love just starting,
and alone now it's hard to cope,
The solution you must be charting,
hidden in the trunk of rope?
Affix us soon,
Jacqueline

Never one for poetry, I thought my poem hokey and yet it certainly made my point. I thought he would get a kick out of it and at the least appreciate the effort.

On my way to his house to loop the knot over his door knob, I decided to swing by my mother's house before heading back to my apartment. I quickly hung the rope with the tag on his door, ran back to my car and peeled out. Seeing him would not help my resolve.

I parked my VW along the road next to my mother's home. A car I didn't recognize sat in the driveway. Peering into the mirror on the visor, I took in my reflection. I could still see the pain in my blue-green eyes and hoped my mother would miss it. After ringing the doorbell, I heard feet shuffling and a child's laugh. Samantha opened the door.

"I wasn't expecting to see you," I said as I stepped inside.

"I'm living here now." She placed Sarah down, and my niece tottered over to me.

"How is the cutest girl I know?" I lifted her into the air and she giggled.

"Momma is the pretty," she said and squirmed to have me put her down.

"Your mother is pretty, that's true, but you're still the

cutest, smartest little girl I know."

She gave me a smile filled with mischief and ran off toward the kitchen.

"She's really got the walking down," I said.

Samantha paused and tilted her head. "What is it?"

"I don't want to talk about it."

"We used to talk about everything."

"That was ages ago and I came by to see Mom. How's she doing?"

"Believe it or not, we're both doing great. I know Mom asked you to talk to Lainie, but I called her myself. She's going to give me a shot on a trial basis."

"Don't you fuck this up. I'll never forgive you if you fuck this up."

"Look Jacqs, I know I've given you reasons—"

"Plenty of reasons—"

"Yeah, I know. I get it. I am attending meetings now but not AA or NA." She scrunched her face as if the very idea pained her. "It's a group through the therapist I'm seeing and I think it's helping. I mean, Mom and I are getting along, and that must mean progress, right?"

"What changed?"

"Darren wanted me to stop seeing Sarah and went so far as demanding I give her up. He did me a favor in a way because his insistence that Sarah was the cause of my drinking made me really stop and take stock. I realized it was preposterous and decided it was time to get some help, from a female therapist this time."

"Sounds like a move in the right direction. I want things to be better between us, and that's going to take some time. My trust level with you is pretty low." I perched on the arm of the couch next to me and looked up at her.

"You can talk to me, you know. I would never, have

never betrayed your confidence. You don't look like yourself today, and I'm worried about you."

I laughed out loud and said, "That's a change, isn't it."

She smiled and took my arm, leading me into the kitchen where mom worked on dinner and chatted with Sarah.

"This is a nice surprise. Will you stay for dinner?"

My first instinct was to say no, but my stomach growled in hunger. "I'd love to." I picked up a stalk of celery and scooped into the dip. "What can I do to help?"

"I'm almost done. Why don't you and Samantha go catch up?" She held her arms out to give me a hug, keeping her wet hands in the air.

I glanced over my mother's shoulder and saw my sister nodding. "I'll be right back," I said to Sarah. Sarah waved to us as I followed Samantha to her room. "Looks pretty much the same."

"Yeah, I'm inclined to change it, but Sarah loves the purple walls," she said as she sat down on her queen size bed. She smoothed the patchwork quilt on either side of her. "It's not like I plan to bring anyone home anyway. I'm done with men for a while."

"That seems wise." I turned her white desk chair around and sat facing her.

"So what gives? Bond again?"

"Yes and no and ... it's way more complicated than that."

"Did Red finally make a move?"

I crossed my legs and hunched forward. "Jesus! Am I the only person who had no idea?"

"It's not like I was one hundred percent sure, but I did see him watching you a lot."

My eyes watered against my control, and Samantha reached out to touch my hand.

"I'm in love with Red and—"

"And Bond?"

"Him too, but he seems determined to rip our group apart." I breathed out heavily, trying to release the pressure in my chest. "He fucked Blue recently and yet Red is off limits to me. Of course, he was shitfaced when he did it and there were extenuating circumstance but—"

"You know I'm not a fan of AA, but he's a perfect candidate. We addicts recognize each other."

"I don't think he'd ever go. He'd actually have to look at himself, and I'm not sure he's capable of it." I blinked several times, not wanting to give into the tears.

"I probably understand that better than anyone. So where do things stand now?" She swept her blond hair to the side and ran her finger through it.

"Nowhere. I told them that they have to work out their friendship first, and so far Bond is unwilling."

"How much time will you give him?"

I uncrossed my legs and rubbed my thighs. "I don't know. It's not just him, you know. I don't want our group to have to pick sides."

"You have no control over that. My therapist says that I need to stop focusing on the things I have no control over and concentrate on the things I do."

"Maybe you can ask her what someone should do if they love two men."

Samantha laughed, which made me smile. It was the first time in forever I heard a sober chuckle from her.

"What's so funny?" I asked in faux indignation.

"I'm finding some stability in my life and you're mired in chaos."

"You don't know the half of it."

"Well, I appreciate you sharing what you have. I'll do my best not to let you down again."

"Mom's probably holding dinner for us," I said and

stood up, stretching out my lower back.

"Yeah, probably." Samantha rose and stepped forward for a hug. "I've missed you."

"Me too. Thanks for listening."

We walked out of her room into the main part of the house. Sarah was climbing up in the chairs, placing napkins over the flatware.

"Ready, girls?"

"Definitely," I said, taking my usual seat.

Samantha placed Sarah in the highchair next to her. It had been years since the three of us, and now with Sarah, sat down for a meal. My mother seemed beside herself with joy. I realized that my mother's pain wasn't just the loss of my father, but of her youngest daughter as well. Maybe she was right and letting Samantha move back home would prove to be a good decision. I certainly hoped it would.

Family time, which in the past few years had been mostly stressful, turned out to be the very thing I needed. Watching Samantha take care of Sarah melted more of my anger toward my sister.

I left full and feeling somewhat better. Desperately needing a good night of sleep, I planned to crash as soon as I slipped off my clothes and crawled into bed.

On my doorstep rested a noose around an octopus's neck. I laughed so hard, clutching my belly. I knew Red referenced Bond's fascination with all things 007. *Octopussy*. Apparently it was Red's idea of "affixing" the problem. I picked up the stuffed octopus and found a note safety-pinned to the back of its head. After removing it from the toy, I unfolded the paper and read:

Dearest Budding Poetess and Knotter,

Thank you for the adjustable bend. Expect me to use those knots the next time we're alone. The poem was clever, Little One, and the whole presentation not only cracked me up but provided me much needed hope of my own.

I'm certain the octopus is self-explanatory but might I remind you that Bond's clock is ticking? One week from Monday you'll be in my domain and avoiding each other is neither practical nor desired. My patience, waning with each moment we are apart, will come at a cost. I hope that little ass of yours is prepared for the fallout.

Your Neanderthal,
Aidan

I skipped inside with a smile on my face. Somehow I had let it slip my mind that I would be working at Aidan's office. Bond did have a deadline of sorts, and I thought it best to make him aware of it. It certainly didn't resolve the issue of our mutual friends and I wouldn't ignore my sister's advice. I would focus on the things I could control.

After changing into my PJs, I turned on my iPod. Sitting on my bed, I contemplated reaching out to Bond. I woke up my phone and dialed Lainie first.

"Hey girl," she said as she answered.

"How goes it?" I lay back against my pillows and turned down the volume on the music.

"I'm more concerned about you. How are you?"

"Better than you'd expect. I went by my mother's and had dinner with her, Sam, and Sarah. It was a nice change. Sam said you offered her a job."

"On a trial basis. Hopefully it'll work out. She has some great ideas for the window displays and I could use the help." Lainie inhaled, and I wondered if she'd started smoking cigarettes again.

"As long as you know what you're doing. She could start using again anytime and—"

"I'm willing to take the risk as long as she is attending group and working on herself. She understands this."

"Thank you, Lainie. I'm still not sure it's the best idea, but I'm counting on Sam to prove me wrong."

"Back to you, how are you?"

I sat up and said, "I've been better, but as Red pointed out, we'll be working in the same office come a week from Monday. Bond's time is running out. I'm considering calling him but wanted to talk to you first."

"Calling Red or Bond? You've seen Red?"

"Talk to Bond and no, I haven't seen Red but we have been leaving messages for each other. He started with a bouquet of roses."

"Ah," Lainie said. "Now I see why you're feeling better. What'll you say to Bond?"

"I have no idea really. He left me several texts that pulled on my heart so I stopped reading them and three voicemails which I haven't listened to."

"Be honest and maybe shoot him an email instead of a phone call. That way you're sure to say everything you need to."

"Bond isn't much for the online stuff, but maybe I'll send a long text."

"I think that's better than talking to him. He's proficient at manipulating your heart even over the phone. Plus making him wait—"

"I'm worried he'll show up here if he doesn't hear from me." I stood up and began pacing. I thought I heard Lainie inhaling again and said, "Are you back to smoking?"

"Let's focus on you, Jacqs."

"Bullshit, girl. What's going on?" I stopped pacing

and sat on the edge of the bed.

"I think you should text Bond and get some sleep. I know you didn't sleep much last night."

"This day does seem endless, but you have to promise to tell me what gives soon. I love you, and I'm worried about you."

"I know. We'll talk soon. Let me know how it goes with Bond. Are we still on for Sunday?"

"Yeah, see you then and expect to tell me what the hell's going on with you."

"Bye, Jacqs."

"Bye."

What the fuck, I thought. Lainie was supposed to be the together one. I would get to the bottom of it on Sunday.

I brought my feet up onto the bed and started a very long text to Bond:

> **Me:** I read some of your text but not all of them and did not listen to your voicemails. I'm still alive. I left work early and went to a hot yoga class. I really
> **Me:** needed it. It's not that I thought this would be easy and when I first started considering Red I was so hurt by you that I didn't care what you might think.
> **Me:** Honestly, at first I didn't think you would care since you'd taken me for granted for so long. I see now that you really believe that you care. I'm not sure
> **Me:** what to say other than that I want you to sort out your friendship with Red. I start working at his company in a week and ½ and therefore will see him.
> **Me:** If you want to be a part of my life, you need

to start looking at yourself and what you bring,
have brought to the table. I don't want what we've
had and at
Me: this point I'm not looking for exclusivity with
you. Our friendship hangs in the balance here,
Bond, and if you can't find a way to be happy for
me and still
Me: be in my life, then I'm worried about our
friendship. Do not come by here or contact me
until something has changed. I love you and
always will but it's time for
Me: me to love myself more.

I reread the long text and hit send before I could change my mind. Turning up the music to drown out my thoughts, I stripped off my PJs and climbed under the covers.

CHAPTER FIFTEEN

I'm Not Calling You a Liar (Ghost)

by Florence + the Machine

M usic swirled around me as I drifted off to sleep.

Bang, bang, bang startled me and I slipped on my robe—it floated over my shoulders—as I ran to answer the door. While running the silk peeled off me and rained down around my feet causing me to stumble. I caught the doorknob in my hand as I fell forward and pushed my body upright. I untangled myself and slipped the robe back on.

Opening the front door wide, I watched Bond and Red storm into my apartment. Red showed up dressed as a biker in black leather boots and jacket and Bond wore chinos and a button down short-sleeved plaid shirt.

"What the hell is going on?" I asked as I shut the front door.

"You can no longer call him Red," Bond shouted. "I take the name back."

"Whatever you say, *Mitchell*," Red responded sarcastically, drawing out his name.

I glanced down at my body, and found I was naked once again. I wrapped my right arm around my breasts and covered my mound with my left hand. Jerking my head toward the door, I said, "I want you both to leave. I told you to work things out between you first."

"I know how to sort this out, here and now," Red said, taking a giant step toward me. "We will fuck her together."

"What? No, definitely not!" I yelled as I ran to my room, trying to shut and lock the door behind me.

Bond shoved his arm in the door, barring me from closing it. "I agree with Aidan. Don't fight it; it will happen, one way or another."

"Leave me alone!" I shouted.

"Leave me alone," Bond and Red mocked me simultaneously. They laughed and slapped each other on the back as Bond pushed open the door.

"Shh, Little One," Red said as he entered the room and stood like a sentinel at my side. "Don't fight us," he whispered softly.

I stood up tall and straightened my back, trying not to be intimidated. "No. I want you both to leave," I said, pointing to the door.

Red patted me on the head and said, "She has rope here somewhere."

"I know where to look," Bond said, and left the room.

"This is a really bad idea, please take Bond and go."

Red lifted me under my arms and pressed my back against the wall. As soon as his lips lowered to mine, I became supple and willing. "That's better," he said.

Wetness gathered in my pussy, my desire and need flaring. I felt suspended in air, light as a feather.

Red pressed his hardness against me and whispered, "Just remember whom you belong to."

Before I had a chance to respond, Bond returned with the same rope I had used to tie the adjustable bend. "I want to fuck her mouth first. Put her down." Bond spun me around and started to tie my wrists together behind my back.

"Let me do that, you have no finesse." Red took over and crisscrossed the rope over my chest and upper back, making double loops around my upper arms to constrain them.

I felt the rope drop down my sides.

Coiling the cordage about my forearms, he constructed a tight knot and finally bound my wrists together with a last tug. He positioned me in front of my full length mirror so I could see the art in his handy work. In front an *X* crossed my chest and in the back another crossed my upper back followed by a diamond shape down to my wrist.

"On your knees," Bond ordered. "I'll be right back."

Lowering down to my carpeted bedroom floor, I peered up and saw a stern look on Red's face. "It's not my fault," I said, starting to shake.

"Are you calling me a liar?" His green eyes grew dark, and I could feel his love slipping away.

"No, no, of course not. Please. But why like this?"

"It's the only way—"

Bond came back into the room naked, cock erect and throbbing, holding a flogger.

"Oh, no," I said in desperation, trying to scoot away in my kneeling position.

Not giving me a chance to escape, he clutched the nape of my neck and hoisted his hard erection into the back of my throat. "Oh, yes, just where I belong."

271

I squirmed, trying to catch a breath and a glimpse of Red. *He must be steaming mad*, I thought.

Bond garnered my full attention by whipping the flogger against my back and ass several times.

"Ahhh," I groaned, half in pain and half in pleasure.

Red escalated my body's torment by kneeling behind me and wrapping his arms around my sides so he could yank on my nipples.

"See if you use her just right," Bond said to Red, "you can have your way with her."

Red got up, stood in my line of sight and said, "What makes you think I haven't?"

Bond forced his cock deeper into my throat, stroking hard back and forth, causing my eyes to water. "Like this? I don't think so."

"No, but she's taken my cock in her ass over and over, stretching her deep and filling her full of my come."

I jerked my head back and lowered down onto my butt. "That's not true, only once!" I screamed.

"Are you calling me…"

I awoke with tears in my eyes and my heart pounding rapidly. Relief flowed over me and once my equilibrium returned, I realized the dream had aroused my body. *That's what I get for researching bondage online and listening to Florence and the Machine while I'm falling asleep.* I shut off the music feeling disgusted with myself.

Stress caused me to remember my twisted dreams. My mind worried me sometimes. Red in Bond's clothes looked ridiculous, and I couldn't fathom what it might mean. The whole scene seemed out of some horrible spoof movie. I had to accept that sharing me would never be an option. Even in my dream life it didn't turn out well.

Rolling onto my stomach, I tried to get comfortable enough to fall back to sleep. After tossing and turning for about thirty minutes, I still couldn't get the dream out of my head. I felt exhausted and spent and really wanted all of the drama gone.

Giving into my amped up libido, I spread my thighs wide, shoved a pillow under my right knee and snaked my hand down my stomach to my pussy and thought about the good parts of the dream: Red's kiss and how wet it made me, my hardened nipples when Red bound my arms behind me, Bond's cock down my throat, his masculine scent filling my nose, the anticipation of them both taking me at once and filling my pussy and ass.

I smothered my orgasmic cries into my pillow, riding the tidal wave of release. I fell on my arm, rolled to the side and hugged the pillow to me. After a few minutes, I finally drifted back to sleep, still floating in the high of my climax.

I still remembered the crazy dream I had with Red and Bond, but thankfully couldn't recall any more once my alarm sounded.

Training didn't start until Monday so I spent my time at the office helping Tom with marketing. Henry left me alone, and when I saw him duck out early, I also left for the day.

On my way to my car I received a call from my doctor's office. The STD test results came back negative. I stopped by the store on my way home and shopped for dinner. I planned to attempt, once again, the perfect pan-seared scallops.

After re-watching the segment on the Food Network, I tried to replicate what I saw. First I fixed the wilted greens with garlic, shallots, wine, soy sauce and spices. As I spooned the butter repeatedly over the shellfish, I fantasized about having a dinner party at Red's like he and I discussed. Bond and Red had forgiven each other and all our friends, including Samantha, attended. We extended the tablecloth covered dining room table to accommodate everyone. In my daydream, I observed all the people closest to me enjoying the food and having a good time.

However, I knew it wouldn't be that simple. Nothing ever was. I tried my best to savor the meal, but I felt lonely, tired, and scared. I should have gone to another hot yoga class on my way home to burn off some of my anxieties.

Cleaning the kitchen distracted me for a bit, but after I put away the last dish, the rest of the night loomed in front of me like an endless trek through the desert. I decided to tackle my ever growing pile of laundry. Right after adding the detergent and setting the load to wash, my phone rang. I ran out into the living room and answered without looking.

"Jacqs," a voice said.

"Yeah," I responded, plopping down on the couch.

"It's Stay."

"Hey Stay, what's up?"

"Bond is a wreck and won't be able to work tonight."

For a fraction of a second I was relishing Stay's interruption. That ended quickly. "It's not like I can fill in for him."

"That's not what I meant."

"Okay, so what did you mean?" I hunched forward and rested my forehead in my palm.

"Bond showed me your text and he's falling apart."

"Fuck, Stay. I don't know what to tell you." I popped up and started pacing. "I'm a wreck too."

"He loves you, Jacqs, he's just—"

"He's just what? According to my sister, and she probably knows better than anyone, Bond's an alcoholic and not a very well-functioning one."

"So am I."

"Get the fuck out of town. Is that why you never drink?"

"I don't broadcast it, but yes. I learned back in college that I couldn't control myself, so I stopped several years ago. In all honesty, I'm not sure he's an alcoholic in the traditional sense, but I think getting off alcohol for a while will help him deal with what's hiding underneath. He's already promised he would come to a meeting with me tonight."

"While he was drunk? He probably won't even remember and doubt that he would ever go."

"He's not drunk, Jacqs. At this point, he's willing to do just about anything and he said he planned to do whatever it took to fix things between you."

"Great, he just has to make up with Red and all will be well."

"I don't see that happening anytime soon."

"Then clearly he didn't mean *whatever it takes*." I hated being sarcastic and felt my venom surfacing. "Look, I don't want to take this out on you. I'm just not sure why you called me."

"If you would talk to him, I think it would help."

"I didn't fall in love with Red to spite Bond. I'm not even seeing Red right now and I have no idea why I'm punishing myself this way other than out of respect for Bond and our friends. I'm sorry, I don't see how talking to him is going to help either of us."

"I think if he hears your voice, it will calm him down."

"I don't know—hey, I have another call. Can you hold for a sec?" I clicked over and said, "Hi, this is Jacqs."

"Hi Jacqueline, this is Ted. I'm sorry to bother you on a Friday evening, but something has come up with Cynthia and I wanted to catch you before Monday."

"Oh." My stomach dropped, and I thought he would tell me he no longer needed me.

"She's having some complications with her pregnancy and her doctor would like her to stop working as soon as she can. Is it possible for you to come in this week for a few hours each day? We can work around your schedule."

I paused for a moment and said, "I'll figure something out. Expect me in the afternoon on Monday. I'll send an email when I have a better idea of what time I'll make it."

"You're a lifesaver. Thank you so much and see you on Monday."

I clicked back over to my call with Stay and said, "Give him the phone."

"You're the best!" Stay said.

"Jacqs," Bond said.

"It's me."

"Baby, I'm sorry." He breathed out heavily, and I heard the pain in his voice. "I know I'm not making this easy on you. I just can't lose you. My life doesn't make any sense without you in it."

"I'm not sure what to say to you. I understand you need time to forgive Red but I'm asking you to try. This isn't easy for any of us."

"Just hearing your voice has helped. Thank you for taking the call. If you give me a chance, I promise I won't hurt you again."

"I think we all need some time."

"Okay, I'll give you space. I love you, baby." I heard him hand the phone back to Stay.

"Listen, I need to go and send some emails," I said. "I'll be seeing Red sooner than I thought. That was his office calling, and I need to go in next week."

"Thank you for talking to him," Stay said.

"I'm not sure it helped anything. I don't want to hurt

him. It's the last thing I want. I must say I hope you're putting as much pressure on Bond to resolve his issues with Red."

"I'm working on it."

"Got to go."

"I'll be in touch."

I emailed Cara and Star, the two part-timers in the office, and Steven to try to cover the afternoons of training starting Monday. Anticipating Henry's wrath from my early departure and abandonment of my duties, I emailed him as well so it wouldn't come as a surprise.

I broke down and texted Red:

> **Me:** I will be at the office starting Monday afternoon.
> **Red:** I heard from Ted as well. Lunch before or dinner after.
> **Me:** Red!
> **Red:** We can't avoid each other at the office. Plus, Little One, I need you in my bed. I need you in my life.
> **Me:** I got a call from Stay pleading with me to talk to Bond.
> **Red:** What did you do?
> **Me:** I spoke to him briefly because I hate to know he's hurting so badly. I don't think it changed anything.
> **Red:** He needs time.
> **Me:** I need to get out of here. I'm going to text Lainie and see if she'll meet me for a drink. See you Monday.

I didn't wait for his response.

> **Me:** Hey girl, are you out tonight? Want to get a

> drink or catch a movie or something? I need to get
> the hell out of the house.

I switched the wash into the dryer and waited to hear back from Lainie. Plopping down on the couch, I put a pillow under my head and zoned out to the TV until I dozed off.

> Looking back, I saw my younger self watch as my father and Samantha climbed out of the station wagon, freshly caught fish in hand. I forced down my feeling of inadequacy and smiled as they approached.
>
> "Look Jackie, we caught four today! I reeled one in myself," Samantha said, her chest out in pride.
>
> "I can see that," I said as I followed them into the house.
>
> "Be nice to your sister," Dad admonished.
>
> My smile vanished, and I steamed with anger.
>
> "Give these to your mom," he said, handing the fish over to Samantha and pushing her on her way.
>
> He rested his hands on my shoulders and leered down at me. "She needs more attention than you do, Jacqs. There are just some people you should put ahead of yourself, put ahead of yourself, put ahead of yourself, put ahead of yourself."
>
> "Stop it, Dad, you're repeating yourself again."
>
> "There are just some people who matter more than you, more than you, way more than you, Jacqueline."
>
> "That's not true," my nine-year-old self screamed. I shifted left and right, jostling to get out from under his grip. The struggle caused me to wake up.

My father never said those things to me in real life,

but it didn't stop me from feeling them. I sat up on the couch, dazed. My brain spun frantically until my pulse settled down. I grabbed my phone from the coffee table seeing that it was already 1:45 a.m. I didn't care. I called Red deciding to put myself first for a change.

"Hello," a groggy Red answered.

"Is it okay if I come over?"

I could hear him moving around and what sounded like him rubbing his beard. "Of course, Jacqs. Are you okay?"

"Not really. I keep having these bad dreams, and I want to be in your arms. I want to feel safe."

"When are you leaving?"

"In five minutes?"

"Great. Can't wait to have you back in my bed. Drive safe."

I hung up the call, changed into street clothes and brushed my teeth. A spontaneous smile crossed my face when I realized I would soon be with the man I loved ... at least one of them.

CHAPTER SIXTEEN

Stay

by Rihana (ft. Mikky Ekko)

Not one to overanalyze dreams or my motivations, I couldn't help but clearly see what my psyche shouted to me. I had been trained to put everyone before me, and it was high time for that to stop.

Hopping on the highway to Red's, my heart jumped in excitement. I could almost feel the warmth of his arms wrapped around me. As I drove down the exit and entered the empty road, I sang along with Rihana.

The light changed, and I pulled into the intersection just before noticing bright lights to my right. Although every single second seemed to be slow and exacting, I had no chance to react. As I crossed the intersection, a vehicle without form, floating through the haze of light, hit the back passenger side of my car. My car spun and I could hear myself scream but I felt far away from the sound. The first car I had ever bought for myself crashed against a light post on the right side of the road. The airbags deployed just as my head smacked against the driver's side window. I passed out.

A man clad in white spread my eye wide open and waved a flash light in front of me. I blinked my eyes rapidly and tried to sit up.

"Don't," he said, pressing my shoulder back down.

"I need to go, someone is waiting for me." I pushed at

his arm.

"Sh. All you need to do is relax. We're taking you to the hospital, and we've already let your family know."

"But how?"

"You gave us the numbers," he said and strapped my head down to the board underneath me.

"I did? I don't remember—" I tried to shift my head but it was locked in place. Lights flashed all around me, and as they lifted me into the ambulance, I saw the wreck that was once my car and started to panic. "Am I okay? Why don't I feel any pain?"

"It's self-protection, your body's chockfull of adrenaline right now. Let's get you to the hospital and have you checked out."

"Okay," I mumbled and drifted away again.

The next time I came to, I lay in a white room with equipment bleeping around me. I noticed Bond crying in a chair to the right of me. In all the years I had known him, I had never seen him shed a tear. My mother, Lainie and Stay were huddled by the door whispering. Red sat hunched over in the chair beside me and held my hand.

"I'm okay," I whispered but only Red seemed to hear. He lifted a cup of water with a straw and brought it to my mouth. The relief on his face caused my eyes to water.

"Bond," Red said, as he brushed my hair away from my face.

"Holy hell, Jacqs," Bond said as he scooted his chair up next to me.

"So is this what I have to do to get you guys in the same room?" I laughed slightly, but it caused my head to hurt.

"You're in pain," Red said, standing. "I'll go get the nurse."

"I'll do it," Bond said, new tears wetting his cheeks. He

dashed to the door and tapped my mother on the shoulder.

She approached me and kissed me on the forehead. "I'm so relieved. I'll be right back. I promised to call your sister. She's worried sick."

"Girl, you gave us a fright," Lainie said, crouching down beside me. "Don't do that again."

"Yes, ma'am," I said.

She leaned in close to my ear and said, "Bond and Red have been civil with each other. I even saw them hug."

"All part of my master plan." I closed my eyes against the bright lights.

I felt a vise grip squeeze on my hand, and I croaked, "Hey!"

"You need to stay awake, Jacqs," Red said. "They did a CAT scan and that lovely head of yours is fine, but they don't like that you keep checking out for spans of time.

"How long have I been out?"

"I've been here for at least three hours," Stay said. "Red called me at about two-thirty."

I held my hand out to him. "Thank you for coming. For me and for Bond."

"Always."

Bond came back in with a nurse in tow.

"I hear you've got a pretty good headache. That's not surprising." To Red she said, "I suggest we ice the left side of her head again, and I'll give her something for the pain after I take her vitals."

"Sounds good," Red said.

I found it unexpected and heartwarming that Red seemed to be in charge of my care.

As if he could hear my thoughts, he said, "You're coming home with me once they let you out."

"Will you be my personal nurse?"

"You'll get a full dose of my bedside manner." He

twitched his eyebrows.

"Don't make me laugh," I said, struggling to suppress a giggle.

After the nurse took my blood pressure and temperature she injected something into my IV causing me to immediately relax.

"Get some of that stuff," I mumbled to Red.

"I'll be right back with a bag of ice," the nurse said as she passed my mother on the way out of the room.

"How's she doing?" my mother asked Red.

"She has no choice other than to live because Bond and I would chase her to hell and back if she left us."

"Absolutely," Bond said.

Their solidarity stunned me.

"Me too," Lainie said.

"Me three," Stay said, catching Lainie's eye. Something passed between them, and I hoped Lainie would give him a chance.

"Jacqueline, I promised Samantha that as soon as I knew you were going to be okay I would come back home and let her come here."

"Does anyone know when they'll be letting me out of this place?"

"I'll go find out," Red said.

"Maybe Sam can come to Red's once I get out of here? What time is it now?"

"It's almost six in the morning," Lainie said.

"You have to open the shop soon, girl."

"You let me worry about that. You scared the shit out of me—out of all of us. Don't do it again."

"I have no intention. How is the other driver?"

Red strolled back and tossed the bag of ice to Bond who held it against my head. "They'll let you go today but the doctor has to be the one to sign you out. It could still be a few hours."

"You're in good hands," my mother said. "I need to go have a good cry and get some sleep before Samantha goes into work."

"I love you, Mom. I'm sorry to have worried you."

She stared at me for a moment, smoothed my hair and said, "Take care of her." She seemed to be struggling not to cry as she headed for the door.

"I'll walk out with you," Lainie said. She bent down and embraced me gently. "Call me after you get settled at Red's."

"I will," I said, hugging her back.

Lainie grabbed Stay's arm, and he winked at me, his half-cocked smile lighting up his face.

After they all had left, an awkward silence filled the room. I peered up at Bond and really took in his appearance. His arrogant veneer seemed to be missing. Touching his hand, I guided the ice away from my head. "It's getting too cold."

"Damn, Jacqs." Bond breathed out heavily. "Red said I can stay with him until you're well."

"You would do that?" I asked with my eyes opened wide.

"At this point, I'd do just about anything. I can't lose you too." Tears regrouped in the wells of his eyes and threatened to spill over again.

I glanced over to Red and he nodded.

"I'll be happy to have you there, but how will you get to and from work."

"We'll sort that out," Red said.

Alone with Red and Bond, butterflies started to dance in my stomach. "Maybe I'm still passed out, because this doesn't seem real. I mean I'm happy you're both here, ecstatically so— Maybe I should just shut the fuck up." Was it too soon for me to hope that we would all be friends in the end?

"One day at a time," Bond said.

I reached out and held his hand. "No one has said. What happened to the other driver?"

"He is fine, although had Red let me punch him out as I intended, he wouldn't be so fine."

"Well, that's a relief. I saw what my car looked like but not his. I don't remember seeing him at the scene."

"He'll be doing jail time at any rate," Red said.

"Oh shit!" I shouted.

"What?" Bond and Red said simultaneously.

"I have to be juggling two jobs come Monday morning and—"

"Don't worry about that, Jacqs." Red touched my arm and said, "I'll talk to the boss for you. I have an in." He gave me a cheeky grin.

"Very funny," I said, fighting to keep my laugh at bay. Giggles threatened to surface and for a flash of a second, I felt I might be hallucinating. A cacophony of chuckles erupted until they morphed into tears.

Bond swept me up in his arms and held me tight. "You're going to be alright, Jacqs." He soothed my back as the sobs rolled through. The warmth of Red enveloped my back, and I felt his weight on the bed behind me. Sandwiched between the men I loved, I cried out all that had happened over the last few weeks and what I felt at the moment of the crash. My life didn't flash before me like it's told in stories and movies, but I did have one very powerful thought. That I was going to die before I had a chance to have a family, something I had convinced myself I didn't even want.

"We love you," Red whispered into my ear as we all broke apart.

"I need to ... step outside." I heard Bond's voice crack.

I held my arm out to him and said, "Stay. Please stay."

"I'll give you two a few minutes," Red said and stood

to leave.

"Thank you," I mouthed to him. I saw the love radiating from his eyes, and I prayed to the gods of life and love that I would be able to navigate between the two men who held my heart without hurting either of them.

Bond rose and paced away from the bed. He ran his fingers through his long brown hair and breathed out heavily. He pivoted to face me, his palms held out at his sides.

I witnessed a young vulnerable Bond and wanted to rescue him from his pain.

"There's something I need to tell you," he said.

"Okay..." I said, struggling to sit up.

Bond reached for the controls and pressed the button to raise the back of the bed.

"Thanks."

He placed his hands in his pockets and stared down at his feet. "I was in an accident years ago, before we met. I did prison time because the person in the car—" He glanced up at me and continued, "...my fiancé died, and her parents were determined to have me pay for her death. It's not that I blame them ... then or now ... and yes, we had been drinking."

"Bond—" I wanted to spare him the details of telling his story but he stopped me.

"Let me get this out, okay."

I didn't say anything more.

He paused, the pain etched across his forehead. He looked away and continued, "We were arguing as I drove us back to the condo—we lived together—because she kissed a mutual friend to get my attention. Well she got my attention; I put on quite a show before we left the party and decked the guy. I only had a couple of beers, but she had drunk a lot of tequila and when I yelled at her for embarrassing me in front of all of our friends, she punched my arm a bunch of times and I lost control of the car."

He sat down at the end of the bed and took another deep breath.

"I'm not blaming Celeste. I should have pulled over instead of fighting while we were on the road. I loved her, and although furious, I never ever wished her dead. I spent several weeks in the ICU and as soon as I got out, I was arrested for vehicular manslaughter."

We sat quietly for a few minutes until he said, "Well, say something."

"Sorry, I wasn't sure you were done. Please don't be mad at Lily but she told me some of it at Donny's promotion party."

"You've known since then?" He jerked upright and sat in the chair to the left of me.

"Honestly, I had hoped you would tell me yourself and I—I didn't think it was my place to bring it up." I reached out and touched his arm. "Don't be angry with me or Lily. She assumed I knew before I had a chance to stop her."

"And you don't care?" He furrowed his brow and squinted his eyes.

"Of course I care. It explains so much about you; why you would never really let me in; why you don't drive; why one person would never be enough. And I hurt for you, Bond. No one should have to go through such a thing." I patted the bed and Bond scooted in next to me. Throwing my arms around him, I squeezed tightly. "Thank you for telling me and trusting me with the truth." We held onto each other for a few minutes.

Once we broke apart, Bond said, "When Red called me, I let it go to voicemail. I had no intention of speaking to him, ever. He had stolen the one person in the world I could never live—"

"I'm still here—"

"Let me finish," he said, his expression serious.

"Sorry," I said meekly.

"When Stay called me and told me you had been in an accident and that I might lose you for good, I heard the echo of Celeste's voice in my head. She said that it's really up to me whether I lose you or not. Maybe it's the withdrawal from alcohol or my present and past colliding in a way that's too close to the truth—"

"You haven't lost me, Bond."

"In a way, I have, and I'm really the only one to blame. You were right; I didn't want to have to look at myself. Stay pointed that out several times over the last few weeks."

"Remind me that I owe him a big hug." I laughed.

Bond harrumphed and scrunched his eyebrows.

Red ducked his head into the room. "Is safe to enter?"

"Two more minutes and then please come back," I said. I already missed his healing presence.

"Sure," he said and closed the door behind him.

"Are you sure it's a good idea for you to stay at Red's? You'll be trapped there. I mean, it'd be great to have you, but I don't want to restart the feud and I'm not sure I could—"

"As Stay has drilled into me, if I want you in my life, I have to get over my shit. I'm making no promises other than I'm working on it."

"That's good enough for me."

"I love you, Jacqs and I'm going to show you that I mean it."

"Good." Somehow the weight of his disclosures lightened the pain from the past. "I have a question if you're up for it."

"Anything."

"The tattoo that you covered over?"

"I had it done in prison to honor Celeste but it was done so poorly I had it reworked. I consider it fixed not covered over."

"That makes sense. Thanks for telling me. Damn, I'm exhausted. Can you lower the bed down a bit and get Red?"

He kissed me lightly on the lips and stared into my eyes. "Don't go anywhere."

"Where would I go?" I chuckled.

"Just saying..."

Red followed Bond back into the room.

"Are you thirsty? Do you need another pillow?" Red asked.

"Water would be good and maybe some food? My stomach is stirring up a racket."

"I'll go ask the staff about some food," Bond said and left the room.

Red held up the cup with the straw, and I sipped the water. "How did it go?"

"He told me about the accident." I was just about to ask Red to hold me when he slipped in behind me and wrapped me up in his warm embrace.

"I thought he might. That's progress."

Caressing the hair on his forearm, I sighed back into him and closed my eyes.

"No going to sleep," he whispered in my ear. "I'll pinch those big nipples of yours if I have to, to keep you awake."

"You are a meany," I said as I melted into Red, feeling so relaxed.

"You really scared me, Jacqs. I'm not sure I'll ever let you out of my sight again."

"Tie me down to the bed?"

"You have no idea. I need to find out how long we have to wait until I'm allowed to penetrate all of your orifices." He pulled the hair away from my neck and nibbled.

"That's sure ... to keep me awake." I giggled.

"That's a wonderful sound."

"Thank you for being here, Red."

"There is no place I'd rather be than beside you, but I'll be happy once we're back home."

"Yeah, me too. Listen, are you sure about Bond staying at your place? He seems different but I'm worried—"

"Let me do the worrying. All you have to do is recover and let us take care of you."

I turned to the side to see his face. "I love you," I said, cupping his cheeks and pulling his mouth to mine. Even through the haze of the painkiller, the storm of our attraction surged and I could feel my body responding.

"Get a room," Bond said, carrying in a tray of food and placing it on the rolling table.

"We're in one, silly," I said, leaning forward so Red could get out from behind me.

"Good thing you don't have a roommate," Bond said, pointing to the bed on the other side of the room.

"You mean other than yourself?"

"Very funny, Jacqs." Bond pressed the button that caused the bed to tilt upright so I could eat.

I adjusted myself so Bond could roll the food in front of me. Just as I took the first bite of scrambled eggs, the door to the room flung open.

"What the fuck," Cat said as she and Kev rushed into the room. "We just heard the message from Red when we got up."

"I'm okay, as you can see," I said and forked another mouthful of food.

"Don't do that again," Kev said with a look of panic.

"I don't plan on it."

"How's the car?" Cat asked, sitting down on the side of the bed.

"She's a goner."

"Damn, I always loved that car," Cat said, squeezing my leg.

"Yeah, me too."

Kev took my hand as I chewed. "I'm relieved to see you in one piece. I'm sorry to say we have to get going soon. We are off to breakfast at Momma Cat's house, which is always a sordid affair and quite the drive."

"I'm sitting right here," Cat said with displeasure.

"Come on, Cat, you hate being there after the first fifteen minutes. You know she never lets up."

"I'm allowed to diss her, not you."

"Right. Sorry love," he said, touching her shoulder and looking over at me with wide eyes.

I did my best not to laugh.

"When do you get sprung?" Kev asked.

"In a couple more hours," Red said. "She'll be staying at my place."

"That's a good idea," Cat said.

"And so will I," Bond said, folding his arms across his chest.

I touched his leg, trying to let him know that he needn't be defensive.

"That should be interesting," Kev said and flashed me a smile.

The door opened again, and the same nurse entered. "I'm about to go off duty and wanted to check your vitals one last time."

"Okay."

Kev and Cat waved goodbye, and Red shifted the food tray out of the way.

As the nurse took my blood pressure, she said, "The doctor should be in within the hour."

"Thanks," I said.

"Since you've been up for a while, it's fine for you to

sleep. Rest will help you heal."

"I thought she needed to stay awake with a concussion," Red said, stepping closer to the bed.

"No, and I'm sure the doctor will explain it all to you. They were just concerned because they couldn't rouse her for a while."

After the nurse had finished her vitals check, Bond lowered the bed, and I drifted into an easy drug-filled stupor.

"How's our patient doing?" I heard and blinked my eyes against the bright lights.

"Ready to go home," I croaked.

"That's a good sign," a man in a white coat said as he approached. He checked my pupils with his flashlight, causing me to squint. "Head still hurts?"

"I think the medicine the nurse gave me has started to wear off."

He palpated the back of my neck and asked, "Any stiffness?"

"Not that I can tell. Just some pain in my temples and the left side of my head."

"I'll write you a prescription for Tylenol with codeine. If you have a headache, stay away from other types of pain relievers like Motrin and Aspirin. If it's only a slight headache, then take plain Tylenol. You might find that your body is sore over the next few days. That's to be expected. Do what you feel you're up to and rest as often as possible. If you feel dizzy, stop what you're doing and rest. If you experience nausea, feeling like you're about to pass out, or the medicine isn't helping the headache, please come back into the emergency room or call my number."

"Is that likely?" Red asked, taking the prescription and the business card from the doctor.

"Her CAT scan looked fine so I imagine she just needs some rest and will be good as new but it's best to keep an eye on things."

"Thanks, doc," Bond said, shaking his hand.

"An orderly will be in to wheel you out," the doctor said. As he began to depart, Red patted him on the back and followed him out whispering something I couldn't hear.

❀ ❀ ❀ ❀ ❀

Once I was back in the clothes I arrived in, they settled me into the passenger side of Red's SUV. Bond climbed into the back.

"Where are we going?" I asked as I watched Red pull out in the opposite direction of his house.

"We're swinging by your apartment to get some of your things—"

"I have some clothes at your—" I stopped myself when I felt a shift of energy from the backseat. Then I thought of all the stuff I had in my car. "Shit, my bag and backpack, my cell phone and wallet. Where is all that stuff?"

"Probably still with the car," Bond said. He reached forward and touched my shoulder. "We can take care of that on Monday."

"Okay," I said, settling back into my seat.

After they filled my prescription, and we went by my place, Red headed to Bond's apartment.

"Listen, Jacqs..." Bond started.

"This is sounding like bad news," I said. I dropped the visor down so I could see Bond without turning my neck.

"I have to work tonight and pack up a few things. I'm going to sleep at my apartment today, and catch a ride to Red's after work."

"That makes sense." I worried that Bond would morph back into his old self.

"I'll leave work as soon as I can."

"Okay."

Red parked in front of Bond's building and just as Bond got out, he tapped on the glass.

I lowered the window and said, "Thank you so much for being there today ... or last night, I mean."

"Thank you for letting me," he said and bent down, so our eyes were level. "I love you and I'll see you soon." He touched my face and softly kissed my lips.

"Goodbye," I said. As Red pulled out into the road, I was scared to look in his direction. I rested my head against the door and closed my eyes.

CHAPTER SEVENTEEN

Let Her Go

by Jasmine Thompson

I felt real concern when Red settled me into his room. "Wouldn't it be better if I stayed in a neutral room?" I said, sorting through the PJs I had at his place. Although I preferred to sleep in the nude, I thought people might be stopping by.

"Unless you've changed your mind and now feel *neutral* about me—"

"No, of course not. I just meant since Bond will be staying here too."

"Put on the cute pink set with the red lips all over the bottoms," he whispered as hugged me from behind.

I stepped from his embrace and slipped on my low-slung, light-pink bottoms and bright pink top. "None of this is really necessary. I'm feeling fine now."

"Jacqs, you weren't *fine* until I picked up the prescription and you took another painkiller. You need to take a few days to rest. Do you have a hard time letting people take care of you?" He rubbed his beard in frustration.

"Are you missing the obvious?" Settling onto the bed, I yanked another pillow behind me, trying to get comfortable.

"Bond will either deal with it or he'll leave. Plus I want you to get used to being in my bed. I'm not letting you go."

"Well then, stop being all manly and come to bed. You must be exhausted."

"I'm going to take a quick shower and I'll be right back."

I reached for Red's phone that lay on the nightstand. Bringing up the text option, I tapped in Lainie's number.

> **Red:** Hey Lainie, it's me. I'm at Red's. In his bed actually. Are you at the shop? Is Sam with you?
> **Lainie:** Where's your phone? And yes, Sam's here. She just asked if she could stop by at lunch time.
> **Red:** My phone is still with the car. Maybe she can drop by after work? We're about to crash (no pun intended). I feel like I could sleep for a week.
> **Lainie:** Very funny. I'll tell her and thanks for checking in. Love you, girl.
> **Red:** Love you too. ☺

I clicked over to make a call and saw the incoming phone list. The name Tammy showed up six times. *Who the hell is Tammy?*

I dialed my mother and waited for her to pick up.

"Hi Mom."

"Hi Jacqueline," my mother said with a groggy voice.

"Oh, I'm sorry. I didn't mean to wake you."

"Not to worry. I decided to nap when Sarah went down for hers. Are you out of the hospital?"

"Yes, I'm at Red's and we plan to sleep for a while. I don't have my phone so you can reach me on this one."

"Okay. Maybe I can come over around dinner time and make a meal for everyone?"

I must have been overly emotional because her suggestion brought tears to my eyes. "That would be wonderful, Mom."

"Who's that? Are you okay?" Red said as he emerged from the bathroom, a towel low on his hips.

My mouth hung open for a second and I couldn't

believe the sexy, kind man in front of me was mine. "Uh ... it's my mother. She would like to come over later and make us all dinner."

He held his hand out for the phone. "Hi Josephine."

"How do you know my mother's name?" I mouthed.

"Yes, she's doing okay. She still has quite the headache once the meds wear off." He paused and said, "Yes, the doctor said that's to be expected."

I watched him listen to my mother's response.

"I'm hoping to convince her to stay here permanently." He shot me a sexy grin.

I fired back the meanest look I could muster.

He chuckled and said, "Yes, it will take some convincing. Okay, that sounds perfect. See you at five."

"What was that?" I said after he hung up. "And who is Tammy?"

Clutching his stomach and doubling over in laughter, he said, "Damn, Little One, you sure are cute when you get mad."

"Answer the questions," I said, slapping the mattress.

"Please don't get worked up. Your mother likes me. Isn't that a good thing?"

"How did you know her first name and getting her on your side isn't fair fighting."

"Are we fighting? You must've really banged your head. Come here." He dropped his towel and scooped me into his arms.

I couldn't help but relax and sighed, even though I felt cranky. Loving his warm skin from the shower, I snuggled tightly against him.

"That's better," he cooed. He kneaded my neck and rubbed my back. "Tammy is my executive assistant and she calls me often."

"I hope she's an old, ugly woman."

"She's not, but you don't have anything to worry about. You'll meet her as soon as you're well enough to go into the office."

He rolled me over so I lay on my stomach and yanked at my bottoms.

"What are you doing?" I said drowsily. The night had taken its toll. "What if someone comes by?" I waved his hands away.

"No one will be here before dinner time and I'm about to massage you from neck to toe, so just enjoy." He shed me of my PJs.

"You mean, 'shut up and enjoy.'"

"Yes, something like that." His big hands spread out over my body, kneading and smoothing out all the tension.

I dozed off to his gentle manipulations.

A bright light flashed before my eyes and just before my car crashed, I jerked upright in the bed, breathing heavily.

"Are you okay?" Red asked, touching my thigh.

"Just a bad dream."

"The accident?"

"Yeah." I smoothed my hair and took a couple of deep breaths. "What time is it?"

Red checked his phone. "It's just about three."

"I'm going to shower and brush my teeth."

"How's your head?"

"My left side is throbbing a bit, but it's not too bad." I scooted out of the bed and headed for the bathroom.

After washing up, I crawled back into bed, still somewhat in a daze from the events and the pain meds.

"How was the shower?" Red asked. "Did you feel dizzy at all?"

"No, but the side of my head is still a little tender."

"We should ice it *when* we go downstairs."

"Oh yeah, what do you have in mind?"

"Only if you're up for it," he said, snuggling me in close.

"Apparently you are," I said, reaching down to feel his silky hard erection. "Oh that reminds me, the doctor's office called and I'm all clear."

"I wasn't worried or we would have waited. Once I had found out Bond always wears a condom, my concerns lessened."

"Clearly," I said, stroking his steely shaft.

"I'll be gentle and I completely understand if you aren't feeling up for sex right now."

"Can we play it by ear?"

"How about playing it by tongue?" he said with a devilish grin.

"Don't make me laugh," I said, pushing at his chest.

"Lie on your back for me. If, at any point, your head starts to hurt let me know."

I placed a pillow under my head.

Expecting him to tongue my clit, he surprised me by starting at my feet with a luxurious massage. Slowly and thoroughly he kneaded his way up my legs to my upper thighs. Gently stroking the inner crevice leading to my mound, he spread me wide and blew across my growing wetness. He caressed my hips and waist using his big hands to work his way under my breasts.

My nipples strained for attention, and he didn't make them wait. Brushing across my hard tips, he made me crave more. I arched my back toward him, and he lightly rested his palm across my chest.

"Don't strain, love or I'll have to stop."

"Then don't tease me," I said with a pout.

He tilted his mouth to mine and sucked my bottom lip. I gazed up into his eyes, and my heart skipped a beat. *This incredible man loves me, wants me*, I thought.

He seemed to witness the change in my eyes as they started to water. "Am I hurting you?"

The last thing I wanted was to cry. "Not at all, I..."

"I understand." He plied his soothing hands down my shoulders, kissed my forehead and eyes and finally my mouth again.

I let all the tension go and stopped worrying about the tears that fell down the sides of my face, vowing to let his healing love and touch sink in.

He nibbled and sucked my nipples. "I love your petite body."

"She loves you too." I groaned in pleasure as he pushed my legs open wide.

He spread my labia and fingered my wetness. "So wet and your smell is exquisite."

"Exquisite huh? Well then, what are you waiting for?"

"You are the impatient one today. Remind me to spank that beautiful ass of yours once you're all better and I can manhandle you again."

I reached down and brought his head to the promise land. "Oh lord, yesss," I moaned as his tongue lapped at my aching clit.

Lightly he tapped at my bud as he kneaded my lower back and hips. The sensations swirled around me, and I struggled to keep still. He guided my legs so they rested on the bed. "You're so red and your clit so swollen, what a turn on," he said when he replaced his tongue with his fingers.

My nipples strained toward the ceiling as the rush of my impending climax tingled over the surface of my body.

With one hand, he circled around my arousal and with the other he fingered my g-spot just inside the entrance of my pussy.

"Oh lord, don't stop. Please, please don't stop. I'm so

close, Aidan. Yes, oh man, just like that!"

"Shh, lay still."

"I can't. Oh please!" The tremors began in my clit and overtook every inch of my body. My back arched off the bed as I lost control. As bliss enveloped me, my mind quieted, and I floated in the high of my orgasm. "Wow, that was—"

"Are you up for one more? How's your head?"

"Another orgasm? You're sweet, but I don't think so. I'm so relaxed I think I could melt away. He could use some help though," I said, pointing at Red's stiff shaft.

"The doc said we could have sex if you were feeling up to it, but I don't think he counted on you screaming your head off. Are you sure you're okay?"

"Mmmhmm."

"Okay then, scoot your cute little butt to the end of the bed and lie on your side."

I shimmied to the end of the mattress and repositioned the pillow under the right side of my head.

"Let me do all the work," Red said as he slid his warm cock inside my already swollen and receptive pussy.

"Oh yesss," I hissed.

His slow and easy strokes reignited my libido and caused my natural juices to flow. "Oh, you're so wet and tight."

"That feels so good ... oh Aidan."

Back and forth he drove, clutching my shoulder for leverage. "I'm getting close."

"Come for me, big boy."

"Oh hell, here goes!" Red grunted out. The muscles in his chest and stomach flexed as he rode his climax to completion. Perspiration glistened across his chest, and his legs trembled slightly. He fell out beside me, heavily panting.

"Your cock felt amazing. It seems like forever since we've been together. Hard to believe it's only been a few days."

"It felt like a lifetime to me. I'd rather us not part again anytime soon."

"I totally agree."

His naked body languished in the bed, legs over the end, his chest still rising and falling.

I crawled over to him, resting my head on his shoulder and draping my left leg over his thigh.

"How's your head doing?" As he held me close, I could hear the pounding of his heart.

"I won't lie, the left side of my head hurts a bit, but the headache I had before hasn't come back. Right now, I feel satiated and blissful."

"That's what I was going for and I aim to please."

"Well you did good."

I grazed my hand over his downy soft chest hairs and plucked lightly at his nipple.

"You'd better cut that out because we wouldn't want to push our luck. Plus, our friends and your mother might be showing up at any time. The doctor also said no alcohol while you're taking the painkillers."

"Not a problem."

Red took me by surprise by sitting up in the bed and taking me along with him. "Put those cute PJs back on and let's go downstairs." The blue and green plaid pajama bottoms that he slipped on hugged his hips and the green top made his eye color pop.

I loved that he, like me, wore PJs around the house, even with my mother coming over. Circling my arms around his waist, I said, "That's a great color on you."

"Thanks. Did you hear that?"

"Sounds like the doorbell. Did you actually lock the door?"

"I didn't want to be disturbed. I'll go get the door, and you can finish dressing." Peering down at me, I saw the love and caring on his face.

I scurried off to the bathroom and wiped up the come from between my legs, loving the smell of our sex. After I had slipped on my PJs, I looked in the mirror and parted my hair on my left side to see if I could find anything there. It felt swollen and tender to the touch, but I found no break in the skin. I filled a cup with water and took another pain pill.

"Hey you," Bond said, sticking his head into the open bathroom door.

I yelp and said, "Fuck, you scared me."

"Sorry, Jacqs, I—"

"What are you doing here?" I said as I ducked under his extended arm.

"I got my shift covered so I could be here with you."

"Oh, that's sweet," I said, but butterflies fluttered in my stomach.

He sauntered past me and sat on the bed where moments before I had sex with his best friend. Leaning back on his arm, he used his other hand to pat the mattress beside him. He gazed up at me with his sexy grin and said, "Sit with me." The snug jeans did nothing to hide his desire and his tight, black shirt accentuated his well-developed biceps and chest.

I crossed my arms in front of me, willing my body to get herself under control. "Our friends should be arriving soon."

"It's just us so far. Come on, Jacqs."

I looked to the door and back at Bond. Were the same rules still in place? My self-restraint never fared well against Bond's charismatic nature, and he seemed somehow more relaxed and more cocky than usual. It was highly unnerving. I reluctantly took a seat next to him.

"How are you feeling? Is Red taking good care of you?"

Damn, that's a loaded question. "My head still hurts a bit but ... well, yeah."

"That's good." He tugged on my arm. "Come over here, I want to hold you."

"Well ... I—"

He shifted closer to me, his natural scent floating around me, scattering my senses. "Jacqs," he murmured. "I love you more than I've ever let myself really feel— until now." He swept me up in his arms and before I could fight him off, he beguiled me with his lips.

I became pliant in his arms, and all at once I wished that I could have more self-control and just let it all go.

Increasing the intensity of the kiss, he charted us on a voyage away from reality, away from all the past rejection suffered under his neglect. He coaxed my tongue into his mouth, and I danced along with his. Lost in the growing heat and reforged connection, I shuffled tighter against Bond, drifting in a sea of hope.

A light tap on the door brought reality crashing back in, and we broke apart with the haste of children getting caught doing something naughty.

"Shit," I mumbled.

"Your mother is here," Red said, staring directly at me.

I stayed stuck on the spot where I sat.

"I'll go say hi to Mom," Bond said. He smiled boyishly. "Thanks, Jacqs."

"Right," I said, turmoil and pain killer riling my stomach.

"That looked hot and steamy," Red said, still standing by the door. He did not look pleased.

"I don't know what to say." I glanced up at him and awkwardly looked away. "I'm sorry?" I asked.

He stomped aggressively toward me and pushed his body onto mine, pinning me against the mattress. His hard bulge pressed against me. His eyes narrowed; leaving me feeling both turned on and scared. "Just remember whom you belong to."

"You said something like that in a dream I had while we were apart. Are we okay?"

"Tell me you plan to live with me even after you're well."

"Get off me," I said, pushing up on his chest. "That sounded too much like blackmail."

"Not meant to be, but I can tell you that I'll have an easier time sharing you when I know you'll be in my bed every night."

I felt slightly dizzy and squeezed my eyes shut.

"Are you okay?" His tone changed to one of concern.

"I took another pain pill and I think it's getting to me. Maybe some food will help."

"I apologize. Finding you kissing Bond took me by surprise." He lifted me in his arms like a bride and I touched his face.

"I love you, Red and yes, I want to live with you."

"That's all I needed to know."

As he kissed my already swollen lips, my soul acknowledged the difference he and Bond brought to my life and I finally admitted to myself that I wanted them both. I just had no clue how it would all sort out.

No one would allow me to do a single thing to help make dinner, and I was relegated to sitting on the couch and icing the side of my head.

"Here. To tide you over," Red said, handing me half a turkey sandwich with sprouts.

My warm smile radiated up to him. "Thanks. Where's the other half?"

He rubbed his stomach and winked at me. "No sprouts on my half," he said, making a funny face.

I watched in awe at how at ease my mother was with everyone. She moved around the kitchen, totally in her element. After she had placed the chickens in the oven, she came over and sat by me. "Do my eyes deceive me or do you have two men vying for your attention?"

"You would be correct."

"What do you plan to do about it?" she asked, raising her right eyebrow.

"That's becoming very tricky."

"I'm fond of Aidan. He seems ... how do I say? Staid."

"I don't even know what that means."

"Stable, confident, capable."

"Yeah, he's a right Neanderthal, that one."

"Did I hear my name?" Red said.

"Maybe you can explain to my mother our current predicament."

My big toothsome lover actually blushed. "Um, well ... I think I'll leave that to you." He ambled away.

I laughed so hard my eyes closed, and when I reopened them, I saw my mother laughing along with me.

"That wasn't very nice," she said but she continued to chuckle.

"Yeah, well, it's a complicated situation and I think the drug is making me loopy."

"You love them both, I can tell and it's clear they both love you."

"I agreed to move in here with—"

"And Bond is staying here as well?" My mother reached out and touched my knee.

I looked down at her hand, the tumult of our situation stirring in my gut. How do you tell your mother you are considering dating, and living with, two men? "We're trying to work it out, the three of us," I said, avoiding eye contact.

"Well, that certainly is an interesting choice. I had

enough trouble with one man."

"I thought you and Dad had one of those rare kinds of love."

"In a way, that is true, but your father was a handful, Jacqueline. No relationship is ever perfect."

"Yes, I'm well aware of that." Glancing up, I took a deep breath and said, "Would you be okay if I lived with them both?"

"More than anything, I want you to be happy. I can't imagine it'll be easy, but it's your life to live."

"That's a huge relief. I still don't know if it'll be doable but—"

Samantha threw her arms around me, cutting off my words. "I was so scared that, just as we were coming back together, I was going to lose you."

"I'm still here," I said, returning her tight hug. "As you've always known, I have a hard head."

"Thank god for that! You look great for someone who just totaled her car."

"More like it was totaled for me, but thanks. Did Lainie come with you?"

"Yeah, she's in the sitting room with Stay and Bond. Damn it's good to see you, sis."

"You too."

"Can I help with the food?" Samantha asked mom.

My mother rose from the couch, wrapped her arm around Samantha's waist and led her to the kitchen. I could hear her ask Samantha about her work day.

Lying back against the couch, I exhaled loudly. The fatigue in my body started to set in.

"I'm taking you back upstairs," Bond announced, pulling me up from the couch.

"I'm fine, I'm just—" I yawned and said, "A little tired I guess."

Allowing him to draw me upstairs, I realized that I would have to employ—in the future, that is, once I was well—a lot of backbone against these alpha males or they would run roughshod over me.

Bond settled me into Red's bed and said, "Stay agreed to help me practice for my driver's test."

"Wow. I don't know what to say. That's excellent news."

"Go to sleep and there'll be food ready for you when you get up." Bond kissed my forehead and left the room.

I ended up sleeping through dinner, and awoke in the middle of the night. Slight snoring emanated from the right of me and deep breathing to the left. It didn't take a genius to figure out why I was sandwiched in the middle of the bed. My mind thought it might be a good sign but my gut told me otherwise. I scooted off the end of the mattress and used the bathroom.

The dim lights above the bed illuminated Bond and Red as I reentered the room. They sat up with their backs against the headboard.

"This sure is an interesting turn of events," I said, wrapping my arms around my nakedness.

"We couldn't agree where you should sleep," Bond said.

"That seems silly considering I was already asleep. You mean with whom?" My stomach growled loudly, stating its emptiness.

"I'd ask how you're doing but clearly you're hungry," Red said as he rubbed his beard.

"Starving is more like it." I felt more than naked standing in front of them both, and my body responded to their stares. Stepping to the side, I grabbed my PJs off the top of the trunk and slipped them on.

"How's your head?" Bond asked.

"It must be okay because I haven't even thought about it."

"Let's get you some food," Red said as he got up from the bed wearing only pajama bottoms.

I stared at his chest momentarily and glanced over at Bond. *Geeze*, I thought to myself. The hit to my head must have been very hard for me to have considered living with them both. A knife could not cut the tension in the room, but maybe a chainsaw. "Cut it out," I yelped.

"What?" they said.

"I can feel the hostility between you two and I think you should take me home."

"No way," Bond said at the same time Red said, "Definitely not."

"Well then, cut it out!"

Bond took a step towards me in his black boxer briefs and shirt. "She needs some food," he said as if I was the crazy one.

"Yeah, let's feed her before she goes off the deep end," Red said as he pulled on a T-shirt.

"Fuck you both," I said and stormed down the stairs.

"She gets cranky when she's really hungry," Bond said, following behind me.

"And her stomach makes a racket," Red said.

"You two are hysterical in the middle of the night." I opened the refrigerator and made myself a plate of leftovers. "Are you guys going to eat anything or should I put the food away?"

"I'll put it away, you go eat," Red said, passing close by me.

I ducked around him and sat up on the counter with my plate in my lap.

"Here," Red said, handing me a glass of water.

"Thanks." After taking a few bites and a sip of water, my stomach quieted down.

"Feeling better?" Bond asked. He thankfully had pulled on his jeans before descending the stairs.

"I'll feel better once we resolve how this is going to work, *if* this is going to work."

"Let's move over to the couch so we can all sit and talk," Red said, taking my plate from me and helping me down.

We settled on the couch that faced the back of the house.

I ate a few more bites of food and placed my plate on the coffee table. "Well?"

"We need to come up with a schedule and split the time," Bond said.

"Is that what you guys agreed on?" I looked over at Red.

He shook his head. "No."

Looking back and forth between them, I said, "You haven't agreed on anything, have you?"

"He won't agree on equal time," Bond said.

I shifted my plate to the side and sat on the coffee table facing them. "Bond, do you plan to keep dating or doing *whatever* it is you call it?"

"Yes, if you are seeing Red, but I don't see how that should make—"

"I already told Red I'd live with him and he said you could have a room here if you wanted, but I'm not interested in splitting my time as you call it. Red will be my primary relationship, and it will be up to him and me how much time I spend with you as lovers. In turn, you are free to date as you wish."

"And what if I don't date? Does that mean I get equal time?" Bond stood up and started to pace. Circling around, he faced us and said, "Why do you get to make all the decisions and I just have to accept it? What about what I want?"

"What do you want?" I asked. "Do you plan to stop dating?"

"I want you to stop seeing Aidan and date me exclusively."

"That's not going to happen," Red asserted, standing

up with his fists clenched by his sides.

I touched Red's thigh and said, "Please sit down and try to remain calm. Maybe we should wait until morning after you both—"

"No," Bond and Red rumbled.

"Well at least you agree on something. Sit down, the both of you," I said, pointing to the sofa.

They settled down in opposite corners of the couch and crossed their legs at the same time. I almost laughed but stopped myself.

"In a perfect world, we could all spend time together and there wouldn't be a need to split it up … however it's clear to me that we aren't there yet and might never be. There is no way I will stop seeing Red. *I am* moving in with him. You haven't answered me; do you plan to stop dating?" In all honesty, I was scared he might say yes. Not that I thought he truly had it in him to stop, but I wasn't sure I wanted him to try.

"No, not if you plan to be involved with Aidan," Bond said, leaning forward and touching my thigh, trying to rattle me with his touch.

Pushing his hand away, I said, "So what do you suggest?"

"I need to go for a walk and clear my mind." Bond got up and headed for the front door.

"Well, that went well," I mumbled.

"Hardly," Red said, holding out his arms to me.

Snuggling into his lap, I rested my head on his chest. "What're we going to do?"

"Wait for him to sort it out for himself. In the meantime..." Red touched my cheeks and angled my head up to him, kissing me gently. "Thank you." His green eyes tugged at my heart.

"For?" I ran my fingers over his beard and into his hair.

"Putting us first. Once you're all better, you'll have to

decide what you want to move here from your place. There is also room in the garage for the stuff you want to store."

"Yeah, there's still a lot to do. First, I have to tackle getting a new car and then there is my new and old job, but we should have time on the weekends to pack things up."

"As long as you're staying here in the interim." Pulling my hair to the side, he nuzzled my neck.

"You're stuck with me," I muttered. "Oh, that feels good."

"Should we head back up to bed?" he said, raising his eyebrows.

"You're insatiable, Aidan."

"Only with you."

I climbed off his lap and pulled on his arm. Hand in hand, we went up the stairs. "Can I ask you something?"

"Anything," he said as we entered his room.

"How did Bond end up sleeping in here?"

"I didn't want him to wake you and he had no intention of letting you out of his sight for long. He kept checking on you all through dinner."

"I have to admit that's nice to hear, but will it last?"

Red smoothed my hair away from my face and said, "I'm surprised you'd doubt it at this point."

"He walked out again just a few minutes ago."

"Jacqueline, we men have our pride. You told him flat out that you plan to put me first. If it was the other way around, I'm not sure I'd have taken it so well."

Red removed his clothes and positioned himself in the middle of the bed, beckoning me to him.

After stripping off my PJs, I crawled over and straddled his lap. We sat facing one another; lips practically touching, sharing our breath.

"I don't think I'll ever get enough of you," Red said, running his large hands from the base of my neck to my buttocks.

"I sure hope not," I said, leaning into his touch.

"Come closer and drape your legs over mine." As I shifted, he nibbled his way up the right side of my neck and down the left, causing a waterfall of sensation.

"What are we going to do with him?" I said, looking down between us.

"I know just the place."

"I bet you do."

Red helped me lift my pelvis over his cock and slowly lower down until he was fully seated within me.

As he rocked me back and forth, I groaned, "Ohhh, I like this position." I caressed his arms and shoulders, gliding my hands up his neck into his red hair.

"I thought you might like it." He looked deeply into my eyes, drawing me into his domain.

We broke away from our connection when we heard the sound of a throat clearing. My heart plummeted to my stomach and seemed to stop beating altogether.

"I've made up my mind," Bond said and proceeded to strip off his clothes. "I need you in my life as much as I need to breathe, Jacqs."

As Bond approached the bed, I glanced back at Red and felt his cock pulse inside me. "Just know you owe me after this," he said, twitching his eyebrows.

Feeling Bond's weight behind me, I reclined into him. He tilted my head up and lit me on fire with his kiss.

"Oh yesss," I groaned.

Reaching around me, Bond fondled my clit as Red clutched my hips and stroked deeply in and out of me. Bond's other hand grasped my breast and pinched my left nipple between his fingers.

Looking down between us, I watched Red's cock slide in and out and Bond's hand matched his pace. My pussy clutched against the oncoming climax, firing tiny releases on the way up. Locking eyes with Red, I saw the heat and passion along with the love he freely offered me.

"Give it to us," Bond said in my ear. As he bit my neck, shockwaves pulsed and propelled me both deeply into my convulsing body, and out to fly in the ethers of my orgasm. My heart pounded wildly, pulsing hot blood to every tingling surface.

Red continued to stroke, allowing me to ride out my climax. When I peeked up at him, I could see him gritting his teeth to stave off his release. Closing my eyes, I hovered in the high and love that surrounded me. Breathing heavily, my heart still pounding, I prayed to the gods of love and sex that it wasn't another dream.

The caresses of four hands and being sandwiched by the bodies of my two lovers assured me this was no dream. They maneuvered me onto my back, Red settling between my legs and Bond at my head. Bond's manly scent of musky warm skin and sandalwood overwhelmed my senses and I turned my head to get closer to it.

"Oh, oh, oh please," I moaned against Bond's cock as Red's tongue licked my sensitive clit.

"You taste so good, Jacqs," Red said. He swirled his finger inside me as he continued to taste me, capturing my wetness and coating my anus with it.

"Mmm," I murmured, burying my nose in Bond's essence.

He lifted his cock to my mouth and I swirled my tongue around his shaft. Angling my head with his hands, he plunged deeper, owning my mouth as only he could.

I reveled in the duality of pleasuring Bond, while Red stirred another approaching orgasm with his fingers and tongue. My hips arched as Red delved two fingers into my ass and eddied his tongue around my sweet spot. I grunted and groaned until Bond took my throat and stole my breath.

He pulled out of my mouth, giving me time to inhale.

As Red continued his finger fucking and tongue lashing, I screamed, "Oh fuck, I'm going to … come! Oh yes, oh lord, yesss." My hips jerked haphazardly until I finally stilled, sinking into the bed. I heard whispering, but I couldn't make out what they said. Opening one eye, I saw them both peering down at me.

"Are you okay?" Red asked.

"More than." I giggled.

"How's your head?" Bond asked.

"It's still there, I think." I stretched my arms over my head, taking in their worried expressions. "I'm fine ... my head is fine, but look at you." Two hard cocks, along with their owners, waited for me. "What shall we do with those?"

"We have an idea..." Bond said, taking my hand and pulling me into a sitting position.

"I thought you might say that." I smiled up at them through my orgasmic high.

"I want you to straddle me on the bed and Red's going to take you from behind."

My energy ratcheted up over the idea and wondered if my small body could accommodate them both.

Red strode over to the bathroom while Bond positioned himself in the middle of the bed.

"Come here," Bond said, reaching out to me.

I settled myself on his long hard cock, taking him in to the hilt. Not moving, I asked, "Are *you* okay?"

"It's a funny time to ask that, don't you think? My cock is balls deep into you."

I circled my hips, taking in his warm smile and lowered my upper body to kiss him.

"I'm sorry, Jacqs," he whispered against my mouth. "Please be patient with me."

"Mmmhmm." I kissed him, losing myself in a love I

hadn't felt for him in a long time.

Red's weight settled behind me, and I almost yelped when he applied something cold to anus. "Lubrication," he said. After working coconut oil in and around my anal opening, his hard cock pushed in, and I had to will myself to relax.

"Oh lord, oh my god, oh fuck, that's intense." All my nerve endings seem to awaken at the same time and I could hear my pulse running through my ears. I started to pant.

"A little at a time," Red said, slowly moving in and out. He loomed over us both, his chest against my back.

Bond stayed perfectly still while Red attempted to work his thick phallus into my ass.

"Almost there," Red said, wrapping his right arm around my torso and using his left arm to hold up his weight.

"Oh, oh, easy, oh I feel so full," I groaned. The intensity stole my breath, and when they both started to move I thought I might combust in ecstasy.

With every incursion of Red's cock, my bulbous clit hitched into Bond's pelvis causing sparks to shoot up my spine. As Bond threaded his fingers into my hair and captivated my mouth with his lips and tongue, he escorted me on a journey of his redemption. All of the stimulation, almost too overwhelming, somehow worked together, and I gave my body over to the men I loved.

"I'm close," Red grunted. His breath rushed over my neck, and his arm tightened around my stomach.

"Oh yesss, me too," I hissed against Bond's mouth.

"As soon ... as Jacqs starts..." Bond forced out.

Red's cock swelled inside me, tripping over the beginning of my climax. A scream tore out of me but I was deaf to it. Red's hips jerked wildly, and my body thrashed around his rapid penetration. His orgasm fired as he grunted in my ear, filling me with his come.

The roar below began to rumble in Bond's chest, and I watched the exaltation of release flash across his face. Our eyes locked and I cried out with him.

Red collapsed beside us and I rolled off Bond and lay between my two lovers.

"Damn, that was fucking awesome," I mumbled, sighing deeply. Although I could have easily drifted off to sleep, we quickly washed up in the bathroom and brushed our teeth. Back at the bed, I wormed my way in between them. Red spooned me from behind, wrapping his arm around my waist, and Bond faced me, holding my hand.

As I drifted off to sleep I heard Bond whisper, "I love you, Jacqs and thanks for giving me another chance. I promise you won't regret it."

CHAPTER EIGHTEEN

A Little Less Conversation

by Elvis vs JXL (ft. Elvis Presley)

A knock on the bedroom door startled me awake, but didn't rouse Red or Bond. I lifted my head to find Lainie standing in the doorway. I held my pointer finger over my lips. Red's arm still lay across me, so I lifted it slowly and slid out of the bed. "Meet you downstairs," I mouthed.

I grabbed a clean set of PJs and used the bathroom to freshen up. Lainie stood by the couch as I descended the stairs.

"That looked pretty self-explanatory," she said with a grin.

"Would you like some coffee?" I said as I entered the kitchen to start a pot. "We can sit outside and talk."

"Sure. How are you feeling? You seem like your normal self."

"I'm not so sure how normal I am, but I'm feeling fine. No more headaches. I think all the sleep helped."

"And other things from the look of it."

I laughed and said, "Yeah, that too."

We settled on the swinging loveseat out back and waited for the coffee to brew.

"So?" she asked.

"We haven't sorted everything out, but last night was definite progress." I pulled in my legs in and shifted to the side to face Lainie.

"So you're going to do this?"

"If you mean being involved with them both, yes, I'm—"

Red strolled up and lifted me to him. He kissed me

deeply and then said, "Good morning." A warm smile lit his face as he caressed my cheek. "I forgot to tell you that Lainie was coming by for your usual Sunday brunch. Shall I make some eggs and hash browns?"

"That sounds wonderful to me. Lainie?"

"Great."

As Red walked away, Lainie shook her head.

"What?" I asked, pushing my foot against the ground so we rocked.

"I don't know how you're going to manage it. I'm having trouble with just one man."

"Are you ever going to tell me about him?"

"It's hard for me to—"

"Babe," Bond said, dipping his head around the French door. "Coffee's ready."

"I'll get both of us a cup," I said to Lainie.

Before I could get into the doorway, Bond wrapped me up in his arms and carried me inside. I couldn't help but laugh.

"I love you, Jacqs," Bond said. He gave me my morning kiss and left me practically swooning.

"We've plans for you later," Red said as he poured two cups of coffee.

I raised one eyebrow and said, "Oh?" I added cream.

"Yes, lots of plans," Bond said.

Red pulled me to him and whispered, "I love you, Little One, and want to redden that ass of yours."

"I concur," Bond said with a wicked smile.

"No ganging up on me!" I said, giggling and covering my butt with the backs of my hands.

"You don't know what you've started," Bond said, chasing after me.

I held my palm out to him, and said, "I started? I started, really? Leave me alone and let me talk to Lainie."

I tried to hold back my grin. "Maybe she'll knock some sense into me." Taking the two cups of coffee, I strolled back outside with a huge smile on my face.

"Here you go," I said, handing Lainie her cup. "Now spit it out before they interrupt us again."

"I know I have been judgmental of some of your choices—"

"Some?"

"I just wanted what's best for you and hated to see you in pain."

"Yeah, I get that."

Lainie looked at me with a strange expression and blurted out, "I'm seeing a married man."

"Oh fuck, girl, who is it?"

"I can't say—"

"I must know him then," I said, scanning my mind for ideas. "Spill it. I want all the details."

"It's a very long story," she said.

"Do you think it's wise?" I asked, wondering how Lainie had strayed off the straight and narrow.

"Do *you* think it's wise?" she said, swirling her finger in the air toward Bond and Red just inside the house.

"Touché," I said and looked through the French door at the two men I love. "But I must admit, I think I'm going to like being stuck in between."

"Yeah, well, that's yet to be seen."

"Something happened last night, Lainie, and they're both smiling this morning. That has to be a good sign."

"Breakfast is served," Red said, waving us inside.

After we had eaten, I walked Lainie to the door and we hugged goodbye.

"Be careful with those two," she said.

I chuckled and said, "I don't think that's possible. Will you ever tell me about your man? I'm worried about you."

"As soon as I can, I will. Love you, girl."

"I love you too."

When I skipped my way back to the living room, Bond said, "I thought she'd never leave."

"Don't be an ass, she is my best friend," I said, squirming my way between them on the couch.

"And what am I?" Bond asked.

"Impatient I would say, but damn it's good to see you both happy this morning."

"I think it's fair to say I'm considering Red's offer," Bond said, lifting me onto his lap.

I threw my arms around his neck and said, "Which part?" I glanced over at Red to scan his expression.

Red pointed down, and I could see his erection pushing against his PJ bottoms.

"Keeping a room here. It'll be easier going back and forth once I'm driving," Bond said, lifting my shirt over my head.

"What are you doing?" I asked, covering my breasts.

"I think that would be obvious," Red said, shifting closer to me and tickling down my arm.

"I'm trying to have a conversation with Bond to sort out—"

"It's in the doing, not the talking—" Bond started before I cut him off.

"Mr. I-want-to-talk-all-the-time? What the hell?"

"We enjoyed last night. Didn't you?" Red asked, as he uncrossed my arms and squeezed my right nipple.

I slapped Red's hand away and tried to ignore Bond, who had started nibbling up my neck. "But, wait, what about schedules and how this will work."

"Shh," Red whispered. "It *is* working. Just let it. Let us." He clutched the hair at the nape of my neck and tilted my face toward him. His stare, so full of lust and love, I couldn't deny him.

I brought his face to mine and kissed Red right in front of Bond. After a smoldering kiss, I broke away and glanced back at Bond.

"Feel," Bond said, forcing my hand between us.

"You two are more alike than you think," I said, throwing my arms in the air and falling to the side on Red. "I need more healing therapy, just like last night. Doctor's orders."

Red devoured my mouth and Bond pulled off my bottoms.

"Turn over," Bond said.

I flipped onto my knees on the couch, my butt in Bond's direction and my face hovering over Red's lap.

Red yanked his PJs over his hard-on and directed my face down.

I happily kissed around his cock and balls, taking in his natural smell. His citrusy scent amped my desire and I had to have him in my mouth.

The cushion shifted below me with Bond's weight, and I felt his hands grip my waist. His cock dipped into my wetness, and he teased in and out of me.

I groaned as I swirled my tongue around Red's flared head, closing my eyes as Bond increased the pace and depth of his incursion.

Bond suddenly changed to long slow strokes and spanked my ass each time he pulled back.

"Ow, oh my," I cried.

"I've wanted to tan your hide for a long time," Bond said, smacking my butt again.

"My favorite way is over my lap..." Red said, "...with her pert little ass displayed right in front of me."

Bond continued to rock into me as I lifted my mouth off Red's cock and said, "Don't give him any ideas. He's not as gentle as you."

"Are you saying my spankings have been gentle? I can rectify that right now." Red moved to get up.

"Down big boy, before you get all riled up," I said, gripping his manhood to keep him in place. "I'm just saying ... Bond's just—ouch." I covered my buttocks with my hands. Over my shoulder I said, "This is one of the reasons I don't let you use your devices on me."

"Oh, but you will," Bond said, spanking me again but not as hard. "That's all part of the negotiations." He shot me one of his dangerous smiles. "Maybe we should tie her down. What do you think Red?"

"Definitely not!" I yelled, kneeling up right.

Bond and Red chuckled.

"It's time to switch," Bond said as he drew his cock out. "Time for you to taste yourself on me."

"I want her pussy over my face," Red said, lying down the length of the couch and positioning me to straddle his mouth.

I bent forward resting my body against Red's stomach, circling my hand around his cock.

"Perfect," Bond said, standing next to the other side of the couch with one leg resting over the back of it. He held my head up and slid his silky erection into my mouth.

I tasted myself on him, our smells mixing a potent elixir. My breathing accelerated as Bond used my mouth, and Red fingered around my pussy, his warm tongue lapping at my clit.

"Oh yesss," I moaned when Bond pulled out of my mouth and tilted my head up for a kiss.

Bond coaxed with his tongue, possessing my mouth and igniting a new confidence in me. He gathered my hair away from my face and held it behind my head. Just before he took what he needed from me, he shared a penetrating stare of love.

My heart fluttered, and I struggled to keep my eyes

focused against the oncoming orgasm that Red was orchestrating.

Bond mouthed, "I love you," just before he plunged his cock to the back of my throat and rode in and out past my lips.

Up and down I stroked Red's shaft, using my other hand to massage his balls. My nipples rubbed against Red's stomach as the oncoming tsunami approached.

"Pull out," Red ordered. "She's about to explode."

Bond moved back and held his saliva coated erection in the palm of his hand, looking sexy as hell.

I stared up at him as my body shook with the force of my climax. I cried out as the contractions fired one after another, giving myself over to the sex and love surrounding me.

Not giving me a chance to recover, Bond said, "Help me turn her around." He lifted me so my back lay against Red's chest with my head near his.

Red lowered his left leg off the couch, giving room for Bond to mount me. Red held my knees back and wide as Bond sluiced his cock into my swollen wet pussy. Sinking down into me, all the contours of his erection rubbed all the right places.

Sandwiched between Bond above me and Red below, I suffered the joy of my predicament.

"Pull on those big nipples of yours," Red whispered in my ear as he bit his way up the side of my neck.

I complied and yanked my hard peaks, twisting them between my fingers.

"So hot," Red breathed.

"Yesss," Bond agreed.

Gazing up at Bond, I saw real love there, and I never wanted him to look away. I moved my hands to his chest and tugged on his nipple piercings. "Oh yes, oh fuck me, Bond!"

"Oh baby," Bond called out. It didn't take long for the roar to begin deep in his chest and project out as he ejaculated inside me. "Jacqs," he groaned as he knelt back on the end of the couch.

I sat up and kissed Bond, wanting to capture and hold onto the lust and love I saw in his eyes. He took control, deepening the kiss and stealing my breath.

"My turn," Red said, standing next to the couch and holding out his arms to me. He steered me behind the couch and had me lay my body over the top. "So wet and warm," he said as he doused his thick cock into me. In one hand he grabbed my shoulder, using it as leverage and with the other, he reached around my stomach and snaked his fingers over my clit.

"Oh fuck, oh lord ... that feels so good," I mumbled.

Bond knelt on the couch in front of me and yanked on my nipples, garnering my attention with his hot, sultry kisses.

Red rocked into me with force as Bond scorched me with his kisses. Never having considered a threesome before meeting Bond and falling in love with Red, I had to admit their duality seemed to suit me perfectly.

"Tell me when you're close," Red said as he thrashed into me.

"Almost to the edge," I moaned against Bond's mouth.

"You're the sexiest woman I know," Bond said, rubbing my nipples between his fingers.

I reveled in his compliment and love. "Oh please ... oh so, so close."

Red increased his pace, slamming against me so hard, my feet lifted off the ground. His fingers, all the while, mastered my clit.

"Don't stop ... please ... please ... oh lord. Ahhh," I screamed out, Bond's light brown eyes filling my gaze. After my orgasm had ceased I closed my eyes, floating in a sea of satiation. I hung over the couch completely blissful and spent.

Red gently stepped away.

The next thing I felt was a warm washcloth softly cleaning my labia. "Thanks," I mumbled, trying to bring myself back to the surface. I stood, steadying myself on the edge of the couch. "I can see how I'll be getting my exercise with the two of you." I gathered my clothes and put them back on.

"Our pleasure," Red said with a wink.

"Mine too." I smiled contently.

We all relaxed on the couch, staring outside. The south Florida winds blew through the fronds in the palm trees, and the sun made patterns on the surface of the pool.

As the high of the incredible love making started to wear off, I remembered I had no car for work the next day. "I need to call the insurance company and make arrangements for a rental car."

"That shouldn't be a problem," Bond said.

"Well, it wouldn't be if I had my car or my wallet or even my phone."

"Do you know the name of the company?" Red asked. "We can look up the number—"

"Right, good idea. Can I borrow your phone?"

"It's upstairs. I'll go get it," Red said, moving to get up.

I touched his shoulder and said, "I'll go. I want to shower and change anyway and could use a few minutes to myself."

"You know where to find us," Red said, flipping on the TV and changing the channel to the Dolphins' football game.

In the shower, I pondered the recent turn of events and decided to remain positive. My mind tried to point out all the potential pitfalls. I refused to linger there when my body still hummed in contentment. Hope filled me, and I smiled as I washed my tender nipples and well used pussy.

After dressing in my bright yellow empire sundress, no bra and panties, I plopped down on Red's made bed and called the insurance company. I was able to track down my adjuster and arrange for a rental car. I debated between taking a nap and finding a good book to read to fill my time while the boys watched their sports. I decided on the latter and hopped down the stairs.

Both Red and Bond briefly looked up over their shoulders and then groaned as they looked back at the TV.

"I won't bother you guys. Red, I was just wondering if you have any good books to read."

"Check in my office," he said. "On the bookshelf behind the desk." The TV changed to a commercial so he offered, "I'll come with you."

Next to the billiard room was Red's office. A large desk filled up most of the space, bookshelves lining the walls.

"The room suits you," I said, scanning around at all the books.

"How's that?" He perched on the side of the desk and drew me to him. He fondled my rear and said, "No panties? Have we not sufficiently taken care of you?"

"More than," I said, grinning broadly.

He lifted the bottom of the dress and took each buttock in hand with a firm squeeze. "Apparently I need to spank that ass of yours even harder."

"Not at all." I wiggled in his grasp. "You missed the point entirely. You do it perfectly and could teach Bond a thing or two."

He puffed out his chest and said, "You know just what to say."

"I'm sure your ego is in fine shape. Can you direct me to the fiction?"

He pointed to the right and followed me, hugging me

from behind.

I sighed against him. "Replay?" I asked, pulling a book off the shelf.

"That's one of my favorites."

I looked up at him and turned in his arms. "So are you." I reached my arms around his neck with the paperback in hand and stood up on tiptoe to kiss him. "Hmmmm," I moaned into his mouth. When we broke apart, I said, "Things are looking promising. Do you—"

"Red, it's back on," Bond shouted.

"I'll be outside reading." As I strolled away, he smacked my bottom. "Hey," I said and strutted away with a big smile on my face.

Settling on the glider loveseat, I easily became lost in the story about Jeff Winston. Bond and Red's voices traveled outside, and I could hear them intermittently cheering and groaning.

"You ready for some dinner?" Bond asked from the French doors, breaking me out of my reading trance. "We're thinking we could grab a bite at Oasis Cafe."

"Isn't that the place with the swinging booths? Sounds good to me." I stood up and stretched my lower back, twisting to either side. Although my head was fine, my body was starting to feel the effects of the accident.

"That's the one. Red just jumped into the shower and should be ready in a few minutes."

"Are you doing okay?" I asked as I entered into the house.

"I'm working my way through it."

I touched his arm and smiled. "I'm really happy you're here. I need to run upstairs, slip on some panties and grab my hoodie."

"You're not wearing underwear?"

I flipped up the back of my skirt and flashed him,

chuckling as I ran up the stairs.

When we got out of Red's SUV, I kept my arms at my sides not knowing whose hand I should hold. It felt awkward, and no one said anything.

At the restaurant we were led to a swinging booth, and I glanced from Bond to Red wondering over the seating arrangements.

"Let's all sit on one side with you in the middle," Bond suggested. He pulled me in after him and Red followed behind.

As soon as we sat down, I realized the stupidity of it. "We don't have room to move or eat this way. I scooted out past Red and sat on the opposite side. "This way I can see you both."

"This is going to take some negotiating," Red said, reaching his hand across the table for mine.

"I agree. I think we all need to talk and work this out." I patted his hand and placed mine back in my lap.

"Not tonight," Bond said, rocking the table back and forth. "Let's just enjoy ourselves. If we start getting into it now, I'm not sure what'll happen."

My stomach twisted over his pronouncement. "I'm willing to wait if you promise we'll talk this out soon."

"Sure we will," Bond said with his dangerous smile.

Left to wonder about our so called progress, I glanced from Red to Bond, waiting for one of them to speak.

The waitress broke the tension and asked, "Can I get you something to drink?"

"Water for me, thanks," I said. I took the napkin off the table and spread it across my lap.

"Do you have Dos Equis amber?" Red asked.

"We have Fat Tire Amber Ale."

"I'll try that," Red said.

"I'll take a coke," Bond said.

We ordered our dinner when the waitress returned with our beverages.

I tried to enjoy the view of the beach, the relaxed rocking of our swing table, and the cool south Florida breeze. Breaking the silence I said, "Red, can you drop me off at Avis at the Fort Lauderdale Airport on your way in to work tomorrow? Then I'll swing by and get my stuff from the impound. I need to have my phone."

"Sure. What time do you want to leave?" he said, placing the beer bottle down on the table.

"I think if we leave by around seven forty-five I should have plenty of time to deal with the rental and get to work."

"How did Henry take the news of the half days?" Bond asked.

"He never responded to my emails so I guess I'll find out at the office. I'm sure he's not thrilled and will probably talk about cutting my pay, but at this point, I really don't care. I have the afternoons covered between Star, Cara, and Steven. I have a feeling I'm heading into some long—ow," I said when a muscle in my back cramped.

"What is it?" Red said, coming over to my side.

I pointed to the spot on my lower back, and he massaged the muscle.

"You're hurting from the accident and you didn't tell us?" Red scolded me. "We could've ordered in."

"I'll get them to pack the meals to go," Bond said, moving out of the booth.

"I'm not that bad," I insisted.

"You have a long week ahead of you, and you need your rest," Red said, working his hands up my back.

"They said it would be a few more minutes," Bond said, taking his seat.

"After we eat and your food settles, I want you spread

out on my bed, and I'll massage you again," Red said. He reached across for his beer and stayed seated on my side.

I looked over at Bond, and he shrugged his shoulders as if he didn't care.

Back at the house, we ate dinner in relative silence, and Bond hung out in his room while Red, as promised, gave me a very relaxing massage. I read a bit more from my novel and fell asleep before Red came to bed. I positioned myself in the middle in case Bond joined us during the night.

My life was moving faster than my mind seemed capable of handling. I wanted to relax into all the experiences and yet found myself feeling like I was standing at the edge of a cliff, getting set to jump off. I, at once, dreaded going into work on Monday, and looked forward to the distraction.

CHAPTER NINETEEN

At Last

by Etta James

On Monday morning, I smiled up at Red after he had gently shaken me awake. Bond, still asleep on the other side of me, held my hand in his. I slipped out of Red's side of the bed and tiptoed to the bathroom. Red closed the door behind us.

"What time is it?" I whispered.

"It's just before seven."

"I have to hurry," I said while I switched on the shower to warm it up. Standing in front of the mirror over the sink, I brushed my teeth.

"Do you think you'll have time to meet up for lunch today?" He stood behind me and fondled my breasts.

"I don't think we have time for *that now*," I said, but his touch wasn't lost on me. I moan escaped as he stimulated the surface of my skin.

"I know, Jacqs, I just can't help myself. I'll leave you alone in a minute," he said, hugging me to him.

I thawed into his embrace, then bent forward to spit the toothpaste out. "Let's play it by ear. I'm not sure what the day will bring."

"How's your back feeling?"

I stepped over to the shower and said, "I'm sure the hot water will help, and I'll take a couple of Tylenol."

On the way to work I charged my cell phone in the rental car. Busy from the get go, I had no time to think about my aching back or my romantic life. Thankfully the new girl, Serena, was a fast learner. Henry generally ignored me, but my phone chimed incessantly.

"Do you want to try loading a document onto the server?" I asked after I demonstrated the process a few times.

"Sure. I think I have it sorted," Serena said.

I shifted my chair over to the side so she could sit in front of the computer. My phone signaled again, and I took the opportunity to check my messages. I received nine texts from four people, and a voicemail from my mother.

Red: How's it going?
Red: Is your back okay?
Red: Will you have time for lunch?
Red: How's the new girl working out?
Bond: You left without saying goodbye.
Bond: Do you have plans for lunch?
Bond: Can you swing by my place and grab a few things before you go to the other office?
Stay: I haven't heard from Bond. Is everything still okay?
Lainie: Call me later if you have time. I want to hear how the new job goes.

I jointly sent one long text back to Red and Bond.

Me: My body is a bit sore, but I'm feeling okay. The new girl is great. She seems sassy enough to handle Henry. At least I hope so for her sake. I don't really
Me: have time to text back and forth with you guys. No, Red, on lunch. Bond wants me to get some things from his apartment (send me a list). I miss you both.

Me: Got to go.

Separately to Bond I texted:

Me: Thanks for sleeping with me last night.
And to Red I texted:
Me: Thank you so much for the massage. It really helped!

To Stay I text:

Me: Things are looking up, but I'm still holding my breath. He's been with us at Red's. See you on Wednesday?

"Your phone has been going off a lot, is everything okay?" Serena asked.

"I was in an accident on Friday night and my friends and family are checking on me."

"Are you okay?"

"So far so good," I said, shuffling my chair up to the desk. "You seemed to have that down. Let's call some of the vendors and introduce you."

After the first half of the day flew by, I drove across town to Bond's apartment.

Me: I'm absolutely not bringing any of your toys over. You can come get them yourself! I can drive you over tomorrow morning on my way in to work.
Bond: Just get the basics then. I hate Red's shampoo, if you can even call it that.
Me: Okay, I have your toothbrush, shampoo, deodorant, three pairs of boxer briefs, three pairs of jeans, and T-shirts. Anything else?

> **Bond:** My pillow and the two cutoff PJs.
> **Me:** Where are those?
> **Bond:** In the closet in the right cubby close to the top.

I stretched up on tiptoe to reach them and then piled all the folded clothes and cosmetics on top of the pillow. After locking up, I carefully navigated the stairs down to my car, looking around the stack of stuff to see the stairs.

I threw his stuff in the back seat and climbed in the front of my boxy, funny smelling rental car. Shopping for a new car beckoned me, but I had no idea when I would find the time. Plus, I had to wait to see how much I would get for my totaled VW Bug. At least I had more money coming in with the new job.

Before I pulled out, I received another text from Bond.

> **Bond:** I'll handle dinner tonight.
> **Me:** You're cooking? I'm having trouble visualizing it. LMAO! ;)
> **Bond:** I meant ordering pizza! LOL :P
> **Me:** That sounds perfect. I'm already tired and have another half day to go. Miss you.
> **Bond:** We need to figure out how you and I can get some time alone. I'm not complaining. I'm trying not to anyway. I'm aching for you in a new way, Jacqs.

His confession found its way into my heart and inflamed my clit at the same time.

> **Me:** We'll work it out. I have to drive now to my next job. Love you and see you tonight.

I shook off my arousal and called my mother to check

in with her. Putting my cell phone on speaker, I pulled out onto the street.

"I was hoping to hear from you. How are you feeling?" she said.

"My body is a bit sore, but my headache is gone. I'm doing fine, really." I made a U-turn to head back to the highway.

"How is it working out with Mitchell and Aidan?"

"We still haven't sorted out all the logistics. In all honesty, it's going way better than I imagined it might, however, I still feel like the floor can drop out at any moment."

"Give it time, dear. My impression at dinner was that Aidan is committed, and Mitchell is working through something. He seemed ... hmm ... what's the right word? Scared maybe. Or lost. Over the years he was always so confident, almost too confident in my opinion. On Saturday he seemed quite the opposite."

"Thank you so much for coming over. I'm sorry I missed dinner." I accelerated to merge with the highway traffic.

"No need to apologize. We were all happy you were going to be okay, and I rather liked meeting all of your friends. They are good people."

"They are, aren't they? I love you, Mom."

"I love you too. Call me later and give your sister a call."

"I will."

I met Cynthia, who worked in the office next to Ted's. We instantly hit it off as she showed me her daily routine.

"Can I steal her for a minute?" Red asked, poking his head around the door. "I won't keep her long."

"Of course," Cynthia said, waving me away.

Once we were out of earshot, I said, "What are you doing?"

He pulled me along the corridor and said, "Showing

you my office and introducing you to Tammy."

"Uh huh," I said, shuffling to keep up.

He opened his door, and we entered the foyer just outside his office. A woman moved to stand up from behind the desk, and a man in a suit sat in the dark paneled waiting area.

"Tammy, this is Jacqueline," Red said. "She is taking over for Cyndi."

"Nice to meet you," I said, stretching my arm across the large wood desk to shake her hand.

She flashed me a warm smile, and I felt at ease. I wouldn't worry about her phone calls anymore.

To the gentleman in the waiting area, Red said, "I'll be just a minute; I have something quick to take care of."

"No problem," the man said.

Red opened the door to his office with flourish. The space reminded me of the office in his house and had to be at least three times the size.

"Do you think you could have found a bigger desk?" I said, laughing.

"It was the largest one they had."

"I bet," I said, resting my butt on the edge of his conference table. "So what do you need to take care of?"

"You," he said, nibbling up my neck.

His beard tickled me, and I started to laugh. "Don't you have more important things to be doing besides distracting your most recent employ?"

"Most definitely not." His kiss ignited me with his fierce fervency and I let myself forget where I was.

Surrounded by his warmth and passion, I moaned out loud, "Hmmmm."

"Shh." He chuckled next to my cheek.

I leaned back with my palms behind me and said, "This looks like a promising surface."

"Out with you," he said, tugging me forward.

"You're very bossy, you know."

"Wait until I have the time to fuck you on that conference table and you'll see just how bossy I can be, Little One."

"Little One?" I said, straightening my conservative, navy, button-down shirt. "That's Ms. Worth to you!" I tried to suppress the giggles. "Well Mr. Burke, I think it's time for me to get back to Cynthia and for you to take care of that poor man you left waiting. Either that, or I'm going to kneel down in front of you and unbutton your slacks."

"Damn you're sexy. Out with you before I change my mind," he said, directing me to the door.

"Seriously though. Do I look presentable?"

"Presentable and highly fuckable."

"Then it's a good thing Ted is married," I said, laughing on my way out. I waved to Tammy and slipped into the bathroom before returning to Cynthia.

By the time I made it home that night, I was ready to fall over. I threw the keys to the rental to Bond and said, "Your stuff is in the back seat." I took a shower, changed into my night clothes and made my way downstairs.

Bond flashed me his bad boy look, and I knew what he had in mind.

I shook my head. "Not tonight. I'm too tired. I just want to zone out to the TV and eat my dinner."

"We can do that," Red said, handing me a plate of pizza and a glass of water.

"Thanks. I think the new *Bachelor* is starting today."

Bond groaned and said, "You don't really watch that crap, do you?"

"Do you have another TV upstairs?" I asked Red. "I can watch it myself."

"This is the only one. I'll keep you company," Red

said, sitting on the couch next to me.

"Damn it," Bond said, lowering down beside me.

I placed the water glass on the coffee table and took a bite of the spinach and mushroom pizza. "Yum, that's good. I didn't realize how hungry I was."

"How was working with Ted?" Bond asked, laying his arm behind me on the couch.

"Ted seems great although I spent most of my time with Cynthia. I can already tell I'm going to like it there," I said, glancing at Red.

"Ted gave you two thumbs up and said he can't wait for you to go full-time."

"I'll be very happy when I'm only in one place," I said, taking another bite of pizza.

"Speaking of moving—" Red started.

"Can we talk about all of that tomorrow? Cynthia promises to get me out of work earlier."

"Tomorrow it is," Red said.

I looked over at Bond and he nodded.

Red flipped on the TV and we watched as car load after car load of women were introduced to the newest bachelor.

"Why the hell would all these women want to date this one guy?" Bond asked.

"That's sort of funny coming from you," I said, trying not to smirk.

"That's completely different," he said.

"I'm sure some of them just want to be on TV," Red said. "You know, their fifteen minutes of fame."

"That guy is barely even attract—"

"Will you guys shut up? I want to hear what they're saying!"

We watched in silence for ten minutes.

"Do you guys want anything?" Red asked as he got up. "I'm grabbing a beer."

"Nothing for me, thanks," I said, over my shoulder.

"I'm good," Bond said. He drew me back to him, and I extended my legs out on the couch.

When Red came back, he gathered my feet into his lap and massaged them.

"Oh, that feels so good," I said. "It's going to make me fall asleep."

We had only made it halfway through the Bachelor episode before I started to doze off. Bond insisted on carrying me upstairs.

I got ready for bed and climbed into the middle.

"Tonight I want you to sleep with your head on my chest," Bond said.

"Can you guys switch sides? I think you're sleeping on Red's side anyway."

"He is," Red said. "As long as I can spoon you from behind."

I rested my right cheek on Bond's chest as Red snuggled in behind me. Surrounded by their energy, I sighed deeply. I was apprehensive to have the "discussion" and yet I wanted to have it over with as soon as possible.

❀ ❀ ❀ ❀ ❀

On my way into work, I dropped Bond off at his apartment to pack up some more of his belongings.

The day sped by.

Arriving back at Red's house, I found the place empty. I took my time to stretch out my body and do a few yoga poses. The warm shower helped to loosen up my tight muscles. I padded down the stairs in my gray flannel bottoms and red tank top and stared into the open refrigerator. Finding the ingredients I would need for a broccoli and cheese quiche, I set out to prepare our dinner.

I tossed a salad and set the quiche to bake.

"That smells good," Red said, carrying in a large box and placing it next to the stairs.

"Is Bond with—" I started to ask until I saw him lugging in another box.

Fuck, I thought. "Are you moving *all* of your stuff over here?"

"No, why? You don't sound happy about—"

"It's one of the things I wanted to talk about when we have *the talk*," I said, taking a step closer to Bond.

"You don't want me to live here?" He stood there with his palms out. Pain and sadness ran across his face.

I touched Bond's hand and said, "I was hoping you were going to keep your apartment so you have a place to bring your other women. I don't think I could stand to watch you parade around here with them on your arm."

Bond snatched me up in his arms and twirled me around. "You scared me there for a second." Lowering me down his body, his lips touched mine before my feet hit the ground.

"Maybe we should start the conversation now," Red said, clearing his throat.

I stepped back from Bond and said, "The quiche has ten more minutes to bake, and then it should rest for a few minutes."

"We can talk while we eat if necessary," Red said, moving over to the couch that faced the back of the house.

I sat on the coffee table, and Bond found his place across from me.

"Since it's already come up, let's talk about other women," Red said. He reclined against the couch and crossed his legs.

I looked over at Bond and he appeared calm as well.

"Am I the only one that's nervous?"

BLAKELY BENNETT

"No, you're not," Bond said. "As far as me dating other women, right now I seem to have lost interest."

"You haven't been around any," I said, pursing my lips. "You've been holed up here with us. What about on Thursday when you go to work and are surrounded by a bevy of broads?"

"I guess we'll see. I won't bring them here and plan to keep my apartment ... for now." Bond sat back and then hunched forward over his knees.

Red and I waited for him to speak again. Bond seemed as though he had more to say.

"I would ... you guys will have plenty of time to yourself ... on the nights I work. When do I get time alone with you, Jacqs?" He ran his hand over his hair and stretched his arms across the top of the couch. His posture was one of relaxed confidence but his expression said otherwise.

"Red and I haven't discussed this—"

"Isn't that what we're doing now?" Bond asked.

"Yes, we are," Red said. "Go on Jacqs."

"Maybe Bond and I can have a night to ourselves? Monday or Tuesday?" My pulse escalated and I dipped my head, peering up at Red.

"That seems fair," Red said. "I'm not thrilled about it but I'm willing to try it out."

"Or both," Bond said.

"Let's start with one," I said.

"Tonight then," Bond said. "I haven't had any time alone with you since—"

"I think we all remember the day," Red said. "It's what set everything in motion."

"Red do you have anything you want to discuss?" I asked, touching his knee. "I have two more on my list."

"Go for it," he said.

"How do we act in public when the three of us are

342

out? It was a bit awkward last night. I usually hold hands with each of you when we're walking. Do we act platonic?"

"I don't give a shit what other people think," Bond said. Holding my hand in his, he kissed the top of it. "I'm having a hard time focusing, knowing you'll be in my bed tonight."

I squeezed his hand and put it back in his lap. "Red?"

"As long as we aren't at a work function."

"Okay and what about with our friends? Are you two going to take turns or what?"

"That's an interesting question," Red said. "Bond?"

"I say we act like we do when they aren't here, less the wild threesome sex on the couch."

I laughed and said, "Okay." The oven beeped and I went to take the quiche out. My heart raced with excitement believing that we might actually make things work.

"Let's eat quickly," Bond whispered into my ear as I placed the dish on the top of the stove.

"I'd like a few minutes alone with Red before. I haven't seen him all day."

"I would really like that," Red said.

Bond looked from Red to me and said, "That seems fair."

"Phew, that was a lot easier than I anticipated. I'm assuming we'll be totally out about us tomorrow night. I'm thinking of inviting Samantha. Is that cool with you guys?"

"Sounds good, and I'll pick up some food on the way home from work," Red said.

❋ ❋ ❋ ❋ ❋

"I missed you today," Red said, once we entered his bedroom. "And damn, I'm going to miss you in my bed tonight."

"Me too. I don't mean to be cruel, but it was *your* idea." I shifted from one foot to the other, gazing up at him.

"Right at this moment, I'm feeling like an idiot."

I playfully punched him in the stomach and said, "I'll be back in your bed tomorrow. Plus, if I get up during the night to pee, I'll come by and say hi."

"You'd better not. I won't let you leave." He gathered me up in his arms and hugged me.

"Kiss me before I have to go," I said, standing up on my toes, my arms thrown around his neck.

And he did, hard and full of passion. "I love you, Little One." He hugged me tight and pushed me on my way. "Get out of here before I change my mind."

"I love you too, very much," I said, closing his door behind me.

I felt a little shy and overly elated to be spending time alone with Bond. For the first time, I felt real consistent love radiating from him and somehow it scared me too.

"I was about to come get you," Bond said as I entered his room. Bond's smaller space had a queen size bed, brown walls and pale wood furniture.

"Worried I would change my mind?" I said, sitting down on the edge of the chest of drawers.

"Yes, I was."

I undressed and said, "Does it help to know, I'm a bit ... um ... distressed?"

"Distressed? How do you mean?" He lifted me to sit on the top of the dresser.

"You seem different, and I feel myself opening up my heart to you again and it scares me."

"Don't be scared, baby. I love you so much, sometimes it hurts and in the past I've pushed away from you, but I'm not now. Let me show you." He drew me in close, entwining his fingers into my hair. When he kissed me, his soul reaching out to mine, tears fell.

I gazed at him; his light brown eyes were wet as well.

"I'm sorry, Jacqs. I know I haven't been the man

you've needed. I promise you, I'm working on it."

"I see that, and I love you even more for it." I wrapped my legs around his waist, pulled his cock against me, and touched his silky, long, brown hair. After all the years, his light brown eyes still managed to light me on fire. "I need you, Bond."

"You have no idea," he said, grabbing my ass and grinding into my wetness.

I adjusted myself so he easily slid inside. "Ahhh," I groaned. "So good."

When we held eye contact, the connection morphed into something new. Instead of feeling the control that he so needed to maintain, his eyes spoke of love and abandon.

"I love you ... oh god ... Jacqs," Bond called out and slowed his movement. "Lean back against the mirror." He adjusted me slightly so he could reach between us, and fingered my distended bud.

"Hmmmm," I moaned, licking my lips. I tugged on his nipple rings and saw desire flash in his eyes.

"So sexy," he said, timing the rhythm of his strokes with his circles around my clit. "It's excruciating, it's so good."

"Yesss," I hissed. "Oh, just like that ... so, so good. Oh lord!" I cried. My pussy began convulsing around Bond's cock. The climax rocked my body and expanded my heart. I reveled in Bond's ability to elicit explosive orgasms, and when I opened my eyes, I saw him staring down at me.

"Thank you," he whispered.

"For? Shouldn't I be thanking you?"

"Giving me another chance," he said and then he kissed me hard and fast. He lifted me off the dresser and carried me over to the bed. "Lay down for me."

I scooted to the center of the bed and rested on my back.

He climbed up next to me and ran his long hair over the top of my body, causing goose bumps to cover the surface of my skin.

"Oh, that feels good," I moaned.

He took his time, bathing me with the sensuous flow of his hair over all of me. "I want to try something with you. I promise I won't hurt you."

"Okay," I said. I swallowed hard, turned on and nervous.

He opened the drawer on the end table and brought out a black flogger, one I had seen on the rack in his bedroom.

"I don't know," I said, shaking my head.

"Trust me."

Like he did with his hair, he trailed the flogger over my skin, around my breasts and down my stomach. The straps of leather felt exquisite and caused my areolas to tighten around the hard peaks of my nipples. He continued to draw the flogger between my thighs and over my mound.

Shivering in response, I said, "Oh that feels so good."

"Baby, I'm going to try something else now."

"Okay," I said, holding my breath.

He whipped the flogger against my thighs, across my stomach and over my nipples. I watched his lips part and his cheeks flush. When our eyes connected again, the pupils of his eyes appeared dilated. "Are you okay?" he asked.

"Yesss," I breathed.

"I'm going to start again." He gifted me with a rare, private smile that exposed all his secrets. "I love you," he mouthed and resumed the dance of the flogger.

Breathing out heavily, I grunted, "Ah, ah, ah, ohhh."

"Good, right?" he asked.

The titillating sensation caused me to pant. The controlled strikes thrilled me, escalating my fervor.

"Turn over, baby." As soon as I compiled, he treated my backside with the same luscious whipping. He struck my ass harder, and I felt wetness drip down the inside of my thighs. "I knew you would love this," he said when he stopped. "Come to me."

My entire body flamed with desire, raw and pulsing with need. I climbed off the bed.

Bond embraced me, lifting me off the ground. I wrapped my legs around his waist as he pressed my back to the wall. After adjusting so his cock slid inside, he gripped my waist. His eyes bore into me as he pounded against me, rubbing my clit with each stroke.

"Oh yes, take me, Bond," I held onto his shoulders, grinding myself against his penetration. So aroused from the foreplay, I quickly arrived at the edge of a riotous climax. Tiny orgasms fired each time he slammed into me.

"Oh baby, can you come with me?" he asked.

"Oh lord, I'm so close, yes Bond, oh god, don't stop."

We rocked together in unison, forming a stronger connection of trust. My heart opened wide, letting Bond, my best friend, back in. The culmination of my release crested over the top and I cried out at the same time Bond deafened us with his roar. Our chests rapidly rose and fell as we clutched onto one another, eyes locked in the thrill of our unification.

"I love you so much," he said into my hair, holding me close. He kissed me softly as we both came back down to earth.

"God that was good," I mumbled against his mouth.

He surprised me when he carried me into the hall bathroom and placed me down. In the cup on the vanity, I saw the toothbrush I had used at his apartment. I smiled up to him. We got ready for sleep, side by side, and climbed into his bed.

"That was incredible, Jacqs. Thank you for trusting me."

"I love you," I said as I lay my head on Bond's chest and my leg across his waist.

"I love you too. More than you know, but I plan to

show you if you continue to give me the chance."

I truly believed him, for the first time in a long time. As sleep beckoned me, I thought of Red, wondering if he heard us making love and was lonely all by himself in his big bed. I loved my alone time with Bond and understood that it was necessary to continue building the relationship we were all forging. And I wouldn't regret it for a second, but in truth, I missed having Red's presence next to me too.

CHAPTER TWENTY

So High

by John Legend

Red nudged me awake Wednesday morning. I quietly scooted out from the bed and walked across to his room. Before I had a chance to say anything, he swept me up in his arms and hugged me tight.

"I missed you last night," he breathed against my neck.

"Were we too loud? I worried that you could—"

"I had to take care of him myself," he said, pointing down between us.

"I would've loved to watch that," I said with a big grin.

"That can be arranged," he said with a wink.

"What time is it?" I asked, opening the closet to pull out a set of my drab work clothes.

"Seven thirty. Why don't you wear one of your cute, colorful dresses to work?"

I looked over my shoulder and said, "I know what you have on your mind."

"We need to make up for last night," he said, twitching his eyebrows.

I laughed and said, "Are you joining me in the shower?"

"No doubt," he said, lifting me up in his arms.

I giggled as he carried me into the bathroom.

Training continued to go smoothly with Serena and on

my way over to Burke & Associates I called Lainie's store.

"Bella Boutique, Samantha speaking. How can I help you?"

"Hi Sam."

"Hey Jackie, how's it going?"

"Very busy juggling the two jobs—"

"And the two men," Samantha added.

I chuckled. "Yeah, that too. Listen, are you free tonight? I'd love you to come by Red's. Bond hasn't been drinking and neither does Stay so I think—"

"I'd love to," she squealed.

"Drag Lainie along with you, okay? Let me speak to her and I'll see you later."

"Hang on."

I heard her put the phone down.

"What's up, girl?" Lainie said.

"Red's any time after six. You'll be there, right?" I exited the highway and pulled into traffic.

"I wouldn't miss it. It's your coming out party," she said, laughing.

"Very funny. I think Bond outed us last week. Was that just last week? I feel like I've aged a year since then."

"I guess he did already out you, but now everyone gets to see the *happy* family."

"Let's just hope it goes that way." I drove into the parking lot at Red's office. "Hey, I've got to go; I've got another call. See you later." After clicking over, I said, "Hello?"

"Hi baby," Bond said. "I missed waking up next to you."

"I figured you wanted to sleep in." I pulled into a parking spot and grabbed my bag. "Thank you so much for last night. My head is still spinning from it."

"So is my heart," he said.

"I love you and can't wait to see you later." I got out

of the rental car and closed the door. "I'm about to start the second half of my day. Are you ready for tonight?"

"As I'll ever be."

"Yeah, I know what you mean. I'll see you in a few hours?"

"Count on it."

Before I headed to my new office, I stepped into the hall bathroom near Red's office. I slipped off my panties and tucked them into my bag. I took a deep breath to steady myself so I wouldn't chicken out. Standing up tall, I strutted into Red's waiting room, already bristling with wetness and thankfully found it empty. *Tammy must be at lunch*, I thought. I knocked on Red's door.

"Come in," I heard him say.

"It's just me," I said, closing and locking the door behind me.

"Not just, never just. Get over here, you," he said, swiveling his chair to the side.

I climbed onto his lap, and he immediately cupped my naked butt over the colorful mini dress.

"Jacqs, are you trying to kill me here? How am I supposed to concentrate for the rest of the day?"

"I have a few ideas, but we need to be quick," I said, pushing his chair back and kneeling in front of him. "Cynthia is expecting me soon."

"You know my rules," he grunted.

"You'll have to make it up to me later," I said as I unbuckled his belt and unzipped his slacks. "He's clearly up for it." With a huge smile on my face, I lowered my mouth over the head of his cock and breathed in his musky scent. I cupped his balls in my left hand, my right circling around the base of his shaft.

"If we're going to do this," he said, pulling me to my feet, "then we're doing it my way." He lifted his blotter, with the stacks of papers and files on top, and set it down on the ground. Flipping me around, he bent my upper body over the top of the desk. "Spread your legs wide," he ordered.

"Yes, sir!"

"Do you know how much you drive me crazy?" He kicked off his shoes and removed his pants. I felt the cooler air on my ass once he lifted the bottom of my dress. "You owe me for last night."

Something smacked across my bottom and I yelped, "What the hell was that?" I turned my upper body to see what he held. "A ruler? Really?"

"Maybe next time you can wear a school girl uniform and I can be your teacher."

"I didn't think you were into that," I said, laughing.

"Neither did I, but seeing you like this has given me a few ideas. You like my hand better?"

"Much."

As he reddened my ass with a few more spanks, my natural moisture wet the inside of my thighs. "Jesus, Jacqs, you smell so good." He covered me from behind with his body and said, "I can't wait any longer."

"Oh yes ... show me."

He drove into my already hot flesh, and I welcomed him in. Clutching my forearm, he directed my hand to my pussy. "Come with me."

I massaged my clit as he pounded into me, forcing me against the desk. "Yes, please. Oh, Aidan."

He wrapped my long hair around his fist and yanked my head back. "Tell me when you're close," he moaned into my ear and bit my shoulder.

My nipples rubbed against the surface of the desk, Red's weight pinning me down. I frantically rubbed my clit and soon approached the very edge of release.

"Red, I'm there, hovering over the abyss."

"Take me with you," he groaned. He let go of my hair and used my shoulder as leverage, jackhammering into me.

"Oh yes ... oh, oh, oh ... I'm going to—" At the last second I remembered where I was and swallowed my scream. I grunted and groaned as I felt Red's warm come fire inside me.

He collapsed back into the chair with me on top of him as we both struggled to catch our breaths. Reaching over us, he snatched a couple of tissues and handed them to me.

I moved forward off his semi-hard cock and wiped myself. On shaky legs, I stood up and said, "I need to get going."

"You're a very naughty woman, Little One. Come give me a kiss before you go."

After a steamy kiss goodbye, I slipped on my panties and opened the door. Tammy was back behind her desk, and I blushed as I walked out.

❀ ❀ ❀ ❀ ❀

By the time I arrived at Red's house, Lainie and Samantha had already showed up and were coming in the French doors from out back. Bond captured me around the waist and kissed me before I had the chance to put my bag down.

"Hello," I said, hugging him back.

"My turn," Red said. He took my backpack off my shoulder and lifted me onto the kitchen counter. "Hello love." He dipped his head and gave me a warm, gentle kiss. Into my ear he whispered, "You're an occupational hazard."

"Oh?"

"I got nothing done today, and even left the office early so I wouldn't snatch you away from Cynthia and fuck you on my conference table."

A huge smile broke across my face as giggles erupted.

BLAKELY BENNETT

"Oops," I said.

"I'm going to oops your ass again tonight."

"Yes, sir." I saluted and jumped down off the counter, still grinning.

"What was that all about?" Lainie asked, dipping a tortilla chip into the salsa.

"You don't want to know." I glanced back at Red and tried not to laugh.

"You seem happy," Samantha said, stepping forward for a hug.

I glanced to Bond and Red and they both smiled back to me. "I am, very happy."

Bond came up behind me and circled his arms around my waist just as Stay and Blue came around the corner. Bond kissed my head and said, "What can I get you all to drink?"

Blue shot me an annoyed look and Stay winked.

"Water for me, thanks," I said.

"Same for me," Samantha said.

"Mike's Hard Lemonade for me," Lainie said.

"I'm good," Stay said.

Blue said, "I need a margarita."

Stay waved me outside, and I followed him. A slight cool breeze filtered through the palm trees.

I heard Blue say from inside, "What the fuck is going on? Is everyone just one big happy family now?"

"She doesn't seem thrilled," I said, sitting down at the wrought iron table.

"She'll come around," Stay said. "You look great."

"Thanks," I said, blushing.

"I talked to Bond today and he told me he's keeping a room here. He sounded good too. Happy."

I touched Stay's hand and said, "I'm glad you're here. I'm trying to relax into it all and yet there is still a part of me holding my breath. I think tonight will help."

"In what way?"

"If all of our friends, less Blue of course, are fine with the three of us being involved, then I think we have a much better chance of making it."

"You don't need our approval to decide what works for you. Your real friends will love you regardless."

"See why I like you so much." I squeezed his hand.

Red approached the table, placing a plate of nachos and a glass of water in front of me. He stood behind my chair and rested his hands on my shoulders.

"Thanks," I said, tilting my head back and sharing a smile.

Rubbing my neck, he asked, "How are you feeling?"

"Pretty much back to normal. What's up with Blue?"

"Bond took her into the billiard room to talk to her. She seemed surprised to find Bond here."

I stood up and said, "Why don't you sit down and relax?"

"Sure," he said, bringing me down on top of his lap.

"I meant I would get you another chair."

"Nope, this is perfect," he said, nuzzling my neck.

Cat, Kevin, Lainie, and Samantha came outside and dragged the other table and chairs over.

Cat bent down and gave me a hug, "Sorry I couldn't stay longer at the hospital."

"Don't think anything of it. I slept after you left. I really appreciated you guys coming by."

"You look incredible," she said. "I want some of what you're having."

"Being surrounded by love definitely suits you, Jacqs," Kev said, sitting in a chair beside us. He offered his lap to Cat.

Bond and Blue joined us outside, and Bond gave me the thumbs up.

I let my shoulders relax against Red.

"Lane," Bond said. "With your permission, I'd like to

give you a nickname. All my friends have them. I know you and I haven't always gotten along, and it's been entirely my fault. I see how much you care for Jacqs and her happiness, and I want the same thing for her."

"As long as you make sure to keep her smiling and glowing like she is today, I happily accept."

"Woohoo," I called out, clapping. Another seam in the fabric of our family had been stitched together.

"Bond tells me, Jacqs, that you're moving in here," Blue said from across the table.

Red shifted in his seat and said, "She's already living here, and over the weekend we're moving more of her stuff over."

"And Bond's living here too?" Blue asked.

"At least part-time anyway, until I pass my driver's test," Bond said.

"Good god, Jacqs. They're both a pain in the ass individually. I have no idea how you're going to manage them together," Blue said, lifting her glass in my direction.

Everyone broke out in laughter.

Red's arms held me close, and Bond's eye contact warmed my heart. Sitting there surrounded by our friends and Samantha, I knew we would all have many more trials, tribulations, love, and adventures to share. Just as they had been there for me, I would be there for them.

Blakely Bennett grew up in Southeast Florida and has been residing in the great Northwest for over eight years. She graduated from Nova Southeastern University with a degree in psychology, which accounts for her particular interest in crafting the personalities, struggles, and motivations of her characters. She is an avid reader of many genres of fiction, but especially enjoys erotica and romance. Writing has always been her bliss.

Blakely is married to a wonderful, loving, and supportive husband, who is also a writer, and who helps to keep her grounded. She is a mother, a communitarian, a lover of music (it is always on while she is writing thanks to Pandora), and a good friend. An advocate of love and female empowerment, she is also a facilitator for a women's group. She loves to walk and hike for exercise, and finds that, since moving to Seattle, Washington, she is now one of those crazy people who walk in the rain.

Stuck In Between is her fifth novel. She is also the author of the dark erotic suspense My Body Trilogy *(My Body-His, My Body-His (Marcello) and My Body-Mine)* and the co-authored of the contemporary romance, *The Demarcation of Jack* which she wrote with her husband, Dana Bennett.

You can find Blakely on the web at:
www.blakelybennett.com

COMING SOON

The second novel

in the

Bound by Your Love series

Bittersweet Deceit